PENGUIN BOOKS

Assassin's Creed
The Secret Crusade

Also in the *Assassin's Creed* series

Renaissance

Brotherhood

Assassin's Creed
The Secret Crusade

OLIVER BOWDEN

PENGUIN BOOKS

PENGUIN BOOKS

Published by the Penguin Group
Penguin Books Ltd, 80 Strand, London WC2R ORL, England
Penguin Group (USA) Inc., 375 Hudson Street, New York, New York 10014, USA
Penguin Group (Canada), 90 Eglinton Avenue East, Suite 700, Toronto, Ontario, Canada M4P 2Y3
(a division of Pearson Penguin Canada Inc.)
Penguin Ireland, 25 St Stephen's Green, Dublin 2, Ireland (a division of Penguin Books Ltd)
Penguin Group (Australia), 250 Camberwell Road,
Camberwell, Victoria 3124, Australia (a division of Pearson Australia Group Pty Ltd)
Penguin Books India Pvt Ltd, 11 Community Centre,
Panchsheel Park, New Delhi – 110 017, India
Penguin Group (NZ), 67 Apollo Drive, Rosedale, Auckland 0632, New Zealand
(a division of Pearson New Zealand Ltd)
Penguin Books (South Africa) (Pty) Ltd, 24 Sturdee Avenue,
Rosebank, Johannesburg 2196, South Africa

Penguin Books Ltd, Registered Offices: 80 Strand, London WC2R ORL, England

www.penguin.com

First published 2011

023

Typeset by Penguin Books Ltd
Printed in Great Britain by Clays Ltd, St Ives plc

A CIP catalogue record for this book is available from the British Library

ISBN: 978-0-241-95172-9

www.greenpenguin.co.uk

MIX
Paper from
responsible sources
FSC www.fsc.org FSC™ C018179

Penguin Books is committed to a sustainable
future for our business, our readers and our planet.
This book is made from Forest Stewardship
Council™ certified paper.

Contents

Prologue

The majestic ship creaked and groaned; its sails rippled, fat with wind. Days from land, it split the ocean towards the great city in the west, carrying precious cargo: a man – a man the crew knew only as the Master.

He was among them now, alone on the forecastle deck, where he had lowered the cowl of his robes to let himself be lashed by seaspray, sipping at it with his face in the wind. Once a day he did this. He appeared from his cabin to pace the deck, chose a spot to gaze out at sea, then returned below. Sometimes he stood on the forecastle, sometimes on the quarter-deck. Always he stared out at the white-crested sea.

Every day the crew watched him. They worked, calling to one another on deck and in the rigging, each with a job to do, while all the time stealing glances at the solitary, pensive figure. And they wondered, What kind of man was he? What kind of man was in their midst?

Furtively they studied him now as he stepped away from the deck railings and pulled up his hood. He stood there a moment with his head bowed, his arms hanging loosely at his sides, and the crew watched him.

Perhaps a few of them even paled as he strode along the deck past them and back to his cabin. And when the door shut behind him, each man found that he had been holding his breath.

Inside, the Assassin returned to his desk and sat, pouring a beaker of wine before reaching for a book and pulling it towards him. Then opening it. Beginning to read.

Part One

I

19 June 1257

Maffeo and I remain at Masyaf and will stay here for the
time being. At least until one or two – how shall I put
this? – *uncertainties* are resolved. In the meantime we
remain at the behest of the Master, Altaïr Ibn-La'Ahad.
Frustrating as it is to surrender dominion of our own
paths in this way, especially to the leader of the Order,
who in his old age wields ambiguity with the same
ruthless precision he once wielded sword and blade, I
at least benefit from being privy to his stories. Maffeo,
however, has no such advantage and has grown restless.
Understandably so. He tires of Masyaf. He dislikes
traversing the steep slopes between the Assassin's
fortress and the village below, and the mountainous
terrain holds little appeal for him. He is a Polo, he
says, and after six months here the wanderlust is like
the call of a voluptuous woman to him, persuasive
and tempting and not to be ignored. He longs to fill the
sails with wind and set off for new lands, show Masyaf
his back.

His impatience is a vexation I could live without,

quite frankly. Altaïr is on the cusp of an announcement; I can feel it.

So, today I declared, 'Maffeo, I'm going to tell you a story.'

The manners of the man. Are we really kin? I begin to doubt it. For instead of greeting this news with the enthusiasm it so clearly warranted, I could have sworn I heard him sigh (or perhaps I should give him the benefit of the doubt: perhaps he was simply out of breath in the hot sun), before demanding of me, 'Before you do, Niccolò, would you mind telling me, what it is about?' in rather exasperated tones. I ask you.

Nevertheless: 'That is a very good question, brother,' I said, and gave the matter some thought as we made our way up the dreaded slope. Above us the citadel loomed darkly on the promontory, as if it had been hewn from the very limestone itself. I'd decided I wanted the perfect setting to tell my tale, and there was nowhere more apposite than the Masyaf fortress. An imposing castle of many turrets, surrounded by shimmering rivers, it presided over the bustling village below, the settlement a high point within the Orontes Valley. An oasis of peace. A paradise.

'I would say that it's about *knowledge*,' I decided at last. '*Assasseen*, as you know, represents "guardian" in Arabic – the Assassins are the guardians of the secrets, and the secrets they guard are of knowledge, so, yes . . .'

no doubt I sounded very pleased with myself '. . . it's about knowledge.'

'Then I'm afraid I have an appointment.'

'Oh?'

'Certainly I would welcome a diversion from my studies, Niccolò. However, an extension of them I don't desire.'

I grinned. 'Surely you want to hear the tales I've been told by the Master.'

'That all depends. Your pitch makes them sound less than invigorating. You know you say my tastes run to the bloodthirsty when it comes to your stories?'

'Yes.'

Maffeo gave a half-smile. 'Well, you're right, they do.'

'Then you shall have that, too. These are, after all, the tales of the great Altaïr Ibn-La'Ahad. This is his *life story*, brother. Believe me, there is no shortage of event, and much of it, you'll be happy to note, featuring bloodshed.'

By now we had made our way up the barbican to the outer part of the fortress. We passed beneath the arch and through the guard station, climbing again as we headed towards the inner castle. Ahead of us was the tower in which Altaïr had his quarters. For weeks I had been visiting him there, spending countless hours by him, rapt, as he sat with his hands clasped and his elbows on the rests of his tall chair, telling his stories, his old eyes barely visible beneath his cowl. And increasingly I had come to realize that I was being told these stories for a purpose. That for some reason yet unfathomable to me, I had been *chosen* to hear them.

When not telling his stories, Altaïr brooded among his books and memories, sometimes gazing for long hours from the window of his tower. He would be there now, I thought, and hooked a thumb under the band of my cap and shifted it back, shading my eyes to look up at the tower, seeing nothing but sun-bleached stone.

'We've an audience with him?' Maffeo interrupted my thoughts.

'No, not today,' I replied, instead pointing at a tower to our right. 'We're going up there . . .'

Maffeo frowned. The defensive tower was one of the highest in the citadel, and was reached by a series of vertiginous ladders, most of which looked in need of repair. But I was insistent, and I tucked my tunic into my belt then led Maffeo up to the first level, then to the next and finally to the top. From there we looked across the countryside. Miles and miles of craggy terrain. Rivers like veins. Clusters of settlements. We looked over Masyaf: from the fortress to the buildings and markets of the sprawling village below, the wooden stockade of the outer curtain and stabling.

'How high are we?' asked Maffeo, looking a little green, no doubt conscious of being buffeted by the wind and that the ground now looked a long, long way away.

'Over two hundred and fifty feet,' I told him. 'High enough to put the Assassins out of range of enemy archers – but able to rain arrows and more down upon them.'

I showed him the openings surrounding us on all sides. 'From the machicolations here they could launch rocks or oil over their foe, using these ...' Wooden platforms jutted out into space and we moved over to one now, holding on to upright supports either side and leaning out into the air to look down. Directly below us, the tower fell away to the cliff edge. Below that the shimmering river.

The blood draining from his face, Maffeo stepped back on to the safety of the tower floor. I laughed, doing the same (and secretly glad to, feeling a little giddy and sick myself, truth be told).

'And why is it you've brought us up here?' asked Maffeo.

'This is where my story begins,' I said. 'In more ways than one. For it was from here that the lookout first saw the invading force.'

'The invading force?'

'Yes. Salah Al'din's army. He came to lay siege to Masyaf, to defeat the Assassins. Eighty years ago, a bright day in August. A day very much like today ...'

2

First, the lookout saw the birds.

An army on the move attracts scavengers. Of the winged variety, mainly, which swoop upon whatever scraps are left behind: food, waste and carcasses, both horse and human. Next he saw the dust. And then a vast, dark stain that appeared on the horizon, slowly beetling forward, engulfing everything in sight. An army inhabits, disrupts and destroys the landscape; it is a giant, hungry beast that consumes everything in its path and in most cases – as Salah Al'din was well aware – the mere sight of it was enough to move the enemy to surrender.

Not this time, though. Not when his enemies were the Assassins.

For the campaign the Saracen leader had raised a modest force of ten thousand infantry, cavalry and followers. With them he planned to crush the Assassins, who had already made two attempts on his life and would surely not fail a third time. Intending to take the fight to their door he had brought his army into the An–Nusayriyah mountains and to the Assassins' nine citadels there.

Messages had reached Masyaf that Salah Al'din's men had been plundering the countryside, but that none of the forts had fallen. That Salah Al'din was on his way to Masyaf, intent on conquering it and claiming the head of the Assassin leader, Al Mualim.

Salah Al'din was regarded as a temperate and fair-minded leader, but he was as angered by the Assassins as he was unnerved by them. According to reports, his uncle, Shihab Al'din, was advising him to offer a peace agreement. Have the Assassins with them, not against them, was Shihab's reasoning. But the vengeful Sultan would not be moved, and so it was that his army crawled towards Masyaf on a bright August day in 1176, and a lookout in the citadel's defensive tower saw the flocks of birds, the great clouds of dust and the black stain on the horizon, and he raised a horn to his lips and sounded the alarm.

Stockpiling supplies, the townspeople moved into the safety of the citadel, thronging the courtyards, faces etched with fear, but many of them setting up stalls to continue trading. The Assassins, meanwhile, began fortifying the castle, preparing to meet the army, watching the stain spread across the beautiful green landscape, the great beast feeding on the land, colonizing the horizon.

They heard the horns and drums and cymbals. And soon they could make out the figures as they materialized from the heat haze: thousands of them, they saw. The infantry: spearmen, javelinmen and archers, Armenians, Nubians and Arabs. They saw cavalry: Arabs, Turks and Mameluks, carrying sabre, mace, lance and longsword, some wearing chainmail, some leather armour. They saw the litters of the noblewomen, the holy men and the disorderly followers at the rear: the families, children and slaves. They watched as the invading warriors reached the outer curtain and set it ablaze, the stables too, the horns still blaring, cymbals crashing. Inside the citadel, the women of the village began weeping. They expected their homes to be next under the torch. But the buildings were left untouched, and instead the army came to a halt in the village, paying little regard to the castle – so it seemed.

They sent no envoy, no message; they simply made camp. Most of their tents were black, but in the middle of the encampment was a cluster of larger pavilions, the quarters of the great Sultan Salah Al'din and his closest generals. There, embroidered flags fluttered; the tips of the tent poles were gilded pomegranates, and the pavilion covers were of colourful silk.

In the citadel the Assassins mulled over their tactics. Would Salah Al'din assault the fortress or try to starve them out? As night fell they had their answer. Below them the army began work assembling its siege engines. Fires burned long into the night. The sound of sawing and hammering rose to the ears of those manning the citadel ramparts, and to the Master's tower, where Al Mualim called an assembly of his Master Assassins.

'Salah Al'din has been delivered to us,' said Faheem al-Sayf, a Master Assassin. 'This is an opportunity not to be missed.'

Al Mualim thought. He looked from the tower window, thinking of the colourful pavilion in which Salah Al'din now sat plotting his downfall – and that of the Assassins. He thought of the great Sultan's army and how it had laid waste to the countryside. How the Sultan was more than capable of raising an even larger force should his campaign fail.

Salah Al'din had matchless might, he reasoned. But the Assassins, they had guile.

'With Salah Al'din dead, the Saracen armies will crumble,' said Faheem.

But Al Mualim was shaking his head. 'I think not. Shihab will take his place.'

'He is half the leader Salah Al'din is.'

'Then he would be less effective in repelling the Christians,' countered Al Mualim, sharply. He tired sometimes of Faheem's hawklike ways. 'Do we wish to find ourselves at their mercy? Do we wish to find our-selves their unwilling allies against the Sultan? We are the Assassins, Faheem. Our intent is our own. We belong to no one.'

A silence fell over the sweet-scented room.

'Salah Al'din is as wary of us as we are of him,' said

Al Mualim, after reflection. 'We should see to it that he is made even more wary.'

The next morning the Saracens pushed a ram and siege tower up the main slope, and as Turkish horse-archers made passes, showering the citadel with arrows, they attacked the outer walls with their siege engines, under constant fire from Assassin archers and with rocks and oil pouring from the defensive towers. Villagers joined the battle, pelting the enemy with rocks from the ramparts, dousing the fires, while at the main gates, brave Assassins made sorties through the wicket doors, fighting back infantry trying to burn them down. The day ended with many dead on both sides, the Saracens retreating down the hill, lighting their fires for the night, repairing their siege engines, assembling more.

That night, there was a great commotion in the encampment, and in the morning the brightly coloured pavilion belong to the great Salah Al'din was taken down, and he left, taking a small bodyguard force with him.

Shortly after that, his uncle, Shihab Al'din, ascended the slope to address the Master of the Assassins.

3

'His Majesty Salah Al'din has received your message, and thanks you most graciously for it,' called the envoy. 'He has business elsewhere and has left, with instructions for His Excellency Shihab Al'din to enter into talks.'

The envoy stood by Shihab's stallion, cupping a hand to his mouth to call up to the Master and his generals, who were assembled in the defensive tower.

A small force had climbed the hill, two hundred men or so and a litter set down by Nubians, no more than a bodyguard for Shihab, who remained on horseback. On his face was a serene expression, as though he were not unduly concerned about the outcome of the talks. He wore wide white trousers, vest and red twisted sash. Inset into his large, blinding-white turban was a glittering jewel. That jewel would have an illustrious name, thought Al Mualim, gazing down upon him from the top of the tower. It would be called the Star of something or the Rose of something. The Saracens were so fond of naming their baubles.

'Do begin,' called Al Mualim, thinking, *Business elsewhere*, with a smile, his mind going back just a few hours to when an Assassin had come to his chambers, raising him from slumber and calling him to the throne room.

'Umar, welcome,' Al Mualim had said, wrapping his robes around himself, feeling the early-morning chill in his bones.

'Master,' Umar had replied, his voice low and his head bent.

'You've come to tell me of your mission?' Al Mualim said to him. He lit an oil lamp on a chain then found his chair, settling into it. Shadows flitted across the floor.

Umar nodded. There was blood on his sleeve, noticed Al Mualim.

'Was our agent's information correct?'

'Yes, Master. I made my way into their encampment and, just as we were told, the gaudy pavilion was a decoy. Salah Al'din's tent was nearby, a much less conspicuous accommodation.'

Al Mualim smiled. 'Excellent, excellent. And how were you able to identify it?'

'It was protected, just as our spy said it would be, with chalk and cinders scattered on the perimeter so my steps would be heard.'

'But they were not?'

'No, Master, and I was able to enter the Sultan's tent and leave the feather as instructed.'

'And the letter?'

'Pinned by dagger to his pallet.'

'And then?'

'I crept from his tent . . .'

'And?'

There was a pause.

'The Sultan awoke and raised the alarm. I was only just able to escape with my life.'

Al Mualim indicated Umar's blood-stained sleeve. 'And that?'

'I was forced to cut a throat in order to make good my escape, Master.'

'A guard?' asked Al Mualim, hopefully.

Umar shook his head sadly. 'He wore the turban and vest of a nobleman.'

At which Al Mualim closed tired and sorrowful eyes. 'There was no other option?'

'I acted rashly, Master.'

'But otherwise your mission was a success?'

'Yes, Master.'

'Then we shall see what transpires,' he said.

What transpired was the exit of Salah Al'din and the visit from Shihab. And standing tall in his tower, Al Mualim had allowed himself to believe that the Assassins had prevailed. That his plan had worked. Their message had warned the Sultan that he should abandon his campaign against the Assassins, for the next dagger would not be pinned to his pallet but to his genitals. Simply by being able to leave it they had shown the monarch how vulnerable he really was;

how his great force counted for nothing when a lone Assassin could outwit his decoys and guards and steal so easily into his tent as he slept.

And perhaps Salah Al'din was fonder of his genitals than he was of pursuing a long and costly war of attrition against an enemy whose interests only rarely came into conflict with his own. For he had gone.

'His Majesty Salah Al'din accepts your offer of peace,' said the envoy.

On the tower, Al Mualim shared an amused glance with Umar, who stood by his side. Further along was Faheem. His mouth was set.

'Have we his assurance that our sect can operate without further hostilities, and no further interference in our activities?' asked Al Mualim.

'As long as interests allow, you have that assurance.'

'Then I accept His Majesty's offer,' called Al Mualim, pleased. 'You may remove your men from Masyaf. Perhaps you would be good enough to repair our stockade before you leave.'

At that Shihab looked sharply up at the tower, and even from the great height Al Mualim saw anger flash in his eyes. Shihab leaned from his stallion to speak to the envoy, who listened, nodding, then cupped his hand to his mouth to address those in the tower once more.

'During the delivery of the message, one of Salah Al'din's trusted generals was killed. His Majesty requires reparation. The head of the culprit.'

The smile slid from Al Mualim's face. At his side, Umar tensed.

There was silence. Just the snorting of the horses. Birdsong. All waited to hear Al Mualim's response.

'You may tell the Sultan that I reject that demand.'

Shihab shrugged. He leaned over to speak to the envoy, who in turn addressed Al Mualim.

'His Excellency wishes to inform you that unless you agree to the demand a force will remain here at Masyaf, and that our patience is greater than your store of supplies. Would you have the peace agreement count for nothing? Would you allow your villagers and your men to starve? All for the head of one Assassin? His Excellency dearly hopes not.'

'I will go,' hissed Umar to Al Mualim. 'The mistake was mine. It is only right I should pay for it.'

Al Mualim ignored him. 'I will not give up the life of one of my men,' he called to the envoy.

'Then His Excellency regrets your decision and asks that you bear witness to a matter now in need of resolution. We have discovered the existence of a spy in our camp, and he must be executed.'

Al Mualim caught his breath as the Saracens dragged the Assassin agent from the litter. After him came an executioner's block that two Nubians placed on the ground in front of Shihab's stallion.

The spy's name was Ahmad. He had been beaten. His head – battered, bruised and blood-stained – lolled on his chest as he was manhandled to the block, dragged on his knees and draped over it, throat up. The executioner stepped forward: a Turk carrying a glinting scimitar that he grounded, placing both hands on the jewelled hilt. The two Nubians held Ahmad's arms; he groaned a little, the sound rising to the stunned Assassins high in the defensive tower.'Let your man take his place and his life will be spared, the peace treaty honoured,' called the envoy. 'If not he dies, the siege begins and your people starve.'

Suddenly Shihab raised his head to shout, 'Do you want that on your conscience, Umar Ibn-La'Ahad?'

As one the Assassins caught their breath. Ahmad had talked. Under torture, of course. But he had talked.

Al Mualim's shoulders slumped.

Umar was beside himself. 'Let me go,' he urged Al Mualim. 'Master, please.'

Below them the executioner planted his feet wide. Two-handed, he raised the sword above his head. Ahmad pulled feebly at the hands that pinned him. His throat was taut, offered for the blade. The promontory was silent but for his whimpering.

'Your last chance, Assassin,' called Shihab.

The blade shone.

'*Master*,' pleaded Umar, 'let me go.'

Al Mualim nodded.

'*Stop!*' shouted Umar. He moved to a platform of

the tower, calling down to Shihab. 'I am Umar Ibn-La'Ahad. It is my life you should take.'

There was a ripple of excitement among the ranks of Saracens. Shihab smiled, nodded. He indicated to the executioner, who stood down, grounding his sword once more. 'Very well,' he said to Umar. 'Come, take your place on the block.'

Umar turned to Al Mualim, who raised his head to look at him with red-rimmed eyes.

'Master,' said Umar, 'I ask you one final favour. That you see to the care of Altaïr. Accept him as your novice.'

Al Mualim nodded. 'Of course, Umar,' he said. 'Of course.'

There was a hush across the citadel as Umar climbed down the ladders of the tower, then took the slope through the barbican, under the arch and to the main gate. At the wicket gate a sentry came forward to open it, and he bent to go through.

A shout came from behind him: *'Father.'* The sound of running feet.

He paused.

'Father.'

He heard the distress in his son's voice and squeezed his eyes shut against tears as he stepped out of the gate. The sentry closed it behind him.

They pulled Ahmad from the block and Umar tried to give him a reassuring look, but Ahmad could not meet his gaze as he was hauled away and dumped outside the wicket gate. It opened and he was dragged in. It closed again behind him. Arms took hold of Umar. He was pulled to the block, spread as Ahmad had been. He offered his throat and watched as the executioner towered above him. Beyond the executioner the sky.

'*Father*,' he heard from the citadel, as the gleaming blade came slicing down.

Two days later, under cover of darkness, Ahmad left the fortress. The following morning when his disappearance was discovered there were those who wondered how he could bear to leave his son alone – his mother having died of the fever two years previously – while others said the shame was too much for him, that that was why he had been forced to leave.

The truth was a different matter altogether.

4

20 June 1257

This morning I awoke with Maffeo shaking my shoulder – not especially gently, I should add. However, his insistence was prompted by an interest in my story. For that at least I should be grateful.

'So?' he said.

'So what?' If I sounded sleepy, well, that's because I was.

'So what happened to Ahmad?'

'That I was to discover at a later date, brother.'

'So tell me.'

As I pulled myself to a sitting position in my bed I gave the matter some thought. 'I think it best that I tell you the stories just as they were told to me,' I said at last. 'Altaïr, ageing though he is, is quite the teller of tales. I believe I shall adhere to his narrative. And what I related to you yesterday formed the bulk of our very first meeting together. An episode that took place when he was just eleven years old.'

'Traumatic for any child,' reflected Maffeo. 'What of his mother?

'Died in childbirth.'

'Altaïr an orphan at eleven?'

'Indeed.'

'What happened to him?'

'Well, you know what happened. He sits up in his tower and –'

'No, I mean what happened to him *next*?'

'That also will have to wait, brother. The next time I saw Altaïr he had moved the focus of his narrative forward by fifteen years, to a day that found him creeping through the dark, dripping catacombs beneath Jerusalem . . .'

The year was 1191, more than three years since Salah Al'din and his Saracens had captured Jerusalem. In response the Christians had gnashed their teeth, stamped their feet, and taxed their people in order to fund the Third Crusade – and once more men in chainmail had marched upon the Holy Land and laid siege to its cities.

England's King Richard, the one they called the Lionheart – as cruel as he was courageous – had recently recaptured Acre, but his greatest desire was to re-take Jerusalem, a holy site. And nowhere in Jerusalem was more sacred than the Temple Mount and the ruins of the Temple of Solomon – towards which Altaïr, Malik and Kadar crept.

They moved fast but stealthily, clinging to the sides

of the tunnels, their soft boots barely disturbing the sand. Altaïr went ahead, Malik and Kadar a few paces behind, all with senses tuned to their surroundings, their pulses quickening as they came closer to the Mount. The catacombs were thousands of years old and looked every day of it; Altaïr could see sand and dust trickling from unsteady wooden supports, while underfoot the ground was soft, the sand wet with the water that dripped steadily from overhead – some kind of nearby watercourse. The air was thick with the smell of sulphur from the bitumen-soaked lanterns that lined the tunnel walls.

Altaïr was the first to hear the priest. Of course he was. He was the leader, the Master Assassin; his skills were greater, his senses sharper. He stopped. He touched his ear, then held up his hand, and all three became still, like wraiths in the passage. When he glanced back, they were awaiting his next command. Kadar's eyes gleamed with anticipation; Malik's were watchful and flinty.

All three held their breath. Around them the water dripped, and Altaïr listened intently to the priest's mumblings.

The false Christian piety of a Templar.

Now Altaïr placed his hands behind his back and flicked his wrist to engage his blade, feeling the familiar pull on the ring mechanism he wore on his little finger. He kept his blade in good order so that the noise it made when it released was almost inaudible – he timed it to the water droplets just to be sure.

Drip . . . drip . . . *snick*.

He brought his arms forward and the blade at his left hand glittered in the flickering torchlight, thirsty for blood.

Next Altaïr flattened himself to the tunnel wall and moved forward stealthily, rounding a slight bend until he could see the priest kneeling in the tunnel. He wore the robes of a Templar, which could only mean there were more ahead, probably within the ruins of the Temple. In search of their treasure, no doubt.

His heart quickened. It was just as he'd thought. That the city was under Salah Al'din's control wasn't going to stop the men of the red cross. They, too, had business at the Mount. What business? Altaïr intended to find out, but first . . .

First there was the priest to take care of.

Crouched low, he moved behind the kneeling man, who prayed on, unaware of death's proximity. Shifting his weight to his front foot and bending at the knee slightly, Altaïr raised the blade, his hand bent back, ready to strike.

'*Wait!*' hissed Malik from behind him. 'There must be another way . . . This one need not die.'

Altaïr ignored him. In one fluid movement he grasped the priest's shoulder with his right hand and with his left jammed the point of the blade into the back of his neck, slicing between the skull and the first vertebra of the backbone, severing his spine.

The priest had no time to scream: death was almost instantaneous. Almost. His body jerked and tautened but Altaïr held him firm, feeling his life ebb away as he held him with one finger on his carotid artery. Slowly, the body relaxed and Altaïr allowed it to crumple silently to the ground where it lay, a spreading pool of blood blotted by the sand.

It had been quick, soundless. But as Altaïr retracted the blade he saw the way Malik looked at him and the accusation in his eyes. It was all that he could do to suppress a sneer at Malik's weakness. Malik's brother, Kadar, on the other hand, was even now looking down at the priest's body with a mixture of wonderment and awe.

'An excellent kill,' he said breathlessly. 'Fortune favours your blade.'

'Not fortune,' boasted Altaïr, 'skill. Watch a while longer and you might learn something.'

As he said it he watched Malik carefully, seeing the Assassin's eyes flare angrily, jealous, no doubt, at the respect Kadar afforded Altaïr.

Sure enough, Malik turned on his brother. 'Indeed. He'll teach you how to disregard everything the Master taught us.'

Altaïr sneered once more. 'And how would you have done it?'

'I would not have drawn attention to us. I would not have taken the life of an innocent.'

Altaïr sighed. 'It matters not how we complete our task, only that it's done.'

'But that is not the way . . .' started Malik.

Altaïr fixed him with a stare. 'My way is better.'

For a moment or so the two men glared at one another. Even in the dank, cold and dripping tunnel, Altaïr could see in Malik's eyes the insolence, the resentment. He would need to be careful of that, he knew. It seemed that young Malik was an enemy in waiting.

But if he had designs on usurping Altaïr, Malik evidently decided that now was not the right moment to make his stand. 'I will scout ahead,' he said. 'Try not to dishonour us further.'

Any punishment for that particular insubordination would have to wait, decided Altaïr, as Malik left, heading up the tunnel in the direction of the Temple.

Kadar watched him go, then turned to Altaïr. 'What is our mission?' he asked. 'My brother would say nothing to me, only that I should be honoured to have been invited.'

Altaïr regarded the enthusiastic young pup. 'The Master believes the Templars have found something beneath the Temple Mount.'

'Treasure?' gushed Kadar.

'I do not know. All that matters is the Master considers

it important, else he would not have asked me to retrieve it.'

Kadar nodded and, at a wave of the hand from Altaïr, darted off to join his brother, leaving Altaïr alone in the tunnel. He looked down, pondering, at the body of the priest, a halo of blood on the sand around the head. Malik might have been right. There had been other ways of silencing the priest – he hadn't had to die. But Altaïr had killed him because . . .

Because he could.

Because he was Altaïr Ibn-La'Ahad, born of an Assassin father. The most skilled of all those in the Order. A Master Assassin.

He set off, coming to a series of pits, mist floating in their depths, and leaped easily to the first crossbeam, lithely landing and crouching catlike, breathing steadily, enjoying his own power and athleticism.

He jumped to the next and to the next, then came to where Malik and Kadar stood waiting for him. But rather than acknowledge them he ran past, the sound of his feet like a whisper on the ground, barely disturbing the sand. Ahead of him was a tall ladder and he took it at a run, scampering up quickly and quietly, only slowing when he reached the very top, where he stopped, listening and sniffing the air.

Next, very slowly, he raised his head to see an elevated chamber, and there, as he'd expected, stood a guard with his back to him, wearing the outfit of a Templar:

padded gambeson jacket, leggings, chainmail, sword at his hip. Altaïr, silent and still, studied him for a moment, taking note of his posture, the dip of his shoulders. Good. He was tired and distracted. Silencing him would be easy.

Slowly Altaïr pulled himself to the ground where he crouched for a moment, steadying his breathing and watching the Templar carefully, before moving up behind him, straightening and raising his hands: his left a claw; his right ready to reach and silence the guard.

Then he struck, snapping his wrist to engage the blade, which sprang forward in the same instant that he rammed it into the guard's spine, reaching with his right hand to smother the man's scream.

For a second they stood in a macabre embrace, Altaïr feeling the tickle of his victim's final muffled shout beneath his hand. Then the guard was crumpling and Altaïr lowered him gently to the ground, stooping to brush his eyelids closed. He had been punished severely for his failure as a lookout, Altaïr thought grimly, as he straightened from the corpse and moved off, joining Malik and Kadar as they crept beneath the arch that had been so poorly guarded.

Once through, they found themselves on an upper level of a vast chamber, and for a moment Altaïr stood taking it in, feeling suddenly overawed. This was the ruin of the fabled Solomon's Temple, said to have been built in 960 BC by King Solomon. If Altaïr was correct they now stood overlooking the Temple's greater house, its Holy Place. Early writings spoke of the Holy Place as having its walls lined with cedar, carved cherubim, palm trees and open flowers embossed with gold, but the Temple was now a shadow of its former self. Gone were the ornate wood, the cherubim and the gold finishing – to where, Altaïr could only guess, though he had little doubt the Templars had had a hand in it. Yet even stripped of its gilding it was still a place of reverence, and despite himself, Altaïr found himself filled with wonder to see it.

Behind him his two companions were even more awestruck.

'There – that must be the Ark,' said Malik, pointing across the chamber.

'The Ark of the Covenant,' gasped Kadar, seeing it too.

Altaïr had recovered, and glanced over to see the two men standing like a pair of foolish merchants dazzled at the sight of shiny baubles. *Ark of the Covenant?*

'Don't be silly,' he chided. 'There's no such thing. It's just a story.' Looking over, though, he was less sure. Certainly the box had all the properties of the fabled Ark. It was just as the prophets had always described: plated entirely with gold, a golden cover adorned with cherubim, and rings for inserting the poles that would be used to carry it. And there was something about it, Altaïr realized. It had an aura . . .

He tore his eyes away from it. More important matters needed his attention, namely the men who had just entered on the lower level, their boots crunching on what had once been fir-board flooring but was now bare stone. Templars, their leader already barking orders.

'I want it through the gate before sunrise,' he told them, referring no doubt to the Ark. 'The sooner we possess it, the sooner we can turn our attention to those jackals at Masyaf.'

He spoke with a French accent, and as he came into the light, they saw his distinctive cape – that of the Templar Grand Master.

'Robert de Sable,' said Altaïr. 'His life is mine.'

Malik rounded on him angrily. 'No. We were asked to retrieve the treasure and deal with Robert only if necessary.'

Altaïr, tired of Malik's constant defiance, turned on him. 'He stands between us and it,' he hissed angrily. 'I'd say it's necessary.'

'Discretion, Altaïr,' urged Malik.

'You mean cowardice. That man is our greatest enemy – and here we have a chance to be rid of him.'

Still Malik argued: 'You have already broken two tenets of our Creed. Now you would break the third. Do not compromise the Brotherhood.'

Finally Altaïr snapped: 'I am your superior – in both title and ability. You should know better than to question me.' And with that he turned, climbing quickly down the first ladder to a lower balcony, then to the floor where he strode confidently towards the group of knights.

They saw him coming and turned to face him, their hands on the hilts of their swords, their jaws set. Altaïr knew that they would be watching him, watching the Assassin as he glided across the floor towards them, his face hidden by his cowl, his robes and red sash flowing about him, the sword at his hip and the hilts of his short swords showing over his right shoulder. He knew the fear they would be feeling.

And he in turn watched them, mentally assessing each man: which of them was a right-handed swordsman, which fought with his left; who was built for speed and who would be strongest, paying particular attention to their leader.

Robert de Sable was the largest of them, the most powerful. His head was shaved, and etched into his face were years of experience, every one of which had contributed to his legend, that of a knight as famed for his skill with a sword as he was for his cruelty and ruthlessness – and this Altaïr knew above all: that of the men present he was by far the most dangerous; he had to be neutralized first.

He heard Malik and Kadar drop from the ladders and glanced behind to see them following his lead, Kadar swallowing, nervous, Malik's eyes flashing his disapproval. The Templars tensed further at the sight of two more Assassins, the numbers more even now. Four of them surrounded de Sable, each man alert, the air thick with fear and suspense.

'Hold, Templars,' called Altaïr, when he was close enough to the five knights. He addressed de Sable, who stood with a thin smile upon his lips, his hands hanging at his sides. Not like his companions, ready for combat, but relaxed, as though the presence of the three Assassins was of little significance to him. Altaïr would make him pay for his arrogance. 'You are not the only ones with business here,' he added.

The two men weighed each other up. Altaïr moved his right hand, as though ready to grasp the hilt of the sword at his belt, wanting to keep de Sable's attention there when in fact death would snick smoothly from the left. *Yes*, he decided. Feint with the right, strike with the left. Dispatch Robert de Sable with the blade and his men would flee, leaving the Assassins to retrieve the treasure. All would talk of Altaïr's great victory over the Templar Grand Master. Malik – that coward – would be silenced, his brother wonderstruck afresh, and on their return to Masyaf the members of the Order would venerate Altaïr; Al Mualim would honour him personally and Altaïr's path to the position of Master would be assured.

Altaïr looked into the eyes of his opponent. Imperceptibly he flexed his left hand, testing the tension of the blade mechanism. He was ready.

'And what is it you want?' asked de Sable, with that same unconcerned smile.

'Blood,' said Altaïr simply, and struck.

With inhuman speed he leaped at de Sable, flicking the blade at the same moment, feinting with his right hand and striking, as fast and as deadly as a cobra, with his left.

But the Templar Grand Master was quicker and more cunning than he had anticipated. He caught the Assassin mid-attack, seemingly with ease, so that Altaïr was stopped in his tracks, unable to move and suddenly – horrifyingly – helpless.

And in that moment Altaïr realized he had made a grave mistake. A fatal mistake. In that moment he knew that it was not de Sable who was arrogant: it was himself. All of a sudden he no longer felt like Altaïr the Master Assassin. He felt like a weak and feeble child. Worse, a bragging child.

He struggled and found he could barely move, de Sable holding him easily. He felt a sharp stab of shame, thinking of Malik and Kadar seeing him brought low. De Sable's hand squeezed his throat, and he found himself gasping for breath as the Templar pushed his face forward at him. A vein in his forehead throbbed.

'You know not the things in which you meddle, Assassin. I spare you only that you may return to your Master and deliver a message: the Holy Land is lost to him and his. He should flee now, while he has the chance. Stay and all of you will die.'

Altaïr choked and spluttered, the edge of his vision beginning to fade, fighting unconsciousness as de Sable twisted him as easily as though handling a new-born and tossed him towards the back wall of the chamber. Altaïr crashed through the ancient stone and into the vestibule on the other side where he lay stunned for a moment, hearing beams fall and the huge pillars of the chamber crash in. He looked up – and saw that his entrance to the Temple was blocked.

From the other side he heard shouts, de Sable crying, 'Men. To arms. *Kill the Assassins!*' He scrambled to his feet and dashed to the rubble, trying to find a way through. With shame and helplessness burning him, he heard the cries of Malik and Kadar, their screams as they died, and finally, his head low, he turned and began to make his way out of the Temple for the journey to Masyaf – there to bring the Master the news.

The news that he had failed. That he, the great Altaïr, had brought dishonour upon himself and upon the Order.

When he finally emerged from the bowels of the Temple Mount it was into bright sunshine and a Jerusalem that teemed with life. But Altaïr had never felt so alone.

5

Altaïr arrived at Masyaf after an exhausting five-day ride, during which he'd had more than enough time to reflect upon his failure. And thus it was with the heaviest of hearts that he arrived at the gates, was allowed in by the guard and made his way to the stables.

Dismounting and feeling his knotted muscles relax at last, he handed his horse to the stable boy then stopped by the well to take some water, sipping it at first, then gulping and, last, splashing it over himself, gratefully rubbing the dirt from his face. He still felt the grime of the journey upon his body, though. His robes hung heavy and filthy and he looked forward to washing in the shimmering waters of Masyaf, hidden away in an alcove of the cliff face. All he craved now was solitude.

As he made his way through the outskirts of the village, his gaze was drawn upwards – past the stable huts and bustling market to the winding paths that led to the ramparts of the Assassins' fortress. Here was where the Order trained and lived under the command of Al Mualim, whose quarters stood in the centre of the citadel's Byzantine towers. He was often to be seen staring from the window of his tower, lost in thought, and Altaïr pictured him there now, gazing down upon the village. The same village that bustled with life, bright with sunshine and loud with business. To which, ten days ago, Altaïr, leaving for Jerusalem with Malik and Kadar, had planned to return as a triumphant hero.

Never – not in his darkest imaginings – had he foreseen failure, and yet . . .

An Assassin hailed him as he made his way across the sun-dappled marketplace, and he pulled himself together, pushing back his shoulders and holding up his head, trying to summon from within the great Assassin who had left Masyaf, rather than the empty-handed fool who had returned.

It was Rauf, and Altaïr's heart sank further – if that were possible, which he sincerely doubted. Of all the people to greet him on his return it would have to be Rauf, who worshipped Altaïr like a god. It looked as though the younger man had been waiting from him, wiling away the time by a walled fountain. Indeed, he bounded up now with wide and eager eyes, oblivious to the nimbus of failure that Altaïr felt around himself.

'Altaïr – you've returned.' He was beaming, as pleased as a puppy to see him.

Altaïr nodded slowly. He watched as behind Rauf an elderly merchant refreshed himself at the fountain-head then greeted a younger woman, who arrived carrying a vase decorated with gazelles. She placed it on the low wall surrounding the waterhole and they began to talk, the woman excited, gesticulating. Altaïr envied them. He envied them both.

'It is good to see you're unharmed,' continued Rauf. 'I trust your mission was a success?'

Altaïr ignored the question, still watching those at the fountain. He was finding it difficult to meet Rauf's eye. 'Is the Master in his tower?' he asked at last, tearing his gaze away.

'Yes, yes.' Rauf was squinting as though to divine somehow what was wrong with him. 'Buried in his books, as always. No doubt he expects you.'

'My thanks, brother.'

And with that he left Rauf and the chattering village folk at the fountainhead and began to make his way past the covered stalls and hay carts and benches, over the paving, until the dry and dusty ground sloped sharply upwards, the parched grass brittle in the sunshine, all paths leading to the castle.

Never had he felt so much in its shadow, and he found himself clenching his fists as he crossed the plateau and was greeted by the guards at the fortress approach, their hands on the hilts of their swords, their eyes watchful.

Now he reached the grand archway that led to the barbican, and once more his heart sank as he saw a figure he recognized within: Abbas.

Abbas stood beneath a torch that chased away what little dark there was within the arch. He was leaning against the rough dark stone, bare-headed, his arms folded and his sword at his hip. Altaïr stopped, and for a moment or so the two men regarded each other as villagers moved around them, oblivious of the old enmity blooming afresh between the two Assassins. Once they had called each other brother. But that time was long past.

Abbas smiled slowly, mockingly. 'Ah. He returns at last.' He looked pointedly over Altaïr's shoulder. 'Where are the others? Did you ride ahead, hoping to be the first one back? I know you are loath to share the glory.'

Altaïr did not answer.

'Silence is just another form of assent,' added Abbas, still trying to goad him – and doing it with all the cunning of an adolescent.

'Have you nothing better to do?' sighed Altaïr.

'I bring word from the Master. He waits for you in the library,' said Abbas. He ushered Altaïr past. 'Best hurry. No doubt you're eager to put your tongue to his boot.'

'Another word,' retorted Altaïr, 'and I'll put my blade to your throat.'

Abbas replied, 'There will be plenty of time for that later, *brother*.'

Altaïr shouldered past him and continued to the courtyard and training square, and then to the doorway to Al Mualim's tower. Guardsmen bowed their heads to him, affording him the respect a Master Assassin rightfully commanded, and he acknowledged them knowing that soon – as long as it took word to spread – their respect would be a memory.

But first he had to deliver the terrible news to Al Mualim, and he made his way up the steps of the tower towards the Master's chamber. Here the room was warm, the air heavy with its customary sweet scent. Dust danced in shafts of light from the great window at the far end, where the Master stood, his hands clasped behind his back. His master. His mentor. A man he venerated above all others.

Whom he had failed.

In a corner the Master's carrier pigeons cooed quietly in their cage and around him were his books and manuscripts, thousands of years of Assassin literature and learning, either on shelves or stacked in tottering, dusty piles. His sumptuous robes flowed about him, his long hair lay over his shoulders, and he was, as usual, contemplative.

'Master,' said Altaïr, breaking the thick silence. He lowered his head.

Wordless, Al Mualim turned and moved towards his desk, scrolls littered the floor beneath it. He regarded Altaïr with one sharp, flinty eye. His mouth, hidden within his grey-white beard, betrayed no emotion until at last he spoke, beckoning to his pupil. 'Come forward.

Tell me of your mission. I trust you have recovered the Templar treasure . . .'

Altaïr felt a trickle of perspiration make its way from his forehead and down his face. 'There was some trouble, Master. Robert de Sable was not alone.'

Al Mualim waved away the notion. 'When does our work ever go as expected? It's our ability to adapt that makes us who we are.'

'This time, it was not enough.'

Al Mualim took a moment to absorb Altaïr's words. He moved from behind his desk, and when he next spoke, his voice was sharp. 'What do you mean?'

Altaïr found himself having to force out the words. 'I have failed you.'

'The treasure?'

'Lost to us.'

The atmosphere in the room changed. It seemed to tense and crackle as though brittle, and there was a pause before Al Mualim spoke again. 'And Robert?'

'Escaped.'

The word fell like a stone in the darkening space.

Now Al Mualim came closer to Altaïr. His one eye was bright with anger, his voice barely restrained, his fury filling the room. 'I send you – my best man – to complete a mission more important than any that has come before and you return to me with nothing but apologies and excuses?'

'I did –'

'*Do not speak.*' His voice was a whipcrack. '*Not another word.* This is not what I expected. We'll need to mount another force so –'

'I swear to you I'll find him – I'll go and . . .' began Altaïr, who was already desperate to meet de Sable again. This time the outcome would be very different.

Now Al Mualim was looking about himself, as though only just recalling that when Altaïr had left Masyaf he had done so with two companions. 'Where are Malik and Kadar?' he demanded.

A second bead of sweat made its way from Altaïr's temple as he replied, 'Dead.'

'*No,*' came a voice from behind them, 'not dead.'

Al Mualim and Altaïr turned to see a ghost.

6

Malik stood at the entrance to the Master's chamber – stood swaying, a wounded, exhausted, blood-soaked figure. His once-white robes were streaked with gore, most of it around his left arm, which looked badly wounded, dangling uselessly at his side and crusted with blackened, dried blood.

As he moved into the room his injured shoulder dipped, and he hobbled slightly. But if his body was damaged, then his spirit was surely not: his eyes burned brightly with anger and hatred – hatred that he turned on Altaïr with a glare so intense that it was all Altaïr could do not to shrink away.

'*I* still live, at least,' growled Malik, his bloodshot eyes brimming with fury as he stared at Altaïr. He took short, ragged breaths. His bared teeth were bloody.

'And your brother?' asked Al Mualim.

Malik shook his head. 'Gone.'

For a beat his eyes dropped to the stone floor. Then, with a sudden burst of angry energy, he raised his head, narrowed his eyes and raised a trembling finger to point at Altaïr. '*Because of you,*' he hissed.

'Robert threw me from the room.' Altaïr's excuses

sounded feeble, even to his own ears – *especially* to his own ears. 'There was no way back. Nothing I could do –'

'Because you would not heed my warning,' shouted Malik, his voice hoarse. 'All of this could have been avoided. And my brother . . . my brother would still be alive. Your arrogance nearly cost us victory today.'

'Nearly?' said Al Mualim, carefully.

Calming, Malik nodded, the ghost of a smile on his lips – a smile directed at Altaïr, for even now he was beckoning another Assassin, who came forward bearing a box on a gilt tray.

'I have what your favourite failed to find,' said Malik. His voice was strained and he was weak, but nothing was going to sour his moment of triumph over Altaïr.

Altaïr felt his world falling away from him as the Assassin set down the tray on Al Mualim's desk. The box was covered with ancient runes and there was something about it – an aura. Inside it, surely, was the treasure. It had to be. The treasure that Altaïr had been unable to recover.

Al Mualim's good eye was wide and gleaming. His lips were parted, his tongue darting from his mouth. He was entranced by the sight of the box and the thought of what was inside. Suddenly there came an uproar from outside. Screams. Running feet. The unmistakable ring of clashing steel.

'It seems I've returned with more than the treasure,' reflected Malik, as a messenger crashed into the chamber, forgetting all protocol as he breathlessly exclaimed, 'Master, we are under attack. Robert de Sable lays siege to the Masyaf village.'

Al Mualim was snatched from his reverie, in the mood to face de Sable. 'So he seeks a battle, does he? Very well. I'll not deny him. Go. Inform the others. The fortress must be prepared.'

Now he turned his attention to Altaïr, and his eyes blazed as he said, 'As for you, Altaïr, our discussion will have to wait. You must make for the village. Destroy these invaders. Drive them from our home.'

'It will be done,' said Altaïr, who could not help but be relieved at this sudden turn of events. Somehow the attack on the village was preferable to having to endure more of this humiliation. He had disgraced himself in Jerusalem. Now he had the chance to make amends.

He vaulted from the landing behind the Master's chamber to the smooth stone floor and dashed from the tower. As he ran across the training yard and through the main gates, he wondered whether being killed now might provide the escape he desired. Would that be a good death? A proud and noble death?

Enough to exonerate him?

He drew his sword. The sounds of battle were closer now. He could see Assassins and Templars fighting on the upland at the foot of the castle, while further down the hill villagers were scattering under the force of the assault, bodies already littering the slopes.

Then he was under attack. A Templar knight rushed him, snarling, and Altaïr twisted, letting his instincts take over, raising his sword to meet the Christian, who bore down upon him fast and hard, his broadsword slamming into Altaïr's blade with a clash of steel. But Altaïr was braced, feet planted wide apart, the line of his body perfect, and the Templar's attack barely moved him. He swept aside the other's sword, using the weight of the huge broadsword against the knight, whose arm flailed uselessly for a blink that Altaïr used to step forward and plunge his blade into the man's stomach.

The Templar had come at him confident of an easy kill. Easy, like the villagers he had already slaughtered. He'd been wrong. With the steel in his gut he coughed blood and his eyes were wide with pain and surprise as Altaïr yanked the blade upward, bisecting his torso. He fell away, his intestines spilling to the dust.

Now Altaïr was fighting with pure venom, venting all of his frustration in his sword blows, as though he might pay for his crimes with the blood of his enemies. The next Templar traded blows, trying to resist as Altaïr pushed him back, his posture instantly changing from attack to defence, and then into desperate defence, so that even as he parried, he was whimpering in expectation of his own death.

Altaïr feinted, wheeled, and his blade flashed across the Christian's throat, which opened, sheeting blood down the front of his uniform, staining it as red as the cross on his chest. He sank to his knees then fell forward, just as another soldier rushed Altaïr, sunlight glinting from his raised sword. Altaïr stepped aside and buried his steel deep in the man's back so that, for a second, his entire body tautened, the blade protruding from his chestplate, his mouth open in a silent scream as Altaïr lowered him to the ground and retrieved his sword.

Two soldiers attacked together, thinking perhaps that their numbers would overwhelm Altaïr. They reckoned without his anger. He fought not with his usual cold indifference, but with fire in his belly. The fire of a warrior who cared nothing for his own safety. The most dangerous warrior of all.

Around him he saw more corpses of villagers, put to the sword by the attacking Templars, and his anger blossomed, his sword blows becoming even more vicious. Two more soldiers fell beneath his blade and he left them twitching in the dirt. But now more and more knights were appearing, villagers and Assassins alike were rushing up the slope, and Altaïr saw Abbas commanding them to return to the castle.

'Press the attack on the heathen fortress,' cried a knight in response. He was running up the hill towards Altaïr, his sword swinging as he swiped at a fleeing woman. 'Let us bring the fight to the Assassin –'

Altaïr slammed his sword into the throat of the Christian, whose last word was a gurgle.

But behind the escaping villagers and Assassins

came more Templars, and Altaïr hesitated on the slope, wondering if now was the moment to take his final stand – die defending his people and escape his prison of shame.

But no. There was no honour in a wasteful death, he knew, and he joined those retreating to the fortress, arriving as the gates were closing. Then he turned to look out on the scene of carnage outside, the beauty of Masyaf sullied by the bloodied bodies of the villagers, the soldiers and the Assassins.

He looked down at himself. His robes were splashed with Templar blood but he himself was unharmed.

'*Altaïr!*' The cry pierced his thoughts. Rauf again. 'Come.'

He felt weary all of a sudden. 'Where are we going?'

'We have a surprise for our guests. Just do as I do. It should become clear soon enough . . .' Rauf was pointing high above them to the ramparts of the fortress. Altaïr sheathed his sword and followed him up a series of ladders to the tower summit where the Assassin leaders were gathered, Al Mualim among them. Crossing the floor, he looked to the Master, who ignored him, his mouth set. Then Rauf was indicating one of three wooden platforms jutting out into the air, bidding him to take his place on it. He did so, taking a deep breath before he walked carefully to the edge.

And now he stood at the top of Masyaf, able to look down upon the valley. He felt air rushing around him; his robe fluttered in the wind and he saw flocks of birds gliding and swooping on warm pockets of air. He felt giddy with the height yet breathless with the spectacle: the rolling hills of the countryside, cast in lush green; the shimmering water of the river; bodies, now specks on the slopes.

And Templars.

The invading army had gathered on the upland in front of a watchtower, close to the gates of the fortress. At their head was Robert de Sable, who now stepped forward, looking up to the ramparts where the Assassins stood, and addressed Al Mualim.

'*Heretic!*' he roared. 'Return what you have stolen from me.'

The treasure. Altaïr's mind drifted momentarily to the box on Al Mualim's desk. It had seemed to glow . . .

'You've no claim to it, Robert,' replied the Master, his voice echoing across the valley. 'Take yourself from here before I'm forced to thin your ranks further.'

'You play a dangerous game,' replied de Sable.

'I assure you this is no game.'

'So be it,' came the reply.

Something about the tone of his voice – Altaïr didn't like it. Sure enough, de Sable turned to one of his men. 'Bring forward the hostage.'

From among their ranks they dragged the Assassin. He was bound and gagged and he writhed against his bonds as he was hauled roughly to the front of the assembly. His muffled cries rose to where Altaïr stood on the platform.

Then, without ceremony, de Sable nodded to a soldier who stood nearby. He yanked the Assassin's hair so that his throat was exposed and swept his blade across it, opening it, then let the body fall to the grass.

The Assassins, watching, caught their breath.

De Sable moved and stood near the body, resting one foot on the dying man's back with his arms folded like a triumphant gladiator. There was murmur of disgust among the Assassins as he called up to Al Mualim, 'Your village lies in ruins and your stores are hardly endless. How long before your fortress crumbles from within? How disciplined will your men remain when the wells run dry and their food is gone?' He could hardly keep the gloating note from his voice.

But in reply Al Mualim was calm: 'My men do not fear death, Robert. They welcome it – and the rewards it brings.'

'Good,' called de Sable. 'Then they shall have it all around.'

He was right, of course. The Templars could lay siege to Masyaf and prevent the Assassins receiving supplies. How long could they last before they were so weakened that de Sable could safely attack? Two weeks? A month? Altaïr could only hope that whatever plan Al Mualim had in mind was enough to break the deadlock.

As if reading his thoughts, Rauf whispered to him, from a platform to his left, 'Follow me. And do so without hesitation.'

A third Assassin stood further across. They were hidden from de Sable and his men. Looking down, Altaïr saw strategically placed mounds of hay, enough to break a fall. He was beginning to understand what Rauf had in mind. They were to jump, undetected by the Templars. But why?

His robe flapped at his knees. The sound was comforting, like waves or rain. He looked down and steadied his breathing. He focused. He went to a place within himself.

He heard Al Mualim and de Sable trading words but he was no longer listening, thinking only of the jump, composing himself for it. He closed his eyes. He felt a great calm, a peace within.

'Now,' said Rauf, who leaped, followed by the other Assassin. Next, Altaïr.

He jumped.

Time collapsed as he fell, his arms outstretched. With his body relaxed and arcing gracefully through the air, he knew that he had achieved a kind of perfection – it was as though he was detached from himself. And then he landed perfectly, a haystack breaking his fall. Rauf too. Not so the third Assassin, whose leg snapped on impact. Immediately the man screamed and Rauf moved over to quieten him, not wanting the Templars to hear: for the subterfuge to work, the knights needed to believe that the three men had leaped to their death.

Rauf turned to Altaïr. 'I'll stay behind and attend to him. You'll have to go ahead without us. The ropes there will bring you to the trap. Release it – rain death upon our enemies.'

Of course. Altaïr understood now. Briefly he wondered how the Assassins had been able to set a trap without him knowing. How many other facets of the Brotherhood remained a secret to him? Nimbly he made his way along the ropes across the chasm, doubling back across the gorge and to the cliff face behind the watchtower. He climbed on instinct. Fast and lithe, feeling the muscles in his arms sing as he scaled the sheer walls higher and higher until he reached the top of the watchtower. There beneath the boards of the upper level he found the trap rigged and ready to be sprung: heavy greased logs, stockpiled and stacked on a tilted platform.

Silently he moved to the edge, looking over to see the assembled ranks of the Templar knights, scores of them with their backs to him. Here also were the ropes holding the trap in place. He drew his sword, and for the first time in days, he smiled.

7

Later the Assassins were assembled in the courtyard, still savouring their triumph.

The logs had tumbled from the watchtower and into the knights below, most of whom were crushed by the first wave, while others were caught in a second load stacked behind the first. Just moments before, they had been assured of victory. Then their bodies had been pummelled, limbs snapping, the entire force in disarray, Robert de Sable already ordering his men back as the Assassins' archers pressed home their advantage and rained arrows down upon them.

Now, though, Al Mualim commanded a hush over the gathered Assassins, indicating to Altaïr to join him on the rostrum by the entrance to his tower. His eyes were hard, and as Altaïr took his place, Al Mualim beckoned two guards to take their place at either side of him.

Silence replaced the congratulations. Altaïr, with his back to the Assassins, felt all eyes on him. By now they would know what had happened in Jerusalem; Malik and Abbas would have seen to that. Altaïr's efforts in battle, then springing the trap – they would count for nothing now. All he could hope was that Al Mualim would show mercy.

'You did well to drive Robert from here,' said the Master, and it was with a measure of pride that he said it. Enough for Altaïr to hope that he might be forgiven; that his actions since Jerusalem had redeemed him. 'His force is broken,' continued Al Mualim. 'It shall be a long while before he troubles us again. Tell me, do you know why it is you were successful?'

Altaïr said nothing, heart hammering.

'You were successful because you listened,' pressed Al Mualim. 'Had you listened in Solomon's Temple, Altaïr, all of this would have been avoided.'

His arm described a circle, meant to take in the courtyard and all that lay beyond, where even now the corpses of Assassins, of Templars and villagers were being cleared away.

'I did as I was asked,' said Altaïr, trying to choose his words carefully, but failing.

'*No!*' snapped the Master. His eyes blazed. 'You did as you pleased. Malik has told me of the arrogance you displayed. Your disregard for our ways.'

The two guards on either side of Altaïr stepped forward and took his arms. His muscles tensed. He braced himself against them but did not struggle.

'What are you doing?' he said warily.

The colour rose in Al Mualim's cheeks. 'There are rules. We are nothing if we do not abide by the Assassin's

Creed. Three simple tenets, which you seem to forget. I will remind you. First and foremost: stay your blade . . .'

It was to be a lecture. Altaïr relaxed, unable to keep the note of resignation from his voice as he finished Al Mualim's sentence. '. . . from the flesh of an innocent. I know.'

The crack of Al Mualim's palm across Altaïr's face echoed from the stone of the courtyard. Altaïr felt his cheek burn.

'And stay your tongue unless I give you leave to use it,' roared Al Mualim. 'If you are so familiar with this tenet, why did you kill the old man inside the Temple? He was innocent. He did not need to die.'

Altaïr said nothing. What could he say? I acted rashly? Killing the old man was an act of arrogance?

'Your insolence knows no bounds,' bellowed Al Mualim. 'Make humble your heart, child, or I swear I'll tear it from you with my own hands.'

He paused, his shoulders rising and falling as he took hold of his anger. 'The second tenet is that which gives us strength,' he continued. 'Hide in plain sight. Let the people mask you so that you become one with the crowd. Do you remember? Because, as I hear it, you chose to expose yourself, drawing attention *before* you'd struck.'

Still Altaïr said nothing. He felt the shame squat in his gut.

'The third and final tenet,' added Al Mualim, 'the

worst of all your betrayals: never compromise the Brotherhood. Its meaning should be obvious. Your actions must never bring harm upon us – direct or indirect. Yet your selfish act beneath Jerusalem placed us all in danger. Worse still, you brought the enemy to our home. Every man we've lost today was lost because of you.'

Altaïr had been unable to look at the Master. His head had remained on one side, still smarting from the slap. But as he heard Al Mualim draw his dagger he looked at last.

'I am sorry. Truly, I am,' said Al Mualim. 'But I cannot abide a traitor.'

No. Not that. Not a traitor's death.

His eyes widened as they went to the blade in the Master's hand – the hand that had guided him since him childhood. 'I am not a traitor,' he managed.

'Your actions indicate otherwise. And so you leave me no choice.' Al Mualim drew back his dagger. 'Peace be upon you, Altaïr,' he said, and plunged it into Altaïr's stomach.

8

And it was. For a few precious moments when he was dead, Altaïr was at peace.

Then ... then he was coming round, gradually recovering a sense of himself and of where he was.

He was on his feet. How could he be on his feet? Was this death, the afterlife? Was he in Paradise? If so, it looked very much like Al Mualim's quarters. Not only that, but Al Mualim was present. Standing over him, in fact, watching him with an unreadable gaze.

'I'm alive?' Altaïr's hands went to where the knife had been driven into his stomach. He expected to find a ragged hole and feel wet blood but there was nothing. No wound, no blood. Even though he'd seen it. Felt it. He'd felt the pain ...

Hadn't he?

'But I saw you stab me,' he managed, 'felt death's embrace.'

Al Mualim was inscrutable in return. 'You saw what I wanted you to see. And then you slept the sleep of the dead. The womb. That you might awake and be reborn.'

Altaïr shook a fog away from his mind. 'To what end?'

'Do you remember, Altaïr, what it is the Assassins fight for?'

Still trying to readjust, he replied, 'Peace, in all things.'

'Yes. In all things. It is not enough to end the violence one man commits upon another. It refers to peace within as well. You cannot have one without the other.'

'So it is said.'

Al Mualim shook his head, cheeks colouring again as his voice rose. 'So it is. But you, my son, have not found inner peace. It manifests in ugly ways. You are arrogant and over-confident. You lack self-control and wisdom.'

'Then what is to become of me?'

'I should kill you for the pain you've brought upon us. Malik thinks it's only fair – your life in exchange for that of his brother.'

Al Mualim paused to allow Altaïr to understand the full significance of the moment. 'But this would be a waste of my time and your talents.'

Altaïr allowed himself to relax a little more. He was to be spared. He could redeem himself.

'You have been stripped of your possessions,' continued Al Mualim. 'Your rank as well. You are a novice – a child – once more. As you were on the day you first joined the Order. I am offering you a chance of redemption. You'll earn your way back into the Brotherhood.'

Of course. 'I assume that you have something planned.'

'First you must prove to me you remember *how* to be an Assassin. A true Assassin,' said Al Mualim.

'So you would have me take a life?' asked Altaïr, knowing his forfeit would be far more rigorous.

'No. Not yet, at least. For now you are to become a student once again. '

'There is no need for this. I am a Master Assassin.'

'You *were* a Master Assassin. Others tracked your targets for you. But no more. From today on, you will track them yourself.'

'If that is what you wish.'

'It is.'

'Then tell me what it is that I must do.'

'I hold here a list. Nine names adorn it. Nine men who need to die. They are plague-bringers. War-makers. Their power and influence corrupt the land – and ensure the Crusades continue. You will find them. Kill them. In doing so you'll sow the seeds of peace, both for the region and for yourself. In this way, you may be redeemed.'

Altaïr took a long, deep breath. This he could do. This he wanted – *needed* – to do.

'Nine lives in exchange for mine,' he said carefully.

Al Mualim smiled. 'A most generous offer, I think. Have you any questions?'

'Where shall I begin?'

'Ride for Damascus. Seek out the black-market merchant named Tamir. Let him be the first to fall.'

Al Mualim moved to his cage of carrier pigeons, took one and cupped it gently in his palm. 'Be sure to visit the city's Assassin Bureau when you arrive. I'll dispatch a bird to inform the *rafiq* of your arrival. Speak with him. You'll find he has much to offer.'

He opened his hand and the bird disappeared through the window, as though snuffed out.

'If you believe it best,' said Altaïr.

'I do. Besides, you cannot begin your mission without his consent.'

Altair bridled. 'What nonsense is this? I don't need his permission. It's a waste of time.'

'It's the price you pay for the mistakes you've made,' snapped the Master. 'You answer not only to me but to all of the Brotherhood now.'

'So be it,' conceded Altaïr, after a pause long enough to communicate his displeasure.

'Go, then,' said Al Mualim. 'Prove that you are not yet lost to us.'

He paused, then reached for something from beneath his desk that he pushed across to Altaïr. 'Take it,' he said.

Gladly, Altaïr reached for his blade, buckling the brace to his wrist and looping the release over his little finger. He tested the mechanism, feeling like an Assassin once more.

9

Altaïr made his way through the palms and past the stables and traders outside the city walls until he came to the huge, imposing gates of Damascus. He knew the city well. The biggest and holiest in Syria, it had been home to two of his targets the previous year. He cast his gaze up to the surrounding wall and its ramparts. He could hear the life inside. It was as though the stone hummed with it.

First, to make his way in. The success of his mission depended on his ability to move anonymously though the sprawling streets. A challenge from the guards wouldn't be the best start. He dismounted and tethered his horse, studying the gates, where Saracen guards stood watch. He would have to try another way, and that was more easily considered than achieved, for Damascus was famously secure, its walls – he gazed up once more, feeling small – were too high and too sheer to be scaled from the outside.

Then he saw a group of scholars, and smiled. Salah Al'din had encouraged the learned men to visit Damascus for study – there were many *madrasah*s throughout the city – and as such they enjoyed special privileges and were allowed to wander unhindered. He moved over and joined them, assuming his most pious stance, and with them drifted easily past the guards, leaving the desert behind as he entered the great city.

Inside, he kept his head down, moving fast but carefully through the streets, reaching a minaret. He cast a swift look around before leaping to a sill, pulling himself up, finding more handholds in the hot stone and climbing higher and higher. He found his old skills coming back to him, though he wasn't moving as quickly or as surely as he once had. He felt them returning. No – *reawakening*. And with them the old feeling of exhilaration.

Then he was at the very tip of the minaret and there he squatted. A bird of prey high above the city, looking around himself, seeing the domed mosques and pointed minarets that interrupted an uneven sea of rooftops. He saw marketplaces, courtyards and shrines, as well as the tower that marked the position of the Assassins' Bureau.

Again, a sense of exaltation passed through him. He'd forgotten how beautiful cities looked from such a height. He'd forgotten how he felt, looking down upon them from their highest points. In those moments he felt released.

Al Mualim had been right. For years now, Altaïr's targets had been located for him. He would be told where to go and when, his job to kill, nothing more, nothing less. He hadn't realized it but he had missed the thrill of what it really meant to be an Assassin, which wasn't bloodshed and death: it was what was to be found inside.

He crabbed forward a little, looking down into the narrow streets. The people were being called to prayer and the crowds were thinning. He scanned the canopies and rooftops, looking for a soft landing, then saw a hay cart. Fixing his eyes on it, taking deep breaths, he stood, feeling the breeze, hearing bells. Then he took a step forward, tumbling gracefully and hitting his target. Not as soft as he had hoped, perhaps, but safer than risking a landing on a fraying canopy, which was liable to tear and deposit him in a heap on the stall below. He listened, waiting until the street was quieter, then scrambled from the cart and began to make his way to the Bureau.

He reached it from the roof, dropping into a shaded vestibule in which tinkled a fountain, plants deadening the sounds from outside. It was if he had stepped into another world. He gathered himself and went inside.

The leader lounged behind a counter. He stood as the Assassin entered. 'Altaïr. It is good to see you. And in one piece.'

'You as well, friend.' Altaïr eyed the man, not much liking what he saw. For one thing, he had an insolent, ironic manner. There was no doubt, also, that he had been informed of Altaïr's recent . . . *difficulties* – and, by the look of him, planned to make the most of the temporary power the situation afforded him.

Sure enough, when he next spoke it was with a barely disguised smirk. 'I am sorry for your troubles.'

'Think nothing of it.'

The leader assumed a look of counterfeit concern. 'A few of your brothers were here earlier . . .'

So. *That* was how he was so well informed, thought Altaïr.

'If you'd heard the things they said,' the leader continued airily, 'I'm certain you'd have slain them where they stood.'

'It's quite all right,' said Altaïr.

The leader grinned. 'Yes, you've never been one for the Creed, have you?'

'Is that all?' Altaïr found himself longing to slap off the insolent dog's smile. Either that or use his blade to lengthen it . . .

'I'm sorry,' said the leader, reddening, 'sometimes I forget myself. What business brings you to Damascus?' He straightened a little, remembering his place at last.

'A man named Tamir,' said Altaïr. 'Al Mualim takes issue with the work he does and I am meant to end it. Tell me where to find him.'

'You will have to track him.'

Altaïr bridled. 'But that sort of work is best left for . . .' He stopped himself, remembering Al Mualim's orders. He was to be a novice again. Conduct his own investigations. Find the target. Perform the kill. He nodded, accepting his task.

The leader continued: 'Search the city. Determine what Tamir's planning and where he works. Preparation makes the victor.'

'All right, but what *can* you tell me of him?' asked Altaïr.

'He makes his living as a black-market merchant, so the souk district should be your destination.'

'I assume you want me to return to you when this is done.'

'Come back to me. I'll give you Al Mualim's marker. And you'll give us Tamir's life.'

'As you wish.'

Glad to be away from the stultifying Bureau, Altaïr made his way to the rooftops. Once again, he inhaled the city as he stopped to gaze into a narrow street below. A light breeze rippled canopies. Women milled around a stall selling polished oil lamps, chattering wildly, and not far away two men stood arguing. Over what, Altaïr couldn't hear.

He turned his attention to the building opposite, then away over the rooftops. From there he could see the Pasha Mosque and the site of the Formal Gardens in the south but what he needed to locate was the . . .

He saw it, the huge Souk al-Silaah – where, according to the leader, he could begin to learn about Tamir. The leader knew more than he was revealing, of course, but was under strict instructions not to tell Altaïr. He understood that: the 'novice' had to learn the hard way.

He took two steps back, shook the tension from his arms, drew a deep breath, then jumped.

Safely across, he crouched for a moment, listening to the chatter from the lane below. He watched a group of guards as they passed, leading an ass with a cart that sagged beneath the weight of many stacked casks. 'Make way,' the guards were saying, shoving citizens from their path. 'Make way for we come with supplies bound for the Vizier's Palace. His Excellency Abu'l Nuqoud is to throw another of his parties.' Those citizens who were shoved aside hid scowls of displeasure.

Altaïr watched the soldiers pass below him. He had heard the name, Abu'l Nuqoud: the one they called the Merchant King of Damascus. The casks. Altaïr might have been mistaken, but they looked as though they contained wine.

No matter. Altaïr's business lay elsewhere. He straightened and set off at a jog, barely pausing for the leap to the next building and then the next, feeling a fresh surge of power and strength with each jump. Back to doing what he knew.

Seen from above, the souk was like ragged hole that had been punched into the city's rooftops so it was easy to find. The biggest trading centre in Damascus, it lay in the centre of the city's Poor District in the north-east and was bordered on all sides by buildings of mud and timber – Damascus turned into a swamp when it rained – and was a patchwork of carts, stands and merchants' tables. Sweet scents rose to Altaïr on his perch high above: perfumes and oils, spices and pastries. Everywhere customers, merchants and traders were chattering or moving quickly through the crowds. The city's people either stood and talked or hurried from one place to the next. There was no in-between, it seemed – not here, anyway. He watched them for a while, then clambered from the rooftop and, blending into the crowds, listened.

Listening for one word.

'*Tamir.*'

The three merchants were huddled in the shade, talking quietly but with all kinds of wild hand move-ments. It was they who had said the name, and Altaïr sidled over towards them, turning his back and hearing Al Mualim's tutelage in his head as he did so: 'Never make eye contact, always look occupied, stay relaxed.'

'He's called another meeting,' heard Altaïr, unable to place which of the men was speaking. Who was the 'he' they mentioned? Tamir, presumably. Altaïr listened, making a mental note of the meeting place.

'What is it this time? Another warning? Another execution?'

'No. He has work for us.'

'Which means we won't be paid.'

'He's abandoned the ways of the merchant guild. Does as he pleases now . . .'

They began discussing a large deal – the biggest ever, said one, in hushed tones – when suddenly they stopped. Not far away an orator with a close-trimmed black beard had taken his place at his stand, and was now staring at the merchants with dark, hooded eyes. Threatening eyes.

Altaïr stole a glance from beneath his cowl. The three men had gone pale. One scuffed at the dirt with his sandal; the other two drifted away, as though suddenly remembering an important task at hand. Their meeting was at an end.

The orator. One of Tamir's men, perhaps. Evidently the black-marketeer ruled the souk with a firm hand. Altaïr drifted over as the man began to speak, drumming up an audience.

'None knows Tamir better than I,' he announced loudly. 'Come close. Hear the tale I have to tell. Of a merchant prince without peer . . .'

Just the tale Altaïr wanted to hear. He drifted closer, able to play the part of an interested observer. The market swirled around him.

'It was just before Hattin,' continued the speaker. 'The Saracens were low on food, and in desperate need of resupply. But there was no relief in sight. Tamir drove a caravan in those days between Damascus and

Jerusalem. But recent business had been poor. It seemed there were none in Jerusalem who wanted what he had: fruits and vegetables from nearby farms. And so Tamir left, riding north and wondering what would become of his supplies. Soon they would surely spoil. That should have been the end of this tale and the poor man's life . . . But Fate intended otherwise.

'As Tamir drove his caravan north, he came across the Saracen leader and his starving men. Most fortunate for them both – each having something the other wanted.

'So Tamir gave the man his food. And when the battle was finished, the Saracen leader saw to it that the merchant was repaid a thousand times.

'Some say, were it not for Tamir, Salah Al'din's men would have turned on him. It could be that we won the battle because of that man . . .'

He finished his speech and let his audience drift away. On his face was a thin smile as he stepped away from the stand and moved into the market. Off, perhaps, to another stand to make the same speech exalting Tamir. Altaïr followed, keeping a safe distance, once again hearing his tutor's words in his head: 'Put obstacles between yourself and your quarry. Never be found by a backwards glance.'

These skills: Altaïr enjoyed the feeling they brought as they returned to him. He liked being able to shut out the clamour of the day and focus on his quarry.

Then, abruptly, he stopped. Ahead of him the orator had bumped into a woman carrying a vase, which had smashed. She began remonstrating with him, her hand out demanding payment, but he curled a cruel lip and drew back his hand to strike her. Altaïr found himself tensing, but she cowered away and he sneered, lowering his hand, walking on, kicking bits of broken pot as he went. Altaïr moved on, past the woman, who now crouched in the sand, weeping and cursing and reaching for the shards of her vase.

Now the orator turned off the street and Altaïr followed. They were in a narrow, almost empty lane, dark mud walls pressing in on them. A shortcut, presumably, to the next stand. Altaïr glanced behind him, then took a few quick steps forward, grasped the speaker by the shoulder, spun him around and jammed the tips of his fingers beneath his ribcage.

Instantly the orator was doubled up, stumbling back and gasping for breath, his mouth working like that of a grounded fish. Altaïr shot a look to make sure there were no witnesses, then stepped forward, pivoted on one foot and kicked the orator in the throat.

He fell back messily, his *thawb* twisted around his legs. Now his hands went to where Altaïr had kicked him and he rolled in the dust. Smiling, Altaïr moved forward. Easy, he thought. It had been too . . .

The orator moved with the speed of a cobra. He shot up and kicked out, catching Altaïr square in the chest. Surprised, the Assassin staggered back as the other came forward, mouth set and fists swinging. He had a gleam in his eye, knowing he'd rocked Altaïr, who dodged one flailing punch only to realize it was a feint as the orator caught him across the jaw with his other fist.

Altaïr almost fell, tasting blood and cursing himself. He had underestimated his opponent. A novice mistake. The orator looked frantically around himself as though seeking the best escape route. Altaïr shook the pain from his face and came forward, holding his fists high and catching the orator on the temple before he could move off. For some moments the two traded blows in the alley. The orator was smaller and faster, and caught Altaïr high on the bridge of his nose. The Assassin stumbled, blinking away tears that split his vision. Sensing victory, the orator came forward, throwing wild punches. Altaïr stepped to the side, went low and swept the orator's feet from beneath him, sending him crashing to the sand, the breath whooshing out of him as he landed on his back. Altaïr spun and dropped, sinking his knee directly into the speaker's groin. He was gratified to hear an agonized bark in response, then stood, his shoulders rising and falling heavily as he collected himself. The orator writhed soundlessly in the dirt, mouth wide in a silent scream, his hands at his crotch. When he managed a great gasping breath, Altaïr squatted, bringing his face close to him.

'You seem to know quite a bit about Tamir,' he hissed. 'Tell me what he's planning.'

'I know only the stories I tell,' groaned the speaker. 'Nothing more.'

Altaïr scooped up a handful of dirt and let it trickle through his fingers. 'A pity. There's no reason to let you live if you've nothing to offer in return.'

'Wait. Wait.' The orator held up a trembling hand. 'There is one thing . . .'

'Continue.'

'He is preoccupied as of late. He oversees the production of many, many weapons . . .'

'What of it? They're meant for Salah Al'din presumably. This does not help me – which means it does not help you . . .' Altaïr reached . . .

'*No.* Stop. Listen.' The orator's eyes rolled and sweat popped on his brow. 'Not Salah Al'din. They're for *someone else.* The crests these arms bear, they're different. Unfamiliar. It seems Tamir supports another . . . but I know not who.'

Altaïr nodded. 'Is that all?' he asked.

'Yes. Yes. I've told you everything I know.'

'Then it's time for you to rest.'

'No,' began the orator, but there was a snick that sounded as loud as the breaking of crockery in the alley as Altaïr released his blade then drove it through the orator's sternum, holding the dying man as he shuddered, pinned by the blade, blood foaming from the corners of his mouth and his eyes glazing. A quick death. A clean death.

Altaïr laid him on the sand, reached to close his eyes, then stood. His blade slid back into place, and he pushed the body behind a stack of stinking barrels, then turned and left the alley.

IO

'Altaïr. Welcome. Welcome.'

The leader smirked as he walked in, and Altaïr regarded him for a moment, seeing him shrink a little under his gaze. Did he carry the smell of death? Perhaps the Bureau leader had detected it upon him.

'I've done as you asked. Now give me the marker.'

'First things first. Tell me what you know.'

Fresh from taking a life, Altaïr reflected that it would be a small matter to add to his day's tally. He itched to put the man in his place. But no. He had to play his part, no matter how much of a charade he thought it was.

'Tamir rules the Souk al-Silaah,' he said, thinking of the merchants talking in hushed tones, the fear on their faces when they spotted Tamir's orator. 'He makes his fortune selling arms and armour, and is supported by many in this endeavour: blacksmiths, traders, financiers. He's the main death dealer in the land.'

The other nodded, hearing nothing he didn't already know. 'And have you devised a way to rid us of this blight?' he asked superciliously.

'A meeting is being arranged at Souk al-Silaah to

discuss an important sale. They say it's the largest deal Tamir has ever made. He'll be distracted with his work. That's when I'll strike.'

'Your plan seems solid enough. I give you leave to go.'

He reached below his desk and retrieved Al Mualim's marker. A feather from one of the Master's beloved birds. He placed it on the desk between them. 'Let Al Mualim's will be done,' he said, as Altaïr took the marker, stowing it carefully within his robe.

Soon after sunrise he left the Bureau and made his way back to the Souk al-Silaah. When he arrived at the market all eyes seemed to be on a sunken ceremonial courtyard in its centre.

He soon saw why: there stood the merchant Tamir. With two glowering bodyguards at his rear, he commanded the courtyard, towering over a trembling man who stood before him. He wore a chequered turban, smart tunic and leg wrappings. His teeth were bared beneath a dark moustache.

As Altaïr made his way round the outside of the crowd he kept an eye on what was happening. Traders had moved from behind their stalls to see too. The Damascus that either hurried between destinations or stood lost in conversation had come to a temporary standstill.

'If you'd just have a look . . .' said the man cringing before Tamir.

'I've no interest in your calculations,' snapped Tamir. 'The numbers change nothing. Your men have failed to fill the order – which means I have failed my client.'

Client, thought Altaïr. Who might that be?

The merchant swallowed. His eyes went to the crowd looking for salvation. He found none there. The market guards stood with blank expressions and unseeing eyes while the spectators simply stared, agog. Altaïr was sickened by them, all of them: the vultures watching, the guards who did nothing. But most of all Tamir.

'We need more time,' pleaded the merchant. Perhaps he realized that his only chance lay in persuading Tamir to be merciful.

'That is the excuse of a lazy or incompetent man,' returned the black-marketeer. 'Which are you?'

'Neither,' responded the merchant, wringing his hands.

'What I see says otherwise,' said Tamir. He raised a foot to a low wall and leaned on his knee. 'Now, tell me, what do you intend to do to solve this problem of ours? These weapons are needed *now*.'

'I see no solution,' stammered the merchant. 'The men work day and night. But your . . . client requires so much. And the destination . . . It is a difficult route.'

'Would that you could produce weapons with the same skill as you produce excuses,' laughed Tamir.

Playing to the crowd, he was rewarded by a chuckle – born more of fear than the quality of his humour.

'I have done all I can,' insisted the older man. Perspiration was flowing freely from the headband of his turban and his grey beard quivered.

'It is not enough.'

'Then perhaps you ask too much,' tried the merchant.

It was a foolhardy gambit. The crowd-pleasing smile slid from Tamir's face and he turned cold eyes on the old man. 'Too much?' he said, a new chill in his voice. 'I gave you everything. Without me you would still be charming serpents for coin. All I asked in return was that you fill the orders I bring you. And you say I ask *too much*?'

He drew his dagger, the blade winking. Those watching shifted uncomfortably. Altaïr looked at the guards, who stood with their arms folded, sabres in their belts, faces expressionless. Nobody in the souk dared move; it was as though a spell had been cast on them all.

A frightened sound escaped the merchant. He dropped to his knees, holding his clasped hands aloft in supplication. His face was etched with pleading; his eyes gleamed with tears.

Tamir looked down at him, a pathetic creature kneeling before him, and spat. The trader blinked phlegm from his eyes.

'*You dare slander me?*' roared Tamir.

'Peace, Tamir,' whimpered the old man. 'I meant no insult.'

'Then you should have kept your mouth shut,' snarled Tamir.

Altaïr could see the bloodlust in his eyes and knew exactly what was going to happen. Sure enough, Tamir slashed at the merchant with the tip of his dagger, opening a sagging hole in his tunic that was immediately stained red. The merchant fell back to his heels with a keening screech that cut through the marketplace. 'No! Stop!' he squealed.

'Stop?' jeered Tamir. 'I'm just getting started.' He stepped forward, drove his dagger deep into the man's stomach and thrust him to the ground where he screamed like an animal as Tamir stabbed him again. 'You came into *my* souk,' he shouted.

Stab.

'Stood before *my* men.'

Stab. A fourth time. The sound like meat being tenderized. The old man was still screaming.

'And dared to insult me?'

Stab. He punctuated every word with a thrust of his dagger. 'You must learn your place.'

But now the merchant had stopped screaming. Now he was nothing but a battered, bloody corpse sprawled in the courtyard, his head at an odd angle. One of Tamir's bodyguards stepped forward to move the body.

'No,' said Tamir, out of breath. He wiped his beard with the back of his hand. 'Leave it.' He turned to address the crowd. 'Let this be a lesson to the rest of you. Think twice before you tell me something cannot be done. Now get back to work.'

Leaving the old man's body where it was — an interested dog already beginning to sniff around it — the spectators resumed their day, activity in the souk gradually building up so that in a few short moments it was as though nothing had happened. As though the old man was forgotten.

Not by Altaïr, though. He found himself unclenching his fists, letting out a long, slow breath, controlling and harnessing his anger. He bowed his head slightly, eyes hidden by his cowl, and stole through the crowd after Tamir, who was walking through the market, his two bodyguards not far behind. Coming closer to him, Altaïr overheard him talking to the traders, each of whom stared at him with wide, terrified eyes, agreeing fiercely with everything they were told.

'I can't sell this,' snapped Tamir. 'Melt it down and try again. And if it comes out just as poorly it'll be *you* who gets melted down next.'

Wide eyes. Nod, nod, nod.

'I don't understand what you do all day. Your stall is filled with goods. Your purse should be filled with coin. Why can't you sell these things? It isn't difficult. Perhaps, you are not trying hard enough. Do you require *motivation?*'

The trader was nodding before he realized what was

being asked and swiftly amended it to an equally emphatic shake. Tamir moved on. The crowds swirled around him. His bodyguards ... Now, was this an opportunity? With the entire market terrified of Tamir, his men had relaxed their guard. They had remained behind at another stall, where they were demanding goods to give as gifts to their wives. Tamir had fresh victims to terrorize.

And now Altaïr slipped between him and the two bodyguards. He tensed, felt the resistance from his blade mechanism on his little finger. Tamir had his back to him, insulting yet another stallholder.

'You begged me for this position. Swore none could do as well as you. I should –'

Altaïr stepped forward, and – *snick* – his blade sprang out as he swept one arm round Tamir and used the other to drive the weapon deep.

Tamir made a strangulated sound but did not scream, and for a second he writhed, before going limp. Over his shoulder, Altaïr met the wide eyes of the terrified stallholder and saw the man wrestling with what to do: raise the alarm or ... The trader turned his back and moved away.

Altaïr lowered Tamir to the ground between two stalls, out of sight of the bodyguards, who remained oblivious.

Tamir's eyes fluttered.

'Be at peace,' said Altaïr, gently.

'You'll pay for this, Assassin,' rasped Tamir. A fine line of blood ran from his nose. 'You and all your kind.'

'It seems you're the one who pays now, my friend. You'll not profit from suffering any longer.'

Tamir gave a harsh, shallow laugh. 'You think me some petty death-dealer, suckling at the breast of war? A strange target, perhaps? Why me, when so many others do the same?'

'You believe yourself different, then?' asked Altaïr.

'Oh, but I am, for I serve a far nobler cause than mere profit. Just like my brothers . . .'

'Brothers?'

Again Tamir chuckled weakly. 'Ah . . . he thinks I act alone. I am but a piece. A man with a part to play. You'll come to know the others soon enough. They won't take kindly to what you've done.'

'Good. I look forward to ending their lives as well.'

'Such pride. It will destroy you, child,' said Tamir. And he passed.

'People have to die for things to change,' intoned Altaïr, closing the man's eyes.

He took Al Mualim's feather from within his robes and stained it with the blood of Tamir, cast a last look at the bodyguards, then moved off, disappearing into the crowds. He was already a ghost when he heard the cry go up behind him.

Tamir, the first of the nine: Al Mualim had been quietly satisfied, looking from the blood-stained feather on his desk to Altaïr and praising him, before giving him his next undertaking.

Altair had bowed his head in assent and left the Master. And the next day he had gathered his supplies and set off once more, this time for Acre – a city held as tightly by the Crusaders as Damascus was by Salah Al'din's men. A city wounded by war.

Acre had been hard-won. The Christians had retaken it after a prolonged and bloody siege lasting almost two years. Altaïr had played his part, helping to stop the city's water supply being poisoned by the Templars.

He had been unable to do anything about the poisoning that did occur, though: corpses in the water had spread disease to Muslim and Christian alike – both inside and outside the city walls. Supplies had run dry, and thousands had simply starved to death. Then more Crusaders had arrived to construct more machines, and their attacks had punched holes in the city walls. The Saracens had fought back for long enough to repair the breaches, until Richard the Lionheart's army simply wore the Muslims down and they offered surrender. The Crusaders had moved in to claim the city and take its garrison hostage.

Negotiations between Salah Al'din and Richard for the release of the hostages had commenced, the finer points of which had been muddied by a disagreement between Richard and the Frenchman Conrad de Montferrat, who was unwilling to hand over hostages taken by French forces.

Conrad had returned to Tyre; Richard was on his way to Jaffa where his troops would meet those of Salah Al'din. And left in charge was Conrad's brother, William.

William de Montferrat had ordered the Muslim hostages put to death. Almost three thousand were beheaded.

And so it was that Altaïr found himself conducting his investigations in a city scarred by its recent history: of siege, disease, starvation, cruelty and bloodshed. A city whose residents knew suffering all too well, whose eyes hid sorrow and whose shoulders were stooped with sadness. In the poor areas he encountered the worst of the suffering. Bodies wrapped in muslin lined the streets, while drunkenness and violence was rife in the ports. The only area of the city not to reek of despair and death was the Chain District, where the Crusaders were based – where Richard had his citadel and William his quarters. From there the Crusaders had pronounced Acre the capital of the Kingdom of Jerusalem, and had used it to stockpile supplies before Richard had set off on the march to Jaffa, leaving William in charge. So far his reign had simply exacerbated the city's problems, which were all too evident – and pressed in on Altaïr as he made his way through the streets. He was grateful to complete his investigations and make his way to the Assassins' Bureau. There the leader, Jabal, sat cooing gently to a pigeon he held. He looked up as Altaïr entered the room.

'Ah, Altaïr,' he said pleasantly. 'A little bird told me you'd be paying a visit . . .'

He smiled at his own joke, then opened his hands to set the pigeon free. Instead it merely alighted on the counter where it puffed out its chest feathers and began walking to and fro as though mounting an avian guard. Jabal watched it with amused eyes, then adjusted himself on his seat to regard his visitor.

'And who is the poor unfortunate that Al Mualim has chosen to taste your blade, Altaïr?' he asked.

'Al Mualim has ordered the execution of Garnier de Naplouse.'

Jabal started. 'The Grand Master of the Knights Hospitalier?'

Slowly Altaïr nodded. 'Indeed. And I have already determined when and how to strike.'

'Share your knowledge with me, then.' Jabal looked impressed, and with good reason.

Altaïr began: 'He lives and works within his Order's hospital, north-west of here. Rumours speak of atrocities committed within its walls.'

As Altaïr told him what he knew, Jabal nodded thoughtfully, considering his words and asking at length, 'What is your plan?'

'Garnier keeps mainly to his quarters inside the hospital, though he leaves occasionally to inspect his patients. It's when he makes his rounds that I will strike.'

'It's clear you've given this some thought. I give you leave to go.' And with that he handed Altaïr Al Mualim's marker. 'Remove this stain from Acre, Altaïr. Perhaps it will help cleanse your own.'

Altaïr took the marker, fixed Jabal with a baleful look – was every Assassin to be made aware of his shame? – then left, making his way across the city's rooftops until he had sight of the hospital. There he stopped, catching his breath and gathering his thoughts as he looked down upon it.

Altaïr had given Jabal a truncated version of his findings; he had hidden his true feelings of disgust from the Bureau leader. He'd learned that de Naplouse was Grand Master of the Order of the Knights Hospitalier. Originally founded in Jerusalem – their aim to provide care for ailing pilgrims – the Knights had a base in one of Acre's most deprived areas.

And there, according to what Altaïr had learned, de Naplouse was doing anything but providing care.

In the Hospitalier district he had overheard two members of the Order talking about how the Grand Master was turning ordinary citizens away from the hospital, and the people were close to violence because of it. One had said that he feared a repeat of a scandal that had taken place at Tyre.

'What scandal?' his friend had asked.

The man had leaned in close to his companion to finish and Altaïr had been forced to listen hard. 'Garnier once called that city home,' the man had said, 'but he was exiled. It's said he was experimenting on its citizens.'

His companion had looked a little sick. 'What sort of experiments?'

'I don't know the details, but I worry ... Has he begun again? Is that why he locks himself away in the Hospitalier fortress?'

Later, Altaïr had read a scroll that he had pickpocketed from an associate of de Naplouse. The Hospitalier had no intention of healing his patients, he read. Supplied with subjects from Jerusalem, he was conducting tests – tests for some unknown master – aimed at inducing certain states in his subjects. And Tamir – the recently deceased Tamir – had been charged with finding arms for the operation.

One particular phrase in the letter caught his eye: *We should endeavour to reclaim what has been taken from us.* What did that mean? Puzzling over it, he continued his enquiries. The Grand Master allowed 'madmen' to wander the grounds of the hospital, he heard, and he discovered the times at which the archers covering the walkways above the hospital left their posts; he learned that de Naplouse liked to make his rounds without a bodyguard and that only monks were allowed passage.

Then, having all the information he needed, Altaïr had visited Jabal to collect Al Mualim's marker.

I 2

Now he moved around the outside of a building adjacent to the Hospitaliers' fortress. As he had expected, there was a guard, an archer, and Altaïr watched as he paced the walkway, every now and then casting his gaze into the courtyard below, but mainly gazing across the roofline. Altaïr looked at the sun. It should be about now, he thought, smiling to himself as, sure enough, the archer moved to a ladder and let himself down.

Altaïr stayed low. He leaped from the roof to the walkway and quietly scuttled along until he was able to peer over the edge and into the courtyard below. Sheer-walled in dull, grey, forbidding stone, a well stood in its centre, but it was otherwise bare, quite unlike the ornately decorated buildings usually to be found in Acre. There, several guards were wearing the quilted black coats of the Hospitalier knights, the white cross on the chest, and there was also a group of monks. Moving among them were what looked like patients, barefoot and shirtless. Poor wretches who milled aimlessly about, their expressions blank, their eyes glazed.

Altaïr frowned. Even with the walkway unguarded it was impossible to drop into the courtyard unseen. He moved to the entrance wall of the hospital, so that he was able to look into the street outside. On stone painted white by the sun, ailing cityfolk and their families begged the guards to be allowed inside. Others whose minds had gone wandered among the throng, casting their arms into the air, shouting gibberish and obscenities.

And there – Altair smiled to see them – was a group of scholars. They were moving through the crowd as if it wasn't there, heedless of the suffering and tumult around them. They seemed to be going in the direction of the hospital. Taking advantage of the disorder, Altaïr lowered himself into the street unnoticed, joined the ranks of the scholars and lowered his head to concentrate his gaze on his shuffling feet. Every now and then he risked a surreptitious glance to check their bearings and, as he'd hoped, they were heading towards the hospital where the guards stood aside, admitting them to the courtyard.

Altaïr wrinkled his nose. Where the street had held the scent of the city, of baking and perfumes and spices, in here was the stench of suffering, of death and human waste. From somewhere – through a set of closed doors – there came a series of pained cries, then low moaning. That would be the main hospital, he thought. He was proved correct when, suddenly, the doors were flung open and a patient careered madly into the courtyard.

'*No! Help! Help me!*' he screamed. His face was contorted with fear, his eyes wide. '*Help me, please! You must help me!*'

After him came a guard. He had a lazy eye, as though the muscles in his eyelid had once been cut. He ran after the escaping crazy man, catching him. Then, joined by another guard, he began punching and kicking him until the crazy man was subdued and on his knees.

Altaïr watched. He felt his jaw tighten and his fists clench as the guards beat the man, other patients moving forward to get an improved view of the spectacle, watching with faces that registered only mild interest, swaying slightly.

'Mercy!' howled the crazy man, as the blows rained down on him. 'I beg mercy. No more!'

He stopped. Suddenly his pain was forgotten as the doors to the hospital swung open and there stood a man who could only be Garnier de Naplouse.

He was shorter than Altaïr had expected. He was beardless and had close-cropped white hair, sunken eyes and a cruel, downturned mouth, which gave him a cadaverous look. The white cross of the Hospitalier was on his arms and he wore a crucifix around his neck – but whatever God he worshipped had deserted him, Altaïr saw. For he also wore an apron. A dirty, blood-stained apron.

Now he looked darkly at the crazy man prostrate

before him, held by Lazy Eye and the other guard, Lazy Eye raising his fist to punch him again.

'Enough, my child,' ordered de Naplouse. 'I asked you to retrieve the patient, not to kill him.'

Lazy Eye lowered his fist reluctantly as de Naplouse came forward, closer to the crazy man, who moaned and pulled away, like a skittish animal.

De Naplouse smiled, the hardness gone. 'There, there,' he said to the crazy man, almost tenderly. 'Everything will be all right. Give me your hand.'

The crazy man shook his head. 'No – no! Don't touch me. Not again . . .'

De Naplouse furrowed his brow, as though slightly hurt by the man's reaction to him. 'Cast out this fear, else I cannot help you,' he said evenly.

'Help me? Like you helped the others? You took their *souls*. But not mine. No. You'll not have mine. Never, never, never . . . *Not mine not mine not mine not mine* . . .'

The softness was gone as de Naplouse slapped the crazy man. 'Take hold of yourself,' he snarled. His sunken eyes flared and the other's head drooped. 'Do you think this gives me pleasure? Do you think I *want* to hurt you? But you leave me no choice . . .'

Suddenly the crazy man had pulled away from the two guards and tried to run into the watching crowd. 'Every kind word matched by the back of his hand . . .' he screeched, passing close to Altaïr as the two guards

92

rushed after him. 'All lies and deception. He won't be content until all bow before him.'

Lazy Eye caught him, dragged him back before de Naplouse, where he whimpered under the Grand Master's cold gaze.

'You should not have done that,' said de Naplouse, slowly, then to Lazy Eye, 'Return him to his quarters. I'll be along once I've attended to the others.'

'*You can't keep me here!*' shouted the crazy man. '*I'll escape again.*'

De Naplouse stopped. 'No, you won't,' he said evenly, then turned to Lazy Eye. 'Break his legs. Both of them.'

Lazy Eye grinned as the crazy man tried to pull away. Then there were two sickening cracks, like kindling being snapped, as the huge knight stamped first on one leg, then the other. The victim screamed, and Altaïr found himself moving forward, unable to contain himself, seething at the wanton cruelty.

Then the moment had gone: the man had lost consciousness – the pain, no doubt, too much to bear – and the two guards were dragging him away. De Naplouse watched him. The sympathetic look had returned to his face.

'I am so sorry, child,' he said, almost to himself, before turning on the crowd. 'Have you people nothing better to do?' he barked, and stared darkly at the monks and patients, who slowly drifted away. As Altaïr turned his back to join them he saw de Naplouse scanning the throng carefully, as though looking for one who might have been sent to kill him.

Good, thought Altaïr, hearing the door to the hospital close as the Grand Master left the courtyard. Let him be afraid. Let him feel a little of what he inflicts on others. The image warmed him as he joined the scholars, who were moving through a second door. This one led into the main ward, where straw matting did little to hide the reek of suffering and human waste. Altaïr found himself trying not to gag, noticing several of the scholars move the fabric of their robes to their noses to block it out. From in here came the moaning and Altaïr saw hospital beds that contained men who groaned and occasionally cried out with pain. Keeping his head bent, he peered out from beneath his cowl, seeing de Naplouse approach a bed in which an emaciated man lay restrained by leather bindings.

'And how are you feeling?' de Naplouse asked him.

In pain, the patient wheezed, 'What have you done . . . to me?'

'Ah, yes. The pain. It hurts at first, I won't lie. A small price to pay. In time you'll agree.'

The man tried to lift his head from the bed. 'You're . . . a monster . . .'

De Naplouse smiled indulgently. 'I've been called worse.' He moved past a wooden cage that enclosed another bed, peering in at the . . . no, not a patient,

Altaïr realized. These poor wretches were subjects. They were *experiments*. Again he fought to control his anger. He glanced around. Most of the guards had congregated at the other end of the ward. Just as in the courtyard, several disoriented patients were stumbling about, and he saw the same cluster of monks, who seemed to hang on de Naplouse's every utterance while remaining at a respectful distance, talking among themselves as the Grand Master made his rounds.

If he was going to do it – and he *was* going to do it – then it had to be soon.

But then de Naplouse moved over to another bed, smiling at the man who lay there. 'They say you can walk now,' he said kindly. 'Impressive.'

The man looked confused. 'Been ... so long. Almost forgot ... how.'

De Naplouse looked pleased – genuinely pleased. Beaming, he said, 'That's wonderful.'

'I don't ... understand. Why did you help me?'

'Because no one else would,' answered de Naplouse, moving on.

'I owe you my life,' said the man in the next bed. 'I am yours to command. Thank you. Thank you for freeing me.'

'Thank you for letting me,' replied de Naplouse.

Altaïr faltered a moment. Was he wrong? Was de Naplouse *not* a monster? Then just as quickly he cast his doubts away, thinking instead of the crazy man's shrieks of agony as they had snapped his legs, the lifeless patients roaming the hospital. If there were indeed examples of healing here, then surely they were outnumbered by the acts of barbarism.

Now de Naplouse had reached the final bed in the ward. In moments he would leave and Altaïr's chance would be gone. Resolved, the Assassin cast a look behind him: the guards were still occupied at the end of the hall. He moved out of the assembly of scholars, coming up behind de Naplouse as the Grand Master bent to his patient.

Altaïr's blade sprang forth and he rammed it home, reaching for de Naplouse and stifling his cry as he arched his back in pain. Almost gently, the Assassin lowered the skewered doctor to the floor. 'Let go your burden,' he whispered.

De Naplouse blinked and looked up at him – into the face of his Assassin. But there was no fear in those dying eyes: what Altaïr saw was concern. 'Ah . . . I'll rest now, yes?' he said. 'The endless dream calls to me. But before I close my eyes, I must know – what will become of my children?'

Children? 'You mean the people made to suffer your cruel experiments?' Altaïr couldn't keep the disgust from his voice. 'They'll be free now to return to their homes.'

De Naplouse laughed drily. 'Homes? What homes? The sewers? The brothels? The prisons we dragged them from?'

'You took these people against their will,' said Altaïr.

'Yes. What little will there was for them to have,' gasped de Naplouse. 'Are you really so naïve? Do you appease a crying child simply because he wails? "But I want to play with fire, Father." What would you say? "As you wish"? Ah . . . but then you'd answer for his burns.'

'These are not children,' said Altaïr, wanting to understand the dying man, 'but men and women full grown.'

'In body, perhaps. But not in mind. Which is the very damage I sought to repair. I admit, without the artefact – which you *stole* from us – my progress was slowed. But there are herbs. Mixtures and extracts. My guards are proof of this. They were madmen before I found and freed them from the prisons of their minds. And, with my death, madmen will they be again . . .'

'You truly believe you were helping them?'

De Naplouse smiled, the light beginning to leave his eyes. 'It's not what I believe. It's what I know.'

He died. Altaïr lowered his head to the stone and reached for Al Mualim's feather, brushing it with blood. 'Death be not unkind,' he whispered.

In the same moment, a cry went up from the nearby monks. Altaïr straightened from the body and saw guards lumbering down the ward towards him. As they drew their swords he leaped up and ran, heading towards a far door, which, he fervently hoped, led to the courtyard.

It opened and he was pleased to see the courtyard before him.

He was less pleased to see Lazy Eye, who barrelled through the open door, his broadsword drawn . . .

Altaïr drew his own sword and, with the blade at one arm, his sword in the other hand, met Lazy Eye with a clash of steel. For a second the two men were nose to nose, and Altaïr could see up close the scarred skin of the knight's eye. Then Lazy Eye pushed away, immediately stabbing forward, meeting Altaïr's sword but readjusting so quickly that Altaïr almost missed the defence. The Assassin danced away, wanting to put space between him and Lazy Eye, who was a better swordsman than he had anticipated. He was big, too. The tendons of his neck stood out, developed from years of wielding the huge broadsword. From behind him Altair heard the other guards arriving, then stopping at a signal from Lazy Eye.

'I want him,' growled the giant knight.

He was arrogant, over-confident. Altaïr smiled, savouring the irony. Then he came forward, his blade sweeping up. Grinning, Lazy Eye deflected the blow and was grunting as Altaïr skipped to his left, coming at Lazy Eye from the other side – the side of his damaged eye, his weak spot – and slashing at his neck.

The knight's throat opened and blood poured from the wound as he sank to his knees. From behind Altaïr there was a surprised cry so he started running, crashing through a collection of crazy men, who had gathered to watch, then sprinting across the courtyard, past the well and under the arch into Acre.

He stopped, scanning the roofline. Next he was vaulting a stall, the angry merchant shaking his fist as he scaled a wall behind him and took to the roofs. Running, jumping, he left the nightmare hospital behind him and melted into the city still mulling over de Naplouse's last words. The *artefact* he had spoken of. Briefly Altaïr thought of the box on Al Mualim's desk, but no. What possible connection would the Hospitalier have with that?

But if not that, then what?

13

'Garnier de Naplouse is dead,' he had told Al Mualim, days later.

'Excellent.' The Master had nodded approvingly. 'We could not have hoped for a more agreeable outcome.'

'And yet . . .' started Altaïr.

'What is it?'

'The doctor insisted his work was noble,' said Altaïr. 'And, looking back, of those who were supposedly his captives, many seemed grateful to him. Not all of them, but enough to make me wonder . . . How did he manage to turn enemy into friend?'

Al Mualim had chuckled. 'Leaders will always find ways to make others obey them. And that is what makes them leaders. When words fail, they turn to coin. When that won't do, they resort to baser things: bribes, threats and other types of trickery. There are plants, Altaïr – herbs from distant lands – that can cause a man to take leave of his senses. So great are the pleasures they bring that men may even become enslaved by them.'

Altaïr nodded, thinking of the glazed patients. The crazy man. 'You think these men were drugged, then? Poisoned?'

'Yes, if it truly was as you describe it,' Al Mualim said. 'Our enemies have accused me of the same.'

Then he had given Altaïr his next task, and Altaïr had wondered why the Master smiled when he told him to complete his enquiries then report to the Assassins' Bureau *rafiq* in Jerusalem.

Now, walking into the Bureau, he knew why. It was because it amused him to think of Altaïr once more crossing paths with Malik.

The Assassin stood up from behind the desk as Altaïr entered. For a moment the two regarded each other, neither hiding his disdain. Then, slowly, Malik turned, showing Altaïr where his arm had once been.

Altaïr blanched. Of course. Damaged in the fight with de Sable's men, the best surgeons in Masyaf had been unable to save Malik's left arm – and so had been forced to amputate.

Malik smiled the bittersweet smile of victory that had come at too high a price, and Altaïr remembered himself. He remembered that he had no business treating Malik with anything but humility and respect. He bowed his head to acknowledge the other man's losses. His brother. His arm. His status.

'Safety and peace, Malik,' he said at last.

'Your presence here deprives me of both,' spat Malik. He, however, had plenty of business treating Altaïr with disdain – and evidently intended to do so. 'What do you want?'

'Al Mualim has asked —'

'That you perform some task in an effort to redeem yourself?' sneered Malik. 'So. Out with it. What have you learned?'

'This is what I know,' answered Altaïr. 'The target is Talal, who traffics in human lives, kidnapping Jerusalem's citizens and selling them into slavery. His base is a warehouse located inside the barbican north of here. As we speak, he prepares a caravan for travel. I'll strike while he's inspecting his stock. If I can avoid his men, Talal himself should prove little challenge.'

Malik curled his lip. '"Little challenge"? Listen to you. Such arrogance.'

Silently Altaïr rebuked himself. Malik was right. He thought of the orator in Damascus whom he had misjudged and who had almost bested him.

'Are we finished?' he asked, showing none of his thoughts to Malik. 'Are you satisfied with what I've learned?'

'No,' said Malik, handing Altaïr the feather, 'but it will have to do.'

Altaïr nodded. He looked at where Malik's sleeve hung loose and was about to say something before he realized that no words would atone for his failures. He had cost Malik too much ever to hope for forgiveness from him.

Instead, he turned and left the Bureau. Another target was to feel the kiss of his blade.

14

Shortly afterwards Altaïr was stealing into the warehouse where the shipment was being prepared, looking around and not liking what he found.

There were no guards. No acolytes.

He took two steps forward, then stopped. No. What was he thinking? Everything about the warehouse was wrong. He was about to spin and leave when suddenly the door was shut and there was the unmistakable sound of a bolt slamming home.

He cursed and drew his sword.

He crept forward, his senses gradually adjusting to the gloom, the damp, the smell of the torches and . . .

Something else. A livestock smell that Altaïr thought was more human than animal.

Meagre flames from the torches threw light on walls that ran dark and slick, and from somewhere came a drip-drip of water. The next sound he heard was a low moan.

Eyes slowly adjusting, he edged forward, seeing crates and barrels and then . . . a cage. He moved closer – and almost recoiled at what he saw. A man was inside it. A pathetic, shivering man, who sat with his legs pulled to his chest and regarded Altaïr with plaintive, watery eyes. He raised one trembling hand. 'Help me,' he said.

Then, from behind, Altaïr heard another sound and wheeled to see a second man. He was suspended from the wall, his wrists and ankles shackled. His head lolled on his chest and dirty hair hung over his face, but his lips appeared to be moving as though in prayer.

Altaïr moved towards him. Then, hearing another voice from his feet, he looked down to see an iron grille set into the flagstones of the warehouse floor. Peering from it was the frightened face of yet another slave, his bony fingers reaching through the bars, appealing to Altaïr. Beyond him in the pit the Assassin saw more dark forms, heard slithering and more voices. For a moment it was as though the room was filled with the pleading of those imprisoned.

'Help me, help me.'

An insistent, beseeching sound that made him want to cover his ears. Until, suddenly, he heard a louder voice: 'You should not have come here, Assassin.'

Talal, surely.

Altaïr swung in the direction of the noise, seeing the shadows shift in a balcony above him. Bowmen? He tensed, crouching, his sword ready, offering the smallest target possible.

But if Talal wanted him dead, he'd be dead by now. He'd walked straight into the slave trader's trap – the mistake of a fool, of a novice – but it had not yet been fully sprung.

'But you are not the kind to listen,' mocked Talal, 'lest you compromise your Brotherhood.'

Altair crept forward, still trying to place Talal. He was above, that much was certain. But where?

'Did you think I'd remain ignorant of your presence?' continued the disembodied voice, with a chuckle. 'You were known to me the moment you entered this city, such is my reach.'

From below he heard sobbing and glanced down to see more bars, more dirty, tear-streaked faces staring at him from the gloom.

'*Help me . . . Save me . . .*'

Here there were more cages, more slaves, men and women now: beggars, prostitutes, drunkards and madmen.

'Help me. Help me.'

'So there are slaves here,' called Altaïr, 'but where are the slavers?'

Talal ignored him. 'Behold my work in all its glory,' he announced, and more lights flared on, revealing more frightened and beseeching faces.

Ahead of Altaïr a second gate slid open, admitting him to another room. He climbed a flight of steps and walked into a large space with a gallery running along all sides above him. There he saw shadowy figures and adjusted the grip on his sword.

'What now, slaver?' he called.

Talal was trying to frighten him. Some things frightened Altaïr, it was true – but nothing the slave master was capable of, that much he knew.

'Do not call me that,' cried Talal. 'I only wish to help them. As I myself was helped.'

Altair could still hear the low moans of the slaves from the chamber behind. He doubted whether they'd consider it help. 'You do no kindness imprisoning them like this,' he called into the darkness.

Still Talal remained hidden. 'Imprisoning them? I keep them safe, preparing them for the journey that lies ahead.'

'What journey?' scoffed Altaïr. 'It is a life of servitude.'

'You know nothing. It was folly to bring you here. To think that you might see and understand.'

'I understand well enough. You lack the courage to face me, choosing to hide among the shadows. Enough talk. Show yourself.'

'Ah . . . So you want to see the man who called you here?'

Altaïr heard movement in the gallery.

'You did not call me here,' he shouted. 'I came on my own.'

Laughter echoed from the balconies above him.

'Did you?' scoffed Talal. 'Who unbarred the door? Cleared the path? Did you raise your blade against a single man of mine, hmm? No. All this I did for you.'

Something moved on the ceiling above the gallery, throwing a patch of light on to the stone floor.

'Step into the light, then,' called Talal from above, 'and I will grant you one final favour.'

Again, Altaïr told himself that if Talal wanted him dead his archers would have filled him with arrows by now, and he stepped into the light. As he did so, masked men appeared from the shadows of the gallery, jumping down and noiselessly surrounding him. They regarded him with dispassionate eyes, their swords hanging by their sides, their chests rising and falling.

Altaïr swallowed. There were six of them. 'Little challenge' they were not.

Then there came footsteps from above and he looked to the gallery where Talal had moved out of the half-light and now stood gazing down at him. He wore a striped tunic and a thick belt. Over his shoulder was a bow.

'Now I stand before you,' he said, spreading his hands, smiling as though warmly welcoming a guest to his household. 'What is it you desire?'

'Come down here.' Altair indicated with his sword. 'Let us settle this with honour.'

'Why must it always come to violence?' replied Talal, sounding almost disappointed in Altaïr, before adding, 'It seems I cannot help you, Assassin, for you do not wish to help yourself. And I cannot allow my work to be threatened. You leave me no choice: you must die.'

He waved to his men.

Who lifted their swords.

Then attacked.

Altaïr grunted and found himself fending off two at once, pushing them back, then straight away turning his attention to a third. The others waited their turn: their strategy, he quickly realized, was to come at him two at a time.

He could handle that. He grabbed one, pleased to see his eyes widen in shock above his mask, then threw him backwards into a fifth man, the pair of them smashing into a scaffold that disintegrated around them. Altaïr pressed home his advantage and, stabbing with his swordpoint, heard a scream and a death rattle from the man sprawled on the stone.

His assailants reassembled, glancing at one another as they slowly circled him. He turned with them, sword held out, smiling, almost enjoying himself now. Five of them, trained, masked killers, against a lone Assassin. They had thought him easy prey. He could see it in their faces. One skirmish later and they weren't quite so certain.

He chose one. An old trick taught to him by Al Mualim for when facing multiple opponents.

Altaïr very deliberately fixed his gaze on a guard directly in front of him . . .

Don't ignore the others but home in on one. Make him your target. Let him know he's your target.

He smiled. The guard whimpered.

Then finish him.

Like a snake, Altaïr struck, coming at the guard, who was too slow to react – who stared down at Altaïr's blade as it thrust into his chest, then groaned as he sank to his knees. With a tearing of meat, Altaïr withdrew his sword, then turned his attention to the next man.

Choose one of your opponents. . .

The guard looked terrified, not like a killer now, as his sword began trembling. He shouted something in a dialect Altaïr didn't understand, then came forward messily, hoping to bring the battle to Altaïr, who sidestepped, slashing at the man's stomach, gratified to see glistening insides spill from the wound. From above Talal's voice cajoled his men to attack even as another fell and the two remaining attacked at once. They didn't look so intimidating now, masks or not. They looked like what they were: frightened men about to die.

Altaïr took another down, blood fountaining from a slashed neck. The last turned and ran, hoping to find shelter in the gallery. But Altaïr sheathed his sword, palmed a pair of throwing knives, which spun, glittering – *one, two* – into the escaping man's back so that he fell from the ladder. Escaping no more.

Altaïr heard running footsteps from above. Talal

making his escape. Bending to retrieve his knives, he took the ladder himself, reaching the second level just in time to see Talal scramble up a second series of steps to the roof.

The Assassin went after him, arriving through a hatch in the top of the warehouse and only just jerking his head back in time as an arrow smacked, quivering, into the wood beside him. He saw the bowman on a far rooftop, already fitting a second shaft, and pulled himself from the hatch, rolling forward on the rooftop and tossing two knives, still wet with the blood of their previous victim.

The archer screamed and fell, one knife protruding from his neck, the other in his chest. Further across, Altaïr saw Talal darting across a bridge between housing then jumping to a scaffold and shimmying down into the street. There, he craned his neck, saw Altaïr already following him, and set off at a run.

Altaïr was already gaining. He was quick and, unlike Talal, he wasn't constantly looking over his shoulder to see if he was being followed. Which meant he wasn't barrelling into unsuspecting pedestrians as Talal was: women who screeched and reprimanded him, men who swore and shoved him back.

All this slowed his progress through the streets and markets, so that soon he had squandered his lead, and when he turned his head Altaïr could see the whites of his eyes.

'Flee now,' Talal screamed over his shoulder, 'while you still can. My guards will be here soon.'

Altaïr chuckled. Kept running.

'Give up this chase and I'll let you live,' screeched Talal. Altaïr said nothing. Kept up his pursuit. Nimbly, he wove through the crowds, hurdling the goods that Talal pulled behind himself to slow his pursuer. Altaïr was gaining on Talal now, the chase almost done.

Ahead of him Talal turned his head once more, saw that the gap was closing and tried appealing to Altaïr again.

'Hold your ground and hear me out,' he bellowed, desperation in his voice. 'Perhaps we can make a deal.'

Altaïr said nothing, just watched as Talal turned again. The slave trader was now about to collide with a woman whose face was hidden by several flasks. Neither of them was looking where they were going.

'I've done nothing to you,' shouted Talal, forgetting, presumably, that just minutes ago he had sent six men to kill Altaïr. 'Why do you persist in chasing –'

The breath left his body in a whoosh, there was a tangle of arms and legs and Talal crashed to the sand along with the flask woman, whose wares smashed around them.

Talal tried scrambling to his feet but was too slow and Altaïr was upon him. *Snick*. As soon as his greedy blade appeared he had sunk it into the man, and was kneeling beside him, blood already gushing from

Talal's nose and mouth. At their side, the flask woman dragged herself to her feet, red-faced and indignant, about to let fly at Talal. On seeing Altaïr and his blade, not to mention the blood leaking from Talal, she changed her mind and dashed off wailing. Others gave them a wide berth, sensing something was amiss. In Jerusalem, a city accustomed to conflict, the inhabitants preferred not to stand and stare at violence for fear of becoming part of it.

Altaïr leaned close to Talal. 'You've nowhere to run now,' he said. 'Share your secrets with me.'

'My part is played, Assassin,' responded Talal. 'The Brotherhood is not so weak that my death will stop its work.'

Altaïr's mind flashed back to Tamir. He, too, had spoken of others as he died. He, too, had mentioned brothers. 'What Brotherhood?' he pressed.

Talal managed a smile. 'Al Mualim is not the only one with designs upon the Holy Land. And that's all you'll have from me.'

'Then we are finished. Beg forgiveness from your God.'

'There is no God, Assassin.' Talal laughed weakly. 'And if there ever was, he's long abandoned us. Long abandoned the men and women I took into my arms.'

'What do you mean?'

'Beggars. Whores. Addicts. Lepers. Do they strike you as proper slaves? Unfit for even the most menial tasks. No . . . I took them not to sell, but to *save*. And yet you'd kill us all. For no other reason than it was asked of you.'

'No,' said Altaïr, confused now. 'You profit from the war. From lives lost and broken.'

'You would think that, ignorant as you are. Wall off your mind, eh? They say it's what your kind does best. Do you see the irony in all this?'

Altaïr stared at him. It was just as it had been with de Naplouse. The dying man's words threatened to subvert everything Altaïr knew of his target – or thought he knew, at least.

'No, not yet, it seems.' Talal allowed himself one final smile at Altaïr's evident confusion. 'But you will.'

And, with that, he died.

Altaïr reached to close his eyes, murmuring, 'I'm sorry,' before brushing his marker with blood, then standing and losing himself in the crowds, Talal's corpse staining the sand behind him.

15

Altaïr would make camp at wells, waterholes or fountains on his travels; anywhere there was water and shade from palms, where he could rest and his mount graze on the grass, untethered. It was often the only patch of green as far as the eye could see so there was little chance of his horse wandering off.

That night he found a fountain that had been walled and arched to prevent the desert swallowing the precious water spot, and he drank well. Then he lay down in its shelter, listening to dripping from the other side of the rough-hewn stone and thinking of the life ebbing away from Talal. His thoughts went even further back, to the corpses in his past. A life punctuated by death.

As a young boy he had first encountered it during the siege. Assassin and Saracen and, of course, his own father, though mercifully he had been spared the sight of that. He had heard it, though, heard the sword fall, followed by a soft thump, and he'd darted towards the wicket gate, wanting to join his father, when hands had gripped him.

He had squirmed, screaming, 'Let me go! Let me go!'

'No, child.' And Altaïr saw that it was Ahmad, the agent whose life Altaïr's father had traded for his own. And Altaïr stared at him, eyes burning with hatred, not caring that Ahmad had been delivered from his ordeal battered and bloody and barely able to stand, his soul scarred with the shame of having succumbed to the Saracens' interrogation. Caring only that his father had given himself up to die and . . .

'*It's your fault!*' he had screamed, twisting and pulling away from Ahmad, who stood with his head bowed, absorbing the boy's words as if they were punches.

'It's your fault,' Altaïr had spat again, then sat on the brittle grass, burying his head in his hands, wanting to shut out the world. A few steps away, Ahmad, exhausted and beaten, had folded to the ground also.

Outside the citadel walls, the Saracens departed, leaving the headless body of Altaïr's father behind for the Assassins to retrieve. Leaving wounds that would never heal.

For the time being Altaïr had stayed in the quarters he had shared with his father, with their walls of grey stone, rushes on the floor, a simple desk between two pallets, one larger, one smaller. He'd moved beds: he had slept in the larger one, so that he could smell his father's smell, and he had imagined him sometimes, in the room, sitting reading at the desk, scratching away at a roll of parchment, or returning late at night to chide Altaïr for still being awake, then snuffing out his candle before retiring. Imaginings were all he had now, the orphan Altaïr. Those and his memories. Al Mualim had said he would be called in due course, when arrangements had been made for his future. In the meantime, the Master had said, if Altaïr needed anything, he should come to him as his mentor.

Ahmad, meanwhile, had been suffering from a fever. Some nights his ravings were heard throughout the citadel. Occasionally he screamed as if in pain, at other times like a man deranged. One night he was shouting one word over and over again. Altaïr had pulled himself from his bed and gone to his window, thinking that what he heard was his father's name.

It was. '*Umar.*' Hearing it was like being slapped.

'*Umar.*' The shriek seemed to echo in the empty courtyard below. '*Umar.*'

No, not empty. Peering more closely, Altaïr could make out the figure of a child of about his age, who stood like a sentinel in the soft early-morning mist that rippled across the training yard. It was Abbas. Altaïr barely knew him, just that he was Abbas Sofian, the son of Ahmad Sofian. The boy had stood listening to his father's demented ravings, perhaps offering silent prayers for him, and Altaïr had watched him for a few heartbeats, finding something to admire in his silent vigil. Then he had let his curtain drop and returned to his bed, putting his hands over his ears so that he could no longer hear Ahmad calling his father's name. He had tried to breathe in his father's scent and realized that it was fading.

They said that Ahmad's fever had abated the next day, and that he had returned to his quarters, albeit a broken man. Altaïr had heard that he lay on his bed attended to by Abbas. That he had lain that way for two days.

The next night Altaïr was awoken by a sound in his room and lay blinking, hearing somebody moving about, feet that went to the desk. A candle was put down that threw shadows on the stone wall. It was his father, he thought, still half asleep. His father had come back for him, and he sat up, smiling, ready to welcome him home and be chided by him for being awake. At last he had woken from a terrible dream in which his father had died and left him alone.

But the man in his room was not his father. It was Ahmad.

Ahmad was standing at the door, emaciated within his white robe, his face a pale mask. He wore a faraway, almost peaceful expression, and he smiled a little as Altaïr sat up, as though he didn't want to frighten the boy. His eyes, though, were sunken dark hollows as if pain had burned the life from within him. And in his hand he held a dagger.

'I'm sorry,' he said, and they were the only words he spoke, his last words, because next he drew the knife across his throat, opening a gaping red mouth in his own neck.

Blood swept down his robe; bubbles of it formed at the wound on his neck. The dagger dropped with a clunk to the floor and he smiled as he slid to his knees, his gaze fixed on Altaïr, who sat rigid with fear, unable to take his eyes from Ahmad as the blood poured from him, draining out of him. Now the dying man lolled back on his heels, at last breaking that ghastly stare as his head dropped to the side, but he was prevented from falling backwards by the door. And for some heartbeats that was how he remained, a penitent man, kneeling. Then at last he fell forward.

Altaïr had no idea how long he sat there, weeping softly and listening to Ahmad's blood spreading thickly across the stone. At last he found the courage to step out of bed, taking the candle and carefully skirting the bleeding horror that lay on the floor. He pulled his door open, whimpering as it made contact with Ahmad's foot. Outside the room at last, he ran. The candle snuffed out but he didn't care. He ran until he reached Al Mualim.

'You must never tell anyone of this,' Al Mualim had said, the next day. Altaïr had been given a warm spiced drink, then spent the rest of the night in the Master's chambers, where he had slept soundly. The Master himself had been elsewhere, attending to Ahmad's body. So it had proved the next day, when Al Mualim returned to him, taking a seat by his bed.

'We shall tell the Order that Ahmad left under cover of darkness,' he said. 'They may draw their own conclusions. We cannot allow Abbas to be tainted with the shame of his father's suicide. What Ahmad has done is dishonourable. His disgrace would spread to his kin.'

'But what of Abbas, Master?' said Altaïr. 'Will he be told the truth?'

'No, my child.'

'But he should at least know that his father is –'

'*No*, my child,' repeated Al Mualim, his voice rising. 'Abbas will be told by no one, including you. Tomorrow I shall announce that you are both to become novices in the Order, that you are to be brothers in all but blood. You will share quarters. You will train and study and dine together. As brothers. You will look after each other. See no harm comes to the other, either physical or by other means. Do I make myself clear?'

'Yes, Master.'

Later that day Altaïr was installed in quarters with Abbas. A meagre room: two pallets, rush matting, a small desk. Neither boy liked it but Abbas said he would be leaving shortly, when his father returned. At night he was fitful and sometimes called out in his sleep, while in the next bed Altaïr lay awake, afraid to sleep in case the nightmares of Ahmad uncoiled themselves and came to him.

They did. Ahmad had come to him at night ever since. He came with a dagger that gleamed in the dancing candlelight. Slowly he drew the blade across his own throat, grinning as he did so.

Altaïr awoke. The desert was cool and still around him. The palm trees rustled slightly in a breeze and the water drip-dripped behind him. He passed a hand across his brow and realized he had been sweating. He laid his head down again, hoping to sleep at least until light.

Part Two

16

'You've done well,' said Al Mualim, the following day. 'Three of the nine lie dead, and for this you have my thanks.' His smile faded. 'But do not think to rest upon your laurels. Your work has just begun.'

'I am yours to command, Master,' said Altaïr, solemnly. He was exhausted but grateful that he was beginning to redeem himself in Al Mualim's eyes. Certainly he had seen a change in the guards. Where before they had looked at him with disdain, now they gave him grudging respect. Word of his success had reached them, no doubt. Al Mualim, also, had awarded him the beginnings of a smile and indicated for him to sit. *Sit.*

The Master continued: 'King Richard, emboldened by his victory at Acre, prepares to move south, towards Jerusalem. Salah Al'din is surely aware of this, and so he gathers his men before the broken citadel of Arsuf.'

Altaïr thought of Salah Al'din and tensed. His mind went back to that day, the Saracens at the gates of the fortress . . .

'Would you have me kill them both, then?' he said,

relishing the possibility of putting the Saracen leader to his blade. 'End their war before it begins in earnest?'

'No,' snapped Al Mualim, studying him so carefully that Altaïr felt as though his thoughts were being read. 'To do so would scatter their forces – and subject the realm to the bloodlust of ten thousand aimless warriors. It will be many days before they meet, and while they march, they do not fight. You must concern yourself with a more immediate threat: the men who pretend to govern in their absence.'

Altaïr nodded. He put away his visions of revenge to be inspected another day. 'Give me names and I'll give you blood.'

'So I will. Abu'l Nuqoud, the wealthiest man in Damascus. Majd Addin, regent of Jerusalem. William de Montferrat, liege lord of Acre.'

He knew the names, of course. Each of the cities bore its leader's pernicious imprint. 'What are their crimes?' asked Altaïr. He wondered if, like the others, there would be more to these crimes than met the eye.

Al Mualim spread his hands. 'Greed. Arrogance. The slaughter of innocents. Walk among the people of their cities. You'll learn the secrets of their sins. Do not doubt that these men are obstacles to the peace we seek.'

'Then they will die,' said Altaïr, obediently.

'Return to me as each man falls that we might better understand their intentions,' ordered Al Mualim, 'and,

Altaïr, take care. Your recent work has likely attracted the attention of the guards. They'll be more suspicious than they've been in the past.'

So it appeared. For, days later, when Altaïr strode into the Bureau at Acre, Jabal greeted him with 'Word has spread of your deeds, Altaïr.'

He nodded.

'It seems you are sincere in your desire to redeem yourself.'

'I do what I can.'

'And sometimes you do it well. I assume it is work that reunites us?'

'Yes. William de Montferrat is my target.'

'Then the Chain District is your destination . . . But be on your toes. That section of the city is home to King Richard's personal quarters, and it is under heavy watch.'

'What can you tell me of the man himself?'

'William has been named regent while the King conducts his war. The people see it as a strange choice, given the history between Richard and William's son, Conrad. But I think Richard rather clever for it.'

'Clever how?'

Jabal smiled. 'Richard and Conrad do not see eye to eye on most matters. Though they are civil enough in public, there are whispers that each intends evil upon the other. And then there was the business with Acre's captured Saracens . . .' Jabal shook his head. 'In its wake, Conrad has returned to Tyre, and Richard has compelled William to remain here as his guest.'

'You mean his hostage?' asked Altaïr. He was inclined to agree with Jabal. It did indeed look like a wise move on Richard's part.

'Whatever you call it, William's presence should keep Conrad in line.'

'Where would you suggest I begin my search?'

Jabal thought. 'Richard's citadel, south-west of here . . . Or, rather, the market in front of it.'

'Very well. I won't disturb you any further.'

'It's no trouble,' said Jabal, who went back to his birds, cooing gently at them.

He was a man unburdened by many worries, thought Altaïr. For that at least, he envied him.

17

Jabal was right, thought Altaïr, as he made his way through hot, crowded streets tangy with sea air, to the citadel market. There were many more guards about, perhaps double the number since his last visit. Some wore the colours of the Crusaders, and were in full armour. However, if he knew one thing about soldiers it was that they liked to gossip, and the more there were, the more indiscreet they were likely to be. He took a place on a bench, and sat as though to admire the grand citadel with its fluttering pennants, or as if simply to watch the day go by. Not far away an entertainer tried to drum up trade, then shrugged and began anyway, tossing coloured balls into the air. Altaïr pretended to watch him but was listening to a conversation taking place over the way, a couple of Crusaders chattering like washerwomen about William's sword skills.

As Altair watched, a soldier's eye was caught by a friar, a tall man in brown hooded robes, who was signalling discreetly to him. The soldier nodded almost imperceptibly, bade his friend goodbye and moved across the market. Watching from beneath his cowl,

Altaïr stood and followed as the two men met and moved away from the hustle and bustle to talk; Altaïr positioned himself close by, straining to hear as the friar spoke.

'Perhaps it was unwise to embrace William. He is old and thinks too much of himself.'

The soldier pursed his lips. 'His army is large. We'll have need of them. For now, I'll go and visit the other brothers. Make sure they have everything they need.'

'Aye. They must not fall,' agreed the friar.

'Fear not. The Master has a plan. Even now he prepares a way to turn our losses to his advantage, should it come to that.'

Master? Altaïr wondered. *Brothers?* Just who did these men answer to? Acre had more layers than an onion.

'What does he intend?' asked the friar.

'The less you know, the better. Just do as you've been instructed. Deliver this letter to the Master.' He passed it to the friar and Altaïr smiled, already flexing his fingertips. He stood from the bench and followed. One lift later the scroll was his, and he sat once again to read it.

Master:

Work continues in the Chain District of Acre though we are concerned about William's ability to see this through to the end. He takes his duties a bit too seriously, and the people

may reject him when the time comes. Without the aid of the
treasure, we can ill afford an uprising, lest it recall the King
from the field. And then your plan will be for nothing. We
cannot reclaim what's been stolen unless the two sides are
united. Perhaps you might prepare another to take his
place — simply as a precaution. We worry that our man in
the harbour will become increasingly unstable. Already he
talks of distancing himself. And this means we cannot rely on
him should William fall. Let us know what you intend that
we might execute it. We remain ever faithful to the cause.

He folded the letter and pushed it into his robes.
Something to show Al Mualim, perhaps. Then again,
maybe not. So far Altaïr felt Al Mualim had been less
than open with him regarding his targets. Perhaps this
was part of his test. Perhaps.

A group of servants hurried past. The juggler jug-
gled; he had a bigger crowd now. Not far away a
speaker had taken up position in the shade of a tree
and was talking against King Richard.

Next Altaïr's attention was arrested by a young man
with a close-trimmed black beard who seemed to be
appealing to citizens as they passed, at the same time
keeping an eye on a pair of city guards stationed a
short distance away.

'William de Montferrat cares *nothing* for the people
of Acre,' he was saying. Altaïr loitered to listen, careful
not to catch his eye. 'While we starve, the men inside

his keep want for nothing. They grow fat upon the fruits of our labour. He brought us here to rebuild, he said. But now, far from home, and the grace of our king, his true plan becomes apparent. He steals our sons, sending them into battle against a savage enemy. Their deaths are all but guaranteed. Our daughters are taken to service his soldiers, robbed of their virtue. And he compensates us with lies and empty promises of a better morrow – of a land blessed by God. What of now? What of today? How much longer must we go without? Is this truly the work of God – or of a selfish man who seeks to conquer all? Rise up, people of Acre. Join us in our protest.'

'Be quiet,' called a woman passer-by, gesturing in the direction of guards who were peering along the street, perhaps aware that rabble-rousing was afoot.

'You're a fool,' agreed another, harshly. He turned away with a dismissive wave of the hand. Nobody in Acre wanted to witness William's anger, or so it seemed.

'Your words will see you hanged,' whispered another, who slunk away.

Altaïr watched as the rebel cast a wary glance, then stepped into the crowd and joined another man there. 'How many have you called to our cause?' he asked.

'I fear they are all too afraid,' answered his companion. 'None would heed the call.'

'We must keep trying. Find another market. Another square. We must not be silenced.'

With a final backwards glance at the soldiers, they moved off. Altaïr watched them go, satisfied he had discovered all that he needed to know about William de Montferrat.

He took a final look at the citadel, towering over the marketplace, the black beating heart of Acre. In there, somewhere, was his target, he thought, and with William dead, the people of Acre would know less tyranny, less fear. The sooner that happened, the better. It was time to revisit Jabal.

The Bureau leader was, as ever, in a jovial mood. His eyes twinkled as he greeted Altaïr.

'I've done as I was asked,' said Altaïr. 'I've armed myself with knowledge. I know what I must do to reach Montferrat.'

'Speak, then, and I will judge.'

'William's host is large and many men call him master. But he is not without enemies. He and King Richard do not see eye to eye.'

Jabal raised an eyebrow. 'It's true. They've never been close.'

'This works to my advantage. Richard's visit has upset him. Once the King has left, William will retreat into his fortress to brood. He'll be distracted. That is when I will strike.'

'You're sure of this?'

'As sure as I can be. And if things change, I'll adapt.'

'Then I give you leave to go. End the life of de

Montferrat that we may call this city free.' Jabal handed him the feather.

'I'll return when the deed's been done,' answered Altaïr.

18

Altaïr returned to the citadel, expecting it to be just as he had left it. But there was something different now – something he detected as he wove through the streets and came closer to it. It was in the air. Excitement. Expectation. He heard gossip concerning Richard's visit. He was in the fortress now, the citizens said, holding talks with de Montferrat. Apparently the King was furious with him over his treatment of the three thousand held hostage when the Crusaders had retaken the city.

Despite himself, Altaïr felt a thrill. Richard the Lionheart's reputation came before him. His bravery. His cruelty. So to see him in the flesh . . .

He moved through the marketplace. The crowds were thicker now as word spread that Richard had arrived. Acre's citizens, whatever their opinions of the English King, wanted to see him.

'He comes,' whispered a woman nearby. Altaïr felt himself carried by the crowd, and for almost the first time since entering the city he was able to hold up his head. The crowds were his disguise and, anyway, the guards were too occupied with the King's imminent arrival to take any interest in him.

Now the mob surged forward, taking Altaïr with it. He allowed himself to be enclosed by bodies and carried towards the decorated stone gates, where the flags of the Crusaders fluttered in the breeze, as though they, too, were keen to see Richard. At the gates, the soldiers warned the crowds to move back and those at the front began calling for those at the rear to stop pushing forward. Still more citizens arrived, though, surging towards the raised area in front of the main gates. More guards formed a shield around the entrance. Some had their hands on the hilts of their swords. Others brandished pikes menacingly, snarling, 'Back with you,' at the seething, complaining crowd.

Suddenly there was a great commotion from the fortress gates, which, grinding, rose. Altaïr craned his neck to see, first hearing the clip-clop of horses' hoofs, then seeing the helmets of the King's bodyguards. Next the crowd was kneeling, Altaïr following suit, though his eyes were fixed on the arrival of the King.

Richard the Lionheart sat on a splendid stallion adorned with his livery, his shoulders back and his chin high. His face was worn, as though carrying the imprint of every battle, every desert crossed, and his eyes were weary but bright. Around him was his bodyguard, also on their horses, and walking at his side another man, this one, Altaïr realized from the crowd's murmurings, William de Montferrat. He was older than the King, and lacked his bulk and power, but there was a litheness about him; Altaïr could see he might well be a skilled swordsman. There was a look of displeasure about him as he walked by the side of the King, small in his shadow and heedless of the crowds surrounding them. Lost in his own thoughts.

'. . . three thousand souls, William,' the King was saying, loud enough for the entire marketplace to hear. 'I was told they would be held as prisoners – and used to barter for the release of our men.'

'The Saracens would not have honoured their side of the bargain,' replied de Montferrat. 'You know this to be true. I did you a favour.'

The Lionheart roared. 'Oh, yes. A great favour, indeed. Now our enemies will be that much stronger in their convictions. Fight that much harder.'

They stopped.

'I know our enemy well,' said de Montferrat. 'They will not be emboldened but filled with fear.'

Richard looked at him disdainfully. 'Tell me, how is it you know the intentions of our enemy so well? You, who forsake the field of battle to play at politics.'

De Montferrat swallowed. 'I did what was right. What was just.'

'You swore an oath to uphold the work of God, William. But that is not what I see here. No. I see a man who's trampled it.'

De Montferrat looked queasy. Then, sweeping an arm around him, as if to remind the King that their subjects were within earshot, he said, 'Your words are most unkind, my liege. I had hoped to earn your trust by now.'

'You are Acre's regent, William, set to rule in my stead. How much more *trust* is required? Perhaps you'd like my crown.'

'You miss the point,' said Montferrat. Not wanting to lose face before the crowd he added, 'But then again, you always do . . .'

Richard glowered. 'Much as I'd like to waste my day trading words with you, I've a war to fight. We'll continue this another time.'

'Do not let me delay you, then,' said de Montferrat, politely, 'Your Grace.'

Richard afforded de Montferrat one last furious stare — a stare to remind a rebellious underling of exactly who wore the crown — then left, his men falling in behind him.

The crowd began to get to their feet and de Montferrat turned to say something to one of his guards. Altaïr strained to hear.

'I fear there will be no place for men like him in the New World. Send word that I wish to speak with the troops. We must ensure everyone is doing their part. Warn them that any negligence will be severely punished. I'm in no mood to be trifled with today.' Then he turned to the rest of his men. 'Follow me.'

Suddenly there was a great surge towards the fortress,

not just of de Montferrat's guards but of traders hoping to find custom inside. Altaïr joined them, buffeted by their hessian sacks but staying in the crush and just squeezing through the gates before the guardsmen took control and slammed them shut. Inside, traders were being herded by irritated soldiers towards a courtyard, there to display their wares, no doubt. But Altaïr could see de Montferrat making his way along the lower bailey and towards the inner curtain. He ducked to one side and squeezed into a gap between the wall and an inner building, holding his breath, half expecting to hear a shout from a sharp-eyed guard who had seen him slip away. There was none. He looked upwards, and was pleased to see handholds in the sandstone surface of the building. He began to climb.

Archer.

Of course. He'd been so pleased to elude the sentries down below that Altaïr had forgotten to consider those above. He stole another look over the edge of the roof, waiting for the man to turn his back. He needed him in the middle of the roof. Didn't want him falling into the fortress and raising the alarm. When the guard reached the right spot, Altaïr struck, the throwing knife glittering in the sun, then burying itself in the sentry's back. He grunted and fell, thankfully not over the edge, and Altaïr pulled himself up to the roof, crouching low and making his way across, one eye on another archer further across the compound, ready to dive out of view if he turned.

Below him de Montferrat was making his way across the fortress, shouting orders and insults at all who dared be in his vicinity.

Altair came upon the next archer. A knife throw later, the man lay sprawled dead on the roof. Altaïr glanced down at him as he passed, keeping low, seeing the body cease to twitch.

A third archer. Altaïr disposed of him. Now he controlled the roof; he had an escape route for when the deed was done. All that remained was to do it.

Below him, de Montferrat passed through a set of inner gates and Altaïr watched him upbraid the guard for some minor infraction as he did so. Then he was moving into the courtyard of a keep, a kind of inner sanctum for him, perhaps. Altaïr shadowed him from the walkway above. He kept out of sight but nobody looked upwards. They had no need to – or so they thought.

Now de Montferrat took his place behind a table at one side of the courtyard. 'Men,' he was saying, 'gather round. Heed well my words.'

They took positions around him and Altaïr saw that, though they wore the same uniform, they were different from those stationed in the outer curtain. These were more grizzled and looked battle-hardened. If Altaïr was right, they would be de Montferrat's personal force. He wasn't going to make the mistake of thinking them 'little challenge' again.

In the courtyard, de Montferrat continued, 'I come from speaking with the King, and the news is grim. We stand accused of failing in our duties. He does not recognize the value of our contributions to the cause.'

'For shame,' said one of the men.

'He knows nothing,' spat another.

'Peace. Peace. Hold your tongues,' admonished de Montferrat. 'Aye, he speaks falsely, but his words are not without some merit. To tour these grounds, it is easy to find fault. To see imperfection. I fear we have grown slack and lazy.'

Above him, Altaïr allowed himself a smile. The method of his entrance was testament to how slack and lazy de Montferrat's men had become. And as for his half-asleep archers . . .

'Why do you say this?' asked one of de Montferrat's men. They bristled, all of them. Altaïr used the sudden eruption of noise as cover to crab to one side, wanting to position himself above his quarry, very, very carefully moving around the courtyard walls. Now he could see what most of the men below did not. From a door at the opposite end of the courtyard more guards had appeared dragging two men. They wore the outfits of Crusaders but were prisoners.

'I see the way you train,' de Montferrat was shouting down below. 'You lack conviction and focus. You gossip and gamble. Tasks set to you are left unfulfilled or poorly performed. This ends today. I will not suffer further degradation at Richard's hands. Whether or not you see it – and you *should* – this is your fault. You've brought shame upon us all. Skill and dedication are what won us Acre. And they will be required to *keep* it. I have been too lenient, it seems. But no more. You will train harder and more often. If this means missing meals, missing sleep – so be it. And should you fail in these tasks, you will learn the true meaning of discipline . . . Bring them forward.'

Altaïr had reached his position without being spotted. He was close enough now to look down on de Montferrat's balding head and see the flecks of spittle fly from his mouth as he shouted at his men. If one of those below was to look up for any reason he might be spotted, but all attention was now on the area in front of de Montferrat's table, where the soldiers had been dragged before him, frightened and shame-faced.

'If I must make examples of some of you to ensure obedience,' announced de Montferrat, 'so be it,' and he turned to the captives. 'The two of you stand accused of whoring and drinking while on duty. What say you to these charges?

Through wet mouths they mumbled pleas and apologies.

De Montferrat scowled at them. Then, with a wave of his hand, he ordered their execution.

Their throats were cut and they spent their last moments watching their own blood gush on to the stone of the courtyard. De Montferrat gazed at them, gurgling and flapping on the ground, like dying fish. 'Disregard for duty is infectious,' he said, almost sadly. 'It shall be rooted out and destroyed. In this way, we may prevent its spread. Am I understood?'

'Yes, my lord,' came the murmured reply.

'Good, good,' he said. 'Return to your duties, then, filled with a new sense of purpose. Stay strong, stay focused – and we will triumph. Falter, and you *will* join these men. Be sure of it. Dismissed.'

He waved them out of his sight, which cheered Altaïr. Out of sight was where he wanted the men, too. He watched as de Montferrat began sifting through papers on the table, hissing with exasperation, his ill-temper clearly not exhausted. Altaïr crept forward, as close as he dared to the edge of the roof. He saw the two bodies, blood still spreading. Further away, most of the men seemed either to have congregated at the entrance to the keep or were leaving for the outer curtain, no doubt keen to put as much distance between themselves and de Montferrat as possible.

Below him de Montferrat tutted in displeasure, still rattling through the papers, unable to find what he was looking for. He groaned as a wad of them slid from the table to the ground. About to call for assistance he thought better of it and bent to retrieve them. Perhaps he heard the snick of Altaïr's blade in the split-second between Altaïr leaping from the walkway above and embedding it in his neck.

Then the Assassin was straddling the Acre leader's body, his hand over his mouth so as not alert others in the courtyard. He had just moments, he knew, whispering, 'Rest now. Your schemes are at an end.'

'What do you know of my work?' croaked de Montferrat.

'I know that you were going to murder Richard – and claim Acre for your son, Conrad.'

'For Conrad? My son is an arse, unfit to lead his host, let alone a kingdom. And Richard? He is no better, blinded as he is by faith in the insubstantial. Acre does not belong to either of them.'

'Then to whom?'

'The city belongs to its people.'

Altaïr fought the now-familiar sense of his world taking an unexpected lurch. 'How can you claim to speak for the citizens?' he said. 'You stole their food. Disciplined them without mercy. Forced them into service under you.'

'Everything I did, I did to prepare them for the New World,' replied de Montferrat, as though such things should be obvious to Altaïr. 'Stole their food? No. I took possession so that, when the lean times came, it might be rationed properly. Look around. My district is without crime – save that committed by you and your ilk. And as for conscription? They were not being trained to fight. They were being taught the merits of order and discipline. These things are hardly evil.'

'No matter how noble you believe your intentions, your acts were cruel and cannot continue,' said Altaïr, though he felt less certain than he sounded.

'We'll see how sweet they are,' said de Montferrat, fading fast, 'the fruits of *your* labours. You do not free the cities, as you believe, but damn them. And in the end, you'll have only yourself to blame. You who speak of good intentions . . .'

But he never finished

'In death, we are all made equals,' said Altaïr, staining the feather. He scaled the wall behind him and was on the walkway, darting across to the outer curtain. Then away. As if he had never been there.

19

Altaïr felt weary of the task. Tired and increasingly vexed. Each long ride exhausted him further but he was commanded to visit Al Mualim after every kill. And on each occasion the Master was enigmatic, demanding details from him yet holding so much back.

So it would prove on the next occasion they met. 'Word has reached me of your success,' Al Mualim said. 'You've my gratitude – and that of the realm. Freeing these cities from their corrupt leaders will no doubt promote the cause of peace.'

'Can you really be so sure?' asked Altaïr. For his own part, he was sure of less and less.

'The means by which men rule are reflected in their people. As you cleanse the cities of corruption, you heal the hearts and minds of those who live within.'

'Our enemies would disagree,' said Altaïr, his mind going to those whose eyes he had closed.

'What do you mean?'

'Each man I've slain has said strange words to me. They are without regret. Even in death, they seem confident of their success. Though they do not admit it directly, there is a tie that binds them. I am sure of it.'

Al Mualim regarded him carefully. 'There is a difference, Altaïr, between what we are told to be true and what we *see* to be true. Most men do not bother to make the distinction. It is simpler that way. But as an Assassin, it is your nature to notice. To question.'

'Then what is it that connects these men?' pressed Altaïr. The Master had the answers, he was sure of it. All of them.

'Ah. But as an Assassin it is also your *duty* to still these thoughts and trust in your master. For there can be no true peace without order. And order requires authority.'

Altaïr could not keep the exasperation from his voice. 'You speak in circles, Master. You commend me for being aware and then ask me not to be. Which is it?'

'The question will be answered when you no longer need to ask it,' responded Al Mualim, mysteriously.

Altaïr could see he was getting nowhere. 'I assume you called me here for more than a lecture,' he said.

'Yes,' said Al Mualim, and directed him to Damascus once more. The one they called Abu'l Nuqoud. He was to be the next to die. First, though, there was the impertinent Bureau leader to negotiate . . .

'Altaïr, my friend. Welcome. Welcome. Whose life do you come to collect today?'

Altaïr frowned to see the Damascus Bureau leader, insolent as ever, but not enough so to warrant his fury.

It was quite a talent the man had for judging it so well. Perhaps if he had been able to put his skills to better use, he wouldn't be spending his days behind a desk in the Bureau. One day Altaïr might remind him of that fact. In the meantime, he had work to do. A new target.

'His name is Abu'l Nuqoud,' he said. 'What can you tell me about him?'

'Oh, the Merchant King of Damascus,' exclaimed the leader, visibly impressed. 'Richest man in the city. Quite exciting. Quite dangerous. I envy you, Altaïr. Well . . . not the bit where you were beaten and stripped of your rank . . . But I envy everything else. Oh . . . except for the terrible things the other Assassins say about you. But, yes, aside from the failure and the hatred – yes, aside from those things – I envy you very much . . .'

Altaïr imagined how his neck would look with a blade sticking from it. 'I do not care what the others think or say,' he said. 'I am here to do a job. So I ask again: what can you tell me about the Merchant King?'

'Only that he must be a very bad man if Al Mualim has sent you to see him. He keeps to his own kind, wrapped in the finery of this city's noble district. A busy man – always up to something. I'm sure if you spend some time among his type you'll learn all you need to know about him.'

Which was exactly what Altaïr did, going to the Omayyad Mosque and Souk Sarouja, as well as Salah

Al'din's citadel, where he learned that Abu'l Nuqoud was hated by the local populace, that he was corrupt and had been embezzling public money, much of which had been diverted to Jerusalem in payments to William de Montferrat. (Altaïr smiled grimly about that.)

Passing the Madrasah al-Kallasah he came upon scholars talking, and hoped he might hear something of Abu'l Nuqoud. They weren't talking about him but Altaïr hung about anyway, perplexed by their speeches.

'Citizens. Bring forth your writings,' the first was saying. 'Place them in the pile before me. To keep any is a sin. Know and embrace the truth of my words. Free yourselves from the lies and corruption of the past.'

Although he'd been about to move on, Altaïr continued to linger. There was something about that. *Free yourselves from the lies and corruption of the past.* Could it have something to do with the 'new order' he kept hearing about?

Another scholar was talking now: 'If you truly value peace – if you truly wish to see an end to war – give up your books, your scrolls, your manuscripts, for they feed the flames of ignorance and hate.'

Altaïr had heard enough – and he didn't like what he had heard. *Give up your books.* Why?

He put it out of his mind, however, continuing to learn about the Merchant King. Nuqoud rarely left his chambers, he heard. However, he would that very evening to attend a party he was hosting – held, many said, merely to rub his personal wealth in the noses of the citizenry. He had even ordered wine – in contravention of his faith – for the event. If it was to be anything like his previous parties then that was when Altaïr would strike. He had heard of a scaffold left outside the balcony of Abu'l Nuqoud's quarters. It was, he decided, a perfect time to go to a party.

20

The festivities were already in full swing as Altaïr made his way around the palace courtyard, feeling conspicuous in his robes. They seemed dirty and shabby compared to the outfits of the guests. Most wore finery, their robes intricately embroidered with expensive threads, and unlike the majority of Damascus residents, they looked healthy and well fed, talking loudly over the music, laughing even more loudly. Certainly there was no shortage of refreshments. Servants moved through the guests offering bread, olives and delicacies on golden trays.

Altaïr looked around. The dancers were the only women present: six or seven of them, gyrating slowly to the sounds of *al'ud* and *rebec* played by musicians stationed below a grand balcony. The Assassin's gaze travelled up to where a guard stood with his arms folded, looking out dispassionately over the frivolities. This was Abu'l's perch, decided Altaïr. Indeed, as he watched, the tempo of the music seemed to increase, the *al'ud* all but drowned by heavy drumming that began to excite the partygoers, a sense of anticipation building. The dancing girls were forced into faster movements and were glistening with perspiration below their sheer silk outfits as around them guests raised their hands, cheering the drums on to a crescendo that built and built until the very air seemed to vibrate – and suddenly he was there above them: Abu'l Nuqoud.

Altaïr had overheard lurid descriptions of the man's appearance. Of his corpulence – he was as big as three normal men, they said – the shiny trinkets he always wore, his gaudy robes and bejewelled turban, most of which Altaïr had dismissed as the exaggerations of a resentful populace. But he was agog to discover that the gossip had understated the man. His girth, jewellery and robes were bigger and more garish than anything Altaïr could have imagined. He watched as Nuqoud stood, continuing to chew whatever meal he had been enjoying, grease glistening around his mouth. And as he strode the length of the balcony gazing down on his guests, the skin below his chin undulating as he finished his food, his robe fell open to expose his bare chest, a huge expanse of flesh glistening with sweat.

Suddenly he clapped his hands. The music stopped, conversation ended.

'Welcome. Welcome,' he announced. 'Thank you all for joining me this evening. Please, eat, drink. Enjoy the pleasures I have to offer.'

With that he swept his hand and the fountain in the

courtyard's centre sprang to life, gushing with what Altaïr first thought was coloured water. Then came an unseemly dash, and he realized what it was: the wine shipment he'd heard about. Here it was. As he watched, two men approached the fountain, dipped their goblets into the foaming liquid, then toasted one another before hurrying off. More guests arrived, dipping their goblets, while servants stood dispensing cups to those who wanted them. It was as if the Merchant King wanted every single one of his guests to sup from the fountain, and he waited until the stampede had receded before continuing.

'I trust everything is to your satisfaction?' he asked, with a raised eyebrow.

Indeed it was. Goblets were raised and there was a roar of approval, the guests tongues loosening swiftly under the influence of the wine.

'Good, good.' Nuqoud grinned, to reveal bits of food plastered to his teeth. 'It pleases me to see you so happy. For these are dark days, my friends, and we must enjoy this bounty while we still can.'

Close to Altaïr, the toasting men returned from a second visit to the wine fountain and were gulping from their filled goblets, stifling giggles as Nuqoud continued: 'War threatens to consume us all. Salah Al'din bravely fights for what he believes in, and you are always there to support him without question. It is your generosity that allows his campaign to continue.'

Altaïr noticed, though he was almost certainly the only one of those in the courtyard to do so, that the galleries along on one side were beginning to fill with guards. He looked closer. Archers.

Nearby the men were still gulping their wine, as Nuqoud began to speak again. 'So I propose a toast, then,' he said. 'To you, my dear friends, who have brought us to where we are today. May you be given everything you deserve.'

'To your health,' came the cry, as the partygoers drank freely from their cups.

'Such kindness,' Nuqoud was saying above them. 'I didn't think it in you. You, who have been so quick to judge me, and so cruelly.'

Sensing a change in him the crowd murmured its confusion.

'Oh, do not feign ignorance. Do you take me for a fool? That I have not heard the words you whisper behind my back? Well, I have. And I fear I can never forget. But this is not why I called you here tonight. No. I wish to speak more of this war – and your part in it.

'You give up your coin, quick as can be, knowing all too well it buys the deaths of thousands. You don't even know *why* we fight. The sanctity of the Holy Land, you'll say. Or the evil inclination of our enemies. But these are lies you tell yourselves.

'No. All this suffering is born of fear and hate. It

bothers you that they are different. Just as it bothers you that I am different.'

Altaïr's gaze went to the archers in the galleries. Feeling a twinge of disquiet he moved to his side to inspect the galleries on the other side of the courtyard. There, too, the bowmen had lined up. He swung round. It was the same behind them. They were not drawing their bows. Not yet, anyway. But, if Altaïr was right, the moment wouldn't be long in coming. And when it did they had the whole courtyard covered. He moved closer to one of the surrounding walls. Not far away, a man began spluttering and coughing, setting his companion off in more fits of laughter.

'Compassion. Mercy. Tolerance,' continued Nuqoud, from the balcony. 'These words mean nothing to any of you. They mean nothing to those infidel invaders who ravage our land in search of gold and glory. And so I say *enough*. I've pledged myself to another cause. One that will bring about a New World – in which all people might live side by side in peace.'

He paused. Altaïr watched the archers tense. They were about to open fire. He pressed himself against the wall. The man was still coughing. He was bent double now, his face red. His companion went from looking concerned to coughing also.

'A pity none of you will live to see it,' finished Nuqoud.

More guests began to splutter. Some were holding their stomachs. Of course, thought Altair. *Poison*. Around him some guests had fallen to their knees. He saw a corpulent man in golden robes frothing, his eyes rolling up in their sockets as he lurched to the ground and lay dying. The archers had readied their bows now. At least half of the partygoers were in the death throes, but there were plenty who had not supped the wine and were scrambling for the exits.

'Kill anyone who tries to escape,' ordered the Merchant King, and his archers opened fire.

Leaving the carnage behind, Altaïr scaled the wall to the balcony and crept up behind Nuqoud. There was a guard at his side, and Altaïr dispatched him with a slash of his blade. The man fell, twisting, his throat opening, spraying blood across the tiles of the balcony. Nuqoud spun to see Altair and his expression changed. Watching the massacre in the party below, he had been smiling, enjoying the show. Now, Altaïr was gratified to see, he felt only fear.

Then pain, as Altaïr sank the blade into his neck above the clavicle.

'Why have you done this?' gasped the huge man, sinking to the smooth stone of his balcony.

'You stole money from those you claim to lead,' Altaïr told him. 'Sent it away for some unknown purpose. I want to know where it's gone and why.'

Nuqoud scoffed. 'Look at me. My very nature is an

affront to the people I ruled. And these noble robes did little more than muffle their shouts of hate.'

'So this is about vengeance, then?' asked Altaïr.

'No. Not vengeance, but my conscience. How could I finance a war in service to the same God that calls me an abomination?'

'If you do not serve Salah Al'din's cause, then whose?'

Nuqoud smiled. 'In time you'll come to know them. I think, perhaps, you already do.'

Puzzled once again, Altaïr asked, 'Then why hide? And why these dark deeds?'

'Is it so different from your own work? You take the lives of men and women, strong in the conviction that their deaths will improve the lot of those left behind. A minor evil for a greater good? We are the same.'

'No.' Altaïr shook his head. 'We are nothing alike.'

'Ah . . . but I see it in your eyes. You doubt.'

The stink of death was on his breath as he pulled Altaïr closer to him. 'You cannot stop us,' he managed. 'We will have our New World . . .'

He died, a thin trail of blood trickling from his mouth.

'Enjoy the silence,' said Altaïr, and dipped his feather into the Merchant King's blood.

He needed to see Al Mualim, he decided. The time for uncertainty was over.

'Come, Altaïr. I would have news of your progress,' said Al Mualim.

'I've done as you've asked,' replied the Assassin.

'Good. Good.' Al Mualim looked hard him. 'I sense your thoughts are elsewhere. Speak your mind.'

It was true. Altaïr had thought of little else on the return journey. Now he had the opportunity to get it off his mind. 'Each man I'm sent to kill speaks cryptic words to me. Each time I come to you and ask for answers. Each time you give only riddles in exchange. But no more.'

Al Mualim's eyebrows shot up in surprise – surprise that Altaïr should address him in such a way. 'Who are you to say "no more"?'

Altaïr swallowed, then set his jaw. 'I'm the one who does the killing. If you want it to continue, you'll speak straight with me for once.'

'Tread carefully, Altaïr. I do not like your tone.'

'And I do not like your deception,' replied Altaïr, more loudly than he had intended.

Al Mualim darkened. 'I have offered you a chance to restore your lost honour.'

'Not lost,' countered Altaïr. 'Taken. By you. And then you sent me to fetch it again, like some damned dog.'

Now the Master drew his sword, eyes flaring. 'It seems I'll need to find another. A shame. You showed great potential.'

'I think if you had another, you'd have sent him long ago,' said Altaïr, who wondered if he was pushing his mentor too far, but carried on anyway. 'You said the answer to my question would arise when I no longer needed to ask it. So I will not ask. I *demand* you tell me what binds these men.'

He stood prepared to feel the point of Al Mualim's sword, hoping only that the Master considered him too valuable. It was a gamble, he knew.

Al Mualim seemed to consider the options also, his sword wavering, light glancing off the blade. Then he sheathed it and seemed to relax a little.

'What you say is true,' he said at last. 'These men are connected . . . by a blood oath not unlike our own.'

'Who are they?'

'*Non nobis, Domine, non nobis,*' he said. *Not unto us, O Lord.*

'Templars . . .' said Altaïr. Of course.

'Now you see the true reach of Robert de Sable.'

'All of these men – leaders of cities – commanders of armies . . .'

'All pledge allegiance to his cause.'

'Their works are not meant to be viewed on their own, are they?' said Altaïr, thinking. 'But as a whole . . . What do they desire?'

'Conquest,' replied Al Mualim, simply. 'They seek the Holy Land – not in the name of God but for themselves.'

'What of Richard? Salah Al'din?'

'Any who oppose the Templars will be destroyed. Be assured they have the means to accomplish it.'

'Then they must be stopped,' said Altaïr, with resolve. He felt as though a great weight had lifted from him.

'That is why we do our work, Altaïr. To ensure a future free of such men.'

'Why did you hide the truth from me?' he asked the Master.

'That you might pierce the veil yourself. Like any task, knowledge precedes action. Information learned is more valuable than information given. Besides . . . your behaviour had not inspired in me much confidence.'

'I see.' Altair lowered his head.

'Altaïr, your mission has not changed, merely the context within which you perceive it.'

'And armed with this knowledge, I might better understand those Templars who remain.'

Al Mualim nodded. 'Is there anything else you want to know?'

Altaïr had solved the mystery of the Brotherhood to which his targets had referred. But there was something else . . . 'What about the treasure Malik retrieved from Solomon's Temple?' he asked. 'Robert seemed desperate to have it back.'

'In time, Altaïr, all will become clear,' said Al Mualim. 'Just as the role of the Templars has revealed itself to you, so too will the nature of their treasure. For now, take comfort in the fact that it is not in their hands, but ours.'

For a moment Altaïr considered pressing him on the subject but decided against it. He had been lucky once. He doubted it would happen a second time. 'If this is your desire . . .' he said.

'It is.'

The atmosphere in the room relaxed as Altaïr turned to go. His next destination was Jerusalem.

'Altaïr – before you go?'

'Yes?'

'How did you know I wouldn't kill you?'

'Truth be told, Master, I didn't.'

22

Stupid Altaïr. Arrogant Altaïr. He was in trouble. Majd Addin lay dead at his feet, the wood slowly staining with his blood. At his back were the accused, lashed to stakes and hanging from them, limp and bloody. The square was emptying of spectators, but not of Majd Addin's guards, who were advancing on him. Approaching the platform. Beginning to climb the steps at either end while blocking him from jumping at the front. With fierce eyes they were slowly hemming him in, their swords raised, and if they felt fear it didn't show. That their leader had been publicly cut down by an Assassin at Jerusalem's Wailing Wall gallows had not thrown them into panic and disarray as Altaïr had hoped. It hadn't instilled in them a mortal fear of the Assassin who now stood before them, his blade dripping with Addin's blood. It had given them resolve and a need to exact revenge.

Which meant that things hadn't gone according to plan.

Except . . . the first of the guards darted forward, snarling, his job to test Altaïr's mettle. The Assassin retreated, parrying the strikes of the Saracen's blade, steel ringing in the near-empty square. The guard pressed forward. Altaïr glanced behind to see others advancing and replied with an attack of his own, forcing the Saracen back. *One, two, thrust.* Forced hurriedly to defend, the guard tried to skip away, almost backing into one of the bodies hanging from the stakes. Altaïr glanced down and saw his chance, coming forward once again, launching a wild attack aimed at panicking his opponent. Blade met blade and, sure enough, the Saracen was forced messily backwards and into the pool of blood on the platform – just as Altaïr had intended. He slipped, his footing lost, and for a second his guard was down – enough time for Altaïr to dart inside his sword arm, impaling him in the chest. He gurgled. Died. His body slipped to the wood, and Altaïr straightened to face more attackers, seeing doubt and maybe a little fear in their eyes now. The Assassin's mettle had been duly tested and he had not been found lacking.

Still, though, the guards had the advantage of numbers, and more, surely, would be on their way, alerted by the commotion. News of events at the square would have spread throughout Jerusalem: that the city regent had been slain on his own execution scaffold; that his guards had set upon the Assassin responsible. Altaïr thought of Malik's glee at the news.

Yet Malik had appeared changed when Altaïr had last visited the Bureau. It wasn't as though he'd welcomed

Altaïr with open arms but, nevertheless, open hostility had been replaced by a certain weariness, and he had regarded Altaïr with a frown, not a glare.

'Why do you trouble me today?' He'd sighed.

Grateful not to have to spar, Altaïr had told him his target: Majd Addin.

Malik nodded. 'Salah Al'din's absence has left the city without a proper leader, and Majd Addin has appointed himself to play the part. Fear and intimidation get him what he wants. He has no true claim to the position.'

'That ends today,' Altaïr had said.

'You speak too readily. This is not some slaver we're discussing. He rules Jerusalem and is well protected because of it. I suggest you plan your attack carefully. Get to know your prey.'

'That I already have,' Altaïr had assured him. 'Majd Addin is holding a public execution not far from here. It's sure to be well guarded, but nothing I can't handle. I know what to do.'

Malik sneered. 'And that is why you remain a novice in my eyes. You cannot *know* anything. Only suspect. You must expect to be wrong. To have overlooked something. Anticipate, Altaïr. How many times must I remind you of this?'

'As you wish. Are we done?'

'Not quite. There is one more thing. One of the men to be executed is a brother. One of us. Al Mualim wishes him to be saved. Do not worry about the actual rescue – my men will take care of that. But you must ensure Majd Addin does not take his life.'

'I won't give him the chance.'

As he'd left, Malik had warned him, 'Don't foul this, Altaïr,' and Altaïr had mentally scoffed at the thought as he began the walk to the Wailing Wall.

23

As he had approached the Wailing Wall, Altaïr had seen crowds beginning to gather: men, women, children, dogs, even livestock. All were making their way through the surrounding streets of the square towards the execution plaza.

Altaïr joined them, and as he passed along a street that was filling with more and more eager spectators heading in the same direction, he had listened to a town crier whipping up enthusiasm for the coming attraction – though it hardly seemed necessary.

'Take notice,' called the crier. 'Majd Addin, most beloved regent of Jerusalem, will attend a public execution at the western edge of Solomon's Temple. All able citizens are requested to be there. Hurry! Come and witness what becomes of our enemies.'

Altaïr had had an idea of what that might be. He hoped he would be able to change the outcome.

Guards at the entrance to the square were trying to control the flow of the crowd inside, turning some back, allowing others in. Altaïr hung back, watching the masses eddy about the entrance, bodies pressing against him in the street. Children darted through the legs of the spectators, sneaking their way into the plaza. Next he saw a knot of scholars, the crowd parting to make way for them, even dogs seeming to sense the reverence reserved for the holy men. Altaïr rearranged his robes, adjusted his cowl, waited until the scholars were passing and slipped in among them. As he did so, he felt a hand tugging at his sleeve and looked down to see a grubby child staring at him with quizzical eyes. He snarled and, terrified, the boy darted away.

Just in time: they had reached the gates, where the guards parted to allow the scholars through, and Altaïr came upon the square.

There were rough stone walls on all sides. Along the far end was a raised platform and on it a series of stakes. Empty, for now, but not for much longer. Jerusalem's regent, Majd Addin was walking out on to the stage. At his appearance there was a surge, and a shout went up from the entrance as the guards lost control and citizens came pouring in. Altaïr was carried forward on the wave, now much closer to the rostrum and to the feared Majd Addin, who was already stalking the stage, waiting for the square to fill. He wore a white turban and a long, ornately embroidered gown. He moved as though he was angry. As though his temper was just moments from escaping his body.

It was.

'*Silence!* I demand *silence*,' he roared.

With the show about to start, there was a final surge and Altair was carried forward once more. He saw guards stationed by the steps on either side of the platform, two at each end. In front of the platform he saw more, to prevent the crowd scrambling on to the scaffold. Craning his neck, he spotted others around the periphery of the square. At least the latter would find it difficult to move through the crowd, but that still gave just seconds for the kill *and* to fend off the nearest guards – the four at either end of the platform at the very least. Maybe those standing guard on the ground as well.

Could he better them all in that time? Ten or so loyal Saracens? The Altaïr who had attacked Robert de Sable on the Temple Mount would have had no doubts at all. Now, though, he was more wary. And he knew that to attempt the killing immediately was madness. A plan doomed to failure.

Just as he'd made up his mind to wait, the four prisoners were led on to the scaffold and to the stakes where the guards began binding them in place. At one end there was a woman, dirty-faced and weeping. Beside her stood two men, dressed in rags. And finally the Assassin, his head lolling, beaten, obviously. The crowd hissed its displeasure

'People of Jerusalem, hear me well,' shouted Majd Addin, his voice silencing the crowd, which had become excited at the arrival of the prisoners. 'I stand here today to deliver a warning.' He paused. 'There are malcontents among you. They sow the seeds of discontent, hoping to lead you astray.'

The crowd murmured, seething around Altaïr.

Addin continued: 'Tell me, is this what you desire? To be mired in deceit and sin? To live your lives in fear?'

'We do not,' screamed a spectator from behind Altaïr. But Altaïr's attention was fixed on the Assassin, a fellow member of the Order. As he watched, a bloody string of saliva dripped from the man's mouth to the wood. He tried to raise his head and Altaïr caught a glimpse of his face. Ripe purple bruises. Then his head lolled once more.

Majd Addin grinned a crooked grin. His was a face not used to smiling. 'So you wish to take action?' he asked agreeably.

The crowd roared its approval. They were here to see blood; they knew the regent would not leave their thirst unquenched.

'Guide us,' called a voice, as the roar died down.

'Your devotion pleases me,' said Addin, and he turned to the prisoners, indicating them with a sweep of his arm. 'This evil must be purged. Only then can we hope to be redeemed.'

Suddenly there was a disturbance in front of the platform, a voice crying, 'This is not justice.'

Altaïr saw a man in rags. He was shouting at Majd

Addin: 'You twist the words of the Prophet, peace be upon him.'

He had a companion, also clothed in tatters, who was similarly upbraiding the crowd. 'And all of you stand idle, complicit in this crime.'

Altaïr used the disturbance to edge closer. He needed to climb to the platform at the end where the Assassin stood bound to the stake. Couldn't risk having him used as a barrier or hostage.

'God curse you all,' shouted the first man — but they had no supporters. Not among the crowd and certainly not among the guards, who even now were moving forward. Seeing them come, the two hecklers made a run for it, producing daggers and waving them as they made a futile dash towards the platform. One was cut down by an archer. The second found himself pursued by two guards, failing to see a third Saracen who opened his stomach with his sword.

They lay dying in the dust and Majd Addin pointed at them. 'See how the evil of one man spreads to corrupt another?' he shrieked. His black beard quivered with outrage. 'They sought to instil fear and doubt within you. But *I* will keep you safe.'

Now he turned back to the poor unfortunates — who must surely have been praying for the attempt on his life to succeed, but instead watched wide-eyed and terrified as he drew his sword.

'Here are four filled with sin,' called Addin, pointing

first at the woman, then at each one in turn. 'The harlot. The thief. The gambler. The heretic. Let God's judgment be brought down upon them all.'

The heretic. That was the Assassin. Altaïr steeled himself and began to move closer to the steps at the side of the platform, one eye on Addin as he walked first over to the woman. The prostitute. Unable to take her eyes off the sword Addin held – almost casually, hanging at his side – she began wailing uncontrollably.

'*Temptress!*' roared Addin, over her sobs. 'Succubus. Whore. She goes by many names, but her sin remains the same. She turned her back on the teachings of our Prophet, peace be upon him. Defiled her body to advance her station. Each man she touched is for ever stained.'

In response the crowd booed. Altaïr moved a few more feet towards the rostrum steps. He watched the guards and saw that their attention was on Addin. Good.

'Punish her,' screamed an onlooker.

Addin had whipped them into a state of righteous fury.

'She must pay,' agreed another.

The woman stopped snivelling to shout at the crowd baying for her blood. 'This man speaks *lies*. I am here today not because I lay down with other men, for I did not. He means to murder me because I would not *lie down with him*.'

Majd Addin's eyes flared. 'Even now, offered redemption, she continues to deceive. She rejects salvation. There is only one way to deal with this.'

She had time to scream, '*No*,' as his sword flashed and he drove it into her stomach. In the moment of silence that followed there was the sound of her blood splashing to the boards of the platform, before a collective 'ooh' went up from the crowd, which shifted as those at the sides and back tried to get a better view of the gutted woman.

Altaïr was closer to the steps now but the sudden movement of the crowd had left him a little exposed. Relieved, he watched as Addin strode to the next whimpering prisoner and the spectators rolled back again, anticipating the next kill.

Addin indicated the man, a gambler, he explained. A man who could not abstain from intoxicants and wagers.

'For shame,' screeched the crowd. It was they who were intoxicated, thought Altaïr, sickened by their bloodlust.

'A game of chance condemns me to death?' cried the gambler, one last throw of the dice for him. 'Show me where such a thing is written. It is not sin that corrupts our city, but *you*.'

'So you would say to the people it is acceptable to defy the will of our Prophet, peace be upon him?' countered Addin. 'And if we are to ignore this teaching, then what of the others? Where does it end? I say it ends in chaos. And so it cannot be allowed.'

His blade glinted in the afternoon sun. He drove it deep into the belly of the gambler, grunting as he yanked it upwards, opening a vertical wound in the man's abdomen and exposing his entrails. Delighted, the crowd screamed in mock disgust, already seething to the side in order to view the next killing, taking Altaïr closer to the steps.

Addin sauntered to the third prisoner, shaking blood from his blade. 'This man,' he said, indicating the trembling captive, 'took what was not his. Money earned through the labour of another. It could have belonged to any of you. And so you have all been violated. What say you to this?'

'It was a single dinar,' the accused appealed, imploring the crowd for mercy, 'found on the ground. He speaks as though I trespassed, as though I ripped it from the hands of another.'

But the throng was not in a merciful frame of mind. There were calls for his blood, the spectators in a frenzy now.

'Today a dinar,' shrieked Addin, 'tomorrow a horse. The next day, another man's life. The object itself is not of consequence. What matters is that you took what did not belong to you. Were I to allow such behaviour, then others would believe it their right to take as well. Where would it end?'

He moved in front of the thief, whose final pleas were cut short as Addin buried the blade in his belly.

Now he would turn his attention to the Assassin. Altaïr had to act fast. He had just moments. Lowering his head, he began to shoulder his way through the crowd, careful not to appear as though he had any particular intention. Simply that he wanted to get as close to the front of the crowd as possible. By now, Majd Addin had reached the Assassin and sauntered up to him, grabbed his hair and raised his head to show the crowd.

'This man spreads vicious lies and propaganda,' he roared venomously. 'He has only murder on his mind. He poisons our thoughts as he poisons his blade. Turns brother against brother. Father against son. More dangerous than any enemy we face. He is *Assassin*.'

He was rewarded with the crowd's collective intake of breath. Altaïr had reached the steps now. Around him the throng seethed, excitable spectators screaming for the killing blow.

'Destroy the unbeliever!'

'Kill him!'

'Slit his throat!'

The Assassin, his head still held by Addin, spoke: 'Killing me will not make you any safer. I see the fear in your eyes, hear the quiver in your throats. You are afraid. Afraid because you know our message cannot be silenced. Because you know we cannot be stopped.'

Altaïr was at the bottom of the steps. He stood there as if attempting to get a better view. Others had seen him and were doing the same. The two guards had been standing at the top entranced by the action, but slowly became aware of what was happening. One called to the other and they stepped down and began commanding citizens to leave, even as more spectators were pouring up the stairs. All wanted to get as close as possible to the execution and were jostling and shoving, some forced off the steps, including one of the furious guards. Altaïr used the disorder to climb higher until he stood just a few feet away from Addin, who had released the Assassin's head and was preaching to the crowd of his 'blasphemy'. His 'treachery'.

Behind Altaïr the scuffle continued. The two guards were fully occupied. Ahead of him, Addin had finished addressing the crowd, who were suitably whipped up and desperate to see the final kill. Now he turned back to the prisoner, brandishing his sword, its blade already stained red, and moved towards him for the death blow.

Then, as though alerted by some higher sense, he stopped, turned his head and looked straight at Altaïr.

For a moment it was as though the square contracted, as though the disorderly crowd, the guards, the condemned man and the corpses were no longer there. And as they regarded one another Altaïr saw realisation dawn on Addin that death was near. Then

Altaïr flicked his ring finger and the blade sprang forth as he launched himself forward, drawing it back, and sinking it into Addin, the entire movement lasting little longer than the blink of an eye.

The crowd roared and screamed, not knowing what to make of the sudden turn of events. Addin bucked and squirmed, blood pumping from the wound in his neck but Altaïr held him steady with his knees, raising his blade.

'Your work here is finished,' he told Addin, and tensed, about to deliver the final blow. Around them there was pandemonium. The guards were only just realizing what was wrong and trying to fight their way to the platform through a panicked crowd. Altaïr needed to finish this, fast. But he wanted to hear what Addin had to say.

'No. No. It had only just begun,' said Addin.

'Tell me, what is your part in all of this? Do you intend to defend yourself as the others have and explain away your evil deeds?'

'The Brotherhood wanted the city. I wanted power. There was . . . an opportunity.'

'An opportunity to murder innocents,' said Altaïr. He could hear the sound of running feet. The people fleeing the square.

'Not so innocent. Dissident voices cut deep as steel. They disrupt order. In this, I agree with the Brotherhood.'

'You'd kill people simply for believing differently from you?'

'Of course not . . . I killed them because I could. Because it was fun. Do you know what it feels like to determine another man's fate? And did you see the way the people cheered? The way they feared me? I was like a god. You'd have done the same if you could. Such . . . power.'

'Once, perhaps. But then I learned what becomes of those who lift themselves above others.'

'And what is that?'

'Here. Let me show you.'

He finished Addin, then closed the tyrant's eyes. Stained the feather.

'Every soul shall taste death,' he said.

And then he had stood up to face the guards – just as a bell began tolling.

A Saracen came flying at him and he parried, grunting, driving the man back. More were scrambling on to the platform, and he found himself facing three at once. One fell screaming beneath his blade, another lost his footing on the slick of blood, fell, and Altaïr finished him. Seeing a gap, the Assassin jumped from the scaffold, activating his blade and spearing a guard as he landed, the man's sword swiping at thin air.

On the square now he saw his only escape and fended off two more attackers as he edged towards the entranceway. He took a nick and felt warm blood sluice down his arm; then, grasping hold of a swords-man, launched him into the path of the second. Both tumbled, yelling, to the dirt. Altaïr darted towards the doorway, arriving as a trio of soldiers came hurrying through. He had the surprise though, impaling one with his sword, slashing the neck of a second with his blade and shoving the two writhing, dying men into the third.

Entrance clear, he glanced behind at the platform to see Malik's men freeing the Assassin and leading him away, then dashed out into the lane where a fourth guard waited, coming forward with a pike, screaming. Altaïr jumped clear, grasping the edge of a wooden frame and flipping himself up on to the canopy, feel-ing his muscles sing. From below there was a shout of frustration, and as he scrabbled up to the rooftop he glanced down to see a cluster of soldiers following him. To give them pause he killed one with a throwing knife, then dashed off across the rooftops, waited until the bell had stopped ringing, and then disappeared into the crowd, listening as word spread throughout the city: an Assassin had killed the regent.

24

There was still something Altaïr needed to know, though.

And with the last of the city regents dead, now was the time to ask it. He steeled himself as he was ushered once more into Al Mualim's chambers.

'Come in, Altaïr. I trust you are well rested? Ready for your remaining trials?' said the Master.

'I am. But I'd speak with you first. I have questions . . .'

Al Mualim indicated his disapproval by raising his chin and pursing his lips slightly. No doubt he remembered the last occasion when Altaïr had pressed for answers. So did Altaïr, who had decided to tread more carefully this time, keen not to see a reappearance of the Master's blade.

'Ask, then,' said Al Mualim. 'I'll do my best to answer.'

Altaïr took a deep breath. 'The Merchant King of Damascus murdered the nobles who ruled his city. Majd Addin in Jerusalem used fear to force his people into submission. I suspect William meant to murder Richard, and hold Acre with his troops. These men were meant to aid their leaders. Instead they chose to betray them. What I do not understand is *why*.'

'Is the answer not obvious? The Templars desire control. Each man – as you've noted – wanted to claim their cities in the Templar name that the Templars themselves might rule the Holy Land and eventually beyond. But they cannot succeed in their mission.'

'Why is that?' asked Altaïr.

'Their plans depend upon the Templar Treasure . . . the Piece of Eden . . . But we hold it now. And they cannot hope to achieve their goals without it.'

Of course, thought Altaïr. This was the item so many of his targets had referred to.

'What is this treasure?' he said.

Al Mualim smiled, then went to the rear of his chamber, bent and opened a chest. He took a box from it, returned to his desk and placed it down. Altair knew what it was without looking, but still found his gaze drawn to it – no, *dragged* to it. It was the box Malik had retrieved from the Temple, and as before it seemed to glow, to radiate a kind of power. He had known all along, he realized, that this was the treasure they spoke of. His eyes went from the box to Al Mualim, who had been watching his reaction. The Master's face bore an indulgent expression, as though he had seen many behave in this way. And that this was only the beginning.

For now he reached into the box and took from it a globe, about the size of two fists: a golden globe with a mosaic design that seemed to pulse with energy, so that Altaïr found himself wondering if his eyes were deceiving him. If maybe it was . . . *alive* in some way. But he was distracted. Instead he felt the globe pulling at him.

'It is . . . temptation,' intoned Al Mualim.

And suddenly, like a candle snuffed out, the globe stopped pulsing. Its aura was gone. Its draw suddenly non-existent. It was . . . just a globe again: an ancient thing, beautiful in its own way but, still, a mere trinket.

'It's just a piece of silver . . .' said Altaïr.

'Look at it,' insisted Al Mualim.

'It shimmers for the briefest moment, but there's really nothing spectacular about it,' said Altaïr. 'What am I supposed to see?'

'This "piece of silver" cast out Adam and Eve. *This is the Apple*. It turned staves into snakes. Parted and closed the Red Sea. Eris used it to start the Trojan War. And with it, a poor carpenter turned water into wine.'

The Apple, the Piece of Eden? Altaïr looked at it doubtfully. 'It seems rather plain for all the power you claim it has,' he said. 'How does it work?'

'He who holds it commands the hearts and minds of whoever looks upon it – whoever "tastes" of it, as they say.'

'Then de Naplouse's men . . .' said Altaïr, thinking of the poor creatures in the hospital.

'An experiment. Herbs used to simulate its effects . . . To be ready for when they held it.'

Altaïr saw it now. 'Talal supplied them. Tamir equipped them. They were preparing for something . . . But what?'

'War,' said Al Mualim, starkly.

'And the others . . . the men who ruled the cities . . . They meant to gather up their people. Make them like de Naplouse's men.'

'The perfect citizens. The perfect soldiers. A perfect world.'

'Robert de Sable must never have this back,' said Altaïr.

'So long as he and his brothers live, they will try,' said Al Mualim.

'Then they must be destroyed.'

'Which is what I've had you doing,' smiled Al Mualim. 'There are two more Templars who require your attention,' he said. 'One in Acre, known as Sibrand. One in Damascus, called Jubair. Visit the Bureau leaders. They'll instruct you further.'

'As you wish,' said Altaïr, bowing his head.

'Be quick about it,' said Al Mualim. 'No doubt Robert de Sable is made nervous by our continued success. His remaining followers will do their best to expose you. They *know* you come: the man in the white hood. They'll be looking for you.'

'They won't find me. I'm but a blade in a crowd,' said Altaïr.

Al Mualim smiled, proud once more of his pupil.

25

It was Al Mualim who had taught them the Creed, the young Altaïr and Abbas. The Master had filled their young heads with the tenets of the Order.

Every day, after a breakfast of flat bread and dates, stern governesses had seen to it that they were washed and neatly dressed. Then, with books clasped to their breasts, they had hurried along corridors, their sandals slapping on the stone, chatting excitedly, until they reached the door to the Master's study.

Here they had had a ritual. Both passed a hand over his own mouth to go from happy face to serious face, the face the Master expected. Then one would knock. For some reason they both liked to knock, so they took it in turns each day. Then they would wait for the Master to invite them in. There, they would sit cross-legged on cushions that Al Mualim had provided especially for them – one for Altaïr, and one for his brother, Abbas.

When they first began their tutelage they had been frightened and unsure, of themselves, of each other and in particular of Al Mualim, who would tutor them in the morning and at evening, with training in the yard in the afternoon and then again at night. Long hours spent learning the ways of the Order, watching the Master pace the study, his hands behind his back, occasionally stopping to admonish them if he thought they weren't paying attention. They both found Al Mualim's one eye disconcerting and felt fixed in place by it sometimes. Until one night Abbas had whispered across their room, 'Hey, Altaïr?'

Altair turned to him, surprised. Neither had done this before, begun talking after the lights had been snuffed. They had lain in silence, each lost in his own thoughts. Until that night. The moon was full and the sheet at their window glowed white, lighting the room a soft, grey hue. Abbas was lying on his side looking across at Altaïr, and when he had the other boy's attention he placed a hand over one eye, and said, in an almost perfect approximation of Al Mualim, 'We are nothing if we do not abide by the Assassin's Creed.'

Altaïr had dissolved into giggles and from then the two were friends. From now on when Al Mualim admonished them, it was for the stifled laughter he heard when his back was turned. Suddenly the governesses found that their charges weren't quite so meek and acquiescent.

And Al Mualim taught them the tenets. The tenets that Altaïr would neglect later in life, at a cost dear to him. Al Mualim told them that the Assassins were not indiscriminate killers, not as the world at large liked to think, but were tasked only with slaying the evil and corrupt; their mission was to bring peace and stability to the Holy Land, to instil in it a code not of violence and conflict but of thought and contemplation.

He taught them to master their feelings and emotions, to cloak their disposition and be absorbed by the world about them, so that they might move among normal people undetected, a blank space, a ghost in the crowd. To the people, the Assassin must be a kind of magic they did not understand, he said, but that, like all magic, it was reality bent to the will of the Assassin.

He taught them to protect the Order at all times; that the Brotherhood was 'more important than you, Altaïr. It is more important than you, Abbas. It is more important than Masyaf and myself.' Thus, the action of one Assassin should never call harm up upon the Order. The Assassin should never compromise the Brotherhood.

And though Altaïr would one day disregard this doctrine, too, it was not for want of Al Mualim's tutoring. He taught them that men had created boundaries and declared all within those boundaries to be 'true' and 'real', but in fact they were false perimeters, imposed by those who would presume to be leaders. He showed them that the bounds of reality were infinitely broader than mankind's limited imagination was able to conceive, and that only the few could see beyond those boundaries – only a few dared even question their existence.

And they were the Assassins.

And because the Assassins were able to see the world as it truly was, then to the Assassin everything was possible – everything was permitted.

Every day, as Altaïr and Abbas learned more and more about the Order, they also grew closer. They spent almost all day with one another. Whatever Al Mualim taught them, their own day-to-day reality was in fact insubstantial. It consisted of each other, the governesses, Al Mualim's classes and a succession of combat trainers, each with a different speciality. And far from everything being permitted, virtually nothing was. Any entertainment was provided by the boys themselves, and so they spent long hours talking when they should have been studying. A subject they rarely discussed was their fathers. At first Abbas had talked only of Ahmad returning one day to Masyaf, but as the months turned into years he spoke of it less. Altaïr would see him standing at the window, watching over the valley with glittering eyes. Then his friend began to withdraw and become less communicative. He was not so quick to smile any more. Where before he had spent hours talking, now he stood at the window instead.

Altaïr thought: If only he knew. Abbas's grief would flare and intensify, then settle into an ache, just as

Altaïr had experienced. The fact of his father's death hurt him every day, but at least he *knew*. It was the difference between a dull ache and a constant sense of hopelessness.

So one night, after the candles had been snuffed out, he told Abbas. With bowed head, fighting back the tears, he told Abbas that Ahmad had come to his quarters and there he had taken his own life, but that Al Mualim had decided it best to hide this fact from the Brotherhood, 'in order to protect you. But the Master hasn't witnessed your yearning at first hand. I lost my father, too, so I know. I know that the pain of it recedes over time. By telling you, I hope to help you, my friend.'

Abbas had simply blinked in the darkness, then turned over in his bed. Altaïr had wondered how he had expected Abbas to react. Tears? Anger? Disbelief? He had been prepared for them all. Even to bar Abbas in and prevent him going to the Master. What he hadn't expected was this . . . emptiness. This silence.

26

Altaïr stood on a rooftop in Damascus, looking down on his next target.

The smell of burning sickened him. The sight too. Of books being burned. Altaïr watched them crinkle, blacken and burn, thinking of his father, who would have been disgusted; Al Mualim, too, when he told him. To burn books was an affront to the Assassin way. Learning is knowledge, and knowledge is freedom and power. He knew that. He had forgotten it, somehow, but he knew it once more.

He stood out of sight on the ledge of the roof overlooking the courtyard of Jubair's *madrasah* in Damascus. Smoke rose towards where he stood but all of the attention below was focused on the fire, piles of books, documents and scrolls at its centre. The fire and Jubair al-Hakim, who stood nearby, barking orders. All were doing his bidding apart from one, Altaïr noticed. This scholar stood to the side, gazing into the fire, his expression echoing Altaïr's thoughts.

Jubair wore leather boots, a black headcloth and a permanent scowl. Altaïr watched him carefully: he had learned much about him. Jubair was the chief scholar of Damascus but in name only, for it was a most unusual scholar who insisted not on spreading learning but on destroying it. In this pursuit he had enlisted the city's academics, whose presence was encouraged by Salah Al'din.

And why were they doing it, collecting then destroying these documents? In the name of some 'new way' or 'new order', which Altaïr had heard about before. Exactly what it involved wasn't clear. He knew *who* was behind it, though. The Templars, his quarry being one of them.

'Every single text in this city must be destroyed.' Below him Jubair was exhorting his men with a fanatic's zeal. His scholar helpers scurried about, laden with armfuls of papers that they had carried from somewhere hidden from Altaïr. They were casting them into the flames, which bloomed and grew with each fresh delivery. From the corner of his eye he saw the distant scholar becoming more and more agitated, until suddenly, as though he could no longer contain himself, he sprang forward to confront Jubair.

'My friend, you must not do this,' he said, his jovial tone belying his obvious distress. 'Much knowledge rests within these parchments, put there by our ancestors for good reason.'

Jubair stopped, to stare at him with naked contempt. 'And what *reason* is this?' he snarled.

'They are beacons meant to guide us – to save us from the darkness that is ignorance,' implored the scholar. The flames danced tall at his back. Scholars came with more armfuls of books that they deposited on the fire, some casting nervous glances at where Jubair and the protester stood.

'No.' Jubair took a step forward, forcing the naysayer to retreat a step. 'These bits of paper are covered with lies. They poison your minds. And so long as they exist, you cannot hope to see the world as it truly is.'

Trying desperately to be reasonable, the scholar still couldn't hide his frustration. 'How can you accuse these scrolls of being weapons? They're tools of learning.'

'You turn to them for answers and salvation.' Jubair took another step forward, the protester another step back. 'You rely more upon them than upon yourselves. This makes you weak and stupid. You trust in words. Drops of ink. Do you ever stop to think of who put them there? Or why? No. You simply accept their words without question. And what if those words speak falsely, as they often do? This is dangerous.'

The scholar looked confused. As though someone was telling him black was white, night was day. 'You are wrong,' he insisted. 'These texts offer the gift of knowledge. We need them.'

Jubair darkened. 'You love your precious writings? You'd do anything for them?'

'Yes, yes. Of course.'

Jubair smiled. A cruel smile. 'Then join them.'

Planting both hands on the scholar's chest, Jubair shoved him backwards, hard. For a second the scholar was mid-topple, his eyes wide open in surprise and his arms flapping madly, as though he hoped to fly clear of the greedy fire. Then he was claimed by the impetus of the shove, falling into the flames, writhing on a bed of searing heat. He screamed and kicked. His robe caught. For a moment he seemed to be trying to beat out the flames, the sleeves of his tunic already alight. Then his shrieks stopped. And contained in the smoke rising to Altaïr was the nauseating scent of roasting human flesh. He covered his nose. In the courtyard below, the scholars did the same.

Jubair addressed them: 'Any man who speaks as he did is just as much a threat. Does any other among you wish to challenge me?'

There was no reply, fearful eyes looked over hands held to noses. 'Good,' said Jubair. 'Your orders are simple enough. Go out into the city. Collect any remaining writings and add them to the piles in the streets. When you're done we'll send a cart to collect them that they may be destroyed.'

The scholars left. And now the courtyard was empty. A beautiful marbled area for ever tarnished by the obscenity of the fire. Jubair paced around it, gazing into the fire. Every so often he cast a nervous glance around him, and appeared to be listening carefully. But if he heard anything it was the crackle of the fire and the sound of his own breathing. He relaxed a little, which made Altaïr smile. Jubair knew the Assassins were coming for him. Thinking himself cleverer than his executioners he'd sent decoys into the city streets – decoys with his most trusted bodyguards, so that the deception should be complete. Altaïr moved silently around the rooftop until he stood directly above the book-burner. Jubair thought he was safe here, locked in his *madrasah*.

But he wasn't. And he had executed his last underling, burned his last book.

Snick.

Jubair looked up and saw the Assassin descending towards him, blade outstretched. Too late, he tried to dart out of the way as the blade was sinking into his neck. With a sigh he crumpled to the marble.

His eyelids fluttered. 'Why . . . why have you done this?'

Altaïr looked over to the blackened corpse of the scholar in the fire. With the flesh burned away from his skull, it was as though he was grinning. 'Men must be free to do as they believe,' he told Jubair. He withdrew the blade from the other's neck. Blood dripped to the marble. 'It is not our right to punish one for thinking as he does, no matter how much we disagree.'

'Then what?' wheezed the dying man.

'You of all people should know the answer. Educate them. *Teach* them right from wrong. It must be knowledge that frees them, not force.'

Jubair chuckled. 'They do not learn, fixed in their ways as they are. You are naïve to think otherwise. It's an illness, Assassin, for which there is but one cure.'

'You're wrong. And that's why you must be put to rest.'

'Am I not unlike those precious books you seek to save? A source of knowledge with which you disagree? Yet you're rather quick to steal my life.'

'A small sacrifice to save many. It is necessary.'

'Is it not ancient scrolls that inspire the Crusaders? That fill Salah Al'din and his men with a sense of righteous fury? Their texts endanger others. Bring death in their wake. I, too, was making a small sacrifice.' He smiled. 'It matters little now. Your deed is done. And so am I.'

He died, eyes closing. Altaïr stood up. He looked around the courtyard, seeing the beauty and ugliness of it. Then, hearing footsteps approaching, he was gone. Over the rooftops and into the streets. Blending into the city. Becoming but a blade in the crowd . . .

'I have a question for *you*,' said Al Mualim, when they next met. He had restored Altaïr's full status and at last the Assassin was a Master Assassin once more. Still, it was as though his mentor wanted to be sure of it. Wanted to be certain that Altaïr had learned.

'What is the truth?' he asked.

'We place faith in ourselves,' replied Altaïr, eager to please him, wanting to show him that he had indeed changed. That his decision to show mercy had been the right one. 'We see the world as it really is, and hope that one day all mankind might see the same.'

'What is the world, then?'

'An illusion,' replied Altaïr. 'One we can either submit to – as most do – or transcend.'

'And what is it to transcend?'

'To recognize that laws arise not from divinity, but reason. I understand now that our Creed does not command us to be free.' And suddenly he really did understand. 'It commands us to be wise.'

Until now he had believed in the Creed but without knowing its true meaning. It was a call to interrogate, to apply thought and learning and reason to all endeavours.

Al Mualim nodded. 'Do you see now why the Templars are a threat?'

'Whereas we would dispel the illusion, they would use it to rule.'

'Yes. To reshape the world in an image more pleasing to them. That is why I sent you to steal their treasure. That is why I keep it locked away. And that is why you kill them. So long as even one survives, so, too, does their desire to create a New World Order. You must now seek out Sibrand. With his death, Robert de Sable will at last be vulnerable.'

'It will be done.'

'Safety and peace upon you, Altair.'

27

Altaïr made what he hoped was a final trip to Acre –
battle-scarred Acre, over which hung the permanent
pall of death. There, he carried out his investigations,
then visited Jabal in the Bureau to collect his marker.
At mention of Sibrand's name, Jabal nodded sagely.
'I am familiar with the man. Newly appointed leader
of the Knights Teutonic, he resides in the Venetian
Quarter, and runs Acre's port.'

'I've learned as much – and more.'

Jabal raised impressed eyebrows. 'Continue then.'

Altaïr told him how Sibrand had commandeered
the ships in the docks, intending to use them to establish a blockade. But not to prevent an attack by Salah
Al'din. That was the revealing aspect. According to
what Altaïr had learned, Sibrand planned to prevent
Richard's men receiving supplies. It made perfect
sense. The Templars were betraying their own. All was
becoming clear to him, it seemed: the nature of the
stolen artefact, the identity of the Brotherhood binding his targets together, even their ultimate aim. Yet
still . . .

Still there was a feeling he couldn't shake off. A

sense that, even now, uncertainty swirled around him like early-morning mist.

'Sibrand is said to be consumed by fear – driven mad by the knowledge that his death approaches. He has sealed the docks district, and now hides within, waiting for his ship to arrive.'

Jabal considered. 'This will make things dangerous. I wonder how he learned of your mission.'

'The men I've killed – they are all connected. Al Mualim warned me that word of my deeds has spread among them.'

'Be on your guard, Altaïr,' said Jabal, handing him the feather.

'Of course, *rafiq*. But I think it will be to my advantage. Fear will weaken him.'

He turned to leave, and as he did so, Jabal called him back. 'Altaïr . . .'

'Yes?'

'I owe you an apology.'

'For what?'

'For doubting your dedication to our cause.'

Altaïr thought. 'No. It was I who erred. I believed myself above the Creed. You owe me nothing.'

'As you wish, my friend. Go in safety.'

Altaïr went to the docks, slipping through Sibrand's cordon as easily as breathing. Behind him rose the walls of Acre, in various states of disrepair; ahead of him, the harbour was filled with ships and platforms, hulks and wooden carcasses. Some were working vessels, others left behind from the siege. They had transformed the gleaming blue sea into an ocean of brown flotsam.

The grey stone sun-bleached dock was its own city. Those who worked and lived there were dock people – they had the look of dock people. They had an easy manner and weathered faces accustomed to smiling.

Though not today. Not under the command of Sibrand, the Grand Master of the Knights Teutonic. Not only had he ordered the area to be sealed but he had filled it with his guards. His fear of assassination was like a virus that had spread through his army. Groups of soldiers moved through the docks with roving eyes. They were twitchy, their hands constantly flitting at the hilts of their broadswords. They were nervous, sweating under heavy chainmail.

Becoming aware of a commotion, Altaïr walked towards it, seeing citizens and soldiers doing the same. A knight was shouting at a holy man. Nearby his companions watched anxiously, while dock workers and merchants had gathered to view the spectacle.

'Y-you are mistaken, Master Sibrand. I would never propose violence against any man – and most certainly not against you.'

So this was Sibrand. Altaïr took note of the black hair, deep brow and harsh eyes that seemed to spin wildly, like those of a sun-maddened dog. He had armed himself with every weapon he could, and his belts sagged with swords, daggers and knives. Across his back was his longbow, arrow quills peeking over his right shoulder. He looked exhausted. A man unravelling.

'So you say,' he said, showering the priest in spit, 'and yet no one here will vouch for you. What am I to make of this?'

'I-I live a simple life, my lord, as do all men of the cloth. It is not for us to call attention to ourselves.'

'Perhaps.' He closed his eyes. Then they snapped open. 'Or perhaps they do not know you because you are not a man of God, but an Assassin.'

And with that he shoved the priest backwards, the old man landing badly, then scrabbling to his knees. 'Never,' he insisted.

'You wear the same robes.'

The holy man was desperate now. 'If they cover themselves as we do, it is only to instil uncertainty and fear. You must not give in.'

'Are you calling me a coward?" shouted Sibrand, his voice breaking. 'Challenging my authority? Are you, perhaps, hoping to turn my own knights against me?'

'No. *No.* I-I don't understand why you're d-doing this to me . . . I've done nothing wrong.'

'I don't recall accusing you of any wrongdoing, which makes your outburst rather odd. Is it the presence of guilt that compels a confession?'

'But I confess nothing,' said the priest.

'Ah. Defiant till the very end.'

The priest looked horrified. The more he said, the worse it got. 'What do you mean?' Altaïr watched as a succession of emotions passed across the old man's face: fear, confusion, desperation, hopelessness.

'William and Garnier were too confident. And they paid for this with their lives. I won't make the same mistake. If you truly are a man of God, then surely the Creator will provide for you. Let him stay my hand.'

'You've gone mad,' cried the priest. He turned to implore the spectators, 'Will none of you come forward to stop this? He is clearly poisoned by his own fear – compelled to see enemies where none exist.'

His companions shuffled awkwardly but said nothing. So, too, the citizens, who gazed at him dispassionately. The priest was no Assassin, they could see that, but it didn't matter what they thought. They were just glad not to be the target of Sibrand's fury.

'It seems the people share my concern,' said Sibrand. He drew his sword. 'What I do, I do for Acre.'

The priest shrieked as Sibrand drove the blade into his gut, twisted, then removed it and wiped it clean. The old man writhed on the dock, then died. Sibrand's guards picked up his body and tossed it into the water.

Sibrand watched it go. 'Stay vigilant, men. Report any suspicious activity to the guard. I doubt we've seen the last of these Assassins. Persistent bastards ... Now get back to work.'

Altaïr watched as he and two bodyguards made their way to a rowing-boat. The priest's body bumped against the hull as it cast off, then began to float through the debris in the harbour. Altaïr gazed out to sea, seeing a bigger ship further out. That would be Sibrand's sanctuary, he thought. His eyes went back to Sibrand's skiff. He could see the knight pulling himself up to scan the water around him. Looking for Assassins. Always looking for them. As though they might appear from the water around him.

Which was exactly what he was going to do, decided Altaïr, moving to the nearest hulk and jumping to it, easily traversing boats and platforms until he came close to Sibrand's ship. There he saw Sibrand make his way up to the main deck, eyes raking the water around him. Altaïr heard him ordering the guards to secure the lower decks, then moved across to a platform near the ship.

A lookout saw him coming and was about to raise his bow when Altaïr sent him a throwing knife, mentally cursing himself for not having time to prepare the kill. Sure enough, instead of falling silently to the wood of the platform, the sentry fell into the water with a splash.

Altaïr's eyes flicked to the deck of the main ship where Sibrand had heard the splash too, and was already beginning to panic. 'I know you're out there, Assassin,' he screeched. He unslung his bow. 'How long do you think you can hide? I've a hundred men scouring the docks. They'll find you. And when they do, you'll suffer for your sins.'

Altaïr hugged the frame of the platform, out of sight. Water lapped at its struts. Otherwise, silence. An almost ghostly quiet that must have unnerved Sibrand as much as it pleased Altaïr.

'Show yourself, coward,' insisted Sibrand. His fear was in his voice. 'Face me and let us be done with this.'

All in good time, thought Altaïr. Sibrand fired an arrow at nothing, then fitted and fired another.

'On your guard, men,' shouted Sibrand, to the lower decks. 'He's out there somewhere. Find him. End his life. A promotion to whoever brings me the head of the Assassin.'

Altaïr leaped from the platform to the ship, landing with a slight thump that seemed to resonate around the area of still water. He waited, clinging to the hull, hearing Sibrand's panicked shouts from above. Then he began to climb. He waited until Sibrand's back was turned then pulled himself on to the deck, now just a few feet away from the Grand Master of the Knights Teutonic, who was prowling the deck, shouting threats to the empty sea, hurling insults and orders at his guards, who hurried about below.

Sibrand was a dead man, thought Altaïr, as he crept

up behind him. He had died as much from his own fear, though he was too stupid to know it.

'Please . . . don't do this,' he said, as he folded to the deck with Altaïr's blade in his neck.

'You are afraid?' asked the Assassin. He withdrew his blade.

'Of course I am,' said Sibrand, as though addressing a dolt.

Altaïr thought back to Sibrand's callousness before the priest. 'But you'll be safe now,' he said, 'held in the arms of your God . . .'

Sibrand gave a small wet laugh. 'Have my brothers taught you nothing? I know what waits for me. For all of us.'

'If not your God, then what?'

'Nothing. Nothing waits. And that is what I fear.'

'You don't believe,' said Altaïr. Was it true? Sibrand had no faith? No God?

'How could I, given what I know? What I've seen. Our treasure was the proof.'

'Proof of what?'

'That this life is all we have.'

'Linger a while longer, then,' pressed Altaïr, 'and tell me of the part you were to play.'

'A blockade by sea,' Sibrand told him, 'to keep the fool kings and queens from sending reinforcements. Once we . . . Once we . . .' He was fading fast now.

'. . . conquered the Holy Land?' prompted Altaïr.

Sibrand coughed. When he next spoke, his bared teeth were coated with blood. '*Freed* it, you fool. From the tyranny of faith.'

'Freedom? You worked to overthrow cities. Control men's minds. Murdered any who spoke against you.'

'I followed my orders, believing in my cause. Same as you.'

'Do not be afraid,' said Altaïr, closing his eyes.

'We are close, Altaïr.' Al Mualim came from behind his desk, moving through a thick shaft of light shining through the window. His pigeons cooed happily in the afternoon heat and there was that same sweet scent in the air. Yet despite the day – and although Altaïr had once again gained his rank and, more importantly, the Master's trust – he could not yet fully relax.

'Robert de Sable is now all that stands between us and victory,' continued Al Mualim. 'His mouth gives the orders. His hand pays the gold. With him dies the knowledge of the Templar Treasure and any threat it might pose.'

'I still don't understand how a simple bit of treasure could cause so much chaos,' said Altaïr. He had been mulling over Sibrand's final mysterious words. He had been thinking of the globe – the Piece of Eden. He had experienced its strange draw at first hand, of course, but surely it had merely the power to dazzle and divert. Could it really exert a hold above that of any desirable ornament? He had to admit to finding the idea fanciful.

Al Mualim nodded slowly, as though reading his thoughts. 'The Piece of Eden is temptation given form. Look at what it's done to Robert. Once he had tasted its power, it consumed him. He saw not a dangerous weapon to be destroyed, but a tool – one that would help him realize his life's ambition.'

'He dreamed of *power*, then?'

'Yes and no. He dreamed – still dreams – like us, of peace.'

'But this is a man who sought to see the Holy Land consumed by war . . .'

'No, Altaïr,' cried Al Mualim. 'How can you not see when you're the one who opened *my* eyes to this?'

'What do you mean?' Altaïr was puzzled.

'What do he and his followers want? A world in which all men are united. I do not despise his goal. I share it. But I take issue with the *means*. Peace is something to be learned. To be understood. To be embraced, but. . .'

'He would force it.' Altaïr was nodding. Understanding.

'And rob us of our free will in the process,' agreed Al Mualim.

'Strange . . . to think of him in this way,' said Altaïr.

'Never harbour hate for your victims, Altair. Such

thoughts are poison and will cloud your judgement.'

'Could he not be convinced, then? To end his mad quest?'

Al Mualim shook his head slowly and sadly. 'I spoke to him – in my way – through you. What was each killing, if not a message? But he has chosen to ignore us.'

'Then there's only one thing left to do.'

At last he was to hunt de Sable. The thought thrilled Altaïr but he was careful to balance it with notes of caution. He would not make the mistake of underestimating him again. Not de Sable, or anybody.

'Jerusalem is where you faced him first. It's where you'll find him now,' said Al Mualim, and released his bird. 'Go, Altair. It's time to finish this.'

Altaïr left, descending the stairs to the doors of the tower and coming out into the courtyard. Abbas was sitting on the fence, and Altaïr felt his eyes on him as he crossed the courtyard. Then he stopped and turned to face him. Their eyes met and Altaïr was about to say something – he wasn't sure what. But he thought better of it. He had a task ahead of him. Old wounds were exactly that: old wounds. Unconsciously, however, his hand went to his side.

28

The morning after Altaïr had told Abbas the truth about his father, Abbas had been even more withdrawn, and nothing Altaïr said could bring him out of that state. They ate their breakfast in silence, sullenly submitting to the attentions of their governesses, then went to Al Mualim's study and took their places on the floor.

If Al Mualim had noticed a difference in his two charges, he said nothing. Perhaps he was privately pleased that the boys seemed less easily distracted that day. Perhaps he simply assumed that they had fallen out, as young friends were inclined to do.

Altaïr, however, sat with twisted insides and a tortured mind. Why had Abbas said nothing? Why hadn't he reacted to what Altaïr had told him?

He was to get his answer later that day, when they went to the training yard as usual. They were to practise sword together, sparring as always. But today Abbas had decided that he wanted to use not the small wooden swords they normally sparred with but the shiny blades to which they planned to graduate.

Labib, their instructor, was delighted. 'Excellent, excellent,' he said, clapping his hands together, 'but, remember, there is nothing to be gained from drawing blood. We'll not trouble the physicians, if you please. This shall be a test of restraint and of cunning as much as it is of skill.'

'Cunning,' said Abbas. 'That should suit you, Altaïr. You are cunning and treacherous.'

They were the first words he had spoken to Altaïr all day. And as he said them he fixed Altaïr with a look of such contempt, such hatred, that Altaïr knew things would never be the same between them. He looked at Labib, wanting to appeal, to implore him not to allow the contest, but he was hopping happily over the small fence that surrounded the training quadrangle, relishing the prospect of some proper combat at last.

They took up position, Altaïr swallowing, Abbas staring hard at him.

'Brother,' began Altaïr, 'what I said last night, I –'

'*Do not call me brother!*' Abbas's shout rang around the courtyard. And he sprang towards Altaïr with a ferocity the boy had never seen in him before. But though his teeth were bared, Altaïr could see the tears that had formed at the corners of his eyes. There was more to this than simple anger, he knew.

'No, Abbas,' he called, desperately defending. He glanced to his left and saw the instructor's puzzled look – he was clearly not sure what to make of Abbas's outburst or the sudden hostility between the two. Altaïr saw two more Assassins approaching the training area, evidently having heard Abbas's cry. Faces appeared in the window of the defensive tower by the citadel entrance. He wondered if Al Mualim was watching . . .

Abbas jabbed forward with his swordpoint, forcing Altaïr to dodge to the side.

'Now, Abbas . . .' chided Labib.

'He means to kills me, Master,' shouted Altaïr.

'Don't be dramatic, child,' said the instructor, though he didn't sound altogether convinced. 'You could learn from your brother's commitment.'

'*I am not.*' Abbas attacked. '*His.*' The boy's words were punctuated with savage strikes of the sword. '*Brother.*'

'I told you to help you,' shouted Altaïr.

'No,' screamed Abbas. 'You lied.' Again he struck and there was a great chime of steel. Altaïr found himself thrown back by the force, stumbling at the fence and almost falling backwards over it. More Assassins had arrived. Some looked concerned, others ready to be entertained.

'Defend, Altaïr, defend,' roared Labib, clapping his hands with glee. Altaïr threw up his sword, returning Abbas's strikes and forcing him into the centre of the quadrangle once more.

'I told the truth,' he hissed, as they came close, the blades of their swords sliding against one another. 'I told you the truth to end your suffering, just as I would have wanted mine ending.'

'You lied to bring shame upon me,' said Abbas,

falling back and taking up position, crouched, one arm thrown back as they'd been taught, the blade of his sword quivering.

'*No!*' cried Altaïr. He danced back as Abbas thrust forward. But with a flick of his wrist Abbas caught Altaïr with his blade, opening a nick that bled warm down Altaïr's side. He glanced over at Labib with beseeching eyes, but his concerns were waved away. He placed a hand to his side and came away with bloodied fingertips that he held out to Abbas.

'Stop this, Abbas,' he pleaded. 'I spoke the truth in the hope of bringing you comfort.'

'Comfort,' said Abbas. The boy was talking to the assembled crowd now. 'To bring me *comfort* he tells me my father killed himself.'

There was a moment of shocked silence. Altaïr looked from Abbas to those who were now watching, unable to comprehend the turn of events. The secret he had sworn to keep had been made public.

He glanced up to Al Mualim's tower. Saw the Master standing there, watching, his hands behind his back and an unreadable expression on his face.

'*Abbas,*' shouted Labib, at last seeing something was amiss. '*Altaïr.*'

But the two fighting boys ignored him, their swords meeting again. Altaïr, in pain, was forced to defend.

'I thought –' he began.

'You thought you would bring shame upon me,'

shrieked Abbas. The tears were falling down his face now and he circled Altaïr, then pushed forward again, swinging his sword wildly. Altaïr crouched and found space between Abbas's arm and body. He struck, opening a wound on Abbas's left arm that he hoped would at least stop him long enough for Altaïr to try to explain –

But Abbas shrieked. And with a final war cry he leaped towards Altaïr who ducked beneath his flailing blade, using his shoulder to upset Abbas's forward momentum so that now they were rolling in the ground in a mess of dirt and bloodied robes. For a moment they grappled, then Altaïr felt a searing pain in his side, Abbas digging his thumb into the wound and using the opportunity to twist, heaving himself on top of Altaïr and pinning him to the ground. From his belt he produced his dagger and held it to Altaïr's throat. His wild eyes were fixed on Altaïr. They still poured with tears. He breathed heavily through bared teeth.

'*Abbas!*' came the shout, not from Labib or any of those who had gathered to watch. This came from the window of Al Mualim. 'Put away the knife at once,' he roared, his voice a thunderclap in the courtyard.

In response Abbas sounded small and desperate. 'Not until he admits.'

'Admits what?' cried Altaïr, struggling but held firm.

Labib had climbed over the fence. 'Now, Abbas,' he

said, with placating palms held out. 'Do as the Master says.'

'Come any closer and I'll carve him,' growled Abbas.

The instructor stopped. 'He'll put you in the cells for this, Abbas. This is no way for the Order to behave. Look, there are citizens here from the village. Word will spread.'

'I don't care,' wept Abbas. 'He needs to say it. He needs to say he lied about my father.'

'What lie?'

'He told me my father killed himself. That he came to Altaïr's quarters to say sorry, then slashed his own throat. But he *lied*. My father did not kill himself. He left the Brotherhood. That was his apology. Now tell me you lied.' He jabbed the point of the dagger into Altaïr's throat, drawing more blood.

'Abbas, stop this,' roared Al Mualim from his tower.

'Altaïr, did you lie?' asked Labib.

A silence shrouded the training yard: all waited for Altaïr's reply. He looked up at Abbas.

'Yes,' he said. 'I did lie.'

Abbas sat back on his haunches and squeezed his eyes shut. Whatever pain went through him seemed to rack his entire body, and as he dropped the dagger with a clang to the ground of the quadrangle, he began weeping. He was still weeping as Labib came to him and grabbed him roughly by the arm, pulling him to his feet and delivering him to a pair of guards, who came hurrying up. Moments later Altaïr was also grabbed. He, too, was manhandled to the cells.

Later, Al Mualim decided that after a month in the dungeons, they should resume their training. Abbas's crime was deemed the more serious of the two; it was he who had allowed his emotions free rein and by doing so brought disrepute to the Order. His punishment was that his training be extended for an extra year. He would still be on the training yard with Labib when Altaïr was made an Assassin. The injustice increased his hatred of Altaïr, who slowly came to see Abbas as a pathetic, bitter figure. When the citadel was attacked, it was Altaïr who saved the life of Al Mualim and was elevated to Master Assassin. That day, Abbas spat in the dirt at Altaïr's feet but Altaïr just sneered at him. Abbas, he decided, was as weak and ineffectual as his father had been.

Perhaps, looking back, that was how he had first become infected by arrogance.

29

When Altaïr next arrived at the Jerusalem Bureau, it was as a changed man. Not that he would make the mistake of thinking his journey was over – that would have been an error made by the old Altaïr. No, he knew that it was just beginning. It was as though Malik sensed it too. There was something changed about the Bureau leader when Altaïr entered. There was a new respect and accord between them.

'Safety and peace, Altaïr,' he said.

'Upon you as well, brother,' replied Altaïr, and there was an unspoken moment between them.

'Seems Fate has a strange way with things . . .'

Altaïr nodded. 'So it's true, then? Robert de Sable is in Jerusalem?

'I've seen the knights myself.' Malik's hand went to his stump. Reminded of it by mention of the Templar.

'Only misfortune follows that man. If he's here, it's because he intends ill. I won't give him the chance to act,' said Altaïr.

'Do not let vengeance cloud your thoughts, brother. We both know no good can come of that.'

Altaïr smiled. 'I have not forgotten. You have nothing to fear. I do not seek revenge, but knowledge.'

Once he would have said such a thing parrot fashion, knowing the beliefs expected of him. Now he truly believed it.

Again, Malik somehow understood. 'Truly you are not the man I once knew,' he said.

Altaïr nodded. 'My work has taught me many things. Revealed secrets to me. But there are still pieces of this puzzle I do not possess.'

'What do you mean?'

'All the men I've laid to rest have worked together, united by this man. Robert has designs upon the land. This much I know for certain. But how and why? When and where? These things remain out of reach.'

'Crusaders and Saracens working together?' wondered Malik, aloud.

'They are none of these things, but something else. Templars.'

'The Templars are a part of the Crusader army,' said Malik, though the question was written all over his face: how could they be King Richard's men if they were staying in Jerusalem? Walking the city streets?

'Or so they'd like King Richard to believe,' said Altaïr. 'No. Their only allegiance is to Robert de Sable and some mad idea that *they* will stop the war.'

'You spin a strange tale.'

'You have no idea, Malik . . .'

'Then tell me.'

Altaïr began to tell Malik what he had learned so far. 'Robert and his Templars walk the city. They've come to pay their respects to Majd Addin. They'll attend his funeral. Which means so will I.'

'What is this that Templars would attend his funeral?'

'I have yet to divine their true intentions, though I'll have a confession in time. The citizens themselves are divided. Many call for their lives. Still others insist that they are here to parley. To make peace.'

He thought of the orator he'd questioned, who had been adamant that his masters wanted an end to war. De Sable, a Christian, was attending Majd Addin's funeral, he a Muslim. Wasn't that proof that the Templars sought a united Holy Land? The citizens were hostile to the notion of Templars being present in Jerusalem. The Crusader occupation was still fresh in their minds. Unsurprisingly there had been reports of fighting breaking out between Crusaders and Saracens, who took exception to the sight of knights in the streets. The city remained unconvinced by the orators who insisted that they came in the name of peace.

'*Peace?*' said Malik, now.

'I told you. The others I have slain have said as much to me.'

'That would make them our allies. And yet we kill them.'

'Make no mistake, we are nothing like these men. Though their goal sounds noble, the means by which they'd achieve it are not. At least . . . that's what Al Mualim told me.'

He ignored the tiny worm of doubt that slithered in the pit of his stomach.

'So what is your plan?'

'I'll attend the funeral and confront Robert.'

'The sooner the better,' agreed Malik, handing Altaïr the feather. 'Fortune favour your blade, brother.'

Altaïr took the marker. Swallowing, he said, 'Malik . . . Before I go, there's something I should say.'

'Out with it.'

'I've been a fool.'

Malik gave a dry laugh. 'Normally I'd make no argument, but what is this? What are you talking about?'

'All this time . . . I never told you I was sorry. Too damned proud. You lost your arm because of me. Lost Kadar. You had every right to be angry.'

'I do not accept your apology.'

'I understand.'

'No. You don't. I do not accept your apology, because you are not the same man who went with me into Solomon's Temple, so *you* have nothing to apologize for.

'Malik . . .'

'Perhaps if I had not been so envious of you, I

would not have been so careless myself. I am just as much to blame.'

'Don't say such things.'

'We are one. As we share the glory of our victories, so too should we share the pain of our defeat. In this way we grow closer. We grow stronger.'

'Thank you, brother.'

And so it was that Altaïr found himself at the cemetery, a small, unadorned burial ground, joining a sparse crowd of Templars and civilians who had gathered around the burial mound of Majd Addin, the erstwhile city regent.

The body would have been bathed and shrouded and carried in a procession, then buried on its right side and the hole filled, members of the procession adding dirt to the grave. As Altaïr entered, an imam was stepping up to deliver the funeral prayer and a hush had descended over the holy ground. Most stood with their hands clasped in front of them and their heads bowed in respect for the dead, so it was an easy task for Altaïr to slip through the crowd in order to gain a good vantage point. To locate his final target. He who had set Altaïr on this path – whose death would be just retribution for the suffering he had caused and that which had happened in his name: Robert de Sable.

Passing along the rows of mourners, Altaïr realized

it was the first time that he had ever found himself at the funeral of one of his targets, and he cast a look around to see if there were any grieving members of the dead man's family nearby, wondering how he, the killer, would feel to be confronted by their grief. But if Majd Addin had had close relatives they were either absent or kept their sorrow hidden among the crowd; there was no one at the graveside but the imam and . . .

A cluster of Templar knights.

They stood in front of an ornately decorated fountain set into a tall sandstone wall, three of them, wearing armour and full-face helmets, even the one who stood in front of the other two, who also wore a cape. The distinctive cape of the Templar Grand Master.

And yet . . . Altaïr squinted, staring at de Sable. The knight was somehow not as Altaïr remembered him. Had his memory played tricks on him? Had Robert de Sable taken on greater dimensions in his head because he had bested Altaïr? Certainly he seemed to lack the stature that Altaïr remembered. Where, also, were the rest of his men?

Now the imam had begun to speak, addressing the mourners: 'We gather here to mourn the loss of our beloved Majd Addin, taken too soon from this world. I know you feel sorrow and pain at his passing. But you should not. For just as we are all brought forth from the womb, so too must we all one day pass from this world. It is only natural – like the rising and the setting of the sun. Take this moment to reflect on his life and give thanks for all the good he did. Know that one day you will stand with him again in Paradise.'

Altaïr fought to hid his disgust. 'The *beloved* Majd Addin'. The same beloved Majd Addin who had been a traitor to the Saracens, who had sought to undermine trust in them by indiscriminately executing the citizens of Jerusalem? *That* beloved Majd Addin? It was no wonder that the crowd was so sparse, and grief so little in evidence. He was about as beloved as leprosy.

The imam began to lead the mourners in prayer. 'O God, bless Muhammad, his family, his companions, O merciful and majestic. O God, more majestic than they describe, peace on the Prophets, blessings from the God of the Universe.'

Altaïr's gaze went from him to de Sable and his bodyguard. A wink of sun caught his eye and he glanced up at the wall behind the trio of knights to the ramparts that ran along the outside of the courtyard. Was it a movement he'd seen? Perhaps. Extra Templar soldiers could easily take cover in the ramparts.

He glanced again at the three knights – Robert de Sable, as if standing for inspection, offering himself as a target. His build. Too slight, surely. The cape. It looked too long.

No. Altaïr decided to abandon the assassination because there was no ignoring his instinct here. It wasn't telling him something was wrong. It was saying nothing was right. He began to edge back, just as the imam's tone changed.

'As you know, this man was murdered by Assassins. We have tried to track his killer, but it has proved difficult. These creatures cling to the shadows and run from any who would face them fairly.'

Altaïr froze, knowing now that the trap was to be sprung. He tried to push through the crowd more quickly.

'But not today,' he heard the imam call, 'for it seems one stands among us. He mocks us with his presence and must be made to pay.'

Suddenly the crowd around Altaïr opened, forming a circle around him. He wheeled, seeing the graveside where the imam stood pointing – at him. De Sable and his two men were moving forward. Around him the crowd looked fierce, and was closing in to swamp him, leaving him no escape route.

'Seize him. Bring him forward that God's justice might be done,' called the imam.

In one movement Altaïr drew his sword and ejected his blade. He remembered his Master's words: *Choose one*.

But there was no need. The mourners might have been brave and Majd Addin beloved, but nobody was prepared to shed blood to avenge him. Panicked, the crowd broke up, mourners falling over their robes to escape, Altaïr using the sudden confusion to dart to one side, breaking the advancing Templars' line of sight. The first of them just had time to register that one member of the crowd was not escaping, but instead moving towards him, before Altaïr's sword was through his mail and in his gut and he fell away.

Altaïr saw a door in the wall open and more knights come pouring through. Five at least. At the same time there was a hail of arrows from above, and one knight was spinning and falling, the shaft protruding from his neck. Altaïr's eyes shot to the ramparts where he saw Templar archers. On this occasion their aim had favoured him. He was unlikely to be quite so fortunate next time.

The second of the two bodyguards came forward and he swiped with his blade, slicing at the man's neck and sending him down in a spray of blood. He turned to de Sable, who came forward swinging his broadsword hard enough to send Altaïr stumbling back, only just able to deflect the blow. Suddenly there were reinforcements, and he was trading blows with three other knights, all in full-face helmets, and finding that he was now standing on Majd Addin's final resting place. There was no time to enjoy the moment, though: from above came another hail of arrows and, to Altaïr's delight, a second knight was speared, screaming as he fell. The effect on the remaining Templars was to send them into disarray and they scattered a little, less frightened of Altaïr than they were of their own archers, just as de Sable began screeching at the bowmen to stop firing on their own men.

And Altaïr was so surprised that he almost dropped his guard. What he had heard was not the unmistakably male French tones of Robert de Sable but a voice that surely belonged to a woman. An *English* woman.

For a heartbeat he was taken aback by a mixture of bemusement and admiration. This ... *woman*, the stand-in sent by de Sable, fought as bravely as any man, and wielded a broadsword just as adeptly as any knight he had ever encountered. Who was she? One of de Sable's lieutenants? His lover? Keeping close to the cover of the wall, Altaïr felled another of the knights. Just one left. One more, and de Sable's stand-in. The last Templar had less appetite for the fight than she did, though, and he died, thrashing on the point of Altaïr's sword.

Just her now and they traded blows, until at last Altaïr was able to get the better of her, sliding the blade into her shoulder at the same time as he swept her legs from beneath her and she crashed heavily to the ground. Scurrying into cover, he pulled her with him so that they were both out of sight of the archers. Then he leaned over her. Still wearing the helmet, her chest heaved. Blood spread across her neck and shoulder but she would live, thought Altaïr – if he allowed her to, that was.

'I would see your eyes before you die,' he said.

He pulled off the helmet, and was still taken aback to be confronted by the truth.

'I sense you expected someone else,' she said, smiling a little. Her hair was hidden by the chainmail coif she wore, but Altaïr was entranced by her eyes. There was determination behind them, he saw, but something else too. Softness and light. And he found himself wondering if her obvious skills as a warrior belied her true nature.

But why — whatever command of combat she possessed — would de Sable send this woman in his stead? What special abilities might she have? He placed his blade to her neck. 'What sorcery is this?' he asked cautiously.

'We knew you'd come,' she said, still smiling. 'Robert needed to be sure he'd have time to get away.'

'So he flees?'

'We cannot deny your success. You have laid waste our plans. First the treasure — then our men. Control of the Holy Land slipped away ... But he saw an opportunity to reclaim what has been stolen. To turn your victories to our advantage.'

'Al Mualim still holds the treasure and we've routed your army before,' replied Altaïr. 'Whatever Robert plans, he'll fail again.'

'Ah,' she said, 'but it's not just Templars you'll contend with now.'

Altaïr bridled. 'Speak sense,' he demanded.

'Robert rides for Arsuf to plead his case, that Saracen and Crusader unite against the Assassins.'

'That will never happen. They have no reason to.'

Her smile broadened. 'Had, perhaps. But now you've given them one. Nine, in fact. The bodies you've left behind – victims on both sides. You've made the Assassins an enemy in common and ensured the annihilation of your entire Order. Well done.'

'Not nine. Eight.'

'What do you mean?'

He removed his blade from her neck. 'You were not my target. I will not take your life.' He stood. 'You're free to go. But do not follow me.'

'I don't need to,' she said, pulling herself to her feet and clasping one hand to the wound at her shoulder. 'You're already too late . . .'

'We'll see.'

With a final glance at the ramparts, where archers were hurrying to new positions, Altaïr darted off, leaving the cemetery empty, apart from its corpses old and new – and the strange, brave and entrancing woman.

'It was a trap,' he exclaimed to Malik, moments later, the time it had taken him to make his way from the cemetery to the Bureau, his mind working furiously as he did so.

'I had heard the funeral turned to chaos . . . What happened?'

'Robert de Sable was never there. He sent another in his stead. He was expecting me —'

'You must go to Al Mualim,' said Malik, firmly.

Yes, thought Altaïr, he should. But there was that insistent feeling again. The one that told him there was yet more mystery to uncover. And why did he think it somehow involved the Master? 'There's no time. She told me where he's gone. What he plans. If I return to Masyaf, he might succeed . . . And then . . . I fear we'll be destroyed.'

'We have killed most of his men. He cannot hope to mount a proper attack. Wait,' said Malik. 'Did you say she?'

'Yes. It was a woman. Strange, I know. But that's for another time. For now we must focus on Robert. We may have thinned his ranks, but the man is clever. He goes to plead his case to Richard and Salah Al'din. To *unite* them against a common enemy . . . Against us.'

'Surely you are mistaken. This makes no sense. Those two men would never —'

'Oh, but they would. And we have ourselves to blame. The men I've killed — men on both sides of the conflict . . . men important to both leaders . . . Robert's plan may be ambitious, but it makes sense. And it could work.'

'Look, brother, things have changed. You *must* return to Masyaf. We cannot act without the Master's permission. It could compromise the Brotherhood. I thought . . . I thought you had learned this.'

'Stop hiding behind words, Malik. You wield the Creed and its tenets like a shield. He's keeping things from us. Important things. You're the one who told me we can never *know* anything, only suspect. Well, I suspect this business with the Templars goes deeper. When I'm done with Robert I will ride for Masyaf that we may have answers. But perhaps *you* could go now.'

'I cannot leave the city.'

'Then walk among its people. Seek out those who served the ones I slew. Learn what you can. You call yourself perceptive. Perhaps you'll see something I could not.'

'I don't know . . . I must think on this.'

'Do as you must, my friend. But I will ride for Arsuf. Every moment I delay, our enemy is one step further ahead of me.'

Once more he had breached the Creed: unwitting or not, he had put the Order in danger.

'Be careful, brother.'

'I will. I promise.'

30

The armies of Salah Al'din and Richard the Lionheart had met at Arsuf, and as he made his way there Altaïr learned – from the gossip he overheard at blacksmiths' and waterholes along the route – that after a series of minor skirmishes the battle had begun that morning, when Salah Al'din's Turks had launched an attack on the Crusader ranks.

Riding towards it, against the flow of anxious countryfolk wanting to escape the slaughter, Altaïr saw plumes of smoke on the horizon. As he came closer he could make out the soldiers at war on the distant plain. Knots of them, huge, dark clusters in the distance. He saw a long band of thousands of men, moving in fast on horseback, charging the enemy, but was too far away to see whether the charge was Saracen or Crusader. Closer, he could see the wooden frames of war machines, at least one on fire. Now he could discern the tall wooden crucifixes of the Christians, huge crosses on wheeled platforms that the infantry pushed forward, and the flags of the Saracens and the Crusaders. The sky darkened with hails of arrows from archers on either side. He saw knights on horseback with pikes, and packs of Saracen horsemen making devastating sorties into the ranks of the Crusaders.

He could hear the drumming of hoofs on the plain, and the constant crash of Saracen cymbals, drums, gongs and trumpets. He could hear the noise of the battle: the unending all-encompassing din of the shouts of the living, the screams of the dying, the sharp rattle of steel on steel and the pitiful whinnies of wounded horses. He began to come across riderless animals and bodies now, Saracen and Crusader, spreadeagled in the dirt or sitting dead against trees.

He reined back his mount – just in time, because suddenly Saracen archers began to appear from the treeline some way ahead of him. He dropped from his horse and rolled from the main track, taking cover behind an upturned cart. There were maybe a hundred of them all told. They ran across the track and into trees on the other side. They moved quickly and were bent low. They moved as soldiers move when they are stealthily advancing into enemy-held territory.

Altaïr stood and darted into the trees, too, following the bowmen at a safe distance. For some miles he pursued them, the sounds of the battle, the vibrations of it, growing stronger until they came upon a ridge. Now they were above the main battle, which raged below them, and for a moment the sheer size of it took his breath away. Everywhere – as far as the eye could see – there were men, bodies, machines and horses.

As at the Siege of Acre he found himself in the middle of a fierce and savage conflict with no side to call his own. What he had was the Order. What he had was a mission to protect it, to stop the beast that he had unwittingly unleashed from tearing it apart.

All round him on the ridge were bodies, too, as though there had already been a battle a short time ago. And of course there had: whoever held the ridge had the advantage of height, so it was likely to be savagely contested. Sure enough, as they came upon it, the Saracens were met by Crusader infantry and bowmen and a great shout went up from both sides. Salah Al'din's men had the element of surprise and so the upper hand, and the first wave of their attack left the bodies of knights in their wake, some falling from the ridge into the seething war below. But as Altaïr crouched and watched, the Crusaders managed to regroup and the combat began in earnest.

Passing along the ridge was the safest way of moving to the rear of the Crusader lines, where Richard the Lionheart would be stationed. And reaching him was the only hope he had of stopping Robert de Sable. He came closer to the battle and began to move to his left, leaving a wide berth between himself and the combatants. He came upon a Crusader who was crouched in the undergrowth, watching the battle and whimpering, and left him, running onwards.

Suddenly there was a shout and two Crusaders moved

into his path, their broadswords raised. He stopped, crossed his arms and reached to his shoulders, drawing his sword with one hand and flicking a knife with the other. One of the scouts went down and he moved to the other and had felled him when he realized that they weren't scouts. They were sentries.

Still overlooking the battle he found that he was on the brow of a hill. Some distance away he could see the standard of Richard the Lionheart and thought he caught a glimpse of the King himself, sitting astride his distinctive steed, flaming orange beard and hair bright in the afternoon sun. But now more rearguard infantry were arriving and he found himself swamped by knights, chainmail rattling, their swords raised and their eyes full of battle beneath their helmets.

Their task was to protect their liege; Altaïr's was to reach him. For long moments the battle raged. Altaïr danced and ran, sometimes carving himself a route, his bloody sword flashing, sometimes able to make a long dash, coming ever closer to where he could now see Richard. The King was in a clearing. He had dismounted, wary of the commotion approaching, and his immediate bodyguard were forming a ring around him, making him a small target.

Still fighting, his sword still swinging, men falling at his feet, his robes stained with Crusader blood, Altaïr broke clear of an attack and was able to dash forwards. He saw the King's lieutenants draw their swords, eyes fierce under their helmets. He saw archers scrabbling up to surrounding boulders, hoping to find a lofty position in order to pick off the intruder.

'Hold a moment,' called Altaïr. Just a few feet away now, he looked King Richard in the eyes, even as his men came forward. 'It's words I bring, not steel.'

The King wore his regal red, at his chest a gold-embroidered lion. He was the only man among them not cursed by fear or panic and he stood utterly calm at the battle's centre. He raised an arm and his men stopped their advance, the battle dying in an instant. Altaïr was grateful to see his attackers fall back a few paces, giving him room at last. He dropped his sword arm. As he caught his breath, his shoulders rose and fell heavily and he knew that all eyes were on him. Every swordpoint was aimed at his gut; every archer had him in his sights. One word from Richard and he would fall.

Instead, Richard said, 'Offering terms of a surrender, then? It's about time.'

'No. You misunderstand,' said Altaïr. 'It is Al Mualim who sends me, not Salah Al'din.'

The King darkened. '*Assassin*? What is the meaning of this? And be quick with it.' The men pressed forward a little. The archers tensed.

'You've a traitor in your midst,' said Altaïr.

'And he has hired you to kill me?' called the King. 'Come to gloat about it before you strike? I won't be taken so easily.'

'It's not you I've come to kill. It's him.'

'Speak, then, that I may judge the truth.' King Richard beckoned Altaïr forward. 'Who is this traitor?'

'Robert de Sable.'

Richard's eyebrows raised in surprise. 'My lieutenant?'

'He aims to betray,' said Altaïr, evenly. He was trying to choose his words carefully, desperate not to be misunderstood. Needing the King to believe him.

'That's not the way he tells it,' said Richard. 'He seeks revenge against your people for the havoc you've wrought in Acre. And I am inclined to support him. Some of my best men were murdered by some of yours.'

So – Robert de Sable already had the King's ear. Altaïr took a deep breath. What he was about to say could mean his immediate death. 'It was *I* who killed them. And for good reason.' Richard glowered but Altaïr pressed on: 'Hear me out. William of Montferrat. He sought to use his soldiers to take Acre by force. Garnier de Naplouse. He would use his skills to indoctrinate and control any who resisted. Sibrand. He intended to block the ports, preventing your kingdom from providing aid. They betrayed you. And they took their orders from Robert.'

'You expect me to believe this outlandish tale?' said the Lionheart.

'You knew these men better than I. Are you truly surprised to learn of their ill intentions?'

Richard seemed to think for a moment, then turned to one of the men standing at his side, who wore a full-face helmet. 'Is this true?' he said.

The knight removed his helmet, and this time it really was Robert de Sable. Altaïr looked at him with open disgust, remembering his crimes. This man had sent a woman as his stand-in.

For a heartbeat the two stared at one another, the first time they had met since the fight below the Temple Mount. Still breathing hard, Altaïr clenched his fist. De Sable smirked, his lip curling, then turned to Richard. 'My liege . . .' he said, in an exasperated tone '. . . it is an Assassin who stands before us. These creatures are masters of manipulation. Of *course* it isn't true.'

'I've no reason to deceive,' snapped Altaïr.

'Oh, but you do,' sneered de Sable. 'You're afraid of what will happen to your little fortress. Can it withstand the combined might of the Saracen and Crusader armies?' He grinned, as though already imagining the fall of Masyaf.

'My concern is for the people of the Holy Land,' Altaïr countered. 'If I must sacrifice myself for there to be peace, so be it.'

Richard had been watching them with a bemused expression. 'This is a strange place we find ourselves in. Each of you accusing the other . . .'

'There really is no time for this,' said de Sable. 'I must be off to meet with Saladin and enlist his aid. The longer we delay, the harder this will become.' He made to move off, hoping, no doubt, that the matter was at an end.

'Wait, Robert,' said Richard. His eyes went from de Sable to Altaïr and back again.

With a snort of frustration, de Sable snapped, '*Why? What do you intend? Surely you do not believe him?*' He indicated Altaïr, who could see in de Sable's eyes that maybe the King had his doubts. Perhaps he was even inclined to believe the word of the Assassin over that of the Templar. Altaïr held his breath.

'It is a difficult decision,' replied the King. 'one I cannot make alone. I must leave it in the hands of one wiser than I.'

'Thank you.'

'No, Robert, not you.'

'Then who?'

'The Lord.' He smiled, as if pleased to have come to the right decision. 'Let this be decided by combat. Surely God will side with the one whose cause is righteous.'

Altaïr watched Robert carefully. He saw the look that passed across the Templar's face, de Sable no doubt recalling the last time they had met when he had easily bested Altaïr.

Altaïr was recalling the same encounter. He was telling himself that he was a different warrior now: last time he had been handicapped by arrogance, which was why he had been so easily defeated. He was trying not to recall the knight's great strength. How he had picked up and tossed Altaïr as easily as hefting a sack of wheat.

De Sable was remembering that, though, and he turned to King Richard, bowing his head in assent. 'If that is what you wish,' he said.

'It is.'

'So be it. To arms, Assassin.'

The King and his right-hand men stood to one side while the remaining members of the bodyguard formed a ring around Altaïr and the smiling de Sable. Unlike Altaïr he was not already battleworn and weary. He wore armour where Altaïr had only a robe. He had not suffered the cuts and blows that Altaïr had received in his battle to reach the clearing. He knew that, too. As he pulled on chainmail gauntlets and one of the men came forward to help him with his helmet, he knew that he had the advantage in every way.

'So,' he said, taunting, 'we face each other once more. Let us hope you prove more of a challenge this time.'

'I am not the man you faced inside the Temple,' said Altaïr, raising his sword. The thunder of the great battle of Arsuf seemed distant now; his world had shrunk to just this circle. Just him and de Sable.

'You look the same to me,' said de Sable. He raised his sword to address Altaïr. In reply the Assassin did the same. They stood, Robert de Sable with his weight adjusted to his back foot, evidently expecting Altaïr to come forward first.

But the Assassin claimed the first surprise of the duel, remaining unmoved, waiting instead for de Sable's attack. 'Appearances can deceive,' he said.

'True. True,' said de Sable, with a wry smile and, in the very next second, struck, and chopped hard with his sword.

The Assassin blocked. The force of de Sable's strike almost knocked the sword from his hand, but he parried and skipped to the side, trying to find a way inside de Sable's guards. The Templar's broadsword was three times the weight of his blade, and though knights were famed for their dedication to sword training and usually had the strength to match, they were nevertheless slower. De Sable could be more devastating in his attack, but he could never be as fast.

That was how Altaïr could beat him. His mistake before had been to allow de Sable to use his advantages. His strength now was to deny him them.

Still confident, de Sable pressed forward. 'Soon this will be over and Masyaf will fall,' he muttered, so close with the mighty blade that Altaïr heard it whistle past his ear.

'My brothers are stronger than you think,' he replied.

Their steel clashed once more.

'We'll know the truth of that soon enough,' grinned de Sable.

But Altaïr danced. He defended and parried and deflected, cutting nicks in de Sable, opening gashes in the mail, landing two or three stunning blows on the knight's helmet. Then de Sable was backing away to gather his strength, perhaps realizing now that Altaïr wouldn't be the easy kill he had assumed.

'Oh,' he said. 'So the child has learned to use a blade.'

'I've had a lot of practice. Your men saw to that.'

'They were sacrificed in service to a higher cause.'

'As will you be.'

De Sable leaped forward, wielding the great sword and almost knocking Altaïr's blade from his hand. But the Assassin bent and twisted in one easy movement ramming back with the hilt of his weapon so that de Sable was sent stumbling back, falling over his own feet. The wind came out of him and he was only just prevented from falling to the dust by the knights forming the ring, who righted him so that he stood there, bristling with fury and breathing heavily.

'*The time for games is ended!*' he bellowed, as though saying it loudly might somehow make it come true, and he sprang forward, but with no deadly grace now. With nothing more deadly than blind hope.

'It ended long ago,' said Altaïr. He felt a great calmness, knowing now that he was pure – pure Assassin. That he was to defeat Robert de Sable with thought as much as might. And as de Sable pressed forward once more, his attack more ragged this time, more desperate, Altaïr easily fended him off.

'I do not know where your strength comes from . . .' gasped de Sable. 'Some trick. Or is it drugs?'

'It is as your king said. Righteousness will always triumph over greed.'

'*My cause is righteous!*' cried de Sable, grunting now as he lifted his sword, almost painfully slowly. Altaïr saw the faces of his men. Could see them waiting for him to deliver the killing blow.

Which he did. Driving his sword straight through the centre of the red cross de Sable wore, parting the knight's mail and piercing his chest.

De Sable gasped. His eyes widened and his mouth dropped open, hands going to the blade that impaled him, even as Altaïr withdrew it. A red stain spread across his tunic, and he staggered, then sank to his knees. His sword dropped and his arms dangled.

Straight away Altaïr's eyes went to the men forming a ring around them. He was half expecting them to attack at the sight of the Templar Grand Master dying. But they remained still. Past them Altaïr saw King Richard, his chin tilted as though the turn of events had done little more than pique his curiosity.

Now Altaïr bent to de Sable, cradling him with one arm and laying him on the ground. 'It's done, then,' he told him. 'Your schemes – like you – are put to rest.'

In response, de Sable chortled drily. 'You know nothing of schemes,' he said. 'You're but a puppet. He betrayed you, boy. Just as he betrayed me.'

'Speak sense, Templar,' hissed Altaïr, 'or not at all.' He stole a look at the men of the ring. They remained impassive.

'Nine men he sent you to kill, yes?' said de Sable. 'The nine who guarded the Treasure's secret.'

It was always nine who had that task, the responsibility handed down through generations of Templars. Almost a hundred years ago, the Knights Templar had formed and made the Temple Mount their base. They had come together to protect those making the pilgrimage to the holiest of holies and lived their lives as warrior monks – or so they maintained. But, as all but the most gullible knew, the Templars had more on their minds than helpless pilgrims. In fact, they were searching for treasure and holy relics within the Temple of Solomon. Nine, always, were tasked with finding it, and nine had finally done so: de Sable, Tamir, de Naplouse, Talal, de Montferrat, Majd Addin, Jubair, Sibrand, Abu'l Nuqoud. The nine who knew. The nine victims.

'What of it?' said Altaïr carefully. Thoughtfully.

'It wasn't nine who found the Treasure, Assassin,' smiled de Sable. The life force was seeping fast from him now. 'Not nine but ten.'

'A tenth? None may live who carry the secret. Give me his name.'

'Oh, but you know him well. And I doubt very much you'd take his life as willingly as you've taken mine.'

'Who?' asked Altaïr, but he already knew. He understood what it was now that had been bothering him. The one mystery that had eluded him.

'It is your master,' said de Sable. 'Al Mualim.'

'But he is not a Templar,' said Altaïr, still not wanting to believe. Though he knew in his heart it was true. Al Mualim, who had raised him almost as his own son. Who had trained and tutored him. He had also betrayed him.

'Did you never wonder how he knew so much?' pressed de Sable, as Altaïr felt his world falling away from him. 'Where to find us, how many we numbered, what we aspired to attain?'

'He is the Master of the Assassins . . .' protested Altaïr, still not wanting to believe. Yet . . . it felt as though the mystery was finally solved. It was true. He almost laughed. Everything he knew, it *was* an illusion.

'*Oui*. Master of lies,' managed de Sable. 'You and I just two more pawns in his grand game. And now . . . with my death, only you remain. Do you think he'll let you live – knowing what you do?'

'I've no interest in the Treasure,' retorted Altaïr.

'Ah . . . but he does. The only difference between your master and I is that he did not want to share.'

'No . . .'

'Ironic, isn't it? That I – your greatest enemy – kept you safe from harm. But now you've taken my life – and, in the process, ended your own.'

Altaïr took a deep breath, still trying to comprehend what had happened. He felt a rush of emotions: anger, hurt, loneliness.

Then he reached and brushed de Sable's eyelids

closed. 'We do not always find the things we seek,' he intoned, and stood, prepared to meet death if the Crusaders wished. Perhaps even hoping they would.

'Well fought, Assassin,' came the cry from his right, and he turned to see Richard striding over to the ring, which parted to allow him through. 'It seems God favours your cause this day.'

'God had nothing to do with it. I was the better fighter.'

'Ah. You may not believe in him, but it seems he believes in you. Before you go, I have a question.'

'Ask it then,' said Altaïr. He was very weary all of a sudden. He longed to lie in the shade of a palm: to sleep, to disappear. To die, even.

'Why? Why travel all this way, risk your life a thousand times, all to kill a single man?'

'He threatened my brothers and what we stand for.'

'Ah. Vengeance, then?'

Altaïr looked down at the body of Robert de Sable and realized that, no, vengeance had not been on his mind when he had killed him. He had done what he had done for the Order. He gave voice to his thoughts. 'No. Not vengeance. Justice. That there might be peace.'

'This is what you fight for?' said Richard, eyebrows raised. 'Peace? Do you see the contradiction?'

He swept an arm around the area, a gesture that took in the battle still raging below them, the bodies scattered about the clearing and, last, the still-warm corpse of Robert de Sable.

'Some men cannot be reasoned with.'

'Like that madman Saladin,' sighed Richard.

Altaïr looked at him. He saw a fair and just king. 'I think he'd like to see an end to this war as much as you would.'

'So I've heard, but never seen.'

'Even if he doesn't say it, it's what the people want,' Altaïr told him. 'Saracen and Crusader alike.'

'The people know not what they want. It's why they turn to men like us.'

'Then it falls to men like you to do what is right.'

Richard snorted. 'Nonsense. We come into the world kicking and screaming. Violent and unstable. It is what we are. We cannot help ourselves.'

'No. We are what we choose to be.'

Richard smiled ruefully. 'Your kind . . . Always playing with words.'

'I speak the truth,' said Altaïr. 'There's no trick to be found here.'

'We'll know soon enough. But I fear you cannot have what you desire this day. Even now that heathen Saladin cuts through my men and I must attend to them. But perhaps, having seen how vulnerable he is, he will reconsider his actions. Yes. In time what you seek may be possible.'

'You were no more secure than him,' said Altaïr.

'Do not forget that. The men you left behind to rule in your stead did not intend to serve you for longer than they had to.'

'Yes. Yes. I am well aware.'

'Then I'll take my leave,' said Altaïr. 'My master and I have much to discuss. It seems that even he is not without fault.'

Richard nodded. 'He is only human. As are we all. You as well.'

'Safety and peace be upon you,' said Altaïr, and he left, his thoughts going to Masyaf. Its beauty seemed tainted by what he had learned about Al Mualim. He needed to ride for home. He needed to put things right.

32

Masyaf was not as he had left it: that much become clear from the moment he arrived at the stables. The horses pawed and whinnied but there were no stable lads to see to them or to take Altaïr's mount. He ran through the open main gates and into the courtyard, where he was struck by the silence, the complete absence not just of sound but of atmosphere. Here the sun struggled to shine, giving the village a grey, overcast tint. Birds no longer sang. The fountain no longer tinkled and there was none of the hubbub of everyday life. Stalls were set out but there were no villagers hurrying this way and that, talking excitedly or bartering for goods. There were no animal sounds. Just an eerie . . . nothing.

He stared up the hill towards the citadel, seeing no one. As ever, he wondered if Al Mualim was in his tower, looking down upon him. Could he see him? Then his eye was caught by a lone figure making his way towards him. A villager.

'What's happened here?' Altaïr demanded of him. 'Where is everyone?'

'Gone to see the Master,' said the citizen. It sounded

like a chant. Like a mantra. His eyes were glassy, and a rope of drool hung from his mouth. Altaïr had seen that look before. He had seen it on the faces of those in thrall to Garnier de Naplouse. The crazy men – or so he had thought at the time. They had had that empty, glazed look.

'Was it the Templars?' said Altaïr. 'Did they attack again?'

'They walk the path,' replied the villager.

'What path? What are you talking about?'

'Towards the light,' intoned the man. His voice had taken on a singsong quality.

'Speak sense,' demanded Altaïr.

'There is only what the Master shows us. This is the truth.'

'You've lost your mind,' spat Altaïr.

'You, too, will walk the path or you will perish. So the Master commands.'

Al Mualim, thought Altaïr. So it was true. It was all true. He had been betrayed. Nothing was true. 'What has he done to you?' he said to the villager.

'Praise be to the Master, for he has led us to the light . . .'

Altaïr ran on, leaving the man behind, a solitary figure in the deserted marketplace. He ran up the slopes, coming to the upland, and there found a group of Assassins waiting for him, their swords drawn.

He drew his own, knowing he could not use it. Not

to kill anyway. These Assassins, though they meant to kill him, had been brainwashed into doing it. Killing them would breach one of the tenets. He was weary of breaking the Creed. He was never going to do it again. But . . .

With dead eyes they closed in on him.

Were they in a trance like the others? Would their movements be just as sluggish? He dipped his shoulder and charged them, knocking the first one down. Another grabbed at him, but he caught hold of the Assassin's robe, took a bunch of it in his fist and swung him, knocking down two more of his attackers to make a gap that he was able to run through.

Then, from above, he heard his name being called. Malik was standing on the promontory by the fortress approach. With him were Jabal of Acre and two more Assassins he didn't recognize. He found himself studying them. Had they, too, been brainwashed? Drugged? Whatever it was that Al Mualim was doing?

But no. Malik was waving his good arm, and though Altaïr had never conceived of a day when he might be pleased to see Malik, here it was.

'Altaïr. Up here.'

'You picked a fine time to arrive,' grinned Altaïr.

'So it seems.'

'Guard yourself well, friend,' Altaïr told him. 'Al Mualim has betrayed us.' He was prepared for disbelief, even anger from Malik, who trusted and revered

Al Mualim and deferred to him in all matters. But Malik merely nodded sadly.

'Betrayed his Templar allies as well,' he said.

'How do you know?'

'After we spoke I returned to the ruins beneath Solomon's Temple. Robert had kept a journal. Filled its pages with revelations. What I read there broke my heart . . . But it also opened my eyes. You were right, Altaïr. All along our master has used us. We were not meant to save the Holy Land, but deliver it to him. He must be stopped.'

'Be careful, Malik,' warned Altaïr. 'What he's done to the others he'll do to us, given the chance. You must stay far from him.'

'What would you propose? My blade arm is still strong and my men remain my own. It would be a mistake not to use us.'

'Distract these thralls, then. Assault the fortress from behind. If you can draw their attention away from me, I might reach Al Mualim.'

'I will do as you ask.'

'The men we face – their minds are not their own. If you can avoid killing them . . .'

'Yes. Though he has betrayed the tenets of the Creed, it does not mean we must as well. I'll do what I can.'

'It's all I ask,' said Altaïr.

Malik turned to leave him.

'Safety and peace, my friend,' said Altair.

Malik smiled wryly. 'Your presence here will deliver us both.'

Altaïr dashed along the barbican to the main courtyard and now he discovered why there had been no villagers in the marketplace. They were all here, crowded into the courtyard, filling it. The whole village surely. They milled around aimlessly, as though barely able to lift their heads. As Altaïr watched, he saw a man and a woman collide, and the woman fall, landing heavily on her backside. Neither acknowledged it, though. No surprise, no pain, no apologies or angry words. The man staggered a little, then moved off. The woman stayed seated, ignored by the other villagers.

Cautiously, Altaïr moved through them towards the tower, struck by the silence, just the sound of dragging feet and the odd murmur.

'The will of the Master must be obeyed,' he heard.

'O Al Mualim. Guide us. Command us.'

'The world will be cleansed. We will begin anew.'

The new order, he thought, dictated by the Knights Templar, yes, but one Templar above all. Al Mualim.

He came into the entrance hall of the tower, no guards there to greet him. Just the same sense of thick, empty air. As though an invisible mist hung over the entire complex. Looking up he saw that a wrought-iron gate was open. The gate that led to the courtyard and gardens at the rear of the tower. Wisps of light seemed to hang in the air by the portal, as though beckoning him onwards, and he hesitated, knowing that to go through was to play into Al Mualim's hands. Though, surely, if the Master wanted him dead, he'd already be dead. He drew his sword and ascended the stairs, realizing that he'd instinctively thought of Al Mualim as 'the Master' when he was no longer Altaïr's master. He had ceased to be his master the moment Altaïr had discovered that Al Mualim was a Templar. He was the enemy now.

He stopped at the doorway to the garden. Took a deep breath. What lay on the other side he had no idea, but there was only one way to find out.

33

It was dark in the garden. Altaïr could hear the low babble of a stream and the soothing cascade of a waterfall, but otherwise the air was still. He came to a marble terrace, the surface smooth beneath his boots, and he looked around, squinting at the dark, irregular shapes of trees and pavilions dotted about him.

Suddenly he heard a noise from behind him. The gate slammed shut and there was a clank as though a bolt had been thrown by unseen hands.

Altair spun. His eyes went up and he saw Al Mualim standing on the balcony of his library, looking down at him on the terrace. He held something: the Treasure taken from the Temple Mount, the Piece of Eden. It glowed with a power that painted Al Mualim a dusky orange, which intensified as Altaïr watched.

Suddenly the Assassin was gripped by an incredible pain. He screamed – and found that he was being raised from the ground, imprisoned by a shimmering cone of bright light controlled by the outstretched hand of Al Mualim, the Apple pulsing like a muscle flexing and tensing.

'What's happening?' cried Altaïr, defenceless in the artefact's grasp, paralysed by it.

'So the student returns,' said Al Mualim, evenly. He spoke with a victor's assurance.

'I've never been one to run,' returned Altaïr, defiant.

Al Mualim chortled. None of this — none of it — seemed to bother him. 'Never been one to listen, either,' he said.

'I still live because of it.' Altaïr struggled against his invisible bonds. The Apple pulsed in response and the light seemed to press in on him, restricting him even more.

'What will I do with you?' Al Mualim smiled.

'Let me go,' snarled Altaïr. He had no throwing knives but, free of these shackles, he could reach the old man in just a few bounds. Al Mualim would have a few last moments to admire his climbing skills before Altaïr slid his blade into his gut.

'Oh, Altair. I hear the hatred in your voice,' said Al Mualim. 'I feel its heat. Let you go? That would be unwise.'

'Why are you doing this?' asked Altaïr.

Al Mualim seemed to consider. 'I believed once. Did you know that? I thought there was a God. A God who loved and looked after us, who sent prophets to guide and comfort us. Who made miracles to remind us of his power.'

'What changed?'

'I found proof.'

'Proof of what?'

'That it is all an *illusion*.'

And with a wave of his hand he released Altaïr from the imprisoning light. Altaïr expected to drop, then realized he had never been suspended at all. Confused, he looked around himself, sensing a new change in the atmosphere, a building of pressure he felt in his ear-drums, like the moments before a storm. Above him on the library balcony, Al Mualim was raising the Apple above his head, intoning something.

'*Come.* Destroy the betrayer. Send him from this world.'

Suddenly figures were appearing around Altaïr, snarling, teeth bared, ready for combat; figures he recognized but found hard to place at first – but then did: they were his nine targets, his nine victims returned from the other life to this one.

He saw Garnier de Naplouse, who stood wearing his blood-stained apron, a sword in his hand, looking at Altair with pitying eyes. He saw Tamir, who held his dagger, his eyes glinting with evil intent, and Talal, his bow over his shoulder, sword in hand. William de Montferrat, who grinned wickedly, drew his weapon and grounded it, biding his time before the attack. Abu'l Nuqoud and Majd Addin were there, Jubair, Sibrand and, last, Robert de Sable.

All of his targets, sent from the world by Altaïr and summoned back to it by Al Mualim so that they might have their revenge.

And they attacked.

Majd Addin he was pleased to dispatch first, for a second time. Abu'l Nuqoud was as fat and comical in his resurrected form as he had been the first time around. He sank to his knees on the point of Altaïr's sword, but instead of remaining on the ground, he vanished, leaving just a disturbance in the air behind him, a ripple of disrupted space. Talal, de Montferrat, Sibrand and de Sable were the most skilled fighters and, accordingly, they hung back, allowing the weaker among them to go forward first in the hope of tiring Altaïr. The Assassin dashed from the marble terrace and leaped from the ridge, landing on a second square of decorated marble, this one with a waterfall nearby. The targets followed him. Tamir died screaming at one, two slashes of Altaïr's sword. The Assassin felt nothing. No remorse. Not even gratification at seeing the men die a deserved second death. De Naplouse vanished as the others had, his throat cut. Jubair fell. Talal he grabbed, and the two grappled before Altaïr drove his sword deep into his stomach and he, too, was nothing but an absence. Montferrat was next to go. Sibrand followed him, then de Sable, until once more Altaïr was alone in the garden with Al Mualim.

'Face me,' demanded Altaïr, catching his breath.

The sweat poured from him but he knew the battle was far from over. It had only just begun. 'Or are you afraid?'

Al Mualim scoffed. 'I have stood before a thousand men – all of them superior to you. And all of them dead – by my hand.'

With a litheness and athleticism belying his years, he jumped from the balcony, landing in a crouch not far away from Altaïr. He still held the Apple. He clasped it as though he was proffering it to Altaïr and his face was bathed in its light. 'I am not afraid,' said Al Mualim.

'Prove it,' challenged Altaïr, knowing that Al Mualim would see through his ploy – his ploy to bring the traitor close. But if he did – and he surely did – then he cared nothing. He was right. He was unafraid – unafraid because he had the Apple, which was burning even more brightly. Dazzling. The whole of the area was lit up, then just as quickly darkened again. As Altaïr's eyes adjusted he saw copies of Al Mualim appear, as though generated from within the body of the Master himself.

He tensed. He wondered if these copies, like those he had just fought, would be inferior, weaker versions of the original.

'What could I possibly fear?' Al Mualim was mocking him now. (Good. Let him mock. Let him be careless.) 'Look at the power I command.'

The copies came to Altaïr, and once again he was fighting. Once again the garden rang to the chimes of crashing steel – and as the copies fell beneath Altaïr's blade they vanished. Until he was again alone with Al Mualim.

He stood, trying to regain his breath, feeling exhausted now, then once again he was embraced by the power of the Apple, which sparkled and throbbed in Al Mualim's hand.

'Have you any final words?' said Al Mualim.

'You lied to me,' said Altaïr. 'You called Robert's goal foul – when all along it was yours as well.'

'I've never been much good at sharing,' said Al Mualim, almost rueful.

'You won't succeed. Others will find the strength to stand against you.'

At this Al Mualim sighed heavily. 'And that is why, as long as men maintain free will, there can be no peace.'

'I killed the last man who said as much.'

Al Mualim laughed. 'Bold words, *boy*. But just words.'

'Then let me go. I'll put words into action.'

Altaïr's mind was racing now as he searched for something to say that would incite Al Mualim to carelessness.

'Tell me, Master, why did you not make me like the other Assassins? Why allow me to retain my mind?'

'Who you are and what you do are entwined too tightly together. To rob you of one would have deprived me of the other. And those Templars had to die.' He sighed. 'But the truth is, I did try. In my study, when I showed you the Treasure . . . But you are not like the others. You saw through the illusion.'

Altaïr's mind returned to the afternoon when Al Mualim had shown him the Treasure. He had felt its lure then, that was true, but he had resisted temptation. He wondered if he would be able to do so indefinitely. Its insidious powers seemed to work on all who came into contact with it. Even Al Mualim, whom once he had idolized, who had been a father to him, and had been a good man then, fair and just and temperate, concerned only with the well-being of the Order and those who served it – but he had been corrupted. The glow of the Apple cast his face in a ghastly hue. It had done the same to his soul.

'Illusion?' said Altaïr, still thinking of that afternoon.

Al Mualim laughed. 'That's all anything's ever been. This Templar Treasure. This Piece of Eden. This Word of God. Do you understand now? The Red Sea was never parted. Water never turned to wine. It was not the machinations of Eris that spawned the Trojan War, but this . . .' He held up the Apple. 'Illusions – all of them.'

'What you plan is no less an illusion,' insisted Altaïr. 'To force men to follow you against their will.'

'Is it any less real than the phantoms the Saracens and Crusaders follow now? Those craven gods who

256

retreat from this world that men might slaughter one another in their names? They live among an illusion already. I'm simply giving them another. One that demands less blood.'

'At least they *choose* these phantoms,' argued Altaïr.

'Do they? Aside from the occasional convert or heretic?'

'It isn't right,' snapped Altaïr.

'Ah. Now logic has left you. In its place you embrace emotion. I am disappointed.'

'What's to be done, then?'

'You will not follow me and I cannot compel you.'

'And you refuse to give up this evil scheme.'

'It seems, then, we are at an impasse.'

'No. We are at an end,' said Altaïr, and perhaps Al Mualim was correct, for he found himself fighting a wave of emotion. Of betrayal and sadness and something he could not quite place at first but then did. Loneliness.

Al Mualim drew his sword. 'I will miss you, Altaïr. You were my very best student.'

Altaïr watched the years fall away from Al Mualim as he took up position, readying his sword and forcing Altaïr to do the same. He skipped to the side, testing Altaïr's guard, and Altaïr realized he had never seen him move so quickly. The Al Mualim he knew paced slowly, walked unhurriedly across the courtyard, made slow, sweeping gestures. This one moved like a swordsman – who thrust forward, slashing with his blade. Then, as Altaïr defended, he adjusted the attack to a jab. Altaïr was forced to his toes, his arm bent as he swept his blade back to deflect Al Mualim's offensive. The move left him off balance and, with the guard on his left side down, Al Mualim saw his chance and came in with a second quick swipe that met its mark.

Altaïr winced, feeling the wound on his hip leak blood, but dared not look. He couldn't take his eyes from Al Mualim for one second. Opposite him, Al Mualim smiled. A smile that said he had taught the young pup a lesson. He stepped to his side, then feigned an attack, going first one way then the other, hoping to catch Altaïr off guard.

Fighting pain and fatigue, Altaïr came forward with an offensive of his own – taking Al Mualim by surprise, he was pleased to see. But though he made contact – he thought he made contact – the Master seemed to slide away as though transporting.

'Blind, Altaïr,' chuckled Al Mualim. 'Blind is all you've ever been. All you'll ever be.' Again, he attacked.

Altaïr was too slow to react in time, feeling Al Mualim's blade slash his arm and crying out with the pain. He couldn't take much more of this. He was too tired. He was losing blood. It was as though the energy was being slowly drained from him. The Apple, his wounds, his exhaustion: all were combining slowly but surely to cripple him. If he couldn't turn the battle soon he faced defeat.

But the old man was letting the Apple make him careless. Even as he was gloating Altaïr danced forward and struck again, his swordpoint striking home, drawing blood. Al Mualim shouted in pain, transported then reappeared, snarling and launching his next offensive. Feigning an attack to the left he spun, wielding his sword backhand. Desperately Altaïr fended him off, but was almost sent reeling, and for some moments the two traded blows, the salvo ending when Al Mualim ducked, sliced upward and nicked Altaïr's cheek, dancing away before the Assassin could respond.

Altaïr launched a counter-attack and Al Mualim transported. But when he reappeared, Altaïr noticed he looked more haggard, and when he attacked it was a little more carelessly. Less disciplined.

Altaïr came forward slicing with his blade, forcing the Master to transport and materialize several feet away. Altaïr saw a new stoop to his shoulders, and his head was heavy. The Apple was sapping Altaïr's strength but was it doing the same to its user? Did Al Mualim know it? How well did the old man understand the Apple? Its power was so great that Altaïr doubted it was possible ever to truly know it.

So. He had to force Al Mualim to use it and so deplete his own energy. With a yell he leaped forward, slashing at Al Mualim, whose eyes went wide with surprise at the sudden vehemence of Altaïr's approach. He transported away. Altaïr came at him the moment he reappeared and Al Mualim's face now wore anger – frustration that the rules of engagement had changed, needing to find the space to adjust.

He materialized further away this time. It was working: he looked even more tired. But he was ready for Altaïr's undisciplined attack, rewarding the Assassin with another bloody arm. Not serious enough to stop him, though: the younger man pushed forward again, forcing Al Mualim to transport. For the last time.

When he reappeared he staggered slightly, and Altaïr could see that he found his sword heavier to hold. As he raised his head to look at Altaïr, the Assassin saw in his eyes that he knew the Apple had been sapping his strength and that Altaïr had noticed.

And, as Altaïr engaged his blade and leaped, driving it deep into Al Mualim with a roar that was part victory and part grief, perhaps Al Mualim's final thoughts were of pride in his former pupil.

'Impossible,' he gasped, as Altaïr knelt astride him. 'The student does not defeat the teacher.'

Altaïr hung his head, feeling tears prick his cheeks.

'You have won, then. Go and claim your prize.'

The Apple had rolled from Al Mualim's outstretched hand. It sat glowing on the marble. Waiting.

'You held fire in your hand, old man,' said Altaïr. 'It should have been destroyed.'

'Destroy the *only* thing capable of ending the Crusades and creating true peace?' laughed Al Mualim. 'Never.'

'Then I will,' said Altaïr.

'We'll see about that,' chuckled Al Mualim.

Altaïr was staring at it, finding it difficult to drag his gaze away. Gently he rested Al Mualim's head on the stone, the old man fading fast now, stood up and walked towards it.

He picked it up.

It was as if it came alive in his hand. As though a huge bolt of energy flowed from it that lit the Apple and travelled up his arm, right into his chest. He felt a great swelling that was uncomfortable at first, then felt life-giving, washing away the pain of battle, filling him with power. The Apple throbbed and seemed to pulse and Altaïr began to see images. Incredible, incomprehensible images. He saw what looked like cities, vast, glittering cities, with towers and fortresses, as though from thousands of years ago. Next he saw machines and tools, strange contraptions. He understood that they belonged in a future not yet written, where some of the devices brought people great joy while others meant only death and destruction. The rate and intensity of the images left him gasping for breath. Then the Apple was enveloped by a corona of light that spread outwards until Altaïr saw that he was looking at a globe, a huge globe, that hung in the still air of the garden, slowly spinning and radiating warm, golden light.

He was entranced by it. Enchanted. It was a map, he saw, with strange symbols – writing he didn't understand.

Behind him he heard Al Mualim speaking: 'I applied my heart to know wisdom, and to know madness and folly. I perceived that this also was a chasing after wind. For in much wisdom is much grief and he that increaseth knowledge increaseth sorrow.'

Now Malik and his men rushed into the garden. With barely a glance at the body of Al Mualim, they stood hypnotized by the Apple. In the distance Altaïr could hear shouting. Whatever spell had been cast over Masyaf was broken.

He readied himself to dash the Apple against the stone, still unable to take his eyes from the spinning image, finding it hard to make his arm heed the command of his brain.

'*Destroy it!*' called Al Mualim. '*Destroy it as you said you would!*'

Altaïr's hand trembled. His muscles refused to obey the commands of his brain. 'I . . . I can't . . .' he said.

'Yes, you can, Altaïr,' gasped Al Mualim. 'You can. But you won't.' With that, he died.

Altaïr looked up from the body of his mentor to find Malik and his men gazing expectantly at him – waiting for leadership and guidance.

Altaïr was the Master now.

Part Three

34

23 June 1257

Sitting in the shade, safely out of the debilitating heat of the Masyaf marketplace, Maffeo asked me, 'Al Mualim's garden. Is this the same piece of land where his library is situated?'

'Indeed it is. Altaïr decided it a fitting spot to use for the care and storage of his work – thousands of journals filled with Assassin learning, knowledge gleaned from the Apple.'

'So he didn't destroy it?'

'Didn't destroy what?'

Maffeo sighed. 'The Apple.'

'No.'

'Not then or not ever?'

'Brother, please, don't hurry our tale to its conclusion. No, Altaïr did not destroy the Apple straight away. For one thing he had to quell the rebellion that erupted immediately after Al Mualim's death.'

'There was a rebellion?'

'Indeed. There was a great confusion in the immediate aftermath of Al Mualim's death. There were many in the Order who stayed true to Al Mualim. Either they were unaware of the Master's treachery or they refused to accept the truth, but to them Altaïr was staging a coup and had to be stopped. No doubt they were encouraged in this by certain voices on the fringes.'

'Abbas?'

I laughed. 'No doubt. Though one can only imagine Abbas's internal conflict surrounding the turn of events. His resentment of Al Mualim was as strong if not stronger than his resentment of Altaïr.'

'And Altaïr quashed the rebellion?'

'Certainly. And he did so by staying true to the Creed, issuing orders to Malik and those he commanded that none of the rebels be harmed, that not a single man be killed or punished. After he had subdued them, there were no reprisals. Instead he used rhetoric to show them the way, persuading them first of Al Mualim's guilt and then of his own suitability to lead the Brotherhood. Doing this, he secured their love, their faith and loyalty. His first task as the Order's new leader was a demonstration of the very principles he aimed to instil. He brought the Brotherhood back from the brink by showing it the way.

'That resolved, he turned his attention to his journal. In it he wrote his thoughts about the Order, his responsibility to it, even the strange woman he had encountered at the cemetery. Who had . . . More than once Altaïr had gone to write the word "captivated", then stopped himself, changing it instead to "interested" him. Certainly she remained in his thoughts.

'Chiefly he had written of the Apple. He had taken to carrying it with him. At nights when he wrote in his journal it remained on a stand beside him, and when he gazed at it he felt a confused mix of emotions: anger that it had corrupted the one he had thought of as father, who had been a great Assassin and an even greater man; fear of it, for he had experienced its power to give and to take; and awe.

'"If there is good to be found in this artefact, I will discover it,'" he wrote, quill scratching. '"But if it is only capable of inspiring evil and despair, I hope I possess the strength to destroy it."'

Yes, he told his journal, he would destroy the Piece of Eden if it held no good for mankind. Those were the words he wrote. Nevertheless, Altaïr wondered how he would find the strength to destroy the Apple if and when the time came.

The fact was that whoever owned it wielded enormous power, and the Templars would want that power to belong to them. What was more, he wondered, were the Templars hunting for other artefacts? Did they even possess them? After the death of Robert de Sable they had consolidated at Acre port, he knew. Should he attack them there? He was determined that no one else should ever possess the Apple, or any others like it.

Nobody but him.

He mulled over this in his quarters, for too long perhaps, until he became concerned that he was allowing the enemy time to regroup. He called Malik and Jabal to him, placing Malik in temporary command of the Order and informing Jabal that they were to lead a squad riding for Acre port at once, to mount an offensive on the Templar stronghold, kill the plant at the root.

They left shortly afterwards, and as they did so, Altaïr noticed Abbas standing in a doorway at the castle approach, regarding him balefully. Recent events had done nothing to dull the blade of his hatred; it had sharpened to a vicious edge.

35

Night was falling over Acre port, the grey stone harbour bathed in orange, and the last of the sun painting the sea blood red as it melted into the horizon. Water lapped hard at the bulwarks and sea walls, and gulls called from their perches, but otherwise the harbour was empty, strangely so.

Or . . . this one was at least. As he watched over it and puzzled at the absence of Templar soldiers – in marked contrast to the last time he had been there, when Sibrand's men were all over it, like fleas on a dog – something told Altaïr that any industry was to be found at the other side of the docks, and his concern grew. He'd taken too long making his decision. Was he about to pay for that?

But the harbour wasn't quite empty. Altaïr heard the sound of approaching footsteps and hushed talk. He held up a hand and, behind him, his team came to a halt, becoming still shadows in the dark. He crept along the harbour wall until he could see them, pleased to note that they had moved apart. The first was almost directly beneath him now, holding up his torch and peering into the dark nooks and crannies of the damp harbour wall. Altaïr wondered if his thoughts were of home, of England or France and the family he had there, and he regretted that the man had to die. As he silently leaped from the wall, landing on him and driving the blade deep, he wished there was another way.

'*Mon Dieu*,' sighed the guard, as he died, and Altaïr stood.

Ahead, the second soldier moved along the wet stone of the dock, shining his tar-dripping torch around himself, trying to chase away the shadows and cringing at every sound. He was beginning to tremble with fear now. The scuttling of a rat made him jump and he turned quickly, his torch held aloft, seeing nothing.

He moved on, peering into the gloom, looking back for his companion ... Oh, God, where was he? He had been there a moment ago. The two of them had come to the dock together. Now there was no sight of him – no sound of him. The guard began to shake with fear. He heard a whimper and realized it had come from himself. Then from behind came a noise and he wheeled around quickly, just in time to see his death at his heels ...

For a moment or so Altaïr knelt astride the dead guard, listening for reinforcements. But none came and now, as he rose to his feet, he was joined by the other Assassins, dropping from the wall and coming on to the harbour, like him dressed in white robes, peering black-eyed from beneath their cowls. With hardly a sound, they spread out, Altaïr issuing hushed orders and indicating for them to move silently and swiftly along the harbour. Templar guards came running and were dealt with, Altaïr moving among them, leaving the fight to his team and coming to a wall. Worry gnawed at his gut: he had timed the attack badly – the Templars were already on the move. A sentry tried to stop him, but with a slash of Altaïr's blade he was falling, blood spurting from his open neck. The Assassin used his body as a springboard, scrambling to the top of the harbour wall and crouching there, looking over at the adjacent dock, then out to sea.

His fears were realized. He'd waited too long. Ahead of him, on a Mediterranean Sea golden with the dying light of the sun, there was a small fleet of Templar ships. Altaïr cursed and moved quickly along the harbour into the heart of the docks. From behind him he could still hear the sounds of battle as his men were met by reinforcements. The Templar evacuation continued but he had an idea that the key to their departure might be found within the stronghold itself. Carefully, quickly and silently he made his way to the fortress, which loomed darkly over the docks, remorselessly disposing of the few guards he came across, wanting to disrupt the enemy's escape as much as he wanted to learn of its intent.

Inside, the grey stone absorbed the sound of his

footsteps. Templars were notable for their absence here. The place already had an empty and disused feel. He climbed stone stairways until he came to a balcony and there he heard voices: three people in the middle of a heated conversation. One voice in particular he recognized as he took up position behind a pillar to eavesdrop. He had wondered if he would ever hear it again. He had hoped he would.

It was the woman from the graveyard in Jerusalem; the brave lioness who had acted as de Sable's stand-in. She stood with two other Templars and, from her tone, was displeased.

'Where are my ships, soldier?' she snapped. 'I was told there would be another fleet of eight.'

Altaïr glanced over. The Templar ships were silhouetted on the horizon.

'I'm sorry, Maria, but this is the best we could do,' replied one of the soldiers.

Maria. Altaïr savoured her name even as he admired the set of her jaw, the eyes that shone with life and fire. Again he noticed that quality about her – as though she kept most of her true self back.

'How do you propose to get the rest of us to Cyprus?' she was saying.

Now, why would the Templars be relocating to Cyprus?

'Begging your pardon, but it might be better if you stayed in Acre,' said the soldier.

Suddenly she was watchful. 'What is that? A threat?' she asked.

'It's fair warning,' replied the knight. 'Armand Bouchart is Grand Master now and he doesn't hold you in high regard.'

Armand Bouchart, noted Altaïr. So it was he who had stepped into de Sable's shoes.

At the centre of the balcony, Maria was bridling. 'Why, you insolent . . .' She stopped herself. 'Very well. I'll find my own way to Limassol.'

'Yes, milady,' said the soldier, bowing.

They moved away, leaving Maria alone on the balcony where, Altaïr was amused to hear, she began talking to herself. 'Damn . . . I was a single heartbeat from knighthood. Now I'm little more than a mercenary.'

He moved towards her. Whatever he felt about her – and he felt *something*, of that much he was certain – he needed to speak to her. Hearing him approach, she spun round and recognized him instantly. 'Well,' she said, 'it's the man who spared my neck, but stole my life.'

Altaïr had no time to wonder what she meant because with a flash of steel, as swift as a lightning bolt, she'd drawn her sword and was coming at him, attacking him with a speed, skill and courage that impressed him anew. She swapped sword hands, spun to attack him on his weak side, and he had to move fast to defend. She was good, better than some of the men in his command, and for some moments they traded

273

blows, the balcony resounding to the ring and clash of steel, punctuated by her shouts of effort.

Altaïr glanced behind to make sure no reinforcements were arriving. But then again, of course they wouldn't. Her people had left her behind. Clearly her closeness to de Sable had done her no favours with his replacement.

On they fought. For a heartbeat she had him with his back to the balustrade, the dark sea over his shoulder and for the same heartbeat he wondered whether she could best him and what a bitter irony that might be. But her desperation to win made her careless and Altaïr was able to come forward, eventually spinning and kicking her feet from beneath her, then pouncing on her with his blade held to her throat.

'Returned to finish me off?' she said defiantly, but he could see the fear in her eyes.

'Not just yet,' he said, though the blade stayed where it was. 'I want information. Why are the Templars sailing to Cyprus?'

She grinned. 'It's been a long, dirty war, Assassin. Everyone deserves respite.'

He fought a smile. 'The more you tell me, the longer you live. So I ask again, why the retreat to Cyprus?'

'What retreat? King Richard has brokered a truce with Salah Al'din, and your Order is leaderless, is it not? Once we recover the Piece of Eden, *you*'ll be the one running.'

Altaïr nodded, understanding. Knowing, too, that there was much about the Order the Templars presumed to know but did not. The first thing being that the Assassins had a leader, the second that they were not in the habit of running from Templars. He stood and pulled her to her feet. Glaring at him, she brushed herself down.

'The Apple is well hidden,' he told her, thinking that in fact it was not. It remained in his quarters.

'Altaïr, consider your options carefully. The Templars would pay a great price for that relic.'

'They already have, haven't they?' said Altaïr, leading her away.

Moments later, he had gathered with his Assassins, the battle on the harbour over, Acre port theirs. Among them was Jabal, who raised his eyebrows at the appearance of Maria and waved for two Assassins to take her away before he joined Altaïr.

'What's happening on Cyprus that would concern the Templars?' mused Altaïr, as they strode along. He had already decided their next destination and there was no time to waste.

'Civil strife, perhaps?' said Jabal, palms spread. 'Their emperor Isaac Comnenus picked a fight with King Richard many months ago, and now he rots in a Templar dungeon.'

Altaïr thought. 'A pity. Isaac was so easily bent, so willing to take a bribe.'

They stopped at the harbour steps and Maria was led past them, her chin held high.

'Those days are past,' Jabal was saying. 'Now the Templars own the island, purchased from the King for a paltry sum.'

'That's not the kind of governance we want to encourage. Have we any contacts there?' asked Altaïr.

'One in Limassol. A man named Alexander.'

'Send him a message,' said Altaïr. 'Tell him to expect me within the week.'

36

He sailed to Cyprus alone – although not *quite* alone.
He took Maria. He had told Jabal that he could use her
as Templar bait, but he wrote in his journal that he
liked to have her with him; it was as simple and as
complicated as that. There had been too few women
in his life. Those who shared his bed had done little
more than satisfy a need, and he had yet to meet a
woman able to stir those feelings found above waist
height. Had he met her now? He scratched the question
in his journal.

Arriving in Limassol they discovered that the Templars had occupied the island in earnest. As ever the
port was soaked in the orange light of the sun and the
sandstone shone with it; the blue waters glittered and
the gulls wheeling and swooping above their heads
kept up a constant noise. But everywhere there were
the red crosses of the Templars, and watchful soldiers
eyeing a begrudging populace. They lived under the
iron gauntlet of the Templars now, their island sold
from beneath them by a king whose claim to it was
tenuous at best. Most carried on with their lives; they
had mouths to feed. A few plucky souls had formed a

Resistance, though. It was they who would be most sympathetic to Altaïr's mission, they he planned to meet.

He made his way from his ship and along the docks. With him came Maria, her hands bound. He'd made sure she had removed any signs identifying her as a Templar Crusader and, to all intent and purposes, she was his slave. This situation, of course, angered her and she wasn't slow to make it known, grumbling as they passed through the docks, which were quieter than expected. Altaïr was privately amused by her discomfort.

'What if I started screaming?' she said, through gritted teeth.

Altaïr chuckled. 'People would cover their ears and carry on. They've seen an unhappy slave before.'

But what people? The docks were strangely empty, and as they came up into the back-streets, they found the highways deserted too. Suddenly a man stepped out of an alley in front of them, wearing scruffy robes and a turban. Disused barrels and the skeletons of empty crates lay about, and from somewhere they could hear water dripping. They were alone, Altaïr realized, just as two more men stepped out of other alleys around them.

'The port is off-limits,' said the first man. 'Show your face.'

'Nothing under this hood but an ugly old Assassin,'

growled Altaïr, and he raised his head to regard the man.

The thug smirked, a threat no longer, grinning. 'Altaïr.'

'Alexander,' said Altaïr, 'you got my message.'

'I assumed it was a Templar trap. Who is the woman?' He looked Maria up and down, a twinkle in his eye.

'Templar bait,' explained Altaïr. 'She was de Sable's. Unfortunately she's a burden.'

Maria fixed him with a gaze: if looks could kill, it would have tortured him viciously first.

'We can hold her for you, Altaïr,' said Alexander. 'We have a secure safe-house.'

She cursed their rotten souls as they made their way to it, such coarse language for an English woman.

Altaïr asked Alexander why there were so few citizens on the streets.

'Quite a ghost town, eh? People are afraid to leave their homes for fear of breaking some obscure new law.'

Altaïr thought. 'The Templars have never been interested in governing before. I wonder why now.'

Alexander was nodding. As they walked, they passed two soldiers, who looked at them suspiciously. Altaïr steeled himself against Maria giving them away. She didn't, and he wondered whether it had anything to do with her having been abandoned by her own side in Acre. Or perhaps . . . No. He put that thought out of his mind.

They reached the safe-house, a derelict warehouse that Alexander had made his base. There was a storeroom sealed with a barred wooden door but they let Maria remain in the open for the moment; Altaïr checked the rope at her wrists, running a finger between it and her arm to make sure she was comfortable. Now she gave him a look of what he could only describe as appreciative disdain.

'I won't assume you're here out of charity,' said Alexander, when they were settled. 'May I ask your purpose?'

Altaïr wanted to act quickly – he wanted to move in on the Templar base at once – but he owed the Cypriot an explanation. 'It's a complicated story, but can be summed up easily: the Templars have access to knowledge and weapons far deadlier than anyone could have imagined. I plan to change this. One such weapon is in our hands. A device with the ability to warp the minds of men. If the Templars possess more like it, I want to know.'

Maria piped up from behind them: 'And we can certainly trust the Assassins to put the Apple, the Piece of Eden, to better use . . .'

Altaïr suppressed a smile but ignored her, saying to Alexander, 'Where are the Templars holed up now?'

'In Limassol Castle, but they're expanding their reach.'

That had to be stopped, thought Altaïr.

'And how do I get inside?' he asked.

Alexander told him about Osman, a Templar whose sympathies lay with the Cypriot Resistance. 'Kill the captain of the guard,' he said. 'With him dead it's likely Osman will be promoted to the post. And if that happens, well, you could walk straight in.'

'It's a start,' said Altaïr.

As he moved through the streets of the city he marvelled at how quiet it was. As he walked, he thought of Maria and the Apple. He had brought it with him, of course – it remained in the cabin of his ship. Had it been foolish, perhaps, to bring the Treasure into such close proximity with the enemy? Only time would tell.

At the marketplace he located the Templar captain of the guard, who had kindly made himself easy to spot, wearing a red tunic over chainmail and looking as imperious as a king. Altair looked around, seeing other guards in the vicinity. He lowered his head, drawing no attention to himself, avoiding the gaze of a guard who watched him with narrowed, suspicious eyes. When he passed on, he did so looking for all the world like a scholar. Then, very carefully, he began to work his way around, manoeuvring himself to the rear of the captain, who stood at the other end of the lane, barking orders at his men. Apart from the captain and now his killer, the lane was empty.

Altaïr took a throwing knife from the sheath at his shoulder, then, with a flick of his wrist, set it free. The captain sank to the stone with a long groan, and by the time the guards came running, Altaïr had taken an adjoining alley and was melting into the empty side-streets. His task fulfilled, he had now to go in search of Osman, just as Alexander had instructed.

Stealthy and fast, he made his way across the rooftops of the sun-bleached city, scuttling catlike across the wooden beams, until he found himself overlooking a courtyard. There below him was Osman. A Templar, he nevertheless had Assassin sympathies, and Altaïr waited until he was alone before lowering himself into the courtyard.

As he did so, Osman looked from Altaïr to the wall above them, then back again, regarding his visitor with amused eyes. At the very least he had a high regard for the Assassin's stealth.

'Greetings, Osman,' said Altaïr. 'Alexander sends his regards, and wishes your grandmother a joyous birthday.'

Osman laughed. 'The dear lady, may she rest in peace. Now, how may I help you, friend?'

'Can you tell me why the Templars purchased Cyprus? Was it to set up another exchequer?'

'I don't rank high enough to know for certain, but I have heard talk of an archive of some kind,' said Osman, as he looked left, then right. If he was seen talking to Altaïr he would almost certainly be put to death in the market square.

'An archive? Interesting. And who is the ranking Templar in Limassol?'

'A knight named Frederick the Red. He trains soldiers in Limassol Castle. A real brute.'

Altaïr nodded. 'With the castle guard dead, what would it take to get me inside?'

'Assuming I'm appointed to his position, I could find an excuse to reduce the castle watch for a short time. Would that work?''

'I'll make it,' said Altaïr.

Things were moving quickly.

'Osman is making the arrangements,' he told Alexander later, back at the safe-house. While he'd been out, Maria had spent much of the day in the storeroom where she had kept Alexander entertained with a string of insults and wisecracks, her infuriation only increasing when he had asked her to repeat them, a fan of her English diction. Now, however, she had been allowed out to eat and sat on an unsteady wooden chair, glaring at Altaïr and Alexander, who sat talking, and shooting angry glances at any other Resistance men who happened to pass through.

'Excellent. Now what?' said Alexander.

'We give him some time,' said Altaïr. He turned to Maria. 'He also told me about the Templar archive. Have you heard of such a thing?'

'Of course,' said Maria. 'That's where we keep our undergarments.'

Altaïr despaired. Turning back to Alexander, he

said, 'Cyprus would be a good location to safeguard both knowledge and weapons. With the right strategy, it's an easy island to defend.'

He stood. Osman would have had time to clear the castle walls by now. It was time to infiltrate the castle.

37

A short while later he found himself in the courtyard of Limassol Castle, ready for the infiltration. Staying in the shadows, he looked up at the forbidding stone walls, noting the arches that were guarded and timing the movements of the men on the ramparts.

He was pleased to note that there were just a few men: Osman had done his work well. The fortress wasn't completely insecure but Altaïr could get in. And that was all he needed.

He scaled a wall to the ramparts, then crept into the castle. A guard screamed and fell, one of Altaïr's throwing knives in his neck. Another heard the commotion and came running along the hallway, only to meet the Assassin's blade. Altaïr lowered the guard to the stone, placed his foot to his back and retrieved his blade, which dripped blood to the floor. Then he continued making his way through the sparsely inhabited castle, disposing of guards when he saw them. Osman really *had* done his job efficiently. Not only had there been fewer guards on the walls but there seemed to be an absence of men inside as well. Altaïr ignored the uncertainty that formed in his gut. The twinge of disquiet.

Up and up he went, further and further into the castle's inner sections until he came to a balcony overlooking a large courtyard used as a training square.

There he saw Frederick the Red, a huge, bearded giant presiding over a duel between two of his men. The sight of him made Altaïr smile. The genial spy Osman had been right. Frederick the Red was indeed a brute of a man.

'No mercy, men,' he was roaring. 'This is an island of superstitious heathens. Remember, they do not want you here, they do not like you, they do not understand the true wisdom of your cause, and they are scheming at every turn to cast you out. Stay on your guard, and trust no one.'

Both in full armour, the two knights battled it out, the sound of their swords ringing around the yard. Staying out of sight on the balcony above, Altair listened to the Templar leader as he spurred them on.

'Find the chinks in your opponent's armour. Strike hard. Save your celebrations for the tavern.'

Now Altaïr stood and took a step up to the wall, in plain sight of the three men in the training yard below. Still they remained engrossed in the battle. He gauged the height from where he stood to the stone below, then took a deep breath, stretched out his arms and jumped.

With a soft thump he landed directly behind Frederick the Red, his knees bent, arms out for balance.

The bearded leader turned as Altaïr straightened. Eyes blazing, he roared, 'An Assassin on Cyprus? Well, well. How quickly you vermin adapt. I'll put an end to –'

He never finished his sentence. Altaïr, who had wanted to look into the Templar's eyes before he delivered the killing blow, engaged his blade and sliced his neck in one movement, the entire action over in the blink of an eye. With a short, strangulated sound, Frederick the Red crumpled, his neck a gaping red hole and his blood flooding over the stone around him, truly living up to his name.

For a second his men stood silent, their helmets robbing them of any emotion so that Altaïr could only picture the looks of shock behind the steel. Then they recovered – and attacked. Altaïr drove his blade through the eye slit of the first. From behind the helmet there was an agonized choking noise and blood leaked from the visor as the swordsman fell. Then the second of the two duellists struck, wielding his broadsword more in hope than expectation of finding his target. The Assassin sidestepped easily, palming a throwing knife at the same time, then twisting and, in a single motion, ramming upwards with his knife under the knight's chestplate.

Battle over, the three corpses settled on the stone, and Altaïr looked around the yard catching his breath. The castle, being so lightly populated, had its advantages, he thought. He returned to the balcony, letting himself out as he had come in. On his return journey the nagging voice of doubt grew louder. Most of the bodies he passed were those he had left earlier, still undisturbed, and there were no sentries at all now. *None.* Where was everybody?

He got his answer shortly after he had left the fortress and made his way across the rooftops to the safe-house, already looking forward to resting and perhaps some verbal jousting with Maria. Maybe even a little conversation with her. All he'd been able to glean from her so far was that she was English, that she had been de Sable's steward (exactly what *that* meant, Altaïr hadn't asked) and that she had become involved in the Crusades after an incident at home in England. That had intrigued him. He hoped to find out soon what had happened to her.

Suddenly he saw smoke, a thick pillar darkening the sky.

And it was coming from the safe-house.

His heart was hammering as he drew closer. He saw Crusader soldiers standing guard and keeping back anyone trying to get near to the building, which was burning. Fingers of flame reached from the windows and the door, dense curls of black smoke crowning the roof. This was why Frederick's castle has been so poorly guarded.

Altaïr's first thought was not for the safety of the Order, Alexander or any of the other Resistance men who might have been inside. His first thought was for Maria.

Fury ripped through him. He snapped his wrist to eject his blade. In one movement he had leaped down from the rooftop and met two of the Templar guards below. The first died shouting, the second had time to turn, with wide, surprised eyes, as Altaïr's blade opened his throat. The shout went up and more soldiers came running, but Altaïr fought on, desperate to reach the safe-house, not knowing whether Maria was trapped inside, perhaps choking to death. Had she been left in the storeroom? Was she in there now, pounding on the door, gasping for air in the smoke-filled room? If so, he could only begin to imagine the terror she must be feeling. More Templar guards came to him, their swordpoints eager for blood. And he fought on. He battled them with throwing knives and sword until he was exhausted, the street was littered with Templar corpses, bleeding into the dirt, and he was rushing towards the now smouldering safe-house, calling her name.

'*Maria!*'

There was no answer.

More Templars were approaching now. With a heavy heart Altaïr fled to the rooftops, there to take stock and plan his next move.

38

As it turned out, his next move was decided for him. Sitting high in a tower in the shade of a bell, Altaïr had become aware of movement in the streets, which had been so empty. People were leaving their homes. He had no idea where they were going, but decided he wanted to know.

Sure enough, with the smoke was still rising from the charred remains of the safe-house, the Templars were mobilizing. Altaïr used the roofs to follow townspeople as they made their way to the square and saw the expressions they wore, overheard their conversations. Talk was of revenge and reprisals. More than once he heard Armand Bouchart's name. Bouchart had just arrived on the island, they said. He had a fearsome reputation. A cruel reputation.

Altaïr was about to see that reputation in action, but for the time being he was overjoyed to see Maria in the crowd, alive and unharmed. She was flanked by two Templar knights in the gathering crowd – their prisoner by the look of it, though she wasn't bound. Like everybody else in the square, her attention was fixed on the steps of the cathedral.

He kept her in his eyeline, staying out of sight on a rooftop overlooking the square, watching as Osman took up position on the steps, standing slightly to one side, ready for the entrance of Armand Bouchart, the new Templar leader, who strode out and joined him.

Like de Sable before him, Bouchart seemed to have been chosen for his formidable appearance as much as his leadership ability. He wore full armour but looked strong and lithe beneath it. He was hairless with a thick brow that seemed to shade his eyes. Sunken cheeks gave his face a cadaverous look.

'A foul murder has shaken my order,' he bellowed, in a voice that commanded the whole square's attention. 'Dear Frederick the Red . . . slain. He, who served God and the people of Cyprus with honour, is paid tribute by a murderer's blade. Who among you will deliver those responsible to me?'

There was nothing from the crowd but the sound of awkward shuffling. Altair's eyes went back to Bouchart, who was darkening. 'Cowards!' he roared. 'You leave me no choice but to flush out this killer myself. I hereby grant my men immunity until this investigation is concluded.'

Altaïr saw Osman shift uncomfortably. Usually his face wore a twinkly look, but not now. He seemed worried as he stepped forward to speak to the leader. 'Bouchart, the citizens are already restless. Perhaps this is not the best idea.'

Bouchart's face was turned away so Osman might not have seen it twist into an expression of terrible fury. Bouchart was not accustomed to having his orders questioned: that was clear. As to whether he considered it insubordination or not . . .

In one movement he drew his sword and rammed it into Osman's stomach.

With a shout that echoed around the stunned square, the captain folded to the stone, cradling his belly. He writhed on the steps briefly until he died, his death rattle deafening in the shocked hush that blanketed the crowd. Altaïr winced. He hadn't known Osman, of course, but what he'd seen of him, he'd liked. Another good man had died a needless death.

Bouchart reached down and wiped his sword clean on the arm of Osman's tunic. 'If anyone else objects, I invite you to step forward.'

The body shifted slightly and one arm came loose, hanging over the step. Osman's sightless eyes stared at the sky.

There were no objections.

Suddenly there was a shout from Maria, who had pulled free of her two captors. She ran to the steps and threw herself to her knees in front of the leader. 'Armand Bouchart,' she called.

Though he smiled in recognition, it was not the smile of friends meeting. 'Ah,' he sneered, 'an old colleague,' and he replaced his sword in his belt.

'Bouchart,' said Maria, 'an Assassin has come to Cyprus. I managed to escape, but he cannot be far behind.'

Up on his perch, Altaïr's heart sank. He'd hoped . . . No. She was a Templar first. She always would be. Her loyalty was to them.

'Why, Maria,' said Bouchart in high spirits, 'that would make this your second miraculous escape from the Assassins, no? Once when de Sable was the target, and now here on my island.'

Altaïr watched incomprehension join panic on Maria's face. 'I am not in league with the Assassins, Bouchart,' she blurted. 'Please listen.'

'De Sable was a weak-willed wretch. Verse seventy of the founding Templar Rule *expressly* forbids consorting with women . . . for it is through women that the devil weaves his strongest web. De Sable ignored this tenet and paid with his life.'

'How dare you?' she retorted and, despite himself, Altaïr smiled. Any fear Maria experienced was always short-lived.

'Touched a nerve, did I?' roared Bouchart, enjoying himself. Then, 'Lock her up.'

And with that the meeting was over. Bouchart turned and left, leaving the glassy-eyed body of Osman on the steps behind him. Maria was bound and dragged away.

Altaïr's eyes went from the receding figure of Bouchart to Maria. He was torn, trying to decide on his next course of action. Bouchart was close. He might not have this chance again. Strike at him when he least expected it.

But then again – Maria.

He let himself down from the rooftop and followed the men as they led her out of the Cathedral Square, presumably towards the gaol. He kept at a safe distance. Then, when they'd turned off into a quieter street, he struck.

Moments later the two guards were dead and Altaïr was approaching Maria where she had been tossed aside, her hands still bound, struggling to get to her feet. He reached for her and she jerked away from him. 'Get your hands off me,' she snapped. 'They consider me a traitor, thanks to you.'

Altaïr smiled indulgently – even though she had alerted Bouchart to his presence. 'I am only a convenient excuse for your wrath, Maria. The Templars are your real enemy.'

She glowered. 'I will kill you when I get the chance.'

'If you get the chance . . . but then you'll never find the Apple, the Piece of Eden. And which would curry more favour with the Templars right now? My head or that artefact?'

She looked at him with narrowed eyes, seeing that what he said made sense. She seemed to relax.

For the time being.

Much later they met Alexander again. His face showed his concern as he told Altaïr, 'Despite his bravado, Bouchart obviously took Maria's warning seriously.' At this he shot Maria a look so furious that, unusually, she was lost for words. 'My sources tell me that after destroying our safe-house he immediately sailed for Kyrenia.'

Altaïr frowned. 'That's a shame. I was hoping to meet him.' He planned to meet him still. 'What's the fastest route there?' he asked.

39

They travelled as a monk and his companion, able to find space in the hold. Occasionally crew members would descend from the main deck and curl up to sleep there, too, farting and snuffling, paying little attention to the two strangers. As Maria slept, Altaïr found a crate and opened his journal, bringing the Apple out from a pack he wore in his robe.

Free of its swaddling it glowed and he watched it for a moment, then began to write: 'I struggle to make sense of the Apple, the Piece of Eden, its function and purpose, but I *can* say with certainty that its origins are not divine. No ... it is a tool ... a machine of exquisite precision. What sort of men were they who brought this marvel into the world?'

There was a noise behind him. In an instant he had swept up the Apple and covered it once more, hiding it within his robe. It was Maria, stirring from sleep. He closed his journal, stepping over the sleeping bodies of two crew members and crossing the hold to where she sat with her back against a stack of wooden boxes, shivering and yawning. She clasped her knees to her chest, watching as Altaïr sat on the deck beside her.

Her eyes were unreadable. For a moment they listened to the creak of the ship, the suck and slap of the sea on the hull. Neither was sure if it was day or night, or how long they had been sailing.

'How did you find yourself here?' he asked her.

'Don't you remember, holy man?' she said archly. 'You brought me.' She whispered, 'I'm your consort.'

Altaïr cleared his throat. 'I mean here in the Holy Land. In the Crusades.'

'I should be at home with a lap full of crochet and one eye on the gardener?'

'Isn't that what English women do?'

'Not this one. I'm what they call the unusual one in my family. Growing up, I always preferred the boys' games. Dolls weren't for me, much to my parents' continued exasperation. I used to pull their heads off.'

'Your parents?'

She laughed. 'My dolls. So, of course, my parents did everything they could to make me less boisterous, and on my eighteenth birthday they gave me a special present.'

'And what was it?'

'A husband.'

He started. 'You're married?'

'I was. His name was Peter, and he was a most pleasant companion, just . . .'

'What?'

'Well, that was it. Just . . . most pleasant. Nothing else.'

'So, not much use as a playmate.'

'In no sense. My ideal husband would have embraced those aspects of my character that my parents wanted to excise. We would have gone hunting and hawking together. He would have tutored me in sports and combat and imbued me with learning. But he did none of those things. We repaired to his family seat, Hallaton Hall, in Leicestershire, where as chatelaine I was expected to manage the staff, oversee the running of the household and, of course, produce heirs. Three at least. Two boys and a girl, preferably, in that order. But I failed to live up to his expectations as miserably as he had failed to live up to mine. The only thing I cared for less than the hierarchies and politics of the staff was child-rearing and especially the birth that comes beforehand. After four years of prevarication I left. Fortunately the Bishop of Leicester was a close friend of the elderly Lord Hallaton and he was able to grant an annulment rather than risking this silly impetuous girl cause the family further embarrassment. I was of course *persona non grata* at Hallaton Hall – indeed, in the whole of Leicestershire – and, returning home, the situation was no better. Hallaton had demanded his bride price back but Father had already spent it. In the end I decided it was best for everyone if I left so I ran away to the Crusade.'

'As a nurse?'

'No, as a soldier.'

'But you're . . .'

'Adept at disguising myself as a man, yes. Did I have you fooled that day in the cemetery?'

'I knew you weren't de Sable, but . . .'

'You didn't anticipate me being a woman. You see? Years of being boisterous finally paid off.'

'And de Sable? Was he fooled?'

Altaïr sensed her rueful smile, rather than seeing it. 'I liked Robert at first,' she said softly. 'He certainly saw more of my potential than Peter did. But, of course, he also saw how I might be exploited. And it wasn't long before he was doing so.' She sighed. 'It was fitting that you killed him,' she said. 'He was not a good man and was unworthy of whatever feelings I had for him.'

'Did he give you that?' said Altaïr after a time, indicating her hand, the gem that shone there.

She looked at and frowned, almost as though she had forgotten she was wearing it. 'Yes. It was a gift from him when he took me under his wing. This is all I have left of my ties to the Templars.'

There was an awkward silence. Eventually it was broken by Altaïr, who said, 'Did you study philosophy, Maria?'

She looked at him dubiously. 'I've read scraps . . . nothing more.'

'The philosopher Empedocles preached that all life on earth began simply, in rudimentary forms: hands without arms, heads without bodies, eyes without faces. He believed that all these early forms combined, very gradually over time, to create all the variety of life we see before us. Interesting?'

She all but yawned. 'Do you know how ludicrous that sounds?'

'I do . . . but I take comfort in the advice of the philosopher Al Kindi: one must not be afraid of ideas, no matter their source. And we must never fear the truth, even when it pains us.'

'I don't see the point of your ramblings.' She laughed softly, sounding sleepy and warm.

Perhaps he had misjudged her. Maybe she wasn't ready to learn. But just then a bell sounded, the sign that they had docked at Kyrenia. They stood up.

Altaïr tried again. 'Only a mind free of impediment is capable of grasping the chaotic beauty of the world. This is our greatest asset.'

'But is chaos something to be celebrated? Is disorder a virtue?' she asked, and something in him lifted at the question. Perhaps she was receptive to higher knowledge, after all.

'It presents us with challenges, yes,' he said, 'but freedom yields greater rewards than the alternative. The order and peace the Templars seek require servility and imprisonment.'

'Hm,' she said. 'I know that feeling . . .'

He felt a certain closeness towards her as they

reached the steps that led to the upper deck and realized it was the very sensation he had been chasing almost since they had met. Now he had it, he liked it. He wanted to keep it. Even so, he should be careful. Hadn't she already told him that she planned to kill him? Her loyalties to the Templars had been torn but that didn't mean she had suddenly come over to the way of the Assassin. As far as he could tell, her way was the way of Maria.

So it was to prove.

At the ladder she smiled and held out her hands and he regarded them distrustfully. But she couldn't possibly climb with her hands tied and, anyway, they were travelling with pirates: although pirates were notoriously low on ethics, even they might be surprised by a monk who kept his companion bound. The two who had been sleeping were now pulling themselves to their feet, yawning, scratching their groins and casting looks across the hold at the pair of them. Surreptitiously Altaïr flicked out his blade and sliced the rope at her wrists. She shot him a grateful look before beginning to climb the ladder.

Then, he heard something. A murmur. He was alerted more by the tone than what was being said. Without making it obvious, he listened. As he'd thought, the two pirates were talking about them.

'I *knew* it was him,' rasped one. 'I told you.'

Altaïr could feel their eyes on his back.

'I'll bet the Templars would pay a handsome reward for those two.'

Silently the Assassin cursed. If he was right, he'd be needing his blade again at any moment . . .

He heard the sound of scimitars being drawn.

. . . *now*.

Altaïr wheeled to face the two men as his companion decided to pursue the Way of Maria and launched a bid for freedom, kicking out with her trailing foot and sending him stumbling against the side of the hold, pain flaring in his face.

There was pain inside him, too. A different kind of pain.

Then she was gone, disappearing into the square of sunlight at the hold door. Altaïr cursed again but aloud this time and righted himself to meet the attack. The first pirate grinned as he came forward, thinking no doubt of the bounty – the wine and women he would buy when he had collected it.

Altaïr thrust his sword through the man's sternum and he stopped grinning, sliding wetly off the blade. It gave the second pause for thought and he stopped. His eyes narrowed and he swapped his weapon from hand to hand. Altaïr smiled at him and stamped, pleased to see him flinch in response.

Good, he thought. He liked his mercenary pirates to be a little scared before they died.

And die he did. The pirate's eyes rolled up as Altaïr

buried his blade in his side then sawed quickly to the front, opening a vast gash in his flank as he dropped to the deck, joining his companion. Now the Assassin scaled the ladder and then he was blinking in the sunlight as he found himself on the main deck, casting his eyes around in search of his escapee. Pirates, alerted by the sudden presence of Maria, came running. A shout went up as they saw Altaïr and realization dawned on them. He dashed across the deck, ducking beneath rigging, then running nimbly down the gangplank and on to Kyrenia docks, desperately looking for a place to hide where he could let the threat go by.

And then, he thought angrily, he was going to find Maria. This time he wouldn't allow her to escape.

He looked around. Another city held by the Templars. It twinkled in the sun. Somehow it was too beautiful to be in the hands of the enemy.

40

At least finding Maria caused him no difficulty. Trouble came to her like rats to a ship's hold. Sure enough when Altaïr next crossed paths with her, pirate corpses were strewn at her feet and three local men were standing nearby, flicking blood from their swords and recovering their breath after battle. They tensed as Altaïr appeared and he held up his hands in a gesture of good faith, taking in the scene: Maria, the men, the dead bodies.

Once again, it seemed, she'd had a lucky escape.

'I thought I'd seen the last of you,' he said to her, arms still upraised.

She had a gift for refusing to be surprised at any turn of events. 'If only I were so lucky. . .'

He frowned at her, then addressed one of the Cypriot men, the likely leader. 'What is your business with this woman? Are you a Templar lackey?'

'No, sir,' stammered the man. He stood with his sword drawn and Altaïr's hands were empty, but even so, the Cypriot knew a skilled warrior when he saw one. 'The pirates attacked her and I had to help. But I'm no lackey. I hate the Templars.'

'I understand. You're not alone,' replied Altaïr.

The man nodded gratefully, their common purpose established. 'My name is Markos, sir. I'll help in any way I can, if it means ridding my country of these Crusaders.'

Excellent, thought Altaïr. 'Then I need you to keep this woman safe until I return. I have to find someone before the Templars do.'

'We'll be at the harbour all day. She'll be safe here with us,' said Markos, and once again Maria was grumbling as the men hauled her away. She'd be all right, thought Altaïr, watching them go. She'd spend the day between a couple of burly Cypriots, watching the world go by in Kyrenia harbour: there were better ways to waste a few hours, but also far worse. At least he knew she'd be safe while he met with Alexander's Resistance contact, the Barnabas he'd been told about.

He found him at the safe-house, which doubled as a grain store. Walking in, Altair had called out cautiously, hearing nothing but the scuttling of mice and the distant sounds of the street. Then a man had appeared from among the sacks. He had a dark beard and watchful black eyes, and introduced himself as Barnabas. When Altaïr asked him if the safe-house had an area that could be used as a cell, he smiled obsequiously and assured him that of course it did, but then dithered, going first to one door, which he opened and closed, and then to a second, through which he peered before announcing that the drying room had a barred area that could be used as a cell.

'I've been following Armand Bouchart,' Altaïr told Barnabas, moments later, the two of them now sitting on grain sacks in the storeroom.

'Ah . . . Bouchart is in Kyrenia?' said the Resistance man. 'He's probably visiting his prisoners in Buffavento.'

'Is that a keep nearby?'

'A castle, yes. It was once the residence of a wealthy Cypriot noblewoman, until the Templars seized her property.'

Altaïr frowned at their greed. 'Can you take me there?'

'Well . . . I can do more than that. I can get you inside without the guards batting an eyelid. But you must do something for me first. For the Resistance.'

'A familiar request,' said Altaïr. 'What is it?'

'We have a traitor in our midst,' said Barnabas, darkly.

The traitor was a merchant named Jonas, and after Barnabas had given him the necessary details Altaïr tracked him to an amphitheatre in the centre of the city. According to Barnabas, Jonas was feeding secrets to the Templars. Altaïr watched him for a while, meeting other tradesman, looking for all the world like any other businessman. Then, when he turned to go, the Assassin followed him from the amphitheatre and into the back-streets, noting as the merchant slowly became aware that he was being followed. He cast more and more frequent glances behind him at Altaïr, his eyes wilder and more frightened each time. Suddenly he broke into a run and Altaïr was in pursuit, delighted to see Jonas turn into an alleyway.

He speeded up, and raced after his quarry.

The alleyway was empty.

Altaïr stopped, glanced behind to check he was not seen, then – *snick* – engaged his blade. He took two steps forward so that he was level with a large, unsteady pile of crates, which was teetering slightly. He bent slightly, then drove his blade through a crate. The wood splintered and there was a scream. The pile toppled down on to Altaïr, who braced himself, almost losing his footing.

He stayed still, though. And when the wood had settled around him he relaxed, looking along the line of his outstretched arm, to where Jonas was pinned by his blade, blood slowly spreading from the wound at his neck. Still in the crouched position he'd adopted to hide, the merchant cut a desperate, pathetic figure. And though Altaïr knew he was a traitor, and that information he gave to the Templars had no doubt been used to kill, capture and torture members of the Resistance, he pitied him, so much so that he removed the blade gently, shoving aside the remnants of the boxes so that he could lay Jonas down and bend to him.

Blood oozed from the neck wound. 'What's this?' wheezed Jonas. 'An Assassin? Does Salah Al'din have his eyes on poor Cyprus too?'

'The Assassins have no ties to the Saracen. Our business is our own.'

Jonas coughed, revealing bloodied teeth. 'Whatever the case, word of your presence is widespread. The Bull has put a bounty on your head ... and on the head of your female companion.'

Altaïr saw the life bleeding out of him. 'I'm worth more and more every day,' he said, and delivered the killing blow.

When he stood up, it was not with the satisfaction of a job well done, but with a terrible sense that something was amiss. The Bull Jonas had mentioned. Whoever he was, he was loyal to Armand Bouchart and he knew of Altaïr and Maria's presence in Kyrenia. Was that the source of Altaïr's disquiet?

He took to the rooftops, meaning to find Markos and Maria at once.

'Well, Maria, it seems there's a hefty price on both our heads,' said Altaïr, when he'd found her. Just as he'd imagined, she was sitting on a stone bench between Markos and another Resistance man, wearing the glowering look to which he was becoming accustomed.

'A price? Damn Bouchart. He probably thinks I'm your apprentice.'

'Someone called the Bull has dispatched his men to search for us.'

Maria jumped as though stung. 'The Bull? So they gave that zealot his own parish?'

'Is he a friend of yours?' said Altaïr, wryly.

'Hardly. His name is Moloch. He's a pious blowhard with arms like tree trunks.'

Altaïr turned to Markos. 'Do you know the Resistance safe-house in the Commons District?'

'I know where it is, but I've never been inside.' Markos shrugged. 'I'm just a foot soldier for the Resistance.'

Altaïr thought, then said, 'I can't be seen with Maria, so you'll have to take her. Keep her out of sight, and meet me there when you're safe.'

'I know some back alleys and tunnels.'

'It may take longer, but we'll get her there in one piece.'

Separately they made their way to the safe-house, Altaïr arriving first. Barnabas had spread out sacks of grain and had been relaxing, but he pulled himself to his feet as Altaïr entered, stifling a yawn as though roused from slumber.

'I just had word that someone found poor Jonas's body,' he said, with a sneer in his voice. 'What a waste, eh?' He brushed grain from his robes.

'You knew him better than I did,' replied Altaïr. 'I'm sure he understood the risk of working for both sides.'

He looked at Barnabas carefully, taking note of the crooked smile he wore. Altaïr took no pleasure from death – any death – and he was apt to look poorly on those who did, whether they be Templar, Assassin or Resistance. On the one hand Barnabas was an ally. On the other ... If Altaïr knew one thing it was to trust his instincts and his instincts were nagging him now; just a low, hushed nagging, but insistent nonetheless.

Barnabas was continuing: 'Yes ... unfortunately, this has complicated things. Jonas was a respected Cypriot and his death has sparked riots near the Old Church. The public is hungry for revenge and the Bull will tell them you were responsible. You may lose the support of the Resistance.'

What? Altaïr stared at him, hardly able to believe his ears. That instinct of his: it moved from nagging to outright harassment. 'But Jonas was a traitor to the Resistance. Did they not know?'

'Not enough of them, I'm afraid,' Barnabas admitted. 'The Resistance is quite scattered.'

'Well, you'll have the chance to tell them yourself,' said Altaïr. 'Some men are on their way to us now.'

'You're bringing people here?' Barnabas looked concerned. 'People you can trust?'

'I'm not sure who I can trust right now,' said Altaïr, 'but it's worth the risk. Right now I need to see these riots for myself.'

'As for our bargain, I'll see what I can do about getting you close to Bouchart. A deal's a deal, eh?' said Barnabas. He smiled again.

Altaïr didn't care for that smile. He liked it less and less each time he saw it.

41

Altaïr paid a visit to the church and his heart sank at the sight of the unrest. Templar guards had formed a cordon and were holding back marauding citizens, who had been prevented from moving out of the immediate area of the church and were smashing everything in sight. Crates and barrels had been splintered and there were scattered fires on the streets. Streetside stalls had been attacked and dismantled, and the smell of trampled produce mingled with the smoke. Men had gathered in groups and were chanting slogans to the beat of drums and the constant rattle of cymbals, trying to goad the lines of Templar knights, who watched them carefully from behind makeshift barriers, overturned carts and stalls. Every now and then small squads of soldiers would make short, ruthless sorties into the mob, dragging out men who kicked and yelled, and either clubbing them with the hilts of their swords or throwing them behind the barrier to be taken to the cells – not that their raids did anything to frighten the rioters or dampen their temper.

Altaïr watched it all from up high, squatting on the edge of a roof, shrouded in despair. Something had gone wrong. Something had gone terribly wrong. And if the Bull decided to make an announcement naming him as the killer, then things were going to get even worse.

He made his decision. The Bull had to die.

When he arrived back at the safe-house, he looked in vain for Barnabas, who was nowhere to be seen. Now Altaïr was certain that he had been wrong to trust him and was cursing himself. He'd listened to his instinct. Just not hard enough.

Markos was there, though, as was Maria, who had been deposited in the cell, a much sturdier design than the makeshift gaol they had been using in Limassol. The door between the drying room and the storeroom was open so they could see her: she sat behind bars with her back against the wall, occasionally kicking her feet among the rushes spread out on the floor and regarding all goings-on with a baleful, sardonic expression. Altaïr watched her, musing upon all the trouble she had caused.

He learned that she, Markos and several other Resistance men had arrived at the safe-house to find it deserted. Barnabas had been gone when they had got there. How convenient, thought Altaïr.

'What's going on out there?' Markos had exclaimed. 'The city is in turmoil. I've seen riots.'

'The people are protesting the death of a citizen, a man named Jonas. Have you heard of him?'

'My father knew him well. He was a good man. How did he die?'

Altaïr's heart sank even further, and he found himself avoiding Markos's eyes as he replied, 'Bravely. Listen, Markos, things have become complicated. Before I find Bouchart, I need to eliminate the Bull and put an end to his violence.'

'You've quite a taste for chaos, Altaïr,' called Maria from her cell.

He liked the way his name sounded in her mouth. 'The Bull is one man responsible for the subjugation of thousands. Few will mourn his loss.'

She shifted. 'And you propose to fly into Kantara, sting him and exit unnoticed? He surrounds himself with devoted worshippers.' Her voice echoed in the stone prison.

'Kantara . . . that's to the east?' said Altaïr, picking up on her inadvertent slip.

'Yes, it's the best defended . . . You'll see for your-self.'

42

Altaïr did indeed see for himself. Kantara Castle was guarded by Crusader soldiers and Moloch's fanatics. Scaling the walls, then making his way across the ramparts, he stopped occasionally to hear them talking, gleaning the odd bit of information about the man they called the Bull. He learned that he was a religious zealot who attracted like-minded followers, fanatics who either worked as his personal bodyguard, his servants, or who trod the streets of Kyrenia, spreading the word. He was attached to the Templars. His devotion to their leader, Bouchart, was almost as devout as his religious faith, and Kantara Castle was his personal citadel, given to him, presumably, by the Templars. He was known to spend most of his time worshipping at the castle chapel.

Which was where Altaïr hoped to find him.

Moving through the fortress he saw fanatics as well as guards. The fanatics looked . . . well, exactly as he would have expected fanatics to look: jumpy, wide-eyed and zealous. They were held in open contempt by the Christian guards who patrolled in twos and clearly thought it beneath them to be stationed at the castle. As Altaïr pressed himself into a recess two wandered past, one complaining to the other. 'Why do the Templars tolerate this madman? The Bull and his fanatics are more dangerous than the citizens of Cyprus.'

'The Templars have their reasons,' replied the other. 'It's much easier for them to rule by proxy, you see.'

'I suppose so. But how long can it last? The Bull and the Templars do not exactly see eye to eye on matters of faith.'

'Ah, the less you say about that the better,' rejoined the first.

Altaïr let them go past, then moved on, the corridor darkening. Maria had said the castle was well defended, and it certainly was if you had raised an army and planned to storm its walls. For a lone Assassin, though, penetrating the fortress by stealth was an easier task. Especially when you were the Master. When you were Altaïr.

Now he found himself in a vast banqueting hall. At the opposite end stood two guards and he took out two throwing knives. He flicked them: one, two. In moments the men lay twitching on the stone and Altaïr stepped over them, knowing that he was near now, that Moloch couldn't be far away.

He wasn't. Altaïr came to what looked like a dead end and turned, checking behind him – why had this been guarded? Then he saw a trapdoor. Bending to it, he listened, then smiled. He had found the Bull.

Very gently he lifted the trapdoor and lowered himself into the roof beams below. He was in the rafters of the castle's place of worship, a large empty room lit by the fire of a large brazier near the altar.

Kneeling before the fire, tending it, was Moloch.

Maria's description of him had been accurate. He was a bear of a man: bare-headed, drooping moustache, bare-chested, apart from a medallion, and with the tree-trunk arms she'd described. Sweat glistened on him as he stoked the fire, chanting an incantation that sounded as much like a growl as it did pious devotion. Absorbed in his work he didn't move from the fire, didn't look away from it, bathing his face in the heat of the flames, oblivious to anything else in the room, even – especially – his killer.

Good. Moloch looked strong, easily more powerful than Altaïr, who had no desire to engage him in combat. Not only did he have the muscular advantage but it was said that he wielded a weapon like a meteor hammer, with a deadly weight attached to a chain. It was said that he used it with unfailing accuracy, and was ruthless with it.

So, no. Altaïr had no desire to engage him in combat. This was to be a stealth kill. Quick, clean and silent.

Noiselessly, Altaïr made his way along the beams, then dropped silently into the centre of the room behind Moloch. He was slightly further away than he would have liked and he held his breath, tensing. If Moloch had heard him . . .

But no. The brute was still engrossed with the brazier. Altaïr took a few steps forward. Silently he engaged the blade and raised it. Orange light danced on the steel. The Bull now just a heartbeat away from death. Altaïr dipped slightly, his leg muscles bunching, then launched himself, blade about to strike.

He was in mid-air when Moloch spun, far more quickly than his size should have allowed. At the same time he grinned and Altaïr realized that he had known he was there all along; that he had merely let Altaïr come close. Then the Assassin was in the embrace of those huge arms, raising him off the ground, feeling a hand go to his throat and squeeze.

For a moment or so he was held that way, Moloch lifting him one-handed into the air as though he were a trophy to be displayed on the castle steps, and he choked as he struggled. His feet kicked at thin air and his hands scrabbled at Moloch's gauntlet, desperately trying to loosen the monster's grip. His vision began to cloud, blackness closing in. He felt himself losing consciousness. Then Moloch was tossing him backwards and he was sprawling on the chapel floor, his head rebounding painfully off a flagstone, wondering why he had been allowed to live.

Because the Bull wanted more sport. He had produced his meteor hammer and, with a single looping swing above his head, launched it at Altaïr, who only just managed to roll clear as it came smashing down, opening a crater in the flagstone and showering him with stone shards.

Altaïr scrambled to his feet, dazed, shaking his head to clear it. He drew his sword. Blade in one hand, sword in the other. He was darting to the side as the Bull retrieved his hammer and launched it again.

It crashed into a pillar beside Altaïr and once again he was hit by a hail of stone fragments. With Moloch's hammer unspooled, Altaïr had a chance and darted in, jabbing with sword and blade. But, faster than seemed possible, Moloch had retrieved the chain and held it two-handed, blocking Altaïr's sword, then swinging the hammer again and sending the Assassin diving for safety once more.

Altaïr thought of Al Mualim – the Al Mualim who had trained him, not the traitor he had become. He thought of Labib and of his other swordskills tutors. He took a deep breath and backed off, stepping to the side, circling Moloch.

The Bull followed him, knowing he had the Assassin worried. When he smiled he revealed a mouthful of jagged, blackened teeth, most worn down to diseased stumps. From the back of his throat he made a growling sound as Altaïr came closer, needing to coax Moloch into throwing the hammer. The Assassin had an idea. It was a good idea but it had a flaw. It would be fatal if he got it wrong. He needed the Bull to release the hammer — but every time that happened it came dangerously close to caving in Altaïr's skull.

It came. Looping through the air. Smashing into the stone. Altaïr only just leaped clear but he landed on his feet and, instead of taking cover, dashed towards the hammer. He stepped on the weight and ran up the taut chain towards Moloch.

Moloch stopped grinning. He had a second to comprehend the sight of the agile Assassin running up the tightrope of his chain before Altaïr's sword sliced through the front of his throat and exited at the neck. He made a sound that was halfway between a shout and a choke, the sword protruding through his neck as Altaïr let go of the hilt and twisted to straddle the Bull's shoulders, driving his blade deep into the man's spine. Still the Bull fought and Altaïr found himself hanging on for grim life. He grabbed the chain and dragged it up to loop around his victim's neck with his free hand, grunting with the effort of pulling it hard. Moloch twisted and pushed backwards and Altaïr saw that he was being manoeuvred towards the fire.

He felt the heat at his back and redoubled his efforts. The beast would not die. He smelt something burning — the hem of his robe! Yelling with pain and effort, he pulled hard on the chain with one hand, digging the blade deeper with the other until at last something gave, some last life force snapped within Moloch and

Altaïr was riding his bucking shoulders as the brute folded to the floor where he lay, breathing heavily, syrupy blood spreading across the stone, slowly dying.

At last his breathing stopped.

Altaïr heaved a huge sigh of relief. Moloch would not be able to turn the people against the Resistance. His reign of tyranny was over. However, he couldn't help but wonder what might replace it.

He was to get his answer very shortly.

43

Maria was gone. Taken by Crusaders. While Altaïr had been battling at Kantara Castle, soldiers had attacked the safe-house and, despite a battle, had made off with some prisoners, Maria among them.

Markos, one of the few who had escaped capture, was there to greet the Assassin, worry etched into his face, fretting as he babbled, 'Altaïr, we were attacked. We tried to fight them off but – but it was no use.' He dropped his eyes, shame-faced.

Or was he feigning it?

Altaïr looked at the door to the drying room. It was open. Beyond, the door to the barred cell hung open too and he pictured her there, watching him with her almond eyes, her back against the wall and boots scuffing in the rushes strewn on the stone.

He shook his head to rid himself of the image. There was more at stake than his feelings for the English woman: he had no business thinking of her before the concerns of the Order. But . . . he had.

'I wanted to stop them,' Markos was saying, 'but I had to hide. There were too many.'

Altaïr looked at him sharply. Now that he knew of

Barnabas's duplicity he was reluctant to trust anybody. 'This was not your fault,' he said. 'The Templars are crafty.'

'I've heard they harness the power of a Dark Oracle in Buffavento. That must be how they found us.'

Was that so? Altaïr thought about it. Certainly the Templars seemed to know their every move. But maybe that was less to do with an oracle and more to do with the fact that the Resistance was infested with Templar spies.

'That is a curious theory,' he said, wary that Markos might be trying deliberately to mislead him. 'But I suspect it was Barnabas who tipped them off.'

Markos started. 'Barnabas? How can that be? The Resistance leader Barnabas was executed the day before you arrived.'

Of course. Altaïr cursed himself. There *had been* a Barnabas who was loyal to the Resistance but the Templars had replaced him with their own man – a false Barnabas. Altaïr thought of Jonas, executed by him on the orders of the spy, and he hoped one day to be able to make recompense for that. Jonas hadn't deserved to die.

Altaïr left for the harbour district, found where the Resistance prisoners were being held and slipped past the guards to discover them huddled in a cramped, filthy cell.

'Thank you, sir, may God bless you,' said one, as

Altaïr opened the door and allowed him out. He wore the same look of gratitude as the others. Altaïr hated to think what the Templars had planned for them.

He searched the gaol in vain for Maria . . .

'Was there a woman with you when you were taken?'

'A woman? Yes, until the Bull's son Shalim took her away in chains. She didn't go quietly.'

No, thought Altaïr. Going quietly wasn't Maria's style. But who was this son, Shalim? Would he take over the Bull's reign of tyranny?

So it was that Altaïr found himself scaling the walls of the fortress at Buffavento, making his way into the castle, then downwards into its dark, damp and dripping depths where the stone glistened blackly, where the lights from flickering torches barely penetrated the forbidding darkness, where every footstep echoed and there was the constant drip of water. Was this where the Templars kept their famous oracle? He hoped so. All he knew so far was that they were keeping one step ahead of him. Whatever they had in mind, he knew he wouldn't like it: he didn't like the idea of the archive he kept hearing about, or that they kept coming so close to crushing the Resistance. Anything he could do to halt their progress needed to be done. And if that meant a spot of witch-hunting, then so be it.

Now, edging along the corridors in the bowels of the castle, he found himself coming closer to what he assumed was the dungeon. Behind him lay the bodies of two guards he had encountered on his way, both with their throats slit, the corpses hidden from view. Just as with Moloch's castle, he had been able to work his way to its heart using a mixture of stealth and killing. Now he heard voices, one of which he recognized immediately. It was Bouchart's.

He was talking to a man on the other side of a steel gate pockmarked with rust.

'So the girl escaped again, did she?' snapped the Templar.

The other man wore sumptuous fur-lined robes. 'One minute she was chained up, the next she was gone . . .'

'Don't insult me, Shalim. Your weakness for women is well known. You let your guard down and she walked away.'

'I will find her, Grand Master. I swear it.'

So this was Shalim. Altaïr paid him special attention, faintly amused. Nothing about him – not his looks, his build and certainly not his attire – was reminiscent of his father, Moloch.

'Do it quickly,' Bouchart was snapping, 'before she leads the Assassin directly to the archive.'

Shalim turned to go, but Bouchart stopped him. 'And, Shalim, see that this is delivered to Alexander in Limassol.'

He handed Shalim a sack that the other man took,

indicating his assent. Altaïr felt his jaw clench. So Alexander was working with the Templars too. The enemy seemed to have a hand in everything.

Now, though, the two men had moved off, and Altaïr resumed his progress towards the Oracle's cell. Unable to pass through the gates, he clambered on to a balcony and worked his way round the outside of the fortress, then downwards again until he came to the dungeons. More guards fell beneath his blade. Soon the bodies would be discovered and there would be a general alert. He needed to move quickly.

Still, it seemed as though the guards had enough to contend with. He could hear screaming and ranting as he approached what he thought were the dungeons. As he came to the end of a tunnel, which opened into what looked like a gaol area, he realised where Bouchart had been going, because here he was again, talking to a guard. They stood on the other side of a barred partition outside a row of cell doors.

Well, thought Altaïr, at least he'd found his dungeon. He crouched out of sight in an alcove in the tunnel. To a background of shrieks, he heard Bouchart ask, 'What's happening?'

'It's that mad woman, sir,' replied the guard, raising his voice to be heard over the din. 'She's on a rampage. Two of the guards are injured.'

'Let her play,' smiled Bouchart. 'She has served her purpose.'

Yet again Altaïr found the way between himself and Bouchart blocked. He would dearly have liked to finish this now, even with the guard present: he thought he could overwhelm the man first, then take Bouchart. But it was not to be. Instead he was forced to watch, frustrated, as Bouchart and the guard moved off, leaving the area deserted. He came from out of his hiding place and went to the partition, finding a locked gate. Dextrous fingers worked at the mechanism. Then he passed through, and strode towards the door of the Oracle's cell. If anything, her screaming was louder and more unsettling now, and Altaïr swallowed. He was frightened of no man. But this was no man. This was something different altogether. He found himself having to steady his nerves as he worked on the second lock. As the door swung open, with the high-pitched complaint of rusting hinges, his heart was hammering.

Her cell was vast, the size of a banqueting hall — a large banqueting hall over which hung the pall of death and decay, with rippling mist and what looked like patches of foliage among the pillars, as though the outside was intruding, one day to claim it in full.

As his eyes became accustomed to the gloom he looked for her but saw nothing, just heard her infernal screeching. It made the hairs on his arms stand on end and he suppressed a shiver as he trod further into her . . . cell?

This was more like her lair.

Suddenly there was silence. His senses pricked. He swapped his sword from hand to hand, eyes scanning the dark, dimly lit room.

'Pagan blood,' came a voice – a jagged singsong voice straight from a nightmare. He wheeled in the direction of the sound, but then it came again and seemed to have moved. 'I know your name, sinner,' she cackled, 'I know why you're here. God guide my claws. God grant me strength to snap your bones.'

Altaïr just had time to think, *Claws?* Did she really have – She appeared, whirling like a dervish from the darkness, black hair whipping about her, screaming as she came. What she had weren't quite claws: they were long, sharp nails – and just as deadly. He heard their whistle as they sliced in front of his face. He jumped back. Then she was crouching like a cat, looking at him and snarling. He was surprised: he had expected an aged crone, but this woman . . . she had noble looks. Of course. It was the woman Barnabas had told him about, who had once lived in the castle. She was young and had been attractive once. But whatever the Templars had done to her, imprisonment had seemingly sent her mad. He knew that when she grinned, suddenly not so noble as she revealed rows of rotting teeth and a tongue that threatened to loll from her mouth. Giggling she struck once more.

They fought, the Oracle attacking blindly, swinging her nails, slashing Altaïr several times and drawing blood. He kept his distance, coming forward to launch counter-attacks until eventually he managed to over-whelm her and pinned her to a pillar. Desperately he tried to hold her – he wanted to reason with her – but she writhed like a wild animal, even when he pushed her to the ground and straddled her, holding his blade to her throat as she thrashed, muttering, 'Glory of God. I am his instrument. God's executioner. I fear neither pain nor death.'

'You were a Cypriot once,' Altaïr told her, strug-gling to hold her. 'A respected noblewoman. What secrets did you tell those devils?'

Did she know that by helping the Templars she'd betrayed her own people? Did she still have enough reason to understand that?

'Not without purpose do I deal in misery,' she rasped, suddenly becoming still. 'By God's command I am his instrument.'

No, he thought. She didn't. Her mind was gone.

'Whatever the Templars have done to you, my lady, they have done you wrong,' he said. 'Forgive me this.'

It was an act of mercy. He killed her, then fled that terrible place.

Later, back at the safe-house, he opened his journal and wrote,

Why do our instincts insist on violence? I have studied the interactions between different species. The innate desire to survive seems to demand the death of the other. Why can they not stand hand in hand? So many believe the world was created through the works of a divine power — but I see only the designs of a madman, bent on celebrating death, destruction, and desperation.

He mused also upon the Apple:

Who were the Ones That Came Before? What brought them here? What drove them out? What of these artefacts? Messages in a bottle? Tools left behind to aid and guide us? Or do we fight for control over their refuse, giving divine purpose and meaning to little more than discarded toys?

44

Altaïr decided to follow Shalim. Now they were both hunting Maria, and Altaïr wanted to make sure he was around if Shalim found her first.

Not that Shalim was looking especially hard at the moment. Markos had told Altaïr that all Shalim had in common with his father was the fact that he served the Templars and had a fierce temper. In place of religious fervour he had a taste for wine and enjoyed the company of prostitutes. Following him, Altaïr saw him indulge in both. He kept a safe distance as Shalim and two of his bodyguards stalked the streets of Kyrenia like a trio of little despots, angrily upbraiding citizens and merchants, abusing them, taking goods and money in preparation for a visit somewhere.

To a brothel, it seemed. Altaïr watched as Shalim and his men approached a door where a drunk was pawing one of the local whores. Either the man was too stupid or too inebriated to recognize that Shalim's mood was dark, because he lifted his leather flask in greeting to the tyrant, calling, 'Raise a mug, Shalim.'

Shalim did not break stride. He rammed the flat of his hand into the drunk's face so that his head rebounded off the wall behind him with a hollow clunk. The leather flask dropped and the man slid down the wall to a sitting position, his head lolling, hair matting with blood. In the same movement Shalim grabbed the prostitute by the arm.

She resisted. 'Shalim, no. Please don't.'

But he was already dragging her off, looking back over his shoulder and calling to his two companions, 'Have your fun, men. And round up some women for me when you're finished.'

Altaïr had seen enough. Shalim wasn't looking for Maria, that much was certain, and he himself wasn't likely to find her by following Shalim to wherever he was going with his whore: bed or a tavern, no doubt.

Instead he returned to the market district, where Markos was aimlessly wandering between the stalls, his hands clasped behind his back, waiting for news from Altaïr.

'I need to get close to Shalim,' he told Markos, when they'd repaired to the shade, looking for all the world like two traders passing the time of day out of the hot sun. 'If he is as stupid as he is brash, I may be able to get some secrets out of him.'

'Speak to one of the monks near the cathedral.' Markos chuckled. 'Shalim's wayward lifestyle demands frequent confessions.'

So it was that at the cathedral Altaïr found a bench beneath a flapping canopy and sat watching the world go by, waiting until a lone white-robed monk passed him, inclining his head in greeting. Altaïr returned the gesture, then said in a low voice, so that only the monk could hear, 'Does it not trouble you, brother, to suffer the sins of such a vile man as Shalim?'

The monk stopped. Looked one way then the other. Then at Altaïr. 'It does,' he whispered, 'but to oppose him would mean death. The Templars have too much at stake here.'

'You mean the archive?' said Altaïr. 'Can you tell me where it is?'

Altaïr had heard about this archive. Perhaps it held the key to the Templars' activities. But the monk was shaking his head and moving away as, suddenly, a small commotion erupted. It was Shalim, Altaïr saw, with a start. He was mounting an orator's platform. He no longer had the prostitute with him and he seemed a good deal less drunk than he had been previously.

'Men and women of Cyprus,' he announced, as his audience assembled, 'Armand Bouchart sends his blessing, but with a stern provision that all who foment disorder with their support of the Resistance will be caught and punished. Those who seek order and harmony, and pay obeisance to the Lord through good work, will enjoy Bouchart's charity. Now, let us work together as brothers to rebuild what hate and anger have torn down.'

This was most odd, thought Altaïr. Shalim looked

rested and fresh-faced, not how Altaïr would have expected him to appear in view of his recent activities. That Shalim had had all the makings of a man who planned to spend the rest of his day drinking and whoring. This one? He was like a different man – not just in looks but in his manner, his bearing and, judging by the content of his speech, his entire philosophy. And this Shalim had no bodyguards with him either. This Shalim Altaïr could easily overcome, perhaps in one of the alleyways off a main avenue of Kyrenia.

When Shalim stepped down from his platform and moved off, leaving the cathedral behind him and taking to the golden streets, Altaïr followed in pursuit.

He wasn't sure how long they'd been walking when suddenly the giant St Hilarion Castle was looming over them and he saw that Shalim was heading inside. Sure enough, when he reached the huge castle gates he stepped inside a wicket door, disappearing from sight. Altaïr cursed. He had lost his target. Still, the castle was a hive of activity, and even now the doors were opening, both gates swinging back to allow a palanquin carried by four men to come out. It was clearly empty – they were able to jog along quickly – and Altaïr followed them to the sun-dappled harbour where they set down their burden and stood waiting, their arms folded.

Altaïr waited too. He took a seat on a low harbour wall and sat with his elbows on his knees, watching the palanquin and the waiting servants, the merchants and fishermen, the beautiful ships rocking gently in the wash, hulls knocking against the harbour wall. A group of fishermen wrestling with a huge net stopped suddenly, looked over to one of the ships and grinned. Altaïr followed their gaze to see a number of women appear in the sheer silk and chiffon of courtesans and make their way on to the harbour with self-conscious, dainty steps. The fishermen leered and some washer-women tutted as the women crossed the dock with their heads held high, knowing exactly the attention they commanded. Altaïr watched them.

Among them was Maria.

She was dressed as a courtesan. His heart lifted to see her. But what was she doing? She had escaped Shalim's clutches only to step back into danger, or so it seemed. She and the other women climbed aboard the palanquin. The servants waited until they were aboard, then picked it up and turned with it, carrying it much more slowly than before, each man bent beneath its weight, heading out of the harbour and, if Altaïr was right, towards St Hilarion Castle. Where, no doubt, Shalim was already rubbing his hands with glee.

Altaïr turned to follow, scaling the wall of a nearby building, then making his way across the roofs, jumping from one to another, tracking the palanquin, which was below him. As it approached the castle gates he waited, crouching. Then, timing his jump, he dropped on to its roof.

Thump.

The palanquin lurched as the men below adjusted to the new weight. Altaïr had gambled on them being too tyrannized even to look up – and he had been right. They merely shouldered the extra weight and walked on. And if the courtesans inside had noticed, they said nothing either, and the procession crossed safely over the castle threshold and came into a court-yard. Altaïr looked around him, seeing archers on the ramparts. Any moment now he'd be spotted. He dropped off and hid behind a low wall, watching as Maria was taken from the transport and escorted away, leaving the courtyard by a small door.

He scrambled up to the roof of an outhouse. He would have to make his way inside the long way round. But one thing he knew. Now he'd found her he wasn't going to lose her again.

45

On a wide, baking-hot balcony, Maria was ushered in to meet the owner of St Hilarion Castle. One of them, at least. Unknown to Altaïr, Shalim had a twin brother, Shahar. It was Shahar whom Altaïr had seen delivering the speech on charity, which would have answered the Assassin's question as to how a man who had spent the evening drinking and whoring could look so invigorated the next day.

Maria, on the other hand, was acquainted with both twins and, though they were identical, knew how to differentiate them. Of the two Shalim was dark-eyed and bore the looks of a man with his lifestyle; Shahar seemed the more youthful of the two. It was him she approached now. He turned to face her and lit up, smiling, as she crossed the balcony towards him, resplendent in her courtesan's outfit, fetching enough to catch any man's eye.

'I didn't expect to see you again.' He leered. 'How can I help you, little fox?'

He walked past her and back into the hall.

'I'm not here to be flattered,' snapped Maria, despite appearances to the contrary. 'I want answers.'

She stayed at his heels, and when they reached the hall, he eyed her, bemused yet lecherous. She ignored his look. She needed to hear for herself what Altaïr had told her.

'Oh?' said Shahar.

'Is it true what I have heard,' she pressed, 'that the Templars wish to use the Apple, the Piece of Eden, for ill? Not to enlighten the people, but to subdue them?'

He smiled indulgently as though explaining things to an adorable but simple-minded child. 'People are confused, Maria. They are lambs begging to be led. And that's what we offer: simple lives, free of worry.'

'But our Order was created to protect the people,' she persisted, 'not to rob them of their liberty.'

Shahar curled his lip. 'The Templars care nothing for liberty, Maria. We seek order, nothing more.'

He was walking towards her. She took a step back. 'Order? Or enslavement?'

His voice had taken on a darker tone as he replied, 'You can call it whatever you like, my dear . . .'

He reached for her, his intentions – his all-too obvious intentions – interrupted only by Altaïr bursting into the room. Shahar wheeled, exclaiming, '*Assassin!*' He grabbed Maria by the shoulders and tossed her to the floor – she landed painfully. Altaïr decided he would make the bully pay for that.

'My apologies, Shalim, I let myself in,' he said.

Shahar grinned. 'So you're looking for Shalim? I'm sure my brother would be happy to join us.'

From above there was a noise and Altaïr looked up to a gallery where Shalim was approaching, smiling. Then two guards came through the open door, ready to pounce on Maria who, standing now, whirled, snatched one guard's sword from its sheath and used it against him.

He screamed and crumpled just as she spun and, dropping to one knee, thrust again, disposing of the other. In the same moment Shalim bounded down from the gallery, landing in the middle of the hall next to his brother. Altaïr had a moment to see the two side by side, and was amazed by how close in looks they were. Next to him stood Maria, her newly acquired sword dripping with blood, shoulders heaving, the two of them against the twins. Altaïr felt his chest fill with something that was partly pride and partly something he preferred not to name. 'Two of them,' he said, 'and two of us.'

Yet again, however, Maria sprang a surprise. Instead of fighting by his side she simply made a contemptuous sound and darted through the door left open by the guards. Altaïr had a moment to wonder whether he should follow, and then the brothers were upon him and he was fighting for his life against the two skilled swordsmen.

The fight was long and brutal and the twins began confidently, sure that they would swiftly overwhelm the Assassin. After all, there were two of them and both were adept with a blade; rightly, they expected to wear him down. But Altaïr was fighting with a bellyful of anger and frustration. He no longer knew who was friend and who foe. He had been betrayed – men who were supposed to be friends had turned out to be enemies. Those he thought might become friends – or more than friends – had spurned the hand of friendship he offered to them. He knew only that he was fighting a war in which more was at stake than he knew, involving powers and ideologies he had yet to understand. He had to keep fighting, to keep struggling, until he reached the end.

And when the slain bodies of the twins at last lay at his feet, their arms and legs at twisted, wrong angles, their dead eyes wide, he took no pleasure or gratification in his victory. He merely shook the blood from his sword, sheathed it and made his way to the balcony. From behind him he heard more guards arriving as he stood on the balustrade with his arms outstretched. Below him was a cart and he dropped into it, then disappeared into the city.

Later, when he returned to the safe-house, Markos was there to meet him, eager to hear the tale of the brothers' demise. Around them, members of the Resistance were embracing, overjoyed at the news. At last the Resistance could regain control of Kyrenia. And if Kyrenia, then surely there was hope for the whole island.

Markos beamed at him. 'It's happening, Altaïr. The ports are emptying of Templar ships. Kyrenia will be free. Maybe all of Cyprus.'

Altaïr smiled, encouraged by the joy in Markos's eyes. 'Stay cautious,' he advised.

He remembered that he was still no closer to discovering the location of the archive. The Templars' departure was telling him something. 'They wouldn't leave their archive undefended,' he said, 'so it cannot be here.'

Markos considered. 'Most of the ships that left here were headed back to Limassol. Could it be there?'

Altaïr nodded. 'Thank you, Markos. You have served the country well.'

'God speed, Altaïr.'

Later, Altaïr found his way to a ship that would return him to Limassol. There, he hoped to unravel the mystery of the Templars' intentions, to root out the truth about Alexander.

He pondered on it during the crossing, writing in his journal,

I remember my moment of weakness, my confidence shaken by Al Mualim's words. He, who had been like a father, was revealed to be my greatest enemy. Just the briefest flicker of doubt was all he needed to creep into my mind with this device. But I vanquished his phantoms, restored my self-confidence, and sent him from this world.

46

Limassol was much as he'd had left it, rife with Templar men and soldiers, a resentful populace carrying on as normal, discontent on their faces as they continued with their business.

Wasting no time, Altaïr located the new Resistance safe-house, a disused warehouse, and entered it, determined to confront Alexander with what he had learned in the conversation he'd overheard between Bouchart and Shalim. But when he entered the building it was Alexander who reacted to him.

'Stay back, traitor. You have betrayed the Resistance and sold out our cause. Have you been working with Bouchart all this time?'

Altaïr had been prepared for a confrontation with Alexander, perhaps even to meet him in combat, but the sight of the Resistance man in such a state calmed him, made him think that he had misinterpreted what he had seen. All the same he stayed cautious.

'I was about to ask the same of you, Alexander. I overheard Bouchart mention your name. He delivered a package to you, did he not?'

With narrowed eyes, Alexander nodded. The furniture in the safe-house was sparse but there was a low table nearby and on it the small sack Altaïr had seen handed to Shalim by Bouchart in Kyrenia.

'Yes,' said Alexander, 'the head of poor Barnabas in a burlap sack.'

Altaïr walked to it. He pulled the drawstring on the sack and the material fell away to reveal a decapitated head, but . . .

'This was not the man who met me in Kyrenia,' said Altaïr, staring sadly at the severed head. It had begun to discolour and emitted a powerful, unpleasant smell. The eyes were half closed, the mouth hanging slightly open, the tongue visible inside.

'What?' said Alexander.

'The real Barnabas had been murdered before I arrived, replaced by a Templar agent who did much damage before he vanished,' said Altaïr.

'God help us. The Templars have been equally brutal here, with captains roaming the market, the ports and Cathedral Square arresting anyone they see fit.'

'Don't despair,' said Altaïr. 'Kyrenia has already shaken off the Templars. We will expel them from Limassol, too.'

'You must be careful. Templar propaganda has turned some of my men against you, and most others are wary.'

'Thank you for the warning.'

Altaïr conducted a fruitless search of the city for Bouchart, but when he returned to share the bad news with Alexander he found the safe-house empty except for a note. It sat on the table and Altaïr picked it up. Alexander wanted to meet him in the courtyard of the castle. So the note said, anyway.

Altaïr thought. Had he ever seen Alexander's script? He didn't think so. Anyway, the Bureau man might have been coerced into writing a note.

As he made his way to the rendezvous, all his instincts told him that this could be a trap, and it was with a sinking heart that he came across a body in the courtyard where they were due to meet.

No, he thought.

Straight away he looked around him. The empty ramparts surrounding the courtyard stared emptily back. Indeed, the whole area was far quieter than he would have expected. He knelt to the body, his fears realized as he turned it over to see Alexander's lifeless eyes staring back at him.

Then from above him came a voice and he straightened, spinning to see a figure on the ramparts overlooking the courtyard. Dazzled by the sun he put up a hand to shield his eyes, still unable to make out the face of the man standing there. Was it Bouchart? Whoever it was, he wore the red cross of the Crusader and stood with his legs slightly apart, his hands on his hips, every inch of him the conquering hero.

The knight pointed at Alexander's corpse. His voice was mocking: 'A friend of yours?'

Altaïr hoped soon to make the knight pay for that scorn. Now the man shifted slightly and Altaïr was at last able to see him clearly. It was the spy. The one who had called himself Barnabas in Kyrenia – who was probably responsible for killing the real Barnabas. Another good man dead. Altaïr hoped to make him pay for that too. His fists clenched and the muscles in his jaw jumped. For the time being, though, the spy had him at a disadvantage.

'You,' he called up to him. 'I didn't catch your name.'

'What did I tell you in Kyrenia?' chuckled the knight – the spy. 'Barnabas, wasn't it?'

Suddenly a great shout went up and Altaïr turned to see a group of citizens enter the courtyard. He had been set up. The spy had put out the word against him. Now he was being framed for the murder of Alexander, the angry mob having been timed to arrive at exactly the right moment. It was a trap and he had walked straight into it, even though instinct had told him to exercise caution.

Once again he cursed himself. He looked around. The sandstone walls loomed over him. A set of steps led to the ramparts but there at the top stood the spy, grinning from ear to ear, enjoying the show that was about to start in earnest as the citizens came running towards Altaïr, their blood up, the need for revenge and justice burning in their eyes.

'There's the traitor!'

'String him up!'

'You'll pay for your crimes!'

Altaïr stood his ground. His first impulse was to reach for his sword but no: he could not kill any citizen. To do so would be to destroy any faith they had in the Resistance or the Assassins. All he could do was protest his innocence. But they were not to be reasoned with. Desperately he searched for the answer.

And found it.

The Apple.

It was as though it was calling to him. Suddenly he was aware of it in the pack at his back and he brought it out now, holding it so that it was facing towards the crowd.

He had no idea what he was trying to do with it and was not sure what would happen. He sensed that the Apple would obey his commands; that it would understand his intent. But it was just a sense. A feeling. An instinct.

And it did. It throbbed and glowed in his hands. It gave out a strange diaphanous light that seemed to settle around the crowd, which was immediately pacified, frozen to the spot. Altaïr saw the Templar spy recoil with shock. Briefly he felt all-powerful, and in that moment he recognized not only the seductive allure of the Apple and the godlike strength it bestowed, but the terrible danger it posed – in the hands of those who would use it for ill, of course, but also with him.

Even he was not immune to its temptation. He used it now, but he pledged to himself that he would never use it again, not for these purposes anyway.

Then he was addressing the crowd.

'Armand Bouchart is the man responsible for your misery,' he called. 'He hired this man to poison the Resistance against itself. Go from this place and rally your men. Cyprus will be yours once again.'

For a moment or so he wondered whether or not it had worked. When he lowered the Apple, would the angry crowd simply resume their lynching? But lower it he did, and the crowd did not move upon him. His words had swayed them. His words had persuaded them. Without further ceremony, they turned and moved out of the courtyard, leaving as quickly as they had arrived, but subdued, penitent even.

Once more the courtyard was empty and, for a few heartbeats, Altaïr looked at the Apple in his hand, watched it fade, feeling in awe of it, frightened by it, attracted to it. Then he tucked it safely away as the spy said, 'Quite a toy you have there. Mind if I borrow it?'

Altaïr knew one thing: that the Templar would have to take the Apple from his dead body. He drew his blade ready for combat as the Templar smiled, anticipating the fight ahead, about to climb down from the ramparts when . . .

He stopped.

And the smile slid from his face like dripping oil.

Protruding from his chest was a blade. Blood flowered at his white tunic, mingling with the red of the cross he wore. He looked down at himself, confused, as if wondering how the weapon had got there. Below him in the courtyard Altaïr was wondering the same thing. Then the Templar was swaying and Altaïr saw a figure behind him. A figure he recognized: Maria.

She smiled, shoved the spy forward from the courtyard wall and let him tumble heavily to the ground below. Standing there, her sword dripping blood, she grinned at Altaïr, shook it, then replaced it in her sheath.

'So,' she said, 'you had the Apple all along.'

He nodded. 'And now you see what kind of a weapon it could be in the wrong hands.'

'I don't know if I'd call yours the right hands.'

'No. Quite right. I will destroy it . . . or hide it. Until I can find the archive, I can't say.'

'Well, look no further,' she said. 'You're standing on it.'

47

Just then there was great shout at the entranceway to the courtyard and a group of Templar soldiers rushed in, eyes dangerous slits behind their visors.

From above Maria called, 'This way – quickly!' She turned and darted along the ramparts to a door. Altaïr was about to follow when the three men were upon him and he cursed, meeting them with a chiming of steel, losing sight of Maria yet again.

They were skilled and had trained hard – they had the neck muscles to prove it – but even three knights were no match for the Assassin, who danced around them nimbly, cutting into them until all three lay dead at his feet.

He cast a look upwards. The ramparts were empty. Just the dead body of the Templar spy at the top of the steps and no sign of Maria. He bounded up the steps, pausing just a moment to look down at the dead man. If the job of an agent was to disrupt the enemy then this one had done his job well; he had almost turned the people against the Resistance, delivering them into the hands of the Templars – who planned not to enlighten but to subjugate and control them.

Altaïr raced on, reaching the door at the end. This, then, was the entrance to the building housing the archive. He stepped inside.

The door slammed behind him. He found himself on a walkway that ran along the wall of a cavernous shaft, leading downwards. Torches on the walls gave out a meagre light, casting dancing shadows on the Templar crosses that decorated the walls. It was quiet.

No, not quite.

From somewhere far below he could hear shouting. Guards, perhaps, alerted to the presence of . . . Maria? Such a free spirit could never align herself with Templar ideologies. She was a traitor now. She had come over to the way of the Assassin: she had slain a Templar and shown an Assassin the location of the archive. They would kill her on the spot. Although, of course, from what he had seen of her in combat that might be easier said than done.

He began to descend, running down the dark steps, occasionally leaping gaps in the crumbling stonework, until he reached a chamber with a sandy floor. Arriving to meet him were three guards, and he disposed of one with a throwing knife straight away, wrongfooted a second and rammed his sword into the man's neck. He thrust the body into the third, who fell, and as they writhed on the ground, Altaïr finished them. Probing deeper, he heard rushing water, and found himself on a bridge passing between two waterfalls. The sound was enough to smother the noise of his arrival from the two guards at the opposite end of the bridge. He felled them both with two slashes of his blade.

He left them, continuing down and into the bowels of . . . the library. Now he saw shelves of books, rooms full of them. This was it. He was here. What he'd expected to see he wasn't sure, but there were fewer book and artefacts than he had imagined. Did this really constitute the famous archive he'd heard about?

But he had no time to stop and inspect his find. He could hear voices, the anvil sound of sword strikes: two combatants, one of whom was unmistakably female.

Ahead of him a large arch was decorated with the Templar cross at its apex. He went to it and entered a vast chamber, with a ceremonial area at its centre ringed by intricate stone pillars. There, in the middle, were Bouchart and Maria, fighting. She was holding the Templar leader off, but only just, and even as Altaïr entered the chamber he struck her and she tumbled, yelling in pain, to the stone.

Bouchart gave her an indifferent look, already turning to face Altaïr, who had made no sound when he entered the chamber.

'Witless Emperor Comnenus,' announced the Templar, contemptuous of the erstwhile Cypriot leader, 'he was a fool, but he was *our* fool. For almost a decade we operated without interference on this island. Our archive was the best-kept secret on Cyprus.

Unfortunately, even the best-laid plans were not immune to Isaac's idiocy.'

For almost a decade, thought Altaïr. But then . . . He took a step forward, looking from Bouchart to Maria. 'He angered King Richard and brought the English a little too close for comfort. Is that it?'

When Bouchart made no move to stop him, he crossed the floor and bent to Maria. He held her face, looking for signs of life.

Bouchart was talking, enjoying the sound of his own voice. 'Fortunately we were able to convince Richard to sell the island to us. It was the only way to divert his attention.'

Her eyes fluttered. She groaned. *Alive*. Breathing a sigh of relief, Altaïr laid her head gently on the stone and straightened to face Bouchart, who had been watching them with an indulgent smile.

'Purchasing what you already controlled . . .' prompted Altaïr. He understood now. The Templars had purchased Cyprus from King Richard to stop their archive being discovered. Little wonder that they had been aggressive in their pursuit of him when he arrived on the island.

Bouchart confirmed that he was correct. 'And look where that has got us. Ever since you arrived and stuck your nose into too many dark corners, the archive hasn't been safe.'

'I wish I could say I'm sorry. But I tend to get what

I want,' replied Altaïr, sounding confident but knowing something wasn't quite right.

Sure enough, Bouchart was grinning. 'Oh, not this time, Assassin. Not now. Our little detour to Kyrenia gave us just enough time to dismantle the archive and move it.'

Of course. It wasn't a meagre archive he'd been seeing on his way down. It was the unwanted *remnants* of one. They'd distracted him with the business in Kyrenia and used the opportunity to move it.

'You weren't shipping artefacts *to* Cyprus, you were shipping them out,' said Altaïr, as it all became clear.

'Exactly,' said Bouchart, with a complimentary nod. 'But not everything has to go . . . I think we'll leave you here.'

Bouchart leaped forward, jabbing with his sword, and Altair deflected. Bouchart was ready and parried, sustaining his attack, and Altaïr was forced on to the back foot, defending a series of thrusts and slashes. Bouchart was skilled, that was certain. He was fast as well, relying more on grace and footwork than the brute strength most Crusaders brought to a sword-fight. But he came forward expecting to win and to win quickly. His desperation to vanquish the Assassin rendered him oblivious to the physical demands of the fight, so that Altaïr defended, let him come, soaked up his attacks, every now and then offering a short attack of his own, opening wounds. A gash here, a nick there. Blood began to leak from beneath Bouchart's chainmail, which hung heavy on him.

As Altaïr fought, he thought of Maria and of those who had died on the orders of the Templar, but he stopped those memories turning into the desire for vengeance. Instead he let them give him resolve. The smile had fallen from Bouchart's face and, as Altaïr remained silent, the Templar Grand Master was grunting with the exertion – that and frustration. His sword swings were less co-ordinated and failed to meet their target. Sweat and blood poured from him. His teeth were bared.

And Altaïr opened more wounds, cutting him on the forehead so that blood was gushing into his eyes and he was wiping his gauntlet across his face to clear it away. Now Bouchart could barely lift the sword and was bent over, his legs rubbery and his shoulders heaving as he fought for breath, squinting through a mask of blood to find the Assassin, seeing only shadows and shapes. He was a defeated man now. Which meant he was a dead man.

Altaïr didn't toy with him. He waited until the danger was over. Until he was sure that Bouchart's weakness was not feigned.

Then he ran him through.

Bouchart dropped to the ground and Altaïr knelt beside him. The Templar looked at him and Altaïr saw respect in his eyes.

'Ah. You are a . . . a credit to your Creed,' he gasped.

'And you have strayed from yours.'

'Not strayed . . . expanded. The world is more complicated than most dare admit. And if you, Assassin . . . if you knew more than how to murder, you might understand this.'

Altaïr frowned. 'Save your lecture on virtue for yourself. And die knowing that I will never let the Apple, the Piece of Eden, fall into any hands but my own.'

As he spoke of it, he felt it warm against his back, as though it had awoken.

Bouchart smiled ironically. 'Keep it close, Altair. You will come to the same conclusions we did . . . in time . . .'

He died. Altaïr reached to close his eyes, just as the building shook and he was showered with falling debris. Cannon fire. The Templars were shelling the archive. It made perfect sense. They wanted to leave nothing behind.

He scrambled over to Maria and pulled her to her feet. For a moment or so they looked into one another's eyes, some unspoken feeling passing between them. Then she tugged at his arm and was leading him out of the grand chamber just as it was shaken by more cannon fire. Altaïr turned in time to see two of the beautiful pillars crumple and fall, great sections of stone smashing to the floor. Then he was following

Maria as she ran, taking the steps two at a time as they climbed back up the shaft to the sunken archive. It was rocked by another explosion, and masonry smashed into the walkway, but they kept running, kept dodging until they reached the exit.

The steps had fallen away so Altaïr climbed, dragging Maria up behind him to a platform. They pushed their way out into the day as the shelling intensified and the building seemed to fall in on itself, forcing them to jump clear. And there they stayed for some time, gulping clean air, glad to be alive.

Later, when the Templar ships had departed, taking the last of the precious archive with them, Altaïr and Maria were walking in the dying light in Limassol port, both lost in thought.

'Everything I worked for in the Holy Land, I no longer want,' said Maria, after a long pause. 'And everything I gave up to join the Templars ... I wonder where all that went, and if I should try to find it again.'

'Will you return to England?' asked Altaïr.

'No ... I'm so far from home already, I'll continue east. To India, perhaps. Or until I fall off the far edge of the world ... And you?'

Altaïr thought, enjoying the closeness they shared. 'For a long time under Al Mualim, I thought my life had reached its limit, and that my sole duty was to show others the same precipice I had discovered.'

'I felt the same once,' she agreed.

From his pack he took the Apple and held it up for inspection. 'As terrible as this artefact is, it contains wonders . . . I would like to understand it as best I can.'

'You tread a thin line, Altaïr.'

He nodded slowly. 'I know. But I have been ruined by curiosity, Maria. I want to meet the best minds, explore the libraries of the world, and learn all the secrets of nature and the universe.'

'All in one lifetime? It's a little ambitious . . .'

He chuckled. 'Who can say? It could be that one life is just enough.'

'Maybe. And where will you go first?'

He looked at her, smiling, knowing only that he wanted her with him for the rest of his journey. 'East . . .' he said.

Part Four

48

15 July 1257

Maffeo has this habit of looking at me strangely some-times. It's as though he believes I'm not quite furnishing him with all the necessary information. And he has done this several times during our storytelling sessions. Whether watching the world go by in the busy market of Masyaf, enjoying the cool draughts in the catacombs beneath the citadel or strolling along the ramparts, seeing birds wheel and dip across the valleys, he looks at me every now and then, as if to say, 'What is it you're *not* telling me, Niccolò?'

Well, the answer, of course, is nothing, apart from my lingering suspicion that the story will eventually involve us in some way, that I'm being told these things for a reason. Will it involve the Apple? Or perhaps his journals? Or the codex, the book into which he has distilled his most significant findings?

Even so, Maffeo fixes me with the Look.

'And?'

'And what, brother?'

'Did Altaïr and Maria go east?'

'Maffeo, Maria is the mother of Darim, the gentleman who invited us here.'

I watched as Maffeo turned his head to the sun and closed his eyes to let it warm his face as he absorbed this information. I'm sure that he was trying to reconcile the image of the Darim we knew, a man in his sixties with the weathered face to prove it, with someone who had a mother – a mother like Maria.

I let him ponder, smiling indulgently. Just as Maffeo would pester me with questions during the tale, so of course I had pestered the Master, albeit with a good deal more deference.

'Where is the Apple now?' I had asked him once. If I'm honest, I had secretly hoped that at some point he would produce it. After all, he'd spoken about it in terms of such reverence, even sounding fearful of it at times. Naturally I had hoped to see it for myself. Perhaps to understand its allure.

Sadly, this was not to be. He met my question with a series of testy noises. I should not trouble myself with thoughts of the Apple, he had warned, with a wagging finger. I should concern myself with the codex instead. For contained in those pages were the secrets of the Apple, he said, but free of the artefact's malign effects.

The codex. Yes, I had decided, it was the codex that was to prove significant in the future. Significant in *my* future, even.

But anyway: back in the here and now, I watched Maffeo mull over the fact that Darim was the son of Altaïr and Maria; that from adversarial beginnings had flourished first a respect between the pair, then attraction, friendship, love and –

'Marriage?' said Maffeo. 'She and Altaïr were wed?'

'Indeed. Some two years after the events I've described, they were wed at Limassol. The ceremony was held there as a measure of respect to the Cypriots who had offered their island as a base for the Assassins, making it a key stronghold for the Order. I believe Markos was a guest of honour, and a somewhat ironic toast was proposed to the pirates, who had inadvertently been responsible for introducing him to Altaïr and Maria. Shortly after the wedding the Assassin and his bride returned to Masyaf, where their son Darim was born.'

'Their only son?'

'No. Two years after the birth of Darim, Maria gave birth to another, Sef, a brother to Darim.'

'And what of him?'

'All in good time, brother. All in good time. Suffice to say for now that this represented a mainly peaceful and fruitful period for the Master. He talks of it little, as though it is too precious to bring out into the light, but much of it is recorded in his codex. All the time he was making new discoveries and was in receipt of fresh revelations.'

'Such as?'

'He recorded them in his journals. In there you can see not only compounds for new Assassin poisons, but for medicine too. Descriptions of achievements yet to come and catastrophes yet to happen; designs for armour and for new hidden blades, including one that fires projectiles. He mused upon the nature of faith and of humanity's beginnings, forged from chaos, order imposed not by a supreme being but by man.'

Maffeo looked shocked. '"Forged from chaos, order imposed not by a supreme being . . ."'

'The Assassin questions all fixed faith,' I said, not without a touch of pomposity. 'Even his own.'

'How so?'

'Well, the Master wrote of the contradictions and ironies of the Assassin. How they seek to bring about peace yet use violence and murder as the means to do it. How they seek to open men's minds yet require obedience to a master. The Assassin teaches the dangers of blindly believing in established faith but requires the Order's followers to follow the Creed unquestioningly.

'He wrote also of the Ones Who Came Before, the members of the first civilization, who left behind the artefacts hunted by both Templar and Assassin.'

'The Apple being one of them?'

'Exactly. A thing of immense power. Competed for by the Knights Templar. His experiences in Cyprus had shown him that the Templars, rather than trying to wrest control by the usual means, had chosen subterfuge for their strategy. Altaïr concluded that this, too, should be the way of the Assassin.

'No longer should the Order build great fortresses and conduct lavish rituals. These, he decided, were not what makes the Assassin. What makes the Assassin is his adherence to the Creed. That originally espoused by Al Mualim, ironically enough. An ideology that challenged established doctrines. One that encouraged acolytes to reach beyond themselves and make the impossible possible. It was these principles that Altaïr developed and took with him in the years he spent travelling the Holy Land, stabilizing the Order and instilling in it the values he had learned as an Assassin. Only in Constantinople did his attempts to promote the way of the Assassin stumble. There, in 1204, great riots were taking place as the people rose up against the Byzantine emperor Alexius, and not long after that the Crusaders broke through and began a sack of the city. In the midst of such ongoing tumult, Altaïr was unable to carry out his plans and retreated. It became one of his few failures during that era.

'Funny, when he told me that, he gave me an odd look.'

'Because our home is in Constantinople?'

'Possibly. I shall have to give the matter thought at a later date. It may well be that our hailing from Constantinople and his attempt to establish a guild there are not unrelated . . .'

'His only failure, you say?'

'Indeed. In all other ways, Altaïr did more to promote the Order than almost any leader before him. It was only the ascendancy of Genghis Khan that prevented him continuing his work.'

'How so?'

'Some forty years ago, Altaïr wrote of it in his codex. How a dark tide was rising to the east. An army of such size and power that all the land was made quick with worry.'

'He was talking about the Mongol Empire?' asked Maffeo. 'The rise of Genghis Khan?'

'Exactly,' I said. 'Darim was in his early twenties and an accomplished bowman, and so it was that Altaïr took him and Maria and left Masyaf.'

'To confront Khan?'

'Altaïr suspected that Genghis Khan's progress might have been helped by another artefact, similar to the Apple. Perhaps the Sword. He needed to establish whether this was the case, as well as to stop Khan's inexorable march.'

'How was Masyaf left?'

'Altaïr put Malik in charge in his place. He left Sef behind also, to help take care of affairs. Sef had a wife and two young daughters by then, Darim did not, and they were gone for a long time.'

'How long?'

'He was absent for *ten years*, brother, and when he

returned to Masyaf everything there had changed. Nothing would ever be the same again. Do you want to hear about it?'

'Please continue.'

49

From a distance all looked well with Masyaf. None of them – not Altaïr, Maria or Darim – had any idea of what was to come.

Altaïr and Maria rode a little ahead, side by side, as was their preference, happy to be with one another and pleased to be within sight of home, each undulating with the slow, steady rhythm of their horses. Both rode high and proud in the saddle despite the long, arduous journey. They might have been advancing in years – both were in their mid-sixties – but it would not do to be seen slouching. Nevertheless they came slowly: their mounts were chosen for their strength and stamina, not speed, and tethered to each was an ass, laden with supplies.

Behind them came Darim, who had inherited the bright, dancing eyes of his mother, his father's colouring and bone structure, and the impulsiveness of both. He would have liked to gallop ahead and climb the slopes of the village to the citadel to announce his parents' return, but instead trotted meekly behind, respecting his father's wishes for a modest home-coming. Every now and then he swatted the flies from his face with his crop and thought that a gallop would have been the most effective way to rid himself of them. He wondered if they were being watched from the spires of the fortress, from its defensive tower.

Passing the stables, they went through the wooden gates and into the market, finding it unchanged. They came into the village, where children rushed excitedly around them calling for treats – children too young to know the Master. Older villagers recognized him, though, and Altaïr noticed them watching the party carefully, not with welcome but wariness. Faces were turned away when he tried to catch their eye. Anxiety bit into his gut.

Now a figure he knew was approaching them, meeting them at the bottom of the slopes to the citadel. Swami. An apprentice when he'd left, one of those who was too fond of combat, not enough of learning. He had collected a scar in the intervening ten years and it wrinkled when he smiled, a broad grin that went nowhere near his eyes. Perhaps he was already thinking of the teachings he would have to endure with Altaïr, now that he had returned.

But endure them he would, thought Altaïr, his gaze going past Swami to the castle, where a vast flag bearing the mark of the Assassins fluttered in the breeze. He had decreed that the flag be removed: the Assassins were disposing of such empty emblems. But Malik had evidently decided it should fly. He was another who would endure some teaching in the time ahead.

'Altaïr,' said Swami, with a bow of the head, and Altaïr decided to ignore the man's failure to address him by his correct title. For the time being at least. 'How pleasant it is to see you. I trust your travels proved fruitful.'

'I sent messages,' said Altaïr, leaning forward in his saddle. Darim drew up on the other side of him so that the three formed a line, looking down at Swami. 'Was the Order not told of my progress?'

Swami smiled obsequiously. 'Of course, of course. I asked merely out of courtesy.'

'I expected to be met by Rauf,' said Altaïr. 'He is most accustomed to meeting my needs.'

'Ah, poor Rauf.' Swami peered at the ground reflectively.

'Is something wrong?'

'Rauf, I'm afraid is dead of the fever these past few years.'

'Why was I not informed?'

At this Swami merely shrugged. An insolent shrug, as though he neither knew nor cared.

Altaïr pursed his lips, deciding that somebody had some explaining to do, even if it wasn't to be this cur. 'Then let us move on. I trust our quarters are prepared?'

Swami bowed his head again. 'I'm afraid not, Altaïr. Until such time as you can be accommodated I have been asked to direct you to a residence on the western side of the fortress.'

Altaïr looked first at Darim, who was frowning, then at Maria, who gazed at him with eyes that said, *Beware*. Something was not right.

'Very well,' said Altaïr, cautiously, and they dismounted. Swami gestured to some servant boys, who came forward to take the horses, and they began their ascent to the citadel gates. There the guards inclined their heads quickly, as though, like the villagers, they were keen to avoid Altaïr's eye, but instead of proceeding up the barbican, Swami led them around the outside of the inner curtain. Altaïr regarded the walls of the citadel stretching high above them, wanting to see the heart of the Order, feeling irritation build – but some instinct told him to bide his time. When they reached the residence it was a low building sunk into the stone with a short arch at its doorway and stairs leading down to a vestibule. The furniture was sparse and there were no staff to greet them. Altaïr was used to modest accommodation – he demanded it, in fact – but here in Masyaf, as the Assassin Master, he expected his accommodation to be in the Master's tower or equivalent.

Bristling, he turned, about to remonstrate with Swami, who stood in the vestibule with the same obsequious grin on his face, when Maria grabbed his arm and squeezed it, stopping him.

'Where is Sef?' she asked Swami. She was smiling pleasantly, though Altaïr knew that she loathed Swami. Loathed him with every fibre in her body. 'I would like Sef sent here at once, please.'

Swami looked pained. 'I regret that Sef is not here. He has had to travel to Alamut.'

'His family?'

'Are accompanying him.'

Maria shot a look of concern to Altaïr.

'What business did my brother have in Alamut?' snapped Darim, even more put out then his parents by the scant quarters.

'Alas, I do not know,' oozed Swami.

Altaïr took a deep breath and approached Swami. The messenger's scar no longer crinkled as the sycophantic smile slid from his face. Perhaps he was suddenly reminded that this was Altaïr, the Master, whose skill in battle was matched only by his fierceness in the classroom.

'Inform Malik *at once* that I wish to see him,' growled Altaïr. 'Tell him he has some explaining to do.'

Swami swallowed, wringing his hands a little theatrically. 'Malik is in prison, Master.'

Altaïr started. '*In prison?* Why?'

'I'm not at liberty to say, Master. A meeting of the council has been called for tomorrow morning.'

'The what?'

'With Malik imprisoned, a council was formed to

oversee the Order, in accordance with the statutes of the Brotherhood.'

This was true, but even so, Altaïr darkened. 'With *who* as its chairman?'

'Abbas,' replied Swami.

Altaïr looked at Maria, whose eyes showed real concern now. She reached to take his arm.

'And when do I meet this council?' asked Altaïr. His voice was calm, belying the storm in his belly.

'Tomorrow the council would like to hear the tale of your journey and apprise you of events at the Order.'

'And after that the council shall be dissolved,' said Altaïr, firmly. 'Tell your council we shall see them at sunrise. Tell them to consult the statutes. The Master has returned and wishes to resume leadership.'

Swami bowed and left.

The family waited until he had gone before letting their true feelings show, when Altaïr turned to Darim and with urgency in his voice told him, 'Ride to Alamut,' he told him. 'Bring Sef back here. He's needed at once.'

50

The following day, Altaïr and Maria were about to make their way from their residence to the main tower when they were intercepted by Swami, who insisted on leading them through the barbican himself. As they skirted the wall Altaïr wondered why he couldn't hear the usual noise of swordplay and training from the other side. As they came into the courtyard he got his answer.

It was because there *was* no swordplay or training. Where once the inner areas of the citadel had hummed with activity and life, echoing to the metallic chime of sword strikes, the shouts and curses of the instructors, now it lay almost deserted. He looked around him, at the towers overlooking them, seeing black windows. Guards on the ramparts stared dispassionately down at them. The place of enlightenment and training – the crucible of Assassin knowledge he had left – had all but disappeared. Altair's mood darkened further as he was about to make his way to the main tower but Swami directed him instead to the steps that led up to the defence room, then into the main hall.

There, the council was gathered. Ten men were

seated on opposite sides of a table with Abbas at their head, a pair of empty chairs for Altaïr and Maria: wooden, high-backed chairs. They took their seats and, for the first time since entering the room, Altaïr looked at Abbas, his old antagonist. He saw something in him other than weakness and resentment. He saw a rival. And for the first time since the night that Ahmad had come to his quarters and taken his own life, Altaïr no longer pitied Abbas.

Altaïr looked around the rest of the table. Just as he'd thought, the new council was made up of the most weak-minded and conniving members of the Order. Those Altaïr would have preferred to be cast out. All had joined this council, it seemed, or been recruited to it by Abbas. Characteristic of them was Farim, Swami's father, who watched him from beneath hooded lids, his chin tucked into this chest. His ample chest. They had got fat, thought Altaïr, scornfully.

'Welcome, Altaïr,' said Abbas. 'I'm sure I speak for us all when I say that I am looking forward to hearing of your exploits in the east.'

Maria leaned forward to address him. 'Before we say anything of our travels, we would like some answers, please, Abbas. We left Masyaf in good order. It seems that standards have been allowed to slip.'

'*We* left Masyaf in good order?' smiled Abbas, though he had not looked at Maria. He hadn't taken his gaze from Altaïr. The two were staring across the table at each other with open hostility. 'When you left the Brotherhood I seem to recall there being only one Master. Now it appears we had two.'

'Be careful your insolence does not cost you dear, Abbas,' warned Maria.

'*My* insolence?' laughed Abbas. 'Altaïr, please tell the infidel that from now on she may not speak unless directly addressed by a member of the council.'

With a shout of anger, Altaïr rose from his chair, which skittered back and tumbled on the stone. His hand was on the hilt of his sword but two guards came forward, their swords drawn.

'Guards, take his weapon,' commanded Abbas. 'You will be more comfortable without it, Altaïr. Are you wearing your blade?'

Altaïr stretched out his arms as a guard stepped forward to take his sword. His sleeves fell away to reveal no hidden blade.

'Now we can begin,' said Abbas. 'Please do not waste our time further. Update us on your quest to neutralize Khan.'

'Only once you have told me what has happened to Malik,' growled Altair.

Abbas shrugged and raised his eyebrows as if to say they were at an impasse, and of course they were, neither man willing to concede, it seemed. With a grunt of exasperation, Altaïr began his story, rather than prolong the stand-off. He related his journeys to Persia,

India and Mongolia, where he, Maria and Darim had liaised with the Assassin Qulan Gal, and told of how they had travelled to the Xia province nearby to Xing-ging, which was besieged by the Mongolian Army, the spread of Khan's empire inexorable. There, he said, Altaïr and Qulan Gal had planned to infiltrate the Mongolian camp. It was said that Khan was there, too.

'Darim found a vantage point not far from the camp and, armed with his bow, would watch over Qulan Gal and me as we made our way through the tents. It was heavily guarded and we relied on him to dispose of any guards we alerted or who looked as though they might raise the alarm.' Altaïr gazed around the table with a challenging stare. 'And he performed this duty admirably.'

'Like father, like son,' said Abbas, with more than a hint of a sneer in his voice.

'Perhaps not,' said Altaïr, evenly. 'For in the event it was I who was responsible for almost alerting the Mongolians to our presence.'

'Ah,' said Abbas. 'He is not infallible.'

'Nobody is, Abbas,' replied Altaïr, 'least of all me, and I allowed an enemy soldier to come up on me. He wounded me before Qulan Gal was able to kill him.'

'Getting old, Altaïr?' jeered Abbas.

'Everybody is, Abbas,' replied Altaïr. 'And I would have been dead if Qulan Gal had not managed to take me from the camp and bring me to safety. His actions saved my life.' He looked carefully at Abbas. 'Qulan Gal returned to the camp. First he formulated a plan with Darim to flush Khan from his tent. Realizing the danger, Khan tried to escape on horseback, but he was brought down by Qulan Gal. Khan was finished with a shot from Darim.'

'His skills as a bowman are beyond doubt,' smiled Abbas. 'I gather you have sent him away, perhaps to Alamut?'

Altaïr blinked. Abbas knew everything, it seemed. 'He has indeed left the citadel on my orders. Whether to Alamut or not, I will not say.'

'To see Sef at Alamut, perhaps?' pressed Abbas. He addressed Swami. 'You told them Sef was there, I trust?'

'As instructed, Master,' replied Swami.

Altaïr felt something worse than worry in his gut now. Something that might have been fear. He felt it from Maria, too: her face was drawn and anxious. 'Say what you have to say, Abbas,' he said.

'Or what, Altaïr?'

'Or my first task when I resume leadership will be to have you thrown in the dungeon.'

'There to join Malik, maybe?'

'I doubt that Malik belongs in prison,' snapped Altaïr. 'Of what crime is he accused?'

'A murder.' Abbas smirked.

It was as though the word thumped on to the table.

'Murder of whom?' asked Maria.

And the reply when it came sounded as though it was given from far, far away.

'Sef. Malik murdered your son.'

Maria's head dropped into her hands.

'No!' Altaïr heard someone say, then realized his own voice had spoken.

'I am sorry, Altaïr,' said Abbas, speaking as though he was reciting something from memory. 'I am sorry that you have returned to hear this most tragic news, and may I say that I speak for all of those assembled when I extend my sympathy to you and your family. But until certain matters are resolved it will not be possible for you to resume leadership of the Order.'

Altaïr was still trying to unravel the jumble of emotion in his head, aware of Maria beside him, sobbing.

'What?' he said. Then louder: '*What?*'

'You remain compromised at this point,' said Abbas, 'so I have taken the decision that control of the Order remains with the council.'

Altaïr shook with fury. '*I* am the Master of this Order, Abbas. I demand that leadership is returned to me, in line with the statutes of the Brotherhood. They *decree* it be returned to me.' He was shouting now.

'They do not.' Abbas smiled. 'Not any more.'

51

Later, Altaïr and Maria sat in their residence, huddled together on a stone bench, silent in the near dark. They had spent years sleeping in deserts but had never felt so isolated and alone as they did at that moment. They grieved at their lowly circumstances; they grieved that Masyaf had become neglected in their absence; they fretted for Sef's family and Darim.

But most of all they grieved for Sef.

He had been stabbed to death in his bed, they said, just two weeks ago; there had been no time to send a message to Altaïr. The knife was discovered in Malik's quarters. He had been heard arguing with Sef earlier that day by an Assassin. The name of the Assassin who had heard the argument, Altaïr had yet to learn, but whoever it was had reported hearing Sef and Malik arguing over the leadership of the Order, with Malik claiming that he intended to keep it once Altaïr returned.

'It was news of your return that sparked the disagreement, it would seem,' Abbas had gloated, revelling in Altaïr's ashen look, the quiet weeping of Maria.

Sef had been heard threatening to reveal Malik's

plans to Altaïr so Malik had killed him. That was the theory.

Beside him, her head tucked into his chest and her legs pulled up, Maria sobbed still. Altaïr smoothed her hair and rocked her until she quietened. Then he watched the shadows cast by the firelight flickering and dancing on the yellow stone wall, listening to the crickets from outside, the occasional crunch of guards' footsteps.

A short while later Maria awoke with a jump. He started too – he had been falling asleep himself, lulled by the leaping flames. She sat up, shivering, and pulled her blanket tight round herself. 'What are we going to do, my love?' she asked.

'Malik,' he said simply. He was staring at the wall with sightless eyes and spoke as though he hadn't heard the question.

'What of him?'

'When we were younger. The assignment in the Temple Mount. My actions caused him great pain.'

'But you learned,' she said. 'And Malik knew that. From that day a new Altaïr was born, who led the Order into greatness.'

Altaïr made a disbelieving sound. 'Greatness? Really?'

'Not *now*, my love,' she said. 'Maybe not now but you can restore it to how it was before all of this. You are the only one who can do it. Not Abbas.' She said his name as though she had tasted something especially unpleasant. 'Not some *council*. You. Altaïr. The Altaïr I've watched serve the Order for more than thirty years. The Altaïr who was born on that day.'

'It cost Malik his brother,' said Altaïr. 'His arm too.'

'He forgave you, and has served as your trusted lieutenant ever since the defeat of Al Mualim.'

'What if it was a façade?' said Altaïr, voice low. He could see his own shadow on the wall, dark and foreboding.

She jerked away from him. 'What are you saying?'

'Perhaps Malik has nurtured a hatred of me all these years,' he said. 'Perhaps Malik has secretly coveted the leadership and Sef discovered that.'

'Yes, and perhaps I'll grow wings in the night and fly,' said Maria. 'Who do you think *really* nurses a hatred for you, Altaïr? It's not Malik. It's Abbas.'

'The knife was found in Malik's bed,' said Altaïr.

'Put there, of course, to implicate him, either by Abbas or by someone in his thrall. I wouldn't be at all surprised if Swami was the man responsible for it. And what of this Assassin who heard Malik and Sef arguing? When is he to be produced? When we see him, do you think we'll discover that he's an ally of Abbas? Perhaps the son of another council member? And what of poor Rauf? I wonder if he really died of the fever. Shame on you for doubting Malik when all of this is so *obviously* the work of Abbas.'

'Shame on me?' he rounded on her, and she pulled

away. Outside, the crickets stopped their noise as though to hear them argue. 'Shame on me for doubting Malik? Do I not have past experience of those I love turning against me, and for reasons far more fragile than Malik has? Abbas I loved as a brother and I tried to do right by him. Al Mualim betrayed the whole order but it was me he had taken as a son. Shame on me for being suspicious? To be trusting is my greatest downfall. Trusting in the wrong people.'

He looked hard at her and she narrowed her eyes. 'You must destroy the Apple, Altaïr,' she said. 'It's twisting your mind. It is one thing to have a mind that is open. It is quite another to have one so open that the birds can shit into it.'

He looked at her. 'I'm not sure that that's how I would have put it,' he said, a sad smile forming.

'Perhaps not, but even so.'

'I need to find out, Maria,' he said. 'I need to know for sure.'

He was aware that they were being watched, but he was an Assassin and he knew Masyaf better than anyone, so it was not difficult for him to leave the residence, make his way up the wall of the inner curtain and squat in the shadows of the ramparts until the guards had moved past. He controlled his breathing. He was still quick and agile. He could still scale walls. But . . .

Perhaps not with the same ease he once had. He

would do well to remember that. The wound he'd received in Genghis Khan's camp had slowed him down too. It would be foolish to overestimate his own abilities and find himself in trouble because of it, flat on his back like a dying cockroach, hearing guards approach because he'd mistimed a jump. He rested a little before continuing along the ramparts, making his way from the western side of the citadel to the south tower complex. Staying clear of guards along the way, he came to the tower then climbed down to the ground. He moved to the grain stores, where he located a flight of stone steps that led to a series of vaulted tunnels below.

There he stopped and listened, his back flat against the wall. He could hear water flowing along the small streams that ran through the tunnels. The Order's dungeons were not far away, so rarely used that they would have been kept as storerooms were it not for the damp. Altaïr fully expected Malik to be their only occupant.

He crept forward until he could see the guard. He was sitting in the tunnel with his back against a side wall of the cell block, head lolled in sleep. He was some way from the cells, and didn't even have them in his eyeline, so exactly what he thought he was guarding was hard to say. Altaïr found himself simultaneously outraged and relieved at the man's sloppiness. He moved stealthily past him – and it swiftly became clear why he was sitting so far away.

It was the stink. Of the three cells, only the middle one was fastened and Altaïr went to it. He was not sure what he was expecting to see on the other side of the bars, but he was certain of what he could smell, and held a hand over his nose.

Malik was curled up in the rushes that had been spread on the stone – and did nothing to soak up the urine. He was clothed in rags, looking like a beggar. He was emaciated and, through his tattered shirt, Altaïr could see the lines of his ribs. His cheekbones were sharp outcrops on his face; his hair was long, his beard overgrown.

He had been in the cell for far longer than a month. That much was certain.

As he gazed at Malik, Altaïr's fists clenched. He had planned to speak to him to determine the truth, but the truth was there on his jutting ribs and tattered clothes. How long had he been imprisoned? Long enough to send a message to Altaïr and Maria. How long had Sef been dead? Altaïr preferred not to think about it. All he knew was that Malik wasn't spending another moment there.

When the guard opened his eyes it was to see Altaïr standing over him. Then, for him, the lights went out. When he next awoke he would find himself locked inside the piss-stinking cell, fruitlessly shouting for help, with Malik and Altaïr long gone.

'Can you walk, my friend?' Altaïr had said.

Malik had looked at him with blurry eyes. All the pain in those eyes. When he had eventually focused on Altaïr, a look of gratitude and relief had come to his face, so sincere that if there had been the slightest doubt in Altaïr's mind it was banished at once.

'For you, I can walk,' said Malik, and attempted a smile.

But as they made their way back along the tunnel it had soon become clear that Malik did not have the strength to walk. Instead, Altaïr had taken his good arm, brought it around his shoulders and carried his old friend to the ladders of the tower, then across the ramparts, eventually descending the wall on the western side of the citadel, avoiding guards along the way. At last they arrived back at the residence. Altaïr looked first one way, then the other before he let himself in.

52

They laid Malik on a pallet and Maria sat as his side, giving him sips from a beaker.

'Thank you,' he gasped. His eyes had cleared a little. He pulled himself up in the bed, seeming uncomfortable with Maria's proximity, as though he thought it dishonourable to be tended by her.

'What happened to Sef?' asked Altaïr. With three of them inside it, the room was small. Now it became smaller, seeming to close in on them.

'Murdered,' said Malik. 'Two years ago Abbas staged his coup. He had Sef killed, then placed the murder weapon in my room. Another Assassin swore that he'd heard Sef and me arguing, and Abbas brought the Order to the conclusion that it was I who was responsible for Sef's murder.'

Altaïr and Maria looked at one another. For two years their son had been dead. Altaïr felt rage bubbling within him and strove to control it – to control the impulse to turn, leave the room, go to the fortress and cut Abbas, watch him beg for mercy and bleed to death.

Maria put a hand to his arm, feeling and sharing his pain.

'I'm sorry,' said Malik. 'I couldn't send a message while I was in prison. Besides, Abbas controlled all communications in and out of the fortress. No doubt he has been busy changing other ordinances during my imprisonment, for his own benefit.'

'He has,' said Altaïr. 'It seems he has supporters on the council.'

'I'm sorry, Altaïr,' said Malik. 'I should have anticipated Abbas's plans. For years after your departure he worked to undermine me. I had no idea he had managed to command such support. It would not have happened to a stronger leader. It would not have happened to you.'

'Don't trouble yourself. Rest, my friend,' said Altaïr, and he motioned to Maria.

In the next room the two of them sat: Maria on the stone bench, Altaïr on a high-backed chair.

'Do you know what you have to do?' said Maria.

'I have to destroy Abbas,' said Altaïr.

'But not for the purposes of vengeance, my love,' she insisted, looking deep into his eyes. 'For the Order. For the good of the Brotherhood. To take it back and make it great once more. If you can do that, and if you can let it take precedence over your own thoughts of revenge, the Order will love you as a father who shows it the true path. If you let yourself be blinded by anger and emotion, how can you expect them to listen when what you teach is the other way?'

'You're right,' he said, after a pause. 'Then how shall we proceed?'

'We must confront Abbas. We must dispute the accusation made against our son's murderer. The Order will have to accept that, and Abbas will be forced to answer for himself.'

'It will be the word of Malik against Abbas and his agent, whoever that is.'

'A weasel like Abbas? His agent is even less trust-worthy, I should imagine. The Brotherhood will believe you, my love. They will *want* to believe you. You are the great Altaïr. If you can resist your desire for revenge, if you can take back the Order by fair means, not foul, then the foundations you lay will be even stronger.'

'I shall see him now,' said Altaïr, standing.

They checked to make sure that Malik was asleep, then left, taking a torch. With early-morning mist swirling at their feet, they walked fast around the out-side of the inner curtain and then to the main gate. Behind them were the slopes of Masyaf, the village empty and silent, yet to awake from its slumber. A sleepy Assassin guard looked them over, insolent in his indifference, and Altaïr found himself fighting his rage, but they passed the man, climbed the barbican and went into the main courtyard.

A bell sounded.

It was not a signal Altaïr knew. He raised his torch

and looked around, the bell still ringing. Then he sensed movement from within the towers overlooking the courtyard. Maria urged him on and they came to the steps leading to the dais outside the Master's tower. Now Altaïr turned and saw that white-robed Assassins carrying flaming torches were entering the courtyard behind them, summoned by the bell, which stopped suddenly.

'I wish to see Abbas,' Altaïr told the guard at the door to the tower, his voice loud and calm in the eerie silence. Maria glanced behind, and at her sharp intake of breath Altaïr turned. He gasped. The Assassins were assembling. All were looking at himself and Maria. For a moment he wondered if they were in some kind of thrall, but no. The Apple was with him, safely tucked into his robe, and dormant. These men were waiting.

For what? Altaïr had a feeling he was soon to find that out.

Now the door to the tower was opening and Abbas was standing before them.

Altaïr felt the Apple – it was almost as though a person were prodding him in the back. Perhaps it was reminding him of its presence.

Abbas strode on to the platform. 'Please explain why you broke into the Order's cells.'

He was addressing the crowd as much as Altaïr and Maria. Altaïr glanced behind him and saw that the courtyard was full. The Assassins' torches were like balls of flame in the dark.

So Abbas meant to discredit him in front of the Order. But Maria had been correct – he wasn't up to the task. All Abbas had achieved was to accelerate his own downfall.

'I meant to establish the truth about my son,' said Altaïr.

'Oh, really?' smiled Abbas. 'Are you sure it wasn't to exact revenge?'

Swami had arrived. He climbed the steps to the platform. He was holding something in a burlap sack that he handed to Abbas, who nodded. Altaïr looked at the sack warily, his heart hammering. Maria too.

Abbas peered into the sack and gave a look of mock concern at what he saw inside. Then, with a theatrical air, he reached in and paused for a moment to enjoy the frisson of anticipation that ran through the assembly like a shiver.

'Poor Malik,' he said, and pulled out a disembodied head: the skin at the neck was ragged and dripping fresh blood, the eyeballs had rolled up, and the tongue protruded slightly.

'*No!*' Altaïr started forward, and Abbas motioned to the guards, who rushed forward, grabbing Altaïr and Maria, disarming Altaïr and pinning his hands behind his back.

Abbas dropped the head back into the sack and

tossed it aside. 'Swami heard you and the infidel plotting Malik's death. What a shame we could not reach Malik in time to prevent it.'

'*No!*' shouted Altaïr. 'Lies! I would never have killed Malik.' Pulling at the guards who held him, he indicated Swami. 'He's lying.'

'Is the dungeon guard lying, too?' said Abbas. 'The one who saw you drag Malik from his cell. Why did you not kill him there and then, Altaïr? Did you want to make him suffer? Did your English wife want to make vengeful cuts of her own?'

Altaïr struggled. 'Because I did not kill him,' he shouted, 'I learned from him that it was *you* who ordered the murder of Sef.'

And suddenly he knew. He looked at Swami and saw his scorn, and knew that he had killed Sef. He felt the Apple at his back. With it he could lay waste to the courtyard. Kill every treacherous dog among them. They would *all* feel his fury.

But no. He had promised never to use it in anger. He had promised Maria he wouldn't allow his thoughts to be clouded by vengeance.

'It is you who has broken the Creed, Altaïr,' said Abbas. 'Not I. You are unfit to lead the Order. I hereby assume leadership myself.'

'You can't do that,' scoffed Altaïr.

'I can.' Abbas came down from the platform, reached for Maria and pulled her to him. In the same movement he produced a dagger that he held to her throat. She scowled and struggled, cursing him, until he jabbed the dagger at her neck, drawing blood and calming her. She held Altaïr's gaze over his arm, sending messages with her eyes, knowing that the Apple would be calling to him. She, too, had realized that Swami had killed Sef. Just like Altaïr she would crave retribution. Her eyes pleaded with him to keep calm.

'Where is the Apple, Altaïr?' said Abbas. 'Show me, or I shall open the infidel a new mouth.'

'Do you hear this?' called Altaïr, over his shoulder, to the Assassins. 'Do you hear how he plans to take the leadership? He wants the Apple not to open minds but to control them.'

It was searing his back now.

'Tell me now, Altaïr,' repeated Abbas. He prodded harder with the dagger and Altaïr recognized the knife. It had belonged to Abbas's father. It was the dagger Ahmad had used to cut his own throat in Altaïr's room a whole lifetime ago. And now it was being held to Maria's.

He fought to control himself. Abbas pulled Maria along the dais, appealing to the crowd: 'Do we trust Altaïr with the Piece of Eden?' he asked them. In return there was a noncommittal murmur. 'Altaïr who exercises his temper in place of reason? Should he not be *compelled* to hand it over without recourse to this?'

Altaïr craned to see over his shoulder. The Assassins

were shifting uncomfortably, talking among themselves, still in shock at the turn of events. His eyes went to the burlap bag and then to Swami. There was blood on Swami's robes, he noticed, as though he'd been hit by a fine spray of it: Malik's blood. And Swami was grinning, his scar crinkled. Altaïr wondered if he had grinned when he stabbed Sef.

'You can have it,' called Altaïr. 'You can have the Apple.'

'No, Altaïr,' cried Maria.

'Where is it?' asked Abbas. He remained at the end of the dais.

'I have it,' said Altaïr.

Abbas looked concerned. He pulled Maria closer to him, using her as a shield. Blood poured from where he'd nicked her with the knife. At a nod from Abbas the guards loosened their grip on Altaïr, who reached for the Apple, bringing it from within his robe.

Swami reached for it. Touched it.

And then, very quietly, so that only Altaïr could hear, he said, 'I told Sef it was you who ordered his death. He died believing his own father had betrayed him.'

The Apple was glowing and Altair had failed to control himself. Swami, his hand on the Apple, suddenly tautened, his eyes popping wide.

Then his head was tilting to one side, his body shifting and writhing as though it were operated by some

394

force inside. His jaws opened but no words came out. The inside of his mouth glowed gold. His tongue worked within it. Then, compelled by the Apple, he stepped away, and all watched as his hands went to his face and he began to tear at the flesh there, gouging deep trenches in it with his fingernails. Blood ran from the churned skin and still he mauled himself, as though he were attacking dough, ripping at the skin of his cheek and tearing a long flap from it, wrenching at one ear, until it dangled from the side of his face.

Altaïr felt the power coursing through him, as though it leaped from the Apple and spread like a disease through his veins. As though it fed off his hatred and his need for revenge, then flowed from the Apple into Swami. Altaïr felt all of this as an exquisite mix of pleasure and pain that threatened to lift him off his feet – that made his head feel as if it might expand and explode, the sensation at once wonderful and terrible.

So wonderful and terrible that he did not hear Maria screaming to him.

Neither was he aware of her pulling away from Abbas and dashing down the dais towards him.

At the same time Swami had pulled his dagger from its sheath and was using it on himself, cutting himself with wild, broad slashes, opening wounds on his face and body, slicing into himself as Maria reached them, trying desperately to stop Altaïr using the Apple. Altaïr had a second to see what was going to happen but was too late to stop it. He saw Swami's dagger flash, and Maria, her throat exposed, suddenly spinning away with blood shooting from her neck. She folded to the wood, her arms outflung. She breathed once. As blood spread quickly around her, her shoulders heaved with a long, ragged gasp and one hand twitched, knocking at a wooden support on the dais.

At the same time, Swami fell away, his sword clattering to the floor. The Apple glowed brightly once, then dimmed. Altaïr dropped to his knees beside Maria, taking her by the shoulder and turning her over.

She looked at him. Her eyelids fluttered. 'Be strong,' she said. And died.

The courtyard was silent. All that could be heard was Altaïr's sobbing as he gathered Maria to him and held her, a man crushed.

He heard Abbas calling, '*Men. Take him.*'

Then he stood. Through eyes thick with tears he saw Assassins running towards the dais. On their faces was fear. He still held the Apple. The crowd was in disarray. Most had drawn their swords, even though they knew steel would be useless against the Apple, but better that than flee. Suddenly the urge was strong, overpowering almost, to use the Apple to destroy everything he could see, including himself, because Maria was dead at his hands and she had been his light. In one moment – in one blinding flash of rage – he had destroyed what he held most dear.

The Assassins paused. Would Altaïr use the Apple? He could see the question in their eyes.

'Get him!' screeched Abbas, and they came forward cautiously.

Around Altaïr, the Assassins seemed unsure whether to attack him or not, so he ran.

'Archers!' screamed Abbas, and the bowmen snatched their shots as Altaïr raced out of the courtyard. Arrows hailed down around him, one slicing his leg. From left and right more Assassins came running, their robes flowing, swords held. Perhaps now they understood that Altaïr would not use the Apple a second time and they leaped from walls and railings to join the pursuit. Fleeing, Altaïr came to the arch and found it blocked. He turned, doubled back and barrelled through two Assassins in pursuit, one swinging his blade and opening a wound on his arm. He screamed in pain but kept going, knowing they could have had him; he'd surprised them but they were scared to attack him – or reluctant to do so.

He turned again, this time heading for the defensive tower. In it he could see archers taking aim and they were the best, he knew. Trained by the best. They never missed. Not with the amount of time they had to aim and fire.

Except he knew when they would fire. He knew that it took them a heartbeat to find their target and a second heartbeat to steady and breathe, then . . .

Fire.

He swerved and rolled. A volley of arrows slammed into the ground he'd just left, all but one missing him. One of the archers had checked his aim and the arrow grazed Altaïr's cheek. Blood sluiced down his face as he hit the ladder, scampering up it and reaching the first level, where a surprised bowman was dithering over whether to draw his sword. Altaïr dragged him from his perch, and he somersaulted to the ground below. He'd live.

Now Altaïr scrabbled up the second ladder. He was in pain. He was bleeding heavily. He reached the top of the tower from which he had jumped a lifetime ago, disgraced then as he was now. He hobbled to the platform and, as men scrambled to the top of the tower behind him, he spread out his arms.

And dropped.

53

10 August 1257

Altaïr means *us* to spread the word of the Assassin, that is his plan. And not just spread the word but set up an Order in the west.

Shame on me for taking so long to work it out, but now that I have, all seems clear: to us (specifically to *me*, it seems), he is entrusting the spirit of the Brotherhood. He is passing the torch to us.

We have had word that warlike Mongols are approaching the village and he thinks we should leave before hostilities commence. Maffeo, of course, seems rather titillated by the idea of witnessing the action and I rather feel that he would prefer it if we stayed. His former wanderlust? All but gone. Our roles are reversed, it seems, for now it is I who want to leave. Either I am more cowardly than he is or I have a more realistic idea of war's grim reality, for I find myself in accord with Altaïr. Masyaf under siege is no place for us.

In truth I am ready to go, whether the marauding party of Mongols arrives or not. I long for home, these hot nights. I miss my family: my wife and my son, Marco. He will be three years old in a few short months and I am painfully aware that I have seen so little of his very earliest years. I have missed his first steps, his first words.

In short, I feel that our time in Masyaf has reached its natural end. Moreover, the Master has said that he wishes to see us. There is something he must give to us, he says, in a ceremony he would like to conduct with other Assassins present. It is something that must be kept safe, he says, and out of the hands of the enemy: the Mongols or the Templars. This is what his tales have been leading to, I realize, and I have my suspicions as to what this precious thing might be. We shall see.

In the meantime, Maffeo is impatient to hear the rest of my tale, now so close to its conclusion. He pulled a face when I informed him that I planned to shift the narrative forward in time, from the moment that Altaïr leaped from the ramparts of the citadel, a shamed and broken man, to a period some twenty years hence and not to Masyaf, but to a spot in the desert two days' ride away . . .

. . . to an endless plain at dusk, seemingly empty apart from a man on a horse leading another horse, the second nag laden with jugs and blankets.

From a distance the rider looked like a tradesman with his wares, and up close that was exactly what he was, sweating under his turban: a very tired and portly tradesman named Mukhlis.

So, when Mukhlis saw the waterhole in the distance he knew he had to lie down and rest. He'd hoped to reach home without stopping but he had no choice: he was exhausted. So many times during the journey the rhythm of the horse had lulled him and he had felt his chin tucking into his chest, his eyes fluttering and closing. It had been getting more and more difficult to resist sleep. Each time the motion of travel rocked him towards sleep, a fresh battle was fought between heart and head. His throat was parched. His robe hung heavy about him. Every bone and muscle in his body hummed with fatigue. The thought of wetting his lips and lying down with his *thawb* pulled around him, for just a few hours, perhaps, enough to restore some energy before resuming the journey home to Masyaf – well, the thought was almost too much for him.

What gave him pause, however, what made him fearful of stopping was the talk he had heard – talk of bandits abroad, thieves preying on tradesmen, taking their goods and slitting their throats, a band of brigands led by a cutthroat named Fahad, whose legendary brutality was matched only by that of his son, Bayhas.

Bayhas, they said, would hang his victims by their feet before slicing them from throat to belly and letting them die slowly, the wild dogs feasting on their dangling innards. Bayhas would do this, and he'd be laughing.

Mukhlis liked his guts inside his body. Neither did he have any desire to surrender all his worldly goods to brigands. After all, things in Masyaf were hard and getting harder. The villagers were forced to pay higher and higher levies to the castle on the promontory – the cost of protecting the community was rising, they were told; the Master was ruthless in demanding taxes from the people and would often send parties of Assassins down the slopes to force them to pay. Those who refused were likely to be beaten, then cast out of the gates, there to wander in the hope of being accepted at another settlement, or at the mercy of the bandits who made a home of the rocky plains surrounding Masyaf and seemed to become more and more audacious in their raids on travellers. Once, the Assassins – or the threat of them at least – had kept the trade routes safe. No longer, it seemed.

So, to return home penniless, unable to pay the tithes that Abbas demanded of the village merchants and the levies he wanted from the people, Mukhlis might find himself and his family tossed out of the village: him, his wife Aalia and his daughter Nada.

He was thinking about all of this as he approached the waterhole, still undecided whether or not to stop.

A horse was standing beneath a large fig tree that spread over the waterhole, a huge inviting canopy of cool shade and shelter. It was untethered but the blanket on its back showed that it belonged to someone, probably a fellow traveller stopping to drink the water, refill his flasks or, perhaps, like Mukhlis, lay down his head and rest. Even so, Mukhlis was nervous as he approached the waterhole. His horse sensed the proximity of water and snorted appreciatively, so that he had to rein her back from trotting up to the well, where he now saw a figure, curled up asleep. He slept with his head on his pack, his robe wrapped around him, his hood pulled up and his arms crossed over his chest. Little of his face was visible, but Mukhlis saw brown, weathered skin, wrinkled and scarred. He was an old man, in his late seventies or early eighties. Fascinated, Mukhlis studied the sleeper's face – the eyes snapped open.

Mukhlis recoiled a little, surprised and frightened. The old man's eyes were sharp and watchful. He remained absolutely still and Mukhlis realized that, although he himself was much younger, the stranger was not at all intimidated by him.

'I'm sorry if I disturbed you,' said Mukhlis, inclining his head, his voice wavering slightly. The stranger said nothing, just watched as Mukhlis dismounted, then led his horse to the well and retrieved the leather bucket so that they could drink. For a moment or so the only sound was the soft bump of the bucket on the wall of the well as the water was fetched, then the slurping as the horse drank. Mukhlis drank too. He sipped then gulped, wetting his beard and wiping his face.

He filled his flasks and took water to the second horse, tethering them both. When he looked again at the stranger he had fallen asleep once more. All that had changed about him was that he no longer lay with his arms crossed. Instead they were by his head, resting on the pack he was using as a pillow. Mukhlis took a blanket from his own pack, found a spot on the other side of the well, and lay down to sleep.

How much later was it that he heard movement and opened his eyes blearily to see a figure standing over him? A figure lit by the first rays of the morning sun, his black hair and beard wild and unkempt, a gold earring in one ear, and grinning a wide, evil grin. Mukhlis tried to scramble to his feet but the man dropped to his haunches, a glittering dagger going to Mukhlis's neck, so that Mukhlis went still with fright, a whimper escaping from his lips.

'I am Bayhas,' said the man, still smiling. 'I am the last face you will ever see.'

'No,' bleated Mukhlis, but Bayhas was already hauling him to his feet and now the trader saw that Bayhas had two companions, who were stripping his horses of his goods and transferring them to their own beasts.

He looked for the sleeping old man but he was no longer there, although Mukhlis could see his horse. Had they killed him already? Was he lying with his throat slit?

'Rope,' called Bayhas. He still had the dagger held to

Mukhlis's throat as one of his companions tossed him a coil of rope. Like Bayhas, he wore black and had an unkempt beard, his hair covered with a *keffiyeh*. On his back was a longbow. The third man had long hair and no beard, a wide scimitar at his belt, and was busily rooting through Mukhlis's packs, discarding unwanted items in the sand.

'No,' cried Mukhlis, seeing a painted stone fall to the dirt. It had been given to him by his daughter as a good-luck gift on the day he had left, and the sight of it tossed to the ground by the robber was too much for him. He pulled away from Bayhas's grip and rushed to Long Hair, who moved to meet him with a smile, then felled him with a vicious punch to the windpipe. The three robbers roared with laughter as Mukhlis writhed and choked in the dirt.

'What is it?' jeered Long Hair, bending to him. He saw where Mukhlis was looking and picked up the stone, reading the words Nada had painted on. '"Good luck, Papa." Is this it? Is this what's making you so brave all of a sudden, Papa?'

Mukhlis reached for the stone, desperate to have it, but Long Hair batted his hand away with disdain, then rubbed the stone on his backside – laughing more as Mukhlis howled in outrage – and tossed it into the well.

'Plop,' he mocked.

'You . . .' started Mukhlis. 'You . . .'

'Tie his legs,' he heard from behind him. Bayhas threw Long Hair the rope and came round, dropping to his haunches and placing the tip of his knife close to Mukhlis's eyeball.

'Where were you heading, Papa?' he asked.

'To Damascus,' lied Mukhlis.

Bayhas sliced his cheek with the knife and he screamed in pain. 'Where were you going?' he demanded again.

'His cloth is from Masyaf,' said Long Hair, who was winding the rope around Mukhlis's legs.

'Masyaf, eh?' said Bayhas. 'Once you might have counted on the Assassins for support, but no longer. Perhaps we should pay it a visit. We may find ourselves a grieving widow in need of comfort. What do you say, Papa? When we've finished with you.'

Now Long Hair stood and tossed the end of the rope over a branch of the fig tree, hauling back on it so that Mukhlis was pulled up. His world went upside down. He whimpered as Long Hair tied the end of the rope to the well arch, securing him there. Now Bayhas reached and spun him. He revolved, seeing the bowman standing some feet away, rocking back on his heels with laughter. Bayhas and Long Hair closer and laughing too. Bayhas bending to him.

Still revolving, he saw the wall of the well go by, then came round again to see the three robbers, Long Hair and Bayhas, behind them the third man, and –

A pair of legs appeared from the tree behind the third man.

But Mukhlis was still spinning and the wall of the well went by again. He revolved, slowing now, to the front, where all three robbers were oblivious that another man was among them, standing behind them. A man whose face was mostly hidden beneath the cowl of the robe he wore, his head slightly bowed, his arms spread, almost as though in supplication. The old man.

'Stop,' said the old man. Like his face, his voice was weathered with age.

All three robbers turned to face him, tensing, ready to cut down the intruder.

And all three began to snigger.

'What is this?' scoffed Bayhas. 'An aged man comes to stop our fun? What do you plan to do, old man? Bore us to death with your tales of the old days? Fart at us?'

His two companions laughed.

'Cut him down,' said the old man, indicating where Mukhlis still hung upside down, swaying on the rope. 'At once.'

'And why would I want to do that?' asked Bayhas.

'Because I say so,' rasped the old man.

'And who might you be to demand this of me?'

The old man flicked his hand.

Snick.

54

The bowman reached for his bow but in two strides Altaïr reached him, swiping his blade in a wide arc that opened the man's neck, slicing the bow in half and shortening his headdress with one cut. There was a soft clatter as the brigand's bow dropped to the ground, followed by a thump as his body joined it.

Altaïr – who had not known combat for two decades – stood with his shoulders heaving, watching Bayhas and Long Hair as their expressions changed from mocking to wary. At his feet the bowman was twitching and gurgling, his blood blotted by the sand. Without taking his eyes from Bayhas and Long Hair, Altaïr dropped to one knee and drove his blade into him, silencing him. Fear was his greatest weapon now, he knew. These men had youth and speed on their side. They were savage and ruthless, accustomed to death. Altaïr had experience. He hoped it would be enough.

Long Hair and Bayhas shared a look. They were no longer smiling. For a moment the only sound around the waterhole was the soft creaking of the rope on the branch of the fig tree, Mukhlis watching everything upside down. His arms were untied and he wondered whether to try and to get free but judged it better not to draw attention to himself.

The two thugs moved apart, wanting to outflank Altaïr, who watched the ground open up between them, revealing the merchant hanging upside down. Long Hair passed his scimitar from hand to hand with a soft slapping sound. Bayhas chewed the inside of his cheek.

Long Hair took a step forward, jabbing with the scimitar. The air seemed to vibrate with the sound of ringing steel as Altaïr stopped him with his blade, sweeping his arm to push the scimitar aside, feeling his muscles complain. If the thieves made short attacks he wasn't sure how long he could last. He was an old man. Old men tended gardens or spent afternoons pondering in their studies, reading and thinking about those they had loved and lost: they didn't get involved in swordfights. Especially not when they were out-numbered by younger opponents. He stabbed towards Bayhas, wanting to stop the leader outflanking him and it worked – but Bayhas darted close enough with the dagger to slice Altaïr at the chest, opening a wound, drawing the first blood. Altaïr attacked in his turn, and they clashed, trading blows but giving Long Hair a chance to step in before Altaïr could ward him off. Long Hair swiped wildly with his blade, making a large cut in Altaïr's leg.

Big. Deep. It gushed blood and Altaïr almost stumbled. He limped to his side, trying to bring the well to his flank in order to defend from the front only. He got there, the wall of the waterhole at his side, the hanging merchant at his back.

'Have strength,' he heard the merchant say quietly, 'and know that whatever happens you have my gratitude and love, whether in this life or the next.'

Altaïr nodded but did not turn, watching instead the two thugs in front of him. Seeing Altaïr bleed had cheered them and, encouraged, they came forward with more stabbing, stinging sorties. Altaïr fought off three offensives, picking up new wounds, bleeding profusely now, limping, out of breath. Fear was no longer his weapon. That advantage was lost to him. All he had now were long-dormant skills and instincts, and he cast his mind back to some of his greatest battles: overcoming Talal's men, beating Moloch, defeating the Templar knights in the Jerusalem cemetery. The warrior who had fought those battles would have sliced these two dead in seconds.

But that warrior lived in the past. He had aged. Grief and seclusion had weakened him. He had spent twenty years mourning Maria, obsessed with the Apple. His combat skills, great as they were, had been allowed to wither and, so it seemed, die.

He felt blood in his boots. His hands were slick with it. He was swinging wildly with his blade, not so much defending as trying to swat his attackers away. He thought of his pack, secured in the fig tree, the Apple inside. To grasp the Apple would be to emerge the victor, but it was too far away and, anyway, he'd vowed never to use it again; he'd left it in the tree for that very reason, to keep its temptation out of reach. But the truth was that if he'd been able to reach it he would have used it now, rather than die like this and surrender the merchant to them, surely condemning him to an even more painful and tortured death because of Altaïr's actions.

Yes, he would have used the Apple, because he was lost. And he'd allowed them to turn him again, he realized. Long Hair came at him from the periphery of his vision and he shouted with the effort of fending him off, Long Hair meeting his parries with attacking strikes – one, two, three – finding a way beneath Altaïr's guard and cutting yet another wound on his flank, a deep slash that bled copiously at once. Altaïr staggered, gasping with the pain. Better to die this way, he supposed, than to surrender meekly. Better to die fighting.

Long Hair came forward now and there was another clash of the sword. Altaïr was wounded again, this time on his good leg. He dropped to his knees, his arms hanging, his useless blade gouging nothing but the sand.

Long Hair stepped forward but Bayhas stopped him. 'Leave him to me,' he ordered.

Dimly, Altaïr found himself thinking of another time, a thousand lives ago, that his opponent had said the same, and how on that occasion he had made the knight pay for his arrogance. That satisfaction would be denied him this time, because Bayhas was coming forward to Altaïr, who knelt, swaying and defeated, in the dirt, his head hanging. He tried to order his legs to stand, but they would not obey. He tried to lift his blade hand but he could not. He saw the dagger coming towards him and was able to lift his head high enough to see Bayhas's teeth bared, his gold earring shining in the early-morning sun . . .

Then the merchant was bucking, swinging and had embraced Bayhas upside down and from behind, momentarily arresting his progress. With a great shout, a final burst of effort, energy summoned from he knew not where, Altaïr thrust upward, his blade slicing up and into Bayhas's stomach, opening a vertical gash that ended almost at his throat. At the same time Mukhlis had grabbed the dagger just before it dropped from Bayhas's loosening fingers, jerking upwards and slicing at the rope that held him. He dropped, smashing his side painfully against the well wall, but scrambled to his feet and stood side by side with his saviour.

Altaïr was bent almost double, dying on his feet. But he raised his blade and stared narrow-eyed at Long Hair, who suddenly found himself outnumbered and unnerved. Instead of attacking, he backed away until he reached a horse. Without taking his eyes off Altaïr and Mukhlis, he mounted it. He stared at them and they stared back. Then he very deliberately drew a finger across his throat, and rode away.

'Thank you,' said Mukhlis to Altaïr, breathlessly, but the Assassin didn't answer. He had folded, unconscious, to the sand.

55

It was a week later when the envoy from the brigand leader arrived. The people from the village watched him ride through the township and to the hills leading up to the citadel. He was one of Fahad's men, they said, and the wiser among them thought they knew the nature of his business at the fortress. Two days before, Fahad's men had come to the village with news of a reward offered for anyone who identified the man who had killed Fahad's son, Bayhas. He had been helped by a merchant from Masyaf, they said, and the merchant would be unharmed if he produced the cowardly dog who had cut down the brigand leader's beloved son. The villagers had shaken their heads and gone about their business, and the men had left empty-handed, muttering dark warnings about their planned return.

And this was it, said the gossips — at least, this was a precursor to it. Even Fahad wouldn't dare send men into the village when it enjoyed the protection of the Assassins: he would have to ask the permission of the Master. Even Fahad would not have dared make the request of Altaïr or Al Mualim, but Abbas was a different matter. Abbas was weak and could be bought.

So it was that the envoy returned. On the outward journey he had looked serious, if disdainful of the villagers who watched him pass, but now he smirked at them and drew his finger across his throat.

'It seems the Master has given Fahad his blessing to come into the village,' said Mukhlis, later that night, as the candles burned down. He sat at the bedside of the stranger, talking more to himself than to the man in the bed, who had not regained consciousness since the battle at the waterhole. Afterwards Mukhlis had man-handled him over the saddle of his second horse and brought him home to Masyaf in order that he might be healed. Aalia and Nada had attended to him, and for three days they had wondered if he would live or die. Blood loss had left him as pale as mist and he had lain in bed – Aalia and Mukhlis having given up theirs for him – looking almost serene, like a corpse, as though at any moment he might have departed the world. On the third day his colour began to improve. Aalia had told Mukhlis so when he returned from market, and Mukhlis had taken his usual place on a chair by the side of the bed to speak to his saviour in the hope of reviving him. He'd got into the habit of recounting his day, occasionally talking of significant things in the hope of exciting the patient's unconscious mind and bringing him round.

'Abbas has his price, it seems,' he said now. He looked sideways at the stranger, who lay on his back, his wounds healing nicely, growing stronger by the day. 'Master Altaïr would have died rather than allow such a thing,' he said.

He leaned forward, watching the figure in the bed very carefully. 'The Master, Altaïr Ibn-La'Ahad.'

For the first time since he had been brought to Mukhlis's home the stranger's eyes flicked open.

It was the reaction he'd hoped for, but even so Mukhlis was taken aback, watching as the patient's cloudy eyes slowly regained their light.

'It's you, isn't it?' whispered Mukhlis, as the stranger blinked, then turned his gaze on him. 'You are him, aren't you? You're Altaïr.'

Altaïr nodded. Tears pricked Mukhlis's eyes and he dropped from his seat to the stone floor, grasping one of Altaïr's hands in both of his own.

'You've come back to us,' he said, between sobs. 'You've come to save us.' There was a pause. '*Have* you come to save us?'

'Do you need saving?' said Altaïr.

'We do. Was it your intention to come to Masyaf when we met?'

Altaïr thought. 'When I left Alamut it was inevitable I would find myself here. The only question was when.'

'You were in Alamut?'

'These past twenty years or so.'

'They said you were dead. That the morning Maria died you threw yourself from the citadel tower.'

'I did throw myself off the citadel tower,' Altaïr smiled grimly, 'but I lived. I made it to the river outside the village. By chance Darim was there. He was returning from Alamut, where he had found Sef's wife and children. He retrieved me and took me to them.'

'They said you were dead,' said Mukhlis again.

'They?'

Mukhlis waved a hand that was meant to indicate the citadel. 'The Assassins.'

'It suited them to say so, but they knew I was not.'

He disentangled his hand from Mukhlis's grasp, pulled himself to a sitting position and swung his legs out of the bed. He looked at his feet, at their wrinkled old skin. Every inch of his body sang with pain but he felt . . . better. His robe had been washed and replaced on him. He pulled his hood over his head, liking the feel of it and breathing in the scent of the clean cloth.

He put his hands to his face and felt that his beard had been tended. Not far away were his boots, and on a table by the side of the bed he saw his blade mechanism, its new design gleaned from the Apple. It looked impossibly advanced, and he thought of the other designs he had discovered. He needed the assistance of a blacksmith to make the objects. But first . . .

'My pack?' he asked of Mukhlis, who had scrambled to his feet. 'Where is my pack?'

Wordlessly, Mukhlis indicated where it sat on the

stone at the head of the bed and Altaïr glanced at its familiar shape. 'Did you look inside?' he asked.

Mukhlis shook his head firmly and Altaïr looked at him searchingly. Then, believing him, he relaxed and reached for his boots, pulling them on, wincing as he did so.

'I have you to thank for tending me,' he said. 'I would be dead by the waterhole were it not for you.'

Scoffing, Mukhlis retook his seat. 'My wife and daughter cared for you, and *I* must thank *you*. You saved me from a grisly death at the hands of those bandits.' He leaned forward. 'Your actions were those of the Altaïr Ibn-La'Ahad of legend. I've told everyone.'

'People know I'm here?'

Mukhlis spread his hands. 'Of course. The whole village knows the tale of the hero who delivered me from the hands of death. Everybody believes it was you.'

'And what makes them think that?' asked Altaïr.

Mukhlis said nothing. Instead he indicated with his chin the low table where Altaïr's blade mechanism shone dully, wicked and oiled.

Altaïr considered. 'You told them about the blade?'

Mukhlis thought. 'Well, yes,' he said, 'of course. Why?'

'Word will reach the citadel. They will come looking for me.'

'They will not be the only ones,' said Mukhlis, ruefully.

'What do you mean?'

'A messenger from the father of the man you killed visited the fortress earlier.'

'And who was the man I killed?'

'A vicious cutthroat called Bayhas.'

'And his father?'

'Fahad, leader of a band of brigands who roam the desert. It's said they are camped two or three days' ride away. It's from there the envoy came. They say he was asking the Master's blessing to come to the village and hunt the killer.'

'The Master?' said Altaïr, sharply. 'Abbas?'

Mukhlis nodded. 'A reward was offered for the killer, but the villagers spurned it. Abbas has perhaps not been so steadfast.'

'Then the people are of good heart,' said Altaïr, 'and their leader is not.'

'Truer words rarely spoken,' agreed Mukhlis. 'He takes our money and gives us nothing in return, where once the citadel was the heart of the community from which came strength, guidance . . .'

'And protection,' said Altaïr, with a half-smile.

'That too,' acknowledged Mukhlis. 'All those things left with you, Altaïr, to be replaced by . . . corruption and paranoia. They say that Abbas was forced to quell an uprising after you left, a rebellion of Assassins loyal to you and Malik; that he had the ringleaders put to death; that he fears a repeat of the insurrection. His paranoia makes him stay in his tower day and night, imagining plots and putting to death those he thinks responsible. The tenets of the Order are crumbling around him just as surely as the fortress itself falls into disrepair. They say he has a recurring dream. That one day Altaïr Ibn-La'Ahad returns from exile in Alamut with . . .' he paused, looking at Altaïr askance and casting a glance at the pack '. . . an artefact capable of defeating him . . . Is there such a thing? Do you plan an attack?'

'Even if there was, it is not an artefact that will defeat Abbas. It is belief – belief in ourselves and in the Creed – that will accomplish that.'

'Whose faith, Altaïr?'

Altaïr waved an arm. 'Yours. That of the people and of the Assassins.'

'And how will you restore it?' asked Mukhlis.

'By example,' replied Altaïr, 'a little at a time.'

The next day Altaïr went out into the village where he began not simply to preach the way of the Assassins but to demonstrate it.

56

There had been fights in which Altaïr had had to intervene, disputes between traders that had required his moderation, land arguments between neighbours, but none had been as thorny as that of the two women who appeared to be fighting over a man. The man in question, Aaron, sat on a bench in the shade, cowering as the two women argued. Mukhlis, who had walked the village with Altaïr as he went about his business, was trying to intercede, while Altaïr stood at one remove, his arms folded, patiently waiting for a break in hostilities so that he might speak to them. He'd already decided what to say: Aaron would have to exercise free will in this instance, whether he liked it or not. Altaïr's real concerns lay with the boy, whose fever had yet to break and to whom he had administered a potion, its recipe, of course, gleaned from the Apple.

Or with the basket weaver who was creating new tools for himself to specifications given to him by Altaïr, who had transcribed them from the Apple.

Or to the blacksmith, who had cast his eye over the drawings Altaïr had given him, turned them upside down and squinted at them, then laid them out on a table so that Altaïr could point out exactly what needed forging. Soon the Assassin would have new equipment; new weapons, the like of which had never been seen.

Or to the man who had been watching him these past few days, who had moved with him like a shadow, staying out of sight, or so he thought. Altaïr had seen him at once, of course. He had noted his bearing, had known he was an Assassin.

It had had to happen, of course. Abbas would have sent his agents into the village in order to learn about the stranger who fought with the hidden blade of the Assassin. Abbas would surely come to the conclusion that Altaïr had returned to reclaim the Order. Maybe he hoped that the brigands would kill Altaïr for him; maybe he would send a man down the slopes to kill him. Perhaps this shadow was also Altaïr's Assassin.

Still the women argued. Mukhlis said, from the side of his mouth, 'Master, it seems I was mistaken. These women are not arguing about who should *have* the unfortunate Aaron, but who should *take* him.'

Altaïr chuckled. 'My judgment would remain the same,' he said, casting an amused look to where Aaron sat chewing his fingernails. 'It is for the young man to decide his own destiny.' He stole a glance at his shadow, who sat in the shade of the trees, mud-coloured robes pulled around him, looking for all the world like a snoozing villager.

To Mukhlis he said, 'I shall return presently. Their talk is giving me a thirst.'

He turned and left the small group, some of whom were about to follow until Mukhlis surreptitiously waved them back.

Altaïr sensed rather than saw his shadow stand also, following him as he walked into a square and to the fountain at its centre. There he bent, drank, and stood, pretending to take in the view over the village below. Then . . .

'It's all right,' he said, to the man he knew stood behind him. 'If you were going to kill me you would have done it by now.'

'You were just going to let me do it?'

Altaïr chuckled. 'I have not spent my life walking the path of a warrior in order to let myself be taken by a young pup at a fountainhead.'

'You heard me?'

'Of course I heard you. I heard you approach with all the stealth of an elephant and I heard that you favour your left side. Were you to attack I should move to my right in order to meet your weaker side.'

'Wouldn't I anticipate that?'

'Well, that would depend on the target. You would, of course, know your target well and be aware of their combat skills.'

'I know that this one has combat skills unmatched, Altaïr Ibn-La'Ahad.'

'Do you indeed? You would have been but a child when I last called Masyaf my own.'

Now Altaïr turned to face the stranger, who pulled down his hood to reveal the face of a young man, perhaps twenty years old, with a dark beard. He had a set to his jaw and eyes that Altaïr recognized.

'I was,' said the boy. 'I was a new-born.'

'Then were you not indoctrinated against me?' said Altaïr, jutting his chin towards the citadel on the promontory above them. It crouched there as if watching them.

'Some are more easily indoctrinated than others,' said the boy. 'There are many who have remained loyal to the old codes, and greater numbers, as the pernicious effects of the new ways have become more pronounced. But I have even more reason to remain loyal than most.'

The two Assassins stood facing each other by the fountainhead, and Altaïr sensed his world lurch a little. Suddenly he felt almost faint. 'What is your name?' he asked, and his voice sounded disembodied to his own ears.

'I have two names,' said the boy. 'I have the name by which I'm known to most of the Order, which is Tazim. But I have another name, my given name, given to me by my mother to honour my father. He died when I was but a baby, put to death on the orders of Abbas. His name was . . .'

'Malik.' Altaïr caught his breath and came forward, tears pricking his eyes as he took the boy by the shoulders. 'My child,' he exclaimed. 'I should have known. You have your father's eyes.' He laughed. 'His stealth I'm not so sure about, but ... you have his spirit. I didn't know – I never knew he had a son.'

'My mother was sent away from here after he was imprisoned. As a young man I returned to join the Order.'

'To seek revenge?'

'Eventually, maybe. Whatever best suited his memory. Now that you have come, I see the way.'

Altaïr put an arm around his shoulders, steered him from the fountain, and they crossed the square, talking intently.

'How are your combat skills?' he asked the young Malik.

'Under Abbas such things have been neglected, but I have trained. Assassin knowledge has barely advanced in the last twenty years, though.'

Altaïr chuckled. 'Not here, perhaps. But here.' He tapped the side of his head. '*Here* Assassin learning has progressed tenfold. I have such things to show the Order. Plans. Stratagem. Designs for new weapons. Even now the village blacksmith forges them for me.'

Respectful villagers moved out of their way. All knew of Altaïr now, and here, in the foothills of the fortress at least, he was the Master once again.

'And you say there are others in the castle loyal to me?' said Altaïr.

'There are as many who hate Abbas as serve him. More so, now that I have been reporting on what I have seen in the village. News that the great Altaïr has returned is spreading slowly but surely.'

'Good,' said Altaïr. 'And could these supporters be persuaded to rally, so that we might march upon the castle?'

The young Malik stopped and looked at Altaïr, squinting as though to check the older man wasn't joking. Then he grinned. 'You mean to do it. You really mean to do it. When?'

'The brigand Fahad will be bringing his men into the village soon,' he said. 'We need to be in control before that happens.'

57

The next morning, as day broke, Mukhlis, Aalia and Nada went from house to house, informing the people that the Master was to march up the hill. Alive with anticipation, the people gathered in the marketplace, standing in groups or sitting on low walls. After some time, Altaïr joined them. He wore his white robes and a sash. Those who looked closely could see the ring of his wrist mechanism on his finger. He moved into the centre of the square, Mukhlis standing to one side, a trusted lieutenant, and waited.

What would Maria have said to him now? wondered Altaïr, as he waited. The boy Malik: Altaïr had trusted him immediately. He'd placed such faith in him that if he were to prove treacherous Altaïr would be as good as dead, and his plans to regain the Order shown as nothing more than the deluded fantasies of an old man. He thought of those he had trusted before, who had betrayed him. Would Maria have advised caution now? Would she have told him he was foolish to be so unquestioning on such scant evidence? Or would she have said, as she had once, 'Trust your instincts, Altaïr. Al Mualim's teachings gave you wisdom; his betrayal set you on the path to maturity.'

Oh, and I am so much wiser now, my love, he thought to her – to the wisp of her he kept safe in his memory.

She would have approved, he knew, of what he had done with the Apple, of the years spent squeezing it of juice, learning from it. She would not have approved of the blame he had shouldered for her death; the shame he felt at letting his actions be guided by anger. No, she would not have approved of that. What would she have said? That English expression she had: 'Take hold of yourself.'

He almost laughed to think of it. *Take hold of yourself.* He had in the end, of course, but it had taken him years to do it – years of hating the Apple, hating the sight of it, even the thought of it, the malignant power that lay dormant within the ageless, sleek mosaic of its shell. He would stare at it, brooding, for hours, reliving the pain it had brought him.

Neglected, unable to bear the weight of Altaïr's suffering, Sef's wife and two daughters had left. He'd had word that they had settled in Alexandria. A year later Darim had left, too, driven away by his father's remorse and his obsession with the Apple. He had travelled to France and England to warn leaders there that the Mongols were on the march. Left alone, Altaïr's torment had worsened. Long nights he would spend staring at the Apple, as though he and it were two adversaries about to do battle – as though if he slept or even took his eyes from it, it might pounce on him.

In the end he had thought of that night in the garden at Masyaf, his mentor Al Mualim slain on the marble terrace, the waterfall bubbling in the background. He remembered holding the Apple for the first time and feeling from it something not evil but benign. The images it had produced. Strange futuristic pictures of cultures far removed from his own in time and space, beyond the sphere of his knowledge. That night in the garden he had instinctively understood its capacity for good. Ever since then, it had shown only its malign aspects, but that great wisdom was in there somewhere. It had needed to be located and coaxed out. It had needed an agent for its release – and Altaïr had managed to harness its power once before.

Then he had been consumed with grief for Al Mualim. Now he was consumed with grief for his family. Perhaps the Apple first had to take in order to give.

Whatever the answer, his studies had begun and journal after journal was filled with his writings: page after page of philosophies, ideologies, designs, drawings, schematics, memories. Untold candles burned down as he scratched away feverishly, stopping only to piss. For days on end he would write, then for days on end he would leave his desk, riding out from Alamut alone, on Apple errands, collecting ingredients, gathering supplies. Once, even, the Apple had directed him to a series of artefacts that he retrieved and hid, telling no one of their nature or their whereabouts.

He had not stopped mourning, of course. He still blamed himself for Maria's death, but he had learned from it. He felt now a purer kind of grief: a yearning for Maria and Sef, an ache that never seemed to leave him, that one day was as sharp and keen as a blade slicing a thousand cuts on his heart, and the next was a nauseous hollow sensation, as if a sick bird were trying to unfurl its wings in his stomach.

Sometimes he smiled, though, because he thought Maria would have approved of him mourning her. It would have appealed to the part of her that had stayed a spoilt English noblewoman, who had been as adept at fixing a man with a haughty stare as she was of defeating him in combat, her withering put-downs as cutting as her blade. And, of course, she would have approved that he had finally managed to take hold of himself, but most of all she would have approved of what he was doing now: taking his knowledge and learning and bringing them back to the Order. Had he known when he ended his exile that he had been heading back to Masyaf for that reason? He still wasn't sure. All he knew was that, once here, there had been no other option. He had visited the spot where they had buried her; Malik's gravestone was not far away, tended by young Malik. Altaïr had realized that Maria, Sef and Malik, his mother and father, even Al Mualim, were all lost to him for ever. The Brotherhood, though, he could take back.

But only if the young Malik was as good as his word. And standing there, feeling the excitement and expectation of the crowd like a weight he must bear upon his back, Mukhlis hovering nearby, he began to wonder. His eyes fixed on the citadel, he waited for the gates to open and the men to appear. Malik had said there would be at least twenty, all of whom supported Altaïr with the same fervency he did. Twenty warriors and, with the support of the people, Altaïr thought it was enough to overcome the thirty or forty Assassins still loyal to Abbas.

He wondered if Abbas was up there now, in the Master's tower, squinting to make out what was happening below. He hoped so.

Throughout his life, Altaïr had refused to find gratification in the death of another, but Abbas? Despite the pity he felt for him, there were the deaths of Sef, Malik and Maria to take into account; there was also Abbas's destruction of the Order. Altaïr had promised himself that he would take no pleasure – not even satisfaction – from Abbas's death.

But he would take pleasure and satisfaction from the absence of Abbas when he had killed him. He could allow himself that.

But only if the gates opened and his allies appeared. Around him the crowds were becoming restless. He felt the confidence and assurance with which he'd awoken slowly ebbing away.

Then he became aware of a buzz of excitement among the villagers and his eyes went from the gates of the castle – still resolutely closed – to the square. A man in white seemed to materialize from the crowd. A man who walked up to Altaïr with his head bent, then removed his hood, grinning at him. It was young Malik. And behind came others. All, like him, appearing from within the crowd as though suddenly becoming visible. At his side, Mukhlis gasped. The square was suddenly full of men in white robes. And Altaïr began to laugh. Surprise, relief and joy in that laugh as each man came to him, inclining his head in respect, showing him blade or bow or throwing knife. Showing him loyalty.

Altaïr grasped young Malik by the shoulders and his eyes shone. 'I take it back,' he said. 'You and all your men – your stealth is unmatched.'

Grinning, Malik bowed his head. 'Master, we should leave at once. Abbas will soon become aware of our absence.

'So be it,' said Altaïr, and he climbed to the low wall of the fountain, waving away Mukhlis, who had come to his aid. Now he addressed the crowd: 'For too long the castle on the hill has been a dark and forbidding place, and today I hope to make it a beacon of light once again – with your help.' There was a low murmur of appreciation and Altaïr quietened them. 'What we will *not* do, though, is welcome our new dawn through a veil of Assassin blood. Those who remain loyal to Abbas are our enemies today but tomorrow they will be our companions. Their friendship can only be won if our victory is merciful. Kill *only* if it is absolutely necessary. We come to bring peace to Masyaf, not death.'

With that he stepped down from the wall and walked from the square, the Assassins and villagers forming up behind him. The Assassins pulled their cowls over their heads. They looked grim and purposeful. The people hung further back: excited, nervous, fearful. So much depended on the outcome.

Altaïr climbed the slopes that, as a child, he had raced up and down, he and Abbas together. As an Assassin, he had run up and down, training, or on errands for the Master, leaving for a mission or returning from one. Now he felt the age in his bones and in his muscles, struggling a little up the slopes, but kept going.

A small party of Abbas's loyalists met them on the hills, a scouting party sent to test their mettle. At first those men with Altaïr seemed reluctant to engage them: these were comrades they had lived and trained with, after all. Friends were pitched against each other; no doubt, if the fighting continued, family members might find themselves face to face. For long moments the outnumbered scouting party and Altaïr's supporters faced off. The scouting party had the advantage of being on higher ground but otherwise they were lambs sent to the slaughter.

Altaïr's eyes went up to where he could just see the peak of the Master's tower. Abbas would be able to see him now, surely. He would have seen the people coming up the hill towards him. Altaïr's eyes went from the citadel to the scouts, sent to fight in the name of their corrupt master.

'There is to be no killing,' repeated Altaïr, to his men, and Malik nodded.

One of the scouts grinned nastily. 'Then you won't get far, old man.' He darted forward with his sword swinging, coming for Altaïr, perhaps hoping to strike at the roots of the rebellion: kill Altaïr, stop the uprising.

In the flap of a hummingbird's wings, the Assassin had spun away from the attack, drawn his sword and rolled around the forward impetus of his assailant's body to grab him from behind.

The scout's sword dropped as he felt Altaïr's blade held to his throat, and he whimpered.

'There will be no killing in the name of *this* old man,' murmured Altaïr, into the scout's ear, and propelled him forward to Malik, who caught him and wrestled him to the ground. The other scouts came forward but with less enthusiasm, no heart for the fight. They all but allowed themselves to be captured; in moments they were either captive or unconscious.

Altaïr watched the short skirmish. He looked at his hand where the scout's sword had nicked it, and surreptitiously wiped off the blood. You were slow, he thought. Next time leave the fighting to the younger men.

Even so, he hoped Abbas had been watching. Now men were gathering on the ramparts. He hoped also that they had seen the events on the hill, the scouting party treated mercifully.

They continued further up the slope, coming to the upland just as the gates to the fortress finally opened. More Assassins poured through them, yelling and ready for the fight.

Behind him he heard the villagers scream and scatter, although Mukhlis was urging them to stay. Altaïr turned to see him throw up his hands, but he couldn't blame the people for their loss of resolve. They all knew of the fearsome savagery of the Assassin. No doubt they had never seen two opposing Assassin armies fight and neither did they want to. What they saw were marauding Assassins come howling from the gates with bared teeth and flashing swords, their boots drumming on the turf. They saw Altaïr's supporters crouch and tense, readying themselves for action. And they took shelter, some running for cover behind the watchtower, others retreating down the hill. There was a great shout and a crash of steel as the two sides met. Altaïr had Malik as his bodyguard, and he kept an eye on the ramparts as the battle raged – the ramparts where the archers stood, perhaps ten of them. If they opened fire the battle was surely lost.

Now he saw Abbas.

And Abbas saw him.

For a moment the two commanders regarded one another, Abbas on the ramparts, Altaïr down below – strong and still as rock as the battle whirled around him – the best of childhood friends turned the bitterest of enemies. Then the moment was broken as Abbas yelled at the archers to fire. Altaïr saw uncertainty on their faces as they raised their bows.

'No one must die,' called Altaïr, entreating his own men, knowing that the way to win over the archers was by example. Abbas was prepared to sacrifice Assassins; Altaïr was not, and he could only hope that the hearts of the archers were true. He prayed that his supporters would show restraint, that they would give the archers no reason to open fire. He saw one of his men fall, howling, his throat open, and straight away the loyalist Assassin responsible was attacking another.

'Him,' he instructed Malik, pointing in the direction of the battle. 'Take him, Malik, but be merciful I urge you.'

Malik joined the battle and the loyalist was pushed back, Malik swiping at his legs. When his opponent fell, he straddled him and delivered not a killing blow but a strike from the hilt of his sword that knocked him senseless.

Altaïr looked up to the ramparts again. He saw two of the archers lower their bows, shaking their heads. He saw Abbas produce a dagger – his father's dagger – and threaten the men with it, but again they shook their heads, lowering their bows and placing their hands to the hilts of their swords. Abbas wheeled, screaming at the archers along the rampart behind him, ordering them to cut down the defectors. But they, too, were lowering their bows and Altaïr's heart leaped. Now he was urging his men forward, to the gates. Still the battle continued but the loyalists were slowly becoming aware of events on the ramparts. Even as they fought they exchanged uncertain glances, and one by one they stepped back from combat, dropping their swords, arms held out, surrendering. The way was clear for Altaïr's party to advance on the castle.

He led his men to the gates and rapped on the door with his fist. Behind him assembled the Assassins – and the villagers were returning, too, so the upland was thronged with people. From the other side of the castle gate there was a strange stillness. A hush descended over Altaïr's people, the air crackling with expectation, until suddenly bolts were thrown and the great castle gates swung wide, opened by guards who dropped their swords and bent their heads in deference to Altaïr.

He nodded in return, stepped over the threshold, under the arch, and walked across the courtyard to the Master's tower. Behind him came his people; they spread out and flowed around the edges of the courtyard; archers descended the ladders from the ramparts to join them, and the faces of families and servants were pressed to the windows of the towers overlooking the grounds. All wanted to witness Altaïr's return, to see his confrontation with Abbas.

He climbed the steps to the platform, then moved into the entrance hall. Ahead of him, Abbas stood on the steps, his face dark and drawn, desperation and defeat all over him, like a fever.

'It is over, Abbas,' called Altaïr. 'Order those who are still loyal to you to surrender.'

Abbas scoffed, 'Never.' At that moment the tower opened and the last of the loyalists came from the side rooms into the hall: a dozen or so Assassins and man-servants. Some had skittering, frightened eyes. Others were fierce and determined. The battle was not over yet.

'Tell your men to stand down,' commanded Altaïr. He half turned to indicate the courtyard, where the crowds were gathered. 'You cannot possibly prevail.'

'I am defending the citadel, Altaïr,' said Abbas, 'to the last man. Would you not do the same?'

'I would have defended the *Order*, Abbas,' snarled Altaïr. 'Instead you have sacrificed everything we stand for. You sacrificed my wife and son on the altar of your own spite – your blank refusal to accept the truth.'

'You mean my father? The lies you told about him.'

'Isn't that why we're standing here? Isn't that the well-spring of your hatred that has flowed through the years, poisoning us all?'

Abbas was trembling. His knuckles were white on the balustrade of the balcony. 'My father left the Order,' he said. 'He would never have killed himself.'

'He killed himself, Abbas. He killed himself with the dagger that you have concealed within your robe. He killed himself because he had more honour than you will ever know, and because he wouldn't be pitied. He wouldn't be pitied as you will be, by all, as you rot in the citadel dungeon.'

'*Never!*' roared Abbas. He pointed a trembling finger at Altaïr. 'You claim you can retake the Order without loss of Assassin life. Let's see you try. *Kill him.*'

And suddenly the men in the hall were surging forward, when . . .

The sound of the explosion echoed around the hall and silenced everyone – the crowds in the courtyard, the Assassins, the loyalists. All stared in shock at Altaïr, who stood with his arm held up as if pointing at Abbas – as though he had been engaging his blade in the direction of the steps. But instead of a blade at his wrist there was a curl of smoke.

From the steps came a short, strangled cry, and all

watched as Abbas stared down at his chest, where a small patch of blood on his robe was gradually spreading. His eyes were wide with shock. His jaw worked as he tried to form words that wouldn't come.

The loyalist Assassins had stopped. They stared open-mouthed at Altaïr who moved his arm, pointing at them so that now they could see the wrist mechanism he wore.

It was a single shot, and he had used it, but they didn't know that. None had ever seen such a weapon before. Only a few even knew of its existence. And seeing it turned in their direction the loyalists cowered. They laid down their swords. They moved past Altaïr and to the door of the tower to join the crowd, their arms held out in surrender, just as Abbas was pitching forward, tumbling down the steps and landing with a messy thud in the hall below.

Altaïr crouched over him. Abbas lay breathing heavily, one of his arms at an odd angle as though it had snapped in the fall; the front of his robe was wet with blood. He had moments left.

'You want me to ask forgiveness of you?' he asked Altaïr. He grinned, looking skeletal all of a sudden. 'For taking your wife and son?'

'Abbas, please, don't let your dying words be malicious.'

Abbas made a short scoffing sound. 'Still he tries to be virtuous.' He lifted his head a little. 'The first blow was struck by you, Altaïr. I took your wife and son, but only after your lies had taken much more from me.'

'They were not lies,' said Altaïr, simply. 'In all these years, did you never doubt?'

Abbas flinched and squeezed his eyes shut with pain. After a pause he said, 'Did you ever wonder if there is a next world, Altaïr? In moments I shall know for sure. And if there is, I shall see my father, and we will both be there to meet you when it is your time. And then – then there will be no doubt.'

He coughed and gurgled and a bubble of blood formed at his mouth. Altaïr looked into his eyes and saw nothing of the orphan boy he had once known; saw nothing of the best friend he had once had. All he saw was a twisted creature who had cost him so much.

And as Abbas died Altaïr realized that he no longer hated or pitied him. He felt nothing – nothing but relief that Abbas was no longer in the world.

Two days later the brigand Fahad appeared with seven of his men on horseback and was met at the village gates by a party of Assassins, led by Altaïr.

They pulled up at the edge of the marketplace, confronted by a line of men wearing white robes. Some stood with their arms folded, others with their hands on their bows or the hilt of their swords.

'So it is true. The great Altaïr Ibn-La'Ahad has

resumed control of Masyaf,' said Fahad. He looked weary.

Altaïr bowed his head, yes.

Fahad nodded slowly, as if mulling this fact over. 'I had an understanding with your predecessor,' he said at last. 'I paid him a great deal in order that I might enter Masyaf.'

'Which you have done,' said Altaïr, pleasantly.

'Ah, yes, but for a specific reason, I'm afraid,' replied Fahad, with a cloudy smile. He shifted on his saddle a little. 'I am here to find my son's killer.'

'Which you have done,' said Altaïr, just as pleasantly.

The cloudy smile slid slowly from Fahad's face. 'I see,' he said. He leaned forward. 'Then which of you is it?' His eyes moved along the line of Assassins.

'Have you no witness to identify your son's killer?' said Altaïr. 'Can he not point out the culprit among us?'

'I did,' sighed Fahad ruefully, 'but my son's mother had his eyes put out.'

'Ah,' said Altaïr. 'Well, he was a weasel. You may console yourself that he did little to protect your son or, indeed, to avenge him once he was dead. As soon as he had two old men to face, instead of one, he turned tail and ran.'

Fahad darkened.

'You?'

Altaïr nodded. 'Your son died as he lived, Fahad. He enjoyed administering pain.'

'A trait he inherited from his mother.'

'Ah.'

'And she insists, incidentally, that his name be avenged.'

'Then there is nothing left to say,' said Altaïr. 'Unless you intend to make your attempt at this very moment, I shall expect you presently with your army.'

Fahad looked wary. 'You intend to let me leave? No archers to stop me? Knowing that I will return with a force to crush you?'

'If I killed you I would have the wrath of your wife to contend with,' smiled Altaïr, 'and, besides, I have a feeling that you will change your mind about attacking Masyaf by the time you have returned to your camp.'

'And why might that be?'

Altaïr smiled. 'Fahad, if we were to do battle then neither of us would give ground. Both of us would put more at stake than the grievance deserved. My community would be devastated, perhaps irreparably so – but so would yours.'

Fahad seemed to consider. 'It is for me to decide, surely, the price of the grievance.'

'Not long ago I lost my own son,' said Altaïr, 'and because of that I came close to losing my people. I realized it was too high a price to pay, even for my son. If you take up arms against us you risk making such a forfeit. I'm sure that the values of your community differ greatly from mine, but that they are just as prized as they are reluctantly surrendered.'

Fahad nodded. 'You have a wiser head than your predecessor, Altaïr. Much of what you say makes sense, and I shall indeed consider it on the ride back. Also I shall endeavour to explain it to my wife.' He gathered up his reins and turned his horse to go. 'Good luck, Assassin,' he said.

'It's you who will need luck by the sound of it.'

The brigand gave another of his crooked, cloudy smiles, then left. Altaïr chuckled and looked up at the citadel on the promontory.

There was much work to do.

58

12 August 1257

So. We were too late to escape Masyaf before the Mongols arrived. Indeed, they *have* arrived. As a result we leave for Constantinople in a matter of hours and I'm scribbling these words as our possessions are removed by helpers to be loaded on to the carts. And if Maffeo thinks that the sharp looks he insists on throwing my way will be enough to make me lay down my quill and lend a hand then he is mistaken. I know now that these words will be of vital importance to future Assassins. They must be written down at once.

It's a small skirmishing party, or so we're told. But the main force is not far away. In the meantime the skirmishing party seems to want to make a name for itself and has been launching small but fierce attacks, scaling the walls of the village and fighting on the ramparts before retreating. I know little of warfare, thank goodness, but it occurs to me that these short assaults may be a way of gauging our strength, or lack of it. And I wonder if the Master ever regrets his decision to weaken the citadel by disbanding the Assassins. Just two short years ago no mere skirmishing party would have come within ten paces of the castle before falling to the Assassin archers, or beneath the blades of the defenders.

When he had wrested control of the Order from Abbas, Altaïr's first task was to send for his journals: the Master's work was to be a totemic force in the rebuilding of the Order, essential for providing the foundations to stop the rot at Masyaf. Under Abbas's corrupt reign they had had none of the skills or training of old: the Brotherhood had been Assassin in name only. Altaïr's first task was to restore the discipline that had been lost: once again the training yard echoed with the ring of steel and the shouts and curses of the instructors. No Mongol would have dared a skirmish then.

But just as the Brotherhood had been restored in name and reputation, Altaïr decided that the base at Masyaf should no longer exist and removed the Assassin crest from the flagpole. His vision for the Order was that the Assassins should go out into the world, he said. They should operate among the people, not above them. Altaïr's son Darim arrived home in Masyaf to find just a few Assassins left, most of whom were occupied in the construction of the Master's library. When it was complete, Darim was dispatched to Constantinople to locate my brother and me.

Which brings us to our entrance into the story, some eighty years after it began.

'But it is not over yet, I feel,' Maffeo said. He stood waiting for me. We were due to see the Master in the main courtyard. For what was surely the last time, we wound our way through the fortress to the courtyard, led by Altaïr's faithful steward, Mukhlis.

As we arrived I thought, What sights it has seen, this courtyard. Here was where Altaïr first saw Abbas, standing in the dead of night, pining for his stricken father. Here was where the two had fought and become enemies; where Altaïr had been shamed in front of the Order by Al Mualim; where Maria had died, Abbas, too.

None of this would have been lost on Altaïr, who had gathered most of the Assassins to hear what he had to say. Darim was among them, with his bow, the young Malik, too, and Mukhlis, who took his place beside the Master on the dais outside his tower. Nerves fluttered like moths in my stomach and I found myself taking short, jagged breaths to try to control them, finding the background noise of battle disconcerting. The Mongols, it seemed, had chosen this moment to launch another of their attacks on the castle, perhaps aware that its defences were temporarily depleted.

'Brothers,' said Altaïr, standing before us, 'our time together was brief, I know. But I have faith that this codex will answer any questions you have yet to ask.'

I took it and turned it over in my hands, in awe of

it. It contained the Master's most important thoughts, distilled from decades of studying the Apple.

'Altaïr,' I said, barely able to form words, 'this gift is . . . invaluable. *Grazie.*'

At a sign from Altair, Mukhlis stepped forward with a small bag that he handed to the Master.

'Where will you go next?' asked Altaïr.

'To Constantinople for a time. We can establish a guild there before returning to Venice.'

He chuckled. 'Your son Marco will be eager to hear his father's wild stories.'

'He is a little young for such tales. But one day soon, *sì.*' I grinned.

He passed the bag to me and I felt several heavy objects inside it shift.

'A last favour, Niccolò. Take these with you, and guard them well. Hide them if you must.'

I raised my eyebrows, implicitly asking his permission to open the bag and he nodded. I peered inside, then reached in and removed a stone, one of five: like the others it had a hole in its centre. 'Artefacts?' I asked. I wondered if these were the artefacts he had found during his exile at Alamut.

'Of a kind,' said the Master. 'They are keys, each one imbued with a message.'

'A message for whom?'

'I wish I knew,' said Altaïr.

An Assassin came hurrying into the courtyard and

spoke to Darim, who moved forward. 'Father. A van-guard of Mongols has broken through. The village is overrun.'

Altaïr nodded. 'Niccolò, Maffeo. My son will escort you through the worst of the fighting. Once you reach the valley, follow its course until you find a small village. Your horses and provisions are waiting for you there. Be safe, and stay alert.'

'Likewise, Master. Take care of yourself.'

He smiled. 'I'll consider it.'

And with that the Master was gone, already barking orders to the Assassins. I wondered if I would ever see him again as I shouldered the bag of strange stones and held the priceless codex tight. What I remember then is an impression of bodies, of shouting, of the ringing of steel, as we were hurried to a residence, and there I huddled in a corner to scribble these words, even as the battle raged outside – but now I shall have to go. I can only pray that we will escape with our lives.

Somehow I think we will. I have faith in the Assassins. I only hope that I am worthy of Altaïr's faith. In that respect, only time will tell.

1 *January 1258*

The first day of a new year, and it is with mixed emotions that I wipe the dust from the cover of my journal and begin a clean page, unsure whether this entry marks a fresh beginning or acts as a postscript to the tale that precedes it. Perhaps that is for you, the reader, to decide.

The first news I have to impart I deliver with a heavy heart. We have lost the codex. That which was given to us by Altaïr on the day of our departure, entrusted to our care, is in the hands of the enemy. I shall always be tortured by the moment that I lay bleeding and weeping in the sand, watching the dust kicked up by the hoofs of the Mongol attacking party, one of whom brandished the leather satchel in which I kept the codex, its strap cut. Two days out of Masyaf, with our safety assured – or so it had seemed – they had struck.

Maffeo and I escaped with our lives, though only just, and we took a little solace from the fact that our time with the Master had given us, if not the learning we might have taken from the codex, the faculties to seek out and interpret knowledge for ourselves. We resolved that soon we should go east and retrieve it (and thus, alas, delay my earliest opportunity to return to Venice and see my son Marco), but that first we should attend to business in Constantinople, for there was much to do. Ahead of us lay at least two years' work, which would be even more demanding without the wisdom of the codex to guide us. Even so, we decided that, yes, we had lost the book, but in our heads and hearts we were Assassins, and we were to put our freshly acquired experience and knowledge to good use. Thus we have already chosen the site for our trading post, a short jaunt north-west of Hagia Sophia, where we aim to supply the highest quality goods (but of course!). Meanwhile, we shall begin to spread and disseminate the creed of the Assassin, just as we pledged to do.

And at the same time as we begin the process of starting the new guild we have also set about hiding the five stones given to us by Altaïr. The keys. Guard them well, he had said, or hide them. After our experiences with the Mongols we had decided that the keys should be hidden so we set about secreting them around and about Constantinople. We are due to hide the last one today, so by the time you read this, all five keys will be safely hidden from the Templars, for an Assassin of the future to find.

Whoever that may be.

Epilogue

From above him on deck the Assassin heard the sounds of a commotion, the familiar drumming of feet that accompanies the approach to land, crew members rushing from their posts to the prow, shimmying up the rigging or hanging off ropes, shielding their eyes to stare long and hard at the shimmering harbours towards which they were sailing, anticipating adventures ahead.

The Assassin, too, had adventures ahead of him. Of course, his would likely be markedly different from the escapades fondly imagined by the crew, which no doubt consisted primarily of visiting taverns and consorting with whores. The Assassin almost envied them the simplicity of their endeavours. His tasks would be more complicated.

He closed Niccolò's journals and pushed the book away from him on the desk, his fingers running across the ageing cover, mulling over what he had just learned, the full significance of which, he knew, would take time to make itself known. And then, with a deep breath, he stood, pulled on his robe, secured the mechanism of the blade to his wrist and pulled up his cowl.

Next, he opened the hatch of his quarters to appear on deck where he, too, shielded his eyes to cast his gaze upon the harbour as the ship sliced through the sparkling water towards it, people gathered there already to welcome them.

Ezio had arrived in the great city. He was in Constantinople.

Dramatis Personae

Niccolò Polo, the narrator
Maffeo Polo

The Assassins
Altaïr Ibn-La'Ahad
Maria, his wife (née Thorpe)
Darim and Sef, their sons
Al Mualim, the Master
Faheem al-Sayf
Umar Ibn-La'Ahad, Altaïr's father
Abbas Sofian
Ahmad Sofian, Abbas's father
Malik Al-Sayf
Tazim, Malik's son, also known as Malik
Kadar, Malik's brother
Rauf
Jabal
Labib
Swami
Farim

Masyaf villagers
Mukhlis, his wife, Aalia, and daughter, Nada

The Crusades
Richard I of England, 'the Lionheart'
Salah Al'din, Sultan of the Saracens
Shihab Al'din, his son

Altaïr's Nine Targets
Tamir, black-market merchant
Abu'l Nuqoud, the Merchant King of Damascus
Garnier de Naplouse, the Grand Master, the Knights
    Hospitalier
Talal, a slave trader
Majd Addin, regent of Jerusalem
William de Montferrat, lord of Acre
Sibrand, Grand Master, the Knights Teutonic
Jubair al-Hakim, chief scholar of Damascus
Robert de Sable, Grand Master, the Knights Templar

In Cyprus
Osman, Limassol citadel captain
Frederick the Red, ranking Templar knight of Limassol
Armand Bouchart, Robert de Sable's successor
Markos, Resistance
Barnabas, Resistance
Barnabas, imposter
Jonas, a merchant
Moloch, 'The Bull'
Shalim and Shahar, sons of Moloch

The Bandits
Fahad
Bayhas
Long Hair

Acknowledgements

Special thanks to
Yves Guillemot
Jean Guesdon
Corey May
Darby McDevitt
Jeffrey Yohalem
Matt Turner

And also
Alain Corre
Laurent Detoc
Sébastien Puel
Geoffroy Sardin
Xavier Guilbert
Tommy François
Cecile Russeil
Christele Jalady
The Ubisoft Legal Department
Charlie Patterson
Chris Marcus
Etienne Allonier
Maria Loreto
Alex Clarke
Alice Shepherd
Andrew Holmes
Clémence Deleuze
Guillaume Carmona